BREAKING PERFECT

LYDIA MICHAELS

WWW.LYDIAMICHAELSBOOKS.COM

Breaking Perfect

For Trudy,
Because you are an incredible woman
who inspires me and makes me smile every day.
xo

CHAPTER 1

The midday light faded as Liberty pressed her eyes shut. The soft two-hundred count sheets slid beneath her heels as her head sank into the plush pillows. A breathy sigh escaped her lips. So close. Thighs slowly scissoring, her muscles clenched as the pleasure thrumming through her entire being became the central focus of her mind.

Fingers sliding over her flesh goaded the echo of her moans as they filled the quiet bedroom. Building the fantasy, she peeked through her lashes. Soft slices of late afternoon sunshine passed through the drawn curtains painting golden puddles upon her dewy skin.

"Oh, God, yes," Libby whimpered as her body drew up stiffly, a delicious prerequisite that told her she was about to come.

Her vocalizations brought the experience to

life. The faint scent of her arousal built into a pungent fragrance that filled the air. She loved the scent of sex. Licking her lips, she tasted the subtle salt of her skin, imagining it was Mason's authentic flavor as her fingers kept rhythm.

"Mmm, Mason, yes! Lick me..." Her low feminine cry became a begging plea as her hips lifted off the mattress, calves locked, and her slender neck arched. Cream coated her fingers as she pushed into the starburst of pleasure spreading from her sex up her spine.

Her mind chased after the coveted orgasm that seemed just out of reach, limited to those fragile moments she managed to break away from the world and find a shameless shadow dark enough to silence her demons. She strove to surrender her compulsion to always be in control, tempting the ecstasy of release as she fought against every deep-rooted need that burdened her.

Her blood flowed heavily through her veins as her mind ebbed away from the very real pressures of her existence. *Let go.* She held onto the command, never able to fully compromise the overbearing consciousness that blanketed her every thought. *Let go. Let go.*

Unsteady fingers gripped her little trembling vibrator. Provocatively, as if being watched, she dragged her left hand to her breast and squeezed her flesh through her blouse. As her body trembled and fluttered deep within her channel, at that place that only some unknown emotion could fill. She found her nipple and pinched almost painfully so her mind could escape for that one moment where everything was timeless and perfect.

*Shh...*her mind let go and all was quiet.

The room, her responsibilities, her many imperfections, they all fell away as she rode the wave of pleasure washing over her and climaxed. Her muscles seized and her fingers fell from her flesh in an equally emotional and physical release.

Her touch drifted away, hands weightless and numb. The buzzing of the small vibrator was muffled in the soft bedding. Quietly panting, breath sawed through her lungs. She no longer wept like she once did. Tears were useless. Rather, she opened her eyes and took a moment to blindly stare at the chandelier hanging over their bed as she came back to herself.

The peace did not last. Her mind settled into a conscious state, shoving her orgasmic bliss aside. She had things to do.

Inhaling one final satisfied breath, Libby pulled herself into a seated position and adjusted her blouse. As she stood she straightened her A-line skirt and automatically began to remake the bed.

The top sheet floated into place as she methodically folded the corners and tucked them under the mattress, remembering her mother's words. *Always make it tight, Liberty. You should be able to bounce a quarter off of a bed when it's made properly.*

She centered the heavy duvet and carefully fluffed and placed all four pillows and shams. Brushing her palms over the work of perfection, a sense of twisted satisfaction spread in her chest. With a smile she turned, slipped her feet into the designer flats set in perpendicular perfection beside the bed. Adjusted the shades, she raised them only partially so that when the sun set it would illuminate the room in just the right way.

As she scooped her panties off the floor her thumb traced over the moist patch of silk and tucked them into the laundry chute. The sensual slide of fresh silk up her legs reawakened her lulling libido. Years of iron control over her actions forced back the urge to masturbate again and come just one more time. She had forty-three minutes. Plenty of time before Mason returned to walk through the house one last time. Mindful of the passing time, she quickly returned to her duties.

After setting the pan on the stove to simmer and stirring the marinade, Libby left the kitchen. Her feet swiftly climbed the stairs to the highest room of their house. Her tender muscles stretched with each step.

They lived in what was referred to as a "starter mansion" just outside of the more touristy parts of the Outer Banks. Some would consider the size of their home extravagant, but around those parts it was actually modest. Where many rental properties closer to the coast boasted of ten or more bedrooms, their year-round residence had only three. What Libby loved most about her home was the livable quarters decorated with clean, orderly functionality and, of course, the peacefulness.

Built in three stories of staggered variations and shapes with one wide hexagon peak centered over the foyer, their home was a spacious sanctuary. The lack of exterior symmetry sometimes irritated her, so she focused her energy on maintaining the inside of the home. Libby liked things just so and took pride in keeping the house lovely and neat for Mason and herself.

When she reached the third floor she opened what she referred to as the 'tower guestroom'. Dressed completely in pristine shades of white and ivory, the chic French escape was as untouched as the day before when she inspected it. No one had been up there besides her, but it was her routine to scrutinize each and every room each day. It gave her a feeling of rightness. She rotated the ivory lampshade one third of the way around the bulb, altering only one version of perfect for another.

Descending to the second floor, she visited the more masculine guestroom. Flipping the switch at the door, bathing the room in a pale golden glow, she found everything as it should be. *On, off, on, off, on, off. Three on. Three off.* A sense of satisfaction blanketed her.

Stepping quietly over the plush ivory runner, she inspected each area. The soft click of one solid oak door after another and the whisper of her linen skirt, was the only proof the home wasn't vacant. She favored the solitude of her soft intrusion. The sounds of her gentle presence calmed her anxiety.

The casual den, Mason's study, and the powder room were perfectly tidy and freshened. When she reached the entertainment room she pressed the shuffle key on the playlist and moved to the next room. Yesterday was Motown so today would be Jazz. She'd spent hours solving the formula that the iPod followed so that what appear random could actually be predicted and therefore manageable. It was really only a simple matter of altering odd numbers followed by a sequence of altering even numbered tracks.

By the time she reached their bedroom, the rich, cool vocals of Etta James filled the house from small recessed speakers hidden in each corner. She smiled. This album always reminded Liberty of when they saw Ms. James perform at a private concert in New Orleans a few years back.

Believing their room was just as she left it ten minutes ago, she moved past the freshly made bed and straight into the master bath. She adored her bathroom. It was a perfect circle with a glass cathedral ceiling and Parisian chandelier set precisely in the center. Mason referred to the bathroom as her palace of beauty.

Sitting in her skirted diamond-back vanity

stool she reached into the upper drawer of her jewelry box and found two tortoise shell chopsticks. Her blonde hair was something Mason had always adored. It hung to her shoulders in wide unruly curls that only time and patience had taught her to tame. Never satisfied with the way the front settled—given that she had about six cowlicks—she wore her bangs in loose chopped twirls just above her blue eyes. With practiced ease she twisted her hair atop her head and pinned it in place with the identical sticks.

Straightening her posture, elongating her neck, she turned her chin first left then right. Delicately finagling an unruly curl until it fell in line with the others she struggled to find symmetry.

"Perfect," she complimented her reflection.

From her crystal jewelry box she plucked her Mother of Pearl stud earrings and fastened them in her lobes. When finished, she quickly tidied the vanity and returned downstairs.

The scent of apple pie baking in the oven filled the foyer. Visiting the kitchen briefly, she stirred the marinade. Tonight would be chicken sautéed in a marmalade marinade with glazed baby carrots, and fresh spring salad. The apple pie, Mason's favorite, was for dessert. They would be celebrating his thirty-eighth birthday tonight.

She'd polished two silver place settings that morning and dressed the table with a long burgundy runner and a low centerpiece filled with nine ripe green pears. Two ivory chargers from their wedding china, sat upon rich satin place-mats retrieved from the dry cleaner's that morning. Wedding china was only for holidays and birthdays, but the crystal they used daily.

Satin napkins folded in thirds rested half a teaspoon's length to the left of the charger. The butter knife shone under the candlelight, a teacup's diameter from the lip of the placemat. *Perfect.* What Mason would see as merely practical propriety, Liberty secretly drew contentment from, each piece holding a particular place and filling a fastidious hunger.

She understood her methods were not the norm. For years she'd battled her inability to be like everyone else. Never able to bend, she finally found Mason, who not only understood her need for constant order, but fit her perfectly. So flexible and kind, his softness complimented her rigidity beyond anything she ever envisioned.

Once the table was dressed, Libby made her way back to the kitchen and finished preparing their meal. At six o'clock on the dot the low hum of her husband's Mercedes pulling into the garage accompanied a tingle of relief. Mason always had impeccable timing.

She quickly wiped her hands on a dishcloth, rushing to fold the hand towel properly into thirds down the center then three times across the length so that no rough edges showed. After setting it down precisely one inch from the edge of the counter and one from the edge of the sink, she hastily moved to the front door.

Nine feet, exactly three marble tiles, from the front door she stood, ankles together, hands clasped tightly just below the hem of her blouse. A final breath escaped as the knob turned. She savored that last bite of anxiety before meeting her husband's gaze.

"Hey, beautiful girl," Mason greeted as he stepped through the doorway carrying a rumpled newspaper and his briefcase. Calm washed over her at the practiced functionality of this part of their day. Predictable was good. No matter what, he always made her feel cherished.

She smiled, genuine contentment grounding her. "How was your day?"

"Okay. How about you? Good day?" Mason dropped his papers in a pile of disarray on the accent table by the door and Libby released the mental hold on herself, moving to him. Helping him off with his coat, she folded it over her arm, and righted the papers with her free hand.

Smiling up at him expectantly, he placed a soft kiss on her nose. This was the dance they naturally practiced each day since moving into their home. It was routine. It was right.

"Something smells delicious. Did you have time to play?"

Libby moved to the hall closet and hung up his coat. Noticing it was showing lint again, she made a mental note to take it to the cleaners on Monday. "My day was very good. I was able to finish the grocery shopping in under an hour so I managed to fit in three hours of practice."

"That's great." When he smiled at her it was always genuine, always kind. She appreciated his open manner and sincerity. "How long before we eat?"

"Dinner's just about finished. I only need to bring it out to the table. Is that okay?"

"You know it's fine, Liberty," he replied endearingly. "Why don't you bring it out? I'm just going to run upstairs and change. This tie's been choking me all day."

She nodded and quickly did as Mason asked. When he returned in a loose fitting pair of sweats and an old Duke sweatshirt she joined him at the table.

"This looks fantastic, Lib."

"Thank you. I also made apple pie."

Shutting his eyes, Mason gave an almost sexual groan at the mention of dessert. Liberty's mind was immediately flooded with images of her fantasy that afternoon and the memory of coming all over her fingers and thighs. She quickly averted her gaze so he wouldn't sense her guilt.

As they ate they chatted about his day. Liberty meticulously sliced her carrots into thirds. Rather than acknowledge her husband's disordered vegetables, she focused on what he was saying.

It was always a pleasure hearing about all the fascinating people her husband came in contact with in one day. As a trauma surgeon at Faith Baptist Hospital located just over the main bridge into town, he never knew what he was walking into. He had a tolerance for natural chaos she admired and dreaded at the same time.

She took great pride in his success. Mason knew he wouldn't be able to save everyone, but he never lost hope or refused to try. It was inspiring. He was so brave compared to her. He was her strength, her rock.

After dinner was cleared she brought out the pie. Her lips curled into an easy smile as Mason ate two generous slices. A bit of sweet glaze clung to the side of his thumb as he took the last bite. Her mind imagined him leaning over and smearing the golden filling across her lower lip then licking it off. When he removed the smudge from his thumb with the napkin her disappointment tingled.

Recently, she acknowledged that she was becoming a contradiction. While everything in her craved normal, there was one part of her that was suddenly longing for spontaneity, and she'd not yet thought of a way to discuss this with Mason. She needed life to be unsurprising for reasons she didn't like to think too hard about. Mason worked diligently to provide a dependable environment. Asking for something else made her feel like she was betraying his expectations.

He was an incredible husband and provided for her well beyond what she should ever expect.

None of the luxuries they enjoyed were required to love him. She only required him to be true to her, to be the emotional anchor she needed to get through each day.

Her tendency to obsess over making everything perfect drove many people away, but Mason always made her quirks seem inconsequential. Her compulsive side resented her insidious ache to change. Change was sloppy and contagious. One aspect could not be changed without somehow disturbing the general balance of all other things.

Her husband was a beautiful man. His thick dark hair was clipped sophisticatedly short and strong jaw, no matter how frequently he shaved, always appeared to be overdue for another trim. He was tall. Of course, Liberty was only five foot so everyone was taller, but Mason was very tall, over six feet. He dressed impeccably and his well thought out wardrobe set off his swimmers physique. Though she rarely had the opportunity to analyze his nude body in broad daylight, when they used the pool she often admired his broad shoulders and trim abdomen.

They disagreed about plenty of things. They were husband and wife after all, but Mason never once raised his voice to her and was always gentle and in control of himself. She never saw him in a rage.

On days that she knew he'd lost a patient on his table she did everything she could to soothe him. Sometimes it pained her to see that part of her husband that she could never quite reach. It was as if he withheld parts of himself from her, perhaps afraid if he leaned on her too heavily she might break. Perhaps he was right.

She supposed everyone had secrets, but the part of him that he didn't share with her was huge, and for that reason she always ended up crying on the nights Mason needed to be left alone to sort out his emotions.

She wasn't made of glass, but definitely had cracks that burdened her with emotional limits. Still, she wished he would come to her, just once, so that she could be there for him the way he was there for her. In spite of his emotional barriers Mason was a wonderful man and an even better husband. So, yes, she would cry at times, but in the end she would chastise herself for being selfish and a shrew for feeling unsatisfied with all the amazing parts Mason did share.

They had a great marriage. They laughed together, enjoyed the same movies. Her passion was playing the piano and Mason loved to listen. She needed to take care of him and he needed her to make sure he didn't walk out the door with newspaper smudges on his fingers or shaving cream in his ear. Five years together and she was very happy.

"Hello, Earth to Libby..." She drew her gaze from her half-eaten pie and looked into Mason's laughing eyes. "Where'd you go there? I was telling you something and you just zoned out."

"Oh, I—" The sound of the phone ringing

saved her from having to form an excuse. "I'll get that. Excuse me."

He smirked with a raised eyebrow as she quickly removed his dish and scurried to the kitchen.

"Whoever it is, I'm not here. I want a nice evening with my wife, a good movie, and no interruptions."

Libby smiled to herself in the kitchen and grabbed the phone on the third ring. "Hello?" When she heard nothing but dead air she assumed the caller hung up. "Hello?"

"Hi."

Libby smiled and crinkled her brow at the phone. She looked at the caller ID and didn't recognize the number. "Hi. Who is this?"

"This—" The deep voice stumbled as if searching for words. "Um… is this…is this Mrs. Davis?"

"Speaking."

"Wife of Dr. Mason Davis?"

"Yes, this is Liberty, Mason's wife. Can I help you?"

"Liberty." The gravelly voice on the other end said her name slowly as if tasting the word.

"I'm sorry, who is this?"

"Is…Is Dr. Davis home?"

Liberty moved to the counter and grabbed the small tablet she used to write down Mason's messages. Glancing to the clock over the double oven, she wrote the exact time and date in the upper left corner. "No, he's not. May I take a message?"

"Do you know when you expect him back?"

Mason came into the kitchen and hugged her from behind. The act was so unexpected her heart raced and her mind scrambled as her nipples grew suddenly hard. His touch always had an effect on her, but being caught off guard added a new and exciting element of arousal. With her husband, all things sexual were usually limited to their intimate encounters refined to their bedroom, so his sudden affection threw her off balance.

Spontaneity never tempted her before and her desire for such nonsense only frustrated her now. He nuzzled his rough chin across her shoulder and chills chased up her spine as he kissed the flesh that peaked out from beneath the collar of her blouse.

A sense of urgency to get off the phone distracted her from the conversation with the unknown caller. Swallowing, she rasped, "He isn't expected back until late tonight. Who shall I say was calling?" She needed to take advantage of this suddenly affectionate side of her husband before it faded.

"Please tell him Sean O'Malley called."

She quickly jotted down the name and number the man gave then hung up the phone and turned in her husband's arms.

"Dinner was wonderful, Lib. Thank you. You

take such good care of me." His praise washed over her like a cleansing baptism of purpose.

Her lips parted as she blinked up at him, savoring the sudden ache in her breasts. So unbelievably turned on as fantasy after fantasy sprang into her sex-starved mind she could barely form words. "It's my job to take care of you. I'm happy to do it," she whispered.

He smiled and kissed her nose and just that quickly, like a blanket being stripped off of a body in the midst of a dreamy slumber, he emotionally disengaged and stepped away.

I'm not glass she wanted to scream! She wanted to rip off her clothing and demand he fuck her right on the imported countertops until her ass was bruised. Maybe she should take off her clothes right there in the kitchen. Panic choked her. She didn't want him to stop, but internally sobbed, recognizing that he already had.

"What kind of movie do you feel like?" he asked as he stretched.

She didn't feel like watching a movie anymore. She felt like fucking her husband. What if she dropped to her knees and sucked his cock deep in her mouth until he grew so hard it touched the back of her throat? Would he be repulsed? Why was she such a pervert all of a sudden?

Guilt and shame crept over her like the feathery feet of spiders. Stepping back, she folded her hands, and set her ankles side by side. Her physical control helped her settle her frantic mind.

"You pick. It's your birthday. Why don't you go get it set up and I'll meet you up there just as soon as I tidy the kitchen?"

"Okay, don't take too long."

The kitchen was spotless in a matter of minutes, but took an extra five to simply stand with her cheek pressed to the chilled glass of the poolroom so that she would cool off. She was twenty-eight. According to her understanding she was still years away from hitting her prime. Why then, was she thinking like such a whore? It was a horrible feeling, wanting her husband to fuck and grope her like an animal. Her mind was suddenly hosting fantasies she shouldn't recognize. Yet they seemed perfectly at home in her head.

She'd been masturbating in secret every day for weeks. Sometimes two or three times a day. And still her panties would need to be changed because one thought would have her soaking wet again. Why? Why was this happening to her? She didn't want to want the things her body was craving. Such fantasies could never exist with Mason. If this kept up she would only find herself resenting a perfectly lovely marriage.

Grabbing hold of the soft skin under her arm, she pinched until tears prickled her eyes. The action had a grounding result. The sharp bite of pain centered her being in a way that didn't require too much time, time she didn't want to spare at the moment.

Clamping her tender flesh between her fingers, knowing she was developing a bruise, she waited until the pain became so much that her body went numb. When the pain stopped, a part of her tension broke away. Her mind cleared for a brief moment, much like it did in the eye of an orgasm, and she let out a slow breath. *That's better.*

Releasing her stiff fingers, she pulled her face away from the cool glass and calmed. She swallowed, squared her shoulders, and headed up to the entertainment room to find Mason.

They watched *The Time Traveler's Wife* and in the end Liberty cried. Mason's hand rubbed over her arm as he passed her tissues.

Mason locked up the house while she changed into a white satin nightgown that flowed to the floor. Folding the linens back on Mason's side of the bed, she lowered the lights to the dim/off setting. Within ten minutes the room would be completely black, the way they both preferred to sleep. Mason entered the room just as she climbed into bed.

"That was a good movie, don't you think?"

"Yes. I liked it."

"You always like the sad ones," he teased.

"That's not true." She laughed. "My favorite movie is *Braveheart*. It's brutal and totally a man flick!"

"Lib, he dies a martyr for his widow."

"He wasn't a martyr. The English caught him.

Otherwise he would have kept on fighting. He fought for his widow."

"Same difference. It may have war, but it's still a sad love story."

She sat up on one elbow and shook her head at him. "Well, don't act like you only watch macho stuff. You loved *The Notebook*."

"Now that," he said, leaning over to kiss her lips, "is a great movie." He settled into his side of the bed and adjusted the covers. "Love you, Lib. Thanks for a fantastic birthday."

"We didn't do anything."

"It was perfect. You made it perfect." Her heart swelled at his compliment. For her, there really was no higher praise.

The room dimmed and Liberty waited for Mason to touch her. It was Friday night. They always made love on Friday night. Not to mention that it was his birthday.

Darker and darker the open space grew with the sense of hyperventilation and anticipation. Anxiety closed in and she fought to force it back. *Patience.*

What if he just went to sleep? What if they didn't make love? It was Friday! Why wasn't he touching her? Her heart raced as she fought the urge to cry. She couldn't initiate their lovemaking. It wasn't in her to do so. He needed to start things. He always started things.

When the room submerged into complete blackness and she could hear nothing but her heart pounding in her ears and her mind screaming *Noooo!* Mason was completely silent. And then he touched her. She sighed. A thousand bits of tension scattered away at that single touch of his fingers along her shoulder and down her arm. He didn't forget. Everything would be fine.

His fingers sought out hers. They linked hands and he drew her palm to his mouth and placed a soft kiss there. "Come here, Lib."

Scooting over on the bed, the gentle touch of his right hand coasted over her thighs, gathering and pulling the silk of her gown. A quiet but intentional moan slipped past her lips so he understood she was enjoying herself. Mason was usually very good about preparing her with long moments of caresses and tender petting, but she was already drenched between her thighs, almost embarrassingly so. She wanted him to move ahead, but would never suggest such a thing.

Mason easily pulled her thighs apart and rolled to his side in the dark. As his mouth kissed her shoulder and neck his fingers worked their way to her pussy. He paused for the briefest second as his fingers discovered the wet mark saturating the satin of her panties. He tried to hide his surprise, but she knew him too well. That second of hesitation, processing his discovery, drawing comparisons, was spiked with a moment's shame. She was grateful the darkness hid her mortified expression.

He worked her panties down her narrow hips. The thin satin straps of her gown slipped over her shoulders and she arched as Mason's hand found her breast. Strong palms cupped her flesh. She was only a B cup, but he never complained. However, sometimes Liberty wondered if she had larger breasts if he would play with them more, perhaps pinch and tug at the tips and softly bite the tender parts.

It wasn't long before he was on top of her and fitting his cock into her sex. Shame for how eager she secretly was twisted low in her stomach. A desire to rush warred with her struggle to stay in control of her emotions. Finally, he slid into her.

They fit together nicely. Mason had a large cock, not irregularly so, according to what she learned about the male anatomy in magazines, but it was wide and Liberty loved the way it stretched her. As always he took measured strokes, never going unnecessarily fast and never pressing in too deep. It was pleasant. It was always pleasant—but as always, she never came and Mason never pressed the issue.

A rumble of satisfaction purred from deep within Mason's chest. Warmth spread within her channel and she sighed. Just like always, Mason finished with an affectionate kiss. "I love you."

Like hunger, her need was sated, but not to the degree an exquisite banquet could satisfy her. Pasta with wine was nice, but champagne, filet mignon, and lobster was better.

"I love you, too."

A few moments later, he was falling asleep as she returned from the bathroom. Her panties were on the floor and she tossed them into the laundry chute then slipped a clean pair over her legs.

Climbing into bed, she refused to mourn her lack of release, because Mason was her everything, and her love was enough to sustain her. Softly sighing, she shut her eyes, promising she'd come again tomorrow.

CHAPTER 2

*M*ason awoke to the delicious scent of bacon and had no doubt that Liberty had already been up for hours. Climbing out of bed, he stretched and yawned until his jaw popped. His fingers adjusted his cock as it audaciously bobbed before him as he moved into the bathroom and started the shower. As if she had the hearing of a bat, music filled the house not two minutes after he began to move around. This morning's choice of music—Coldplay. Lovely.

Steam from Libby's shower lingered in the large ultra-feminine bathroom as Mason brushed his teeth. It didn't bother him that his master bath was filled with decadent female frills and luxuries. Liberty was an incredible wife and she deserved to be pampered much more than she ever allowed him to do for her. She took pride in doing for herself and others, so he knew, when he was having their home designed, that the only way to ensure she treated herself to some regular pampering was to make it available to her around the clock.

The best hotels of New York and Paris couldn't claim a bath as luxurious as the one he'd created for his wife. The circular design was one of a kind. The upholstered sitting chair beside the tub was large enough to fit five grown men. It was custom made, as was the vanity seat. The fabrics came from India and the tile from Italy. All of the wide trim work was custom made by a local carpenter who retired years ago, but Mason found his price and tempted him out of retirement.

He rarely wasted money, but when it came to their home and items that would be used well past their prime, he had no qualms about spending it. He made an extremely good living, but he was never a prick about owning or being able to afford luxuries. Every year, he asked Libby to call community centers across the country and learn about those in need. Come Christmas, she would have ten families selected and Mason made it her project to make sure every mother, father, son, and daughter got what they wanted and needed. He loved being able to make a difference and it was something Liberty really benefited from, something she never was permitted to do as a child.

As the hot water sloshed over his body and suds swirled into the drain, Mason worked a lather over his needy cock. His mind went somewhere else for a moment, but he quickly chased it back to where it needed to be. Tugging hard and fast at his slippery flesh, he gritted his teeth.

His balls drew up tight and his ass clenched as his body came alive. Widening his stance, he braced his upper body so that his forehead could rest on the forearm fixed across the tiled wall. His tight calf muscles flexed as his spine began to tingle. Panting through his teeth he grunted. *Almost there.* Tightly, he squeezed his aching cock, needing to experience that heady pain of resistance that only came with certain kinds of raw fucking, the kind he gave up long ago.

Opening his eyes, a pearl of pre-cum slid over his finger and that was all it took. A kaleidoscope of images filled his mind, Libby's sweet pink mouth, her perfect tight cunt, that round apple shaped ass. Oh, God, what it would feel like to grab hold of that thick blonde hair and slowly feed her every inch of his cock.

And then it happened. No matter how hard he fought it a little glimpse always slipped past his guard, that little snippet frozen in time, one moment locked in his memory, a moment that was only one of many, unspectacular and ordinary, but meaningful because it was gone. His mind zeroed in on that forbidden glimpse of his past like a starved vulture over a long dead corpse. Greedily he mindfucked the image and come was suddenly busting from his cock with the force of a bullet.

Mason panted and caught his breath. His eyes

squeezed shut as if that would make him forget what he saw in his mind. "Fuck."

Blinking, he shook his head, clearing away the memories of his past. Like a phantom, they would haunt him for the remainder of the day. His past was not welcome here any more than Liberty's was. The difference, however, was that he knew all about his wife's tainted past. His mental relapse was an indiscretion, a reminder that, in light of his wife's innocent continence, he still kept secrets from her.

Yes, he needed to tell her. For five long years avoided the subject in order to protect her and nurture the neutral sense of regularity she depended on. But lately, as though the universe were warning him of something, the urge to unburden his secrets was stronger than ever. He just needed to find the right time, perhaps tonight.

It had been a while since she'd had an episode, but this might send her to a dark place—something he desperately wanted to avoid. Maybe it was selfish to want to share these irrelevant moments of his past. The ongoing mental debate was beyond tedious.

Confessing who he'd been before her seemed the right thing to do, yet what did it matter at this point? She knew who he was now. Disturbing her progress wouldn't benefit anyone. Perhaps it would be best to continue to bury those memories with the passing of time.

Pushing the dusty recollections back as far as

he could, he focused on the happy life he had in the here and now. He loved his wife. She was a magnificent woman. He could not disrespect her by fantasizing about someone else. Yes, bringing up the past would only complicate the now. She was more than enough to meet his needs both emotionally and sexually.

After drying off and shaving, he moved back into the bedroom. Libby had been there. The evidence was in the freshly made bed, pillows fluffed like plump clouds and blankets smoother than an idle millpond kissing the horizon. She did like to have everything just so.

A few minutes later he walked into the kitchen to find his beautiful wife dropping a dollop of hand whipped cream on a stack of perfectly shaped buttermilk pancakes. Placing a kiss on the side of her neck, he grinned as she shivered. His mouth gently nibbled her there, the motion causing her hand holding the whisk to shake and leave her with a less than perfect tear shaped cloud of cream. She huffed, but smiled at him anyway. There was a teasing sort of pleasure that came with ruffling her feathers, playing with her just enough to keep the atmosphere of their home light and forgiving, while still supporting her need for perfection.

Mason opened the stainless steel fridge and pulled out a quart of orange juice. Just as he brought the bottle to his lips Libby snatched it out of his hands.

"You're picking on me on purpose today," she teased, pouring him a tall glass of juice.

"I just like to give you a challenge."

She rolled her eyes. "Your mother called again this morning. Mase, it isn't fair to blow her off on your birthday. You know she just wants to wish her favorite son a happy fortieth."

"Oh ho! Now look who's picking!" He had two years before he climbed over that hill.

"I'm sorry, I meant fiftieth."

As she tried to sashay by him after returning the juice to the fridge Mason grabbed her wrist and spun her into his hold. Her back pressed against his front. Leaning down, bending over her much smaller form, he pressed his lips into her neck. She squealed as he gave her a slight tickle. He wanted her too much, considering he just had her the night before and jerked off that morning. "Listen here, little girlie, keep being so cheeky and this old man may have to give you a spanking."

Liberty suddenly grew very still. Fuck. Had he taken things too far? Her petite frame radiated with strong emotion as she took deep, slow breaths. Was she scared? Had he frightened her? "Liberty, I was just playing around, baby."

Her body sagged a little and she nodded silently. As he released her she didn't look at him. Cheeks flushed, she seemed intent on busying herself with bullshit that didn't have to be done, like wiping down an immaculate countertop. Little walls, that's what his marriage was contained in. Sometimes their marriage was like navigating his way through a labyrinth he could easily step over alone—but he wanted her by his side.

She cleared her throat softly. "Your messages are by the fridge. Breakfast is ready. If you want to make calls while you eat I can bring your coffee and paper in here."

"No, that's all right. I'll go over them after breakfast. You made a lovely meal. Come on, let's go enjoy it."

By the end of breakfast whatever blip on the radar they experienced was gone. As usual, Libby made sure everything ran smoothly. He had no idea where she found the energy. She seemed extra anxious that morning, perhaps because of his stupid joke. Knowing what kind of odd things she found cathartic, he purposely tipped over the last half of his coffee and pretended regret as it dribbled onto the light carpeting.

"Damn, baby, I'm sorry."

She was up with a rag in her hand before the cup even emptied. "That's all right. Let me just blot up the most of it then I'll get you a fresh cup. Do you want to make calls from the study? I can run your coffee up to you."

Mason stood and picked up his plate and toppled cup. "Don't worry, I'll get the coffee. Why don't we swim this afternoon? I'll make my calls, you tidy up, and then we'll rendezvous here."

"It's a date."

He paused for a moment. Sometimes it still

took his breath away, seeing how beautiful she was. Those soft blue eyes stared up at him with such love and admiration it was sometimes overwhelming. There was something so special about Liberty, something pure and youthful he wanted to protect since the first day he met her. At age twenty-eight she still possessed that charming, nameless quality and he hoped it never faded.

"Mason?"

He shook his head. "Sorry. Right. Okay, I'll grab my coffee and messages and come find you when I'm done."

The smile spread to her eyes and he wished he knew what she was thinking in that moment. What had taken her from amused, to genuinely pleased? Right, coffee. He left her to clean up the intentional spill, glad to see it was already re-laxing her to be of some help, and headed into the kitchen.

He had given her the look, that look that he gave her the first time he told her he needed to have her. Liberty understood that look. She would always recognize it. It was that random glimpse inside of him when all barriers were gone. A moment, just for her, one of life's little gifts, where she was shown that yes, her husband still found her attractive.

Folding up the damp napkin, she headed toward the laundry room and jumped when she heard the sound of glass shattering.

"Mason?" Pivoting, she ran into the kitchen. He was standing with one hand braced on the counter between the fridge and the sink, his face tight with tension. "What's wrong?" she cried and hurried into the room.

"Stop!"

Liberty froze.

"There's glass on the floor and you don't have shoes on your feet."

She shook her head. Something was terribly wrong. Ignoring his warning she carefully walking toward him. "I don't care. What happened? Are you all right?"

"I said, *don't move.*"

Something inside of her went on lockdown. She couldn't move, not after he used such a firm tone of voice. Her body quivered. What the hell? Why was she suddenly getting turned on? She wanted to ask again if he was all right. He hadn't answered her either time. There was no sign of blood. Physically he appeared fine. Emotionally something seemed to have upset him. Yet, she waited, as he commanded.

The glass lay between them like the Red Sea. Only his authority could clear the way. His hand dropped to his side and reached for his messages on the counter. His tense fingers crumpled them as if he were angry. "Is this who called last night?"

"Who? Your mother? I told you she called yesterday and this—"

"Sean. Was it Sean O'Malley who called last night after dinner?"

Was that the guy's name? She had to think for a moment. Mason had been kissing her and she was incredibly distracted as she took the message. "I think that was his name. Do you know him?"

Mason nodded, again appearing as if he were in pain. "I'll be in my study." Without looking at her again he took the messages and walked out of the kitchen.

Liberty stood there for several minutes wondering what she should do. The coffee stain was setting in the carpet and she needed to treat it, but the cleaner was under the sink. She didn't have shoes on and he'd told her not to move. Could she move if she got shoes? Someone had to clean up that glass. It couldn't stay there. Her anxiety over the disorganized state of the room and the inexplicable need to do exactly as her husband asked pushed and tugged at her like similar sides of a magnet. The nagging pull to correct the state of things battled with the need to obey. She didn't want to get glass in her foot and have to explain that she didn't listen to his edict.

Her palms began to sweat and her fingers shook. Biting down on her lip, she whimpered as nausea set in. If she weren't crazy there wouldn't be a problem. If she were a normal person who didn't need everything to be in its rightful place in order to function she wouldn't be standing there. If she weren't a pervert she wouldn't be getting a sexual rush from following her husband's command, a command that was anything but sexual. What the fuck was wrong with her?

A door slammed upstairs and she began to cry. "God damn it!" she snapped and turned to run out of the kitchen. Taking the steps as fast as she could, her small feet rounded the bend and her footfalls grew muffled the moment they landed on the soft runner of the second floor hall.

The office door was closed, thankfully. She made it into her bedroom and out again, with shoes now on her feet in under ten seconds. A minute later and she was standing back in her place in the kitchen.

It took another ten minutes of internal debating that only a psychotic person would suffer through to take a baby step closer to the pieces of broken glass. She debated and looked from the door, to the glass, to the cabinet that held the stain treatment, to the forgotten, soiled napkin on the ground.

Once she was over the humiliation of coming up against a crazy person and acknowledging that it was only herself, she moved onto being upset. Why would he tell her not to move and just leave? Did she do something wrong? He should know she wouldn't be able to deal with such a mess. Was he trying to test her? Push her?

Was he doing this to be punish her for something? Then came anger. How could he leave her?

Wrapped up in such a whirlwind of emotional confusion and rage, she didn't hear him return to the kitchen. Her lips pressed firmly together and trembled as her eyes blinked repetitively, holding back her tears, tears that would surely underscore that she was nuts. Who cried over coffee and glass? And what kind of moron didn't have the common sense to move when something had to be done?

He walked into the room and didn't appear to notice her. It was as if she was invisible—a notion that intensified her pain—until suddenly he stopped. "Oh, Jesus, Libby, fuck, come here, baby."

She turned to him and couldn't hold back the stuttering breath that broke her resolve. Regardless of her silence, she hurled the blame at him. *Bastard!* Only thought, no words needed, because he understood her that well.

He wrapped her in his arms and she crumbled. Too weak to hold it all inside, she couldn't prevent some of the ugliness within her from seeping out. She hated the jagged edges of herself, hated when others saw them too.

Liberty pounded weakly on his chest as she cried. "You just left. You told me not to move and you left! The carpet will be ruined now and that stain will be there forever."

Holding her tightly, he moved to the stools

beside the breakfast nook. "Baby, I'm so sorry." He pulled her onto his lap and tilted her chin so she was facing him. "Liberty, please don't cry. I'm an asshole. I forgot about the stain and I wasn't thinking when I told you not to move. I just didn't want to see you cut your feet."

She couldn't stop shaking or crying. His acknowledgement of forgetting about her only made it more real and more painful. His hands ran over her curls and cupped the back of her head, forcing her gaze to meet his.

"Look at me. I'm a jerk. You did nothing wrong and I'll buy you a new carpet before the end of the week. It isn't your fault. It's mine. *I* spilled the coffee. *I* broke the glass. *I* told you not to move. And *I* was the one who got distracted. *Me*. You did nothing wrong. As a matter of fact, look how hard you pushed yourself just to please me. I don't deserve a wife like you. I know how hard it must have been for you waiting here, alone and unsure. I won't let it happen again."

He spoke slow and calmly. Offering a jagged nod, she rested her head on his shoulder. She needed to cry a little bit longer and once she was done he simply held her. Exhaustion set in. Emotion clouded her mind until numbness took hold and she rested in his arms. Her eyes seemed to be blinking longer and longer each time to stay awake. When she next opened her eyes Mason was laying her in their bed and leaning down over her.

"I need to sweep up the floor," she mumbled tiredly.

He gave her a sympathetic smile and she wanted to cry for him. She hated that he had to suffer a broken wife who was so emotionally unstable she could have a complete episode over one cup of coffee and some broken glass.

Perching on the edge of the bed he brushed her hair off of her face. "What if I told you I wanted you to rest for an hour? What if I said, 'Libby, what I *need* is for you not to get off this bed for one hour so that I can carry out the dining room carpet and sweep the kitchen floor'? What would you do then, baby?"

"But that's *my* job."

He shook his head. "I want to do it. It'll be my penance for getting you upset. Let me do it, Libby. And when I'm done and you wake up in an hour, rather than swim, I want you to play for me. Will you do that for me?"

Playing sounded lovely. The piano was cathartic. He suggested it, not because he wanted her to play for him, but because he wanted her to play for herself. Pounding her frustration out on those black and white keys until they transformed into something beautiful had a soothing effect on her nerves. Mason would've much rather swam, she guessed, but she was grateful for his concession. "Yes, I can do that for you."

He kissed her nose. "Good. Call me if you need anything. Try to sleep. I'll see you in one hour."

~

Mason quietly shut the door and returned to his study. Gazing down at the message he'd been mindlessly staring at for twenty-five minutes while his wife fell to pieces in his absence, he cursed. What a prick he was.

"Fuck!" he hissed as he swept a pile of papers angrily off the small table in front of him.

It had been almost a year since she had an episode and he fucked it all up. How could he have been so absentminded? Maybe because he was a goddamn bastard! He picked the crumpled message up off the floor.

Perhaps it was a good thing he fucked up today. He knew what the message meant. Old Man O'Malley had finally died. But what just happened to his wife was exactly why he had no time to even think on what the other man's passing signified, exactly why his past needed to stay in the past. Her episode was a reminder of where his head should be. His duty was to Liberty and she would break if he told her what was running through his head.

Mason stood and walked over to the empty fireplace. Eying the crumpled note in his hand, he refused to let himself even glance at the number. He sighed and tossed the sheet of paper into the hearth and left the room. The temptation of his past was unwelcome in his present.

~

SUNDAY MORNING WENT a lot better than Saturday morning. By mid-afternoon Mason had Libby laughing and playing in the indoor pool and he was wishing he didn't have to go into work in a few hours. It was moments like this that he recognized how lucky he was. Liberty's vivaciousness kept him young and her kindness never failed to keep him honest. She humbled him with her trust, sometimes to the point of speechlessness.

He dove underwater and swam directly to where her legs dangled under the surface. Reaching for her ankle he tugged her under, hearing her yelp just before the dunk. When she broke the surface she immediately tackled him and tried to force him back down. Her slick flesh slid softly down his chest. They laughed and wrestled for a few minutes longer until they were both out of breath.

Mason swam them over to the lower end, towing Libby by her narrow waist. Once he was standing she wrapped her smooth legs around his torso and smiled at up at him. Her eyes were huge with her hair slicked back from the water, leaving her face without the usual frame of curls. They were easily the prettiest blue that ever existed.

There was a longing in those cerulean eyes. What did his pretty lady Liberty want? "If you could ask for one thing right now and, no matter what it was, no matter how much the cost, I promised to give it to you, what would you request?"

"A kiss."

He laughed long and hard. She was such a girl. "A kiss? Anything in the world and you would ask for a kiss? Not a new designer bag or jewelry or a new car?"

"No. Those bags are ridiculous. Do you know the one you bought me last month cost eight hundred dollars, Mason?" Of course he knew the price. What he'd like to know is who told *her*.

"So?"

"So that could be eight weeks of groceries for a small family or a much needed medical treatment for someone suffering."

At that he did kiss her, and he kissed her well and good. His tongue pressed between soft lips and reached deep inside her warm mouth as if searching for her soul. His body stirred when she suddenly wound her arms around his neck and kissed him back with equal or perhaps more passion than he intended. What had gotten into her? She was curiously stepping out of the shy and reserved persona she maintained for so long. Her diffidence seemed to be fading and he liked it.

Her thighs tightened over his hips and his body grew hard in response to the way she fit the crease of her pussy against his cock. Although they were wearing their swimsuits, the material was thin enough that every cleft and curve was evident.

Libby's tongue pierced past his lips as if she

were on a mission. So unlike the other night, she now met him with vigor. Perhaps this change had been long overdue and his Liberty realized it before him. She had been drenched when he touched her the previous evening, yet somehow he suspected he had missed his mark, always concerned he might push her too far.

Libby continuously reacted to his sexual overtures in a gentle, feminine way. He was satisfied with that. She was his wife and he would never pressure her to do anything that might make her uncomfortable. But, perhaps she *wanted* to be pressured.

She was suddenly like a woman possessed. This was a side of his submissive Libby he'd never seen. It was as if she had just thrown off a mask. He wondered how far he could coax this side of her and was delighted that he discovered it.

Mason's fingers forked into Liberty's wet hair from the base of her neck. Spiked lashes closed over crystal blue eyes. She clung to him with little effort in the waist deep water. His hand coasted up her back and found the threads at the back of her bathing suit top. He tugged. She didn't seem to notice so he found the tie behind her neck and did the same.

Taking control of the kiss he ushered her to the wide stairs of the pool and rested her bottom on the second step down. Holding her at the waist, he broke the kiss and eased away from her. As the space between them grew her top slithered into the water and fell away leaving two perfectly pink tipped nipples.

His handling of her suddenly baffled him. He was a moron. *Why do I fuck her—this beautiful woman who wants* me—*in the dark?* Potent desire filled his gut and tunneled through his cock. *Will she let me fuck her here? Now?*

She gasped, realizing he'd undone her top and moved to cover her body. He caught her delicate wrists and stilled her attempt. "No, let me see you."

She didn't relax in his grip, nor did she struggle. She simply dropped each arm to her side and bared herself just as he asked. Dear God, she was a wet dream. "You're incredible, Lib. I don't know how an old guy like me got so lucky."

"You aren't old, Mason. Thirty-eight is younger than it used to be."

"This, from the wise twenty-eight year old."

"Well, you don't look or act old to me. I think you're in better shape and more handsome than all twenty-something guys I've met. Besides, with you I not only get a hot husband I get all of your wisdom and experiences to learn from. You're one of the smartest men I know."

"Again, I wonder how I got so lucky."

Something lurched between them in that moment. A secret weighing a million pounds in emotion that could never be fully purged, and he sensed he wasn't the only one hiding something. His worry never ended where his wife was concerned. He was the provider, the decision maker, had the final say in their relationship, but she was the soul of everything. He wanted the soul to be happy and unafraid, always, but eternal content was a fairytale and Liberty's entire existence was saturated in internal disquiet. Her disorder left him impotent at times, a useless extension of herself, unable to protect her from the demons that haunted and he hated the hell out of what she suffered.

He looked at her curiously and she bashfully lowered her lashes. "It's almost time for you to get ready for work," she whispered.

He tipped her chin up so she met his gaze. "What would you give me, Liberty? If you could give me anything in the world, no matter the cost, what would you allow me to have?"

A slow smile touched her mouth. "All of it. Whatever you asked for, I would stop at nothing to make you happy. I'd give you my soul."

She might've had more to say, but he needed to kiss her again. He kissed her hard and was delighted when she kissed him back with equal vigor. Mason moved to the step and pulled her onto his lap. She went easily and the new position lifted her body so that her breasts were displayed before him as she straddled his hips.

Wrapping his hands around the tops of her spread thighs, he pulled her close. His cock found a snug crevice, past her pussy, at the cleft of her ass and his mouth found those berry tipped nipples. He sucked one than the other into his mouth, releasing each one with a short pop of suction. Chlorine slightly altered the natural flavor of her flesh. Leaning back he admired his work. Each rosy peak wore his kiss, bore his mark. They were *his* tits.

His hand coasted over her hip and down to her bikini bottom. She trembled above him and his barely contained desire swelled inside of him as a spattering of goose bumps prickled her tender skin. "Are you turned on right now, Liberty?"

"Yes," she breathed.

"Would you let me make love to you right here on these steps if I asked it of you?" She breathed a little harder at the suggestion. Interesting. Perhaps it was time to enrich their intimate relationship. Mason always tried to keep a bead on her limits, but perhaps they were changing. "Answer me."

She moaned. "Yes."

He didn't know if she realized that his position beneath her allowed him to feel every twitch and clench of her pelvic muscles. She was excited. Highly excited and fighting to keep still. What caused this? He wanted to see if he could push her farther out of her typically cautious self.

"And what if I told you I didn't want to make love? What if I told you I wanted to fuck my wife?" His words were out before he considered that they might not get the desired reaction.

A chill visibly traveled up her body causing her to tremble and sigh. Her pupils dilated, as she looked at him with denim blue irises, dark with arousal. Oh, something was definitely going on with her.

His shock at his audacious words disappeared. Calmly, softly, he asked, "Liberty, what if I told you I want to yank this suit aside and shove my cock so far up your pussy you scream with pleasure?" And the most incredible thing happened. He could swear her body tightened so much that she may very well have had a mini-orgasm. They were each full of surprises today. "Well, I guess that's my answer then."

In one quick move he had his swim trunks shucked below his balls and kicked them off under the water as he yanked her suit bottom aside and aligned his engorged cock with her tight pussy. Jesus H. Christ! He froze when he felt more than saw what she had done. He looked down at her.

The expression of drunken lust on her face morphed into panic. She shook her head. "It'll grow back. I'm sorry. I thought you would like it. I should have asked first."

He pressed a finger to her lips to shush her as he looked back down to see her bare lips again. "Stand up for me," he instructed in a hoarse voice.

She timidly climbed off of his lap and stood on the third step. The absence of her body's heat against the weeping head of his cock was now in second place to his curiosity and need to inspect his wife's shaved flesh. Her suit folded back over the naked delta of her pussy as she stood, utopia just a mere inch above the water.

"Take it off."

She swallowed and removed the suit. Her blue gaze avoided his as she quickly folded it and placed it on the side of the pool. Jesus Christ, had she gotten more beautiful. How long had it been since he allowed himself to look at her in all her naked glory? He was a fucking moron for not looking at her like this every day. Fuck that, every hour. He knew if he asked her she would do it too. If he said he thought that would be something he would like she would undress like clockwork for him.

He cleared his dry throat. "Sit on the edge of the pool." She complied. Amazing. More turned on than the first time he discovered an erotic picture of a nude in his father's desk drawer, he instructed, "Spread your legs, Libby."

She hesitated a moment, but then slowly did as he asked. Her gaze remained hidden from him. When her creamy thighs parted so did her outer labia. Like pink petals of a flower, her inner lips parted. Liberty had the most beautiful pussy he'd ever seen. His possessiveness of her body nearly toppled him.

An aura of purity had always surrounded her and he coveted that quality, always careful not to corrupt her innocence, yet, at this moment, he wanted to do very naughty things. He wanted to make his sweet wife scream.

A trickle of white nectar gathered at the seam

of her slit. Without thinking he ran his finger over her opening. Once he breached the small entry, his finger slid right in to the third knuckle. Smooth, hot, thick honey coated his skin.

She groaned and reared back, catching her weight on her palms. He hadn't meant to do that, but she was so wet it just happened. "I'm sorry. Did I hurt you?"

She was panting, neck arched, head hung back, wet curls swaying between her shoulder blades. What happened to his timid little wife? What she said next shocked the ever loving shit out of him.

The long curve of her neck slowly contracted and she tipped her chin to look at him. She was sacred, and so help him god, whatever she asked of him he would do. After one long, needy breath, she sighed, "Don't stop." Her words seemed to reverberate along the tender skin of his cock as if she whispered them over his most sensitive flesh.

He watched her as he pulled his finger out and slid it back into her pussy, this time with his middle finger as well. He cupped the palm of his hand against her sex, keeping his two longest digits buried inside and pressed against her hard little clit peeking out from the shaved hood of her mound. She moaned and her body tightened and pulsed.

"What do you need, Liberty? Tell me what you need."

She took two deep breaths and then, "I need

to come, Mason. Please make me come." She never spoke like that. Words like *come* were simply not part of her vocabulary. Her sudden boldness was likely one of the sexiest things he had ever witnessed.

He loved his tender, feminine wife, but the fact that she had the courage to communicate her needs filled him with pride. His mind briefly touched on their wedding night and the battle they faced with Liberty's shame. She'd come so far, healed so much since those difficult times.

Bringing his wife to orgasm was suddenly the biggest goal of his life. He dove between her thighs and fastened his lips around her peach clit and sucked hard, alternately running his tongue relentlessly over the bundle of nerves located there

She cried out, her moan echoing through the glass enclosed room. His fingers moved in and out, faster and faster. He'd make her come so hard she'd feel the echo of his kiss for days.

It occurred to him that they'd never done this. How does a couple spend five years together, married, and this was the first time he was eating her pussy? He'd always handled their intimacy with kid gloves, needed to, in order to keep Liberty's mind in the present.

Sure, he'd kissed her there in passing while making love, but that was nothing compared to what he was doing to her now. Such a difference, giving, versus taking, and while he'd given her many soft kisses in secret places upon her body, he'd never taken from her with such greed. Today, he feasted.

He was taking away her Madonna status and seeing her as a female made to seek pleasures untold. Taking and giving in a manner of sin that wasn't wholesome, but carnal and driven by greed, hunger, and need. It was freeing to be so uncivilized and finally allow himself to gorge on the woman he craved.

Her cries built and built like a tribal call. He believed she enjoyed herself in their bed, but she'd never offered more than a whisper. His fingers worked as her ass lifted off the tiled poolside. She was freely offering what he needed in that moment with zero inhibitions. Good, because he wanted to swallow every damn drop of her.

She was in a different place, a place he'd never witnessed her go before. It was as if for the first time in her life she allowed herself to be uncontrolled. As if the idea of having a worthwhile orgasm made her illness temporarily go away. He nibbled her clit with his teeth just as he pressed deep and tickled her G-spot and she came.

Pleasure filled cries echoed through the poolroom and he licked up every drop of her sweet come. In absolute awe, he watched as his compulsive wife suddenly let go of all the rules and needs for perfection so that she could experience her climax to its fullest. She was beautiful, because his Liberty was suddenly free.

~

LIBERTY COULDN'T MOVE SO she allowed Mason to lift her and carry her into the house. Her sex-muddled mind could hardly understand why watermarks left by the trail from the pool wouldn't be a good thing.

Her body shivered as the cool central air within the house replaced the warm moist air of the poolroom. By the time Mason laid her on their bed her senses were beginning to return. "You're going to get chlorine on the duvet," she moaned and he laughed.

"I don't care."

"But it'll stain." An uncomfortable ache intruded at the thought of such an imperfection.

"Then we'll send it out to the cleaners. Now, stop worrying and kiss me." His lips gently pressed into hers.

She was exhausted from coming so hard. He'd never done anything like that before in their relationship. Their track record of timid, controlled affection had everything to do with the way she was and the ghosts of her past, but the way he'd just behaved…it was like a fantasy come true. She very well could be dreaming. Hopefully, if she was, she didn't start moaning in her sleep and wake her husband.

He gently coaxed her mouth open and his tongue explored. Her desire rekindled and she found it almost impossible to lie passively beneath his touch. Her thighs rubbed together slowly as friction and sensation built. Mason wedged his muscled thigh between hers and she sighed at the hard contact. Shamelessly, she began to grind against his leg as his heavy cock rested over her hip.

Arousal smeared over her skin and her need doubled. Would Mason ever let her taste him the way he tasted her? She never much considered doing such a thing, found it difficult to understand how putting him in her mouth could bring her pleasure, but after his reaction to her at the pool, she had to wonder.

He kissed a trail down her neck and there was something so different about the way he was touching her, something aggressive and potent—something she—and he—had obviously been starved for. It was as if one of those walls her husband always kept firmly in place had suddenly come down. She wished she could pinpoint what caused this aggressive side of him. If it was something she had done to provoke it, she wanted to know exactly what it was.

Her body arched beneath him when his hot mouth latched onto her aching nipples. *Hard, suck them hard*, she wanted to scream. But she remained silent because that would be like asking for a gift. It would diminish the value somehow if she had to ask. She wanted him to *know*.

Gasping, she twitched when the sharp scrape of teeth abraded the sensitive tip of her breast like a shard of glass pressing against a rose petal.

It was as if he sensed her thoughts, making her feel all the more exposed.

She moaned and he quickly apologized, misinterpreting the sound. When his mouth licked over the sensitized area she wanted to weep with pleasure. Her hands held onto his broad shoulders as he continued to kiss and suck her flesh.

Mason's cock dragged over her bare mound and her clit swelled as if begging and reaching for his contact. Her thighs spread and his body fell into place, all parts aligning just as they should. Her folds were so damp. The tip of his length slowly penetrated.

Oh, God, yes!

His hips moved, making deliberate, shallow dips into her folds. She wanted him to fill her, stretch her, be a part of her. "Please, Mason."

He moaned and nudged deeper as his hot mouth left wet marks over her breasts and shoulders. He was only halfway in. She never understood why he held back with her. Sure he was a large man and she was a petite woman, but she had no doubt she could take all of him. Mason would never be brutal with her or intentionally cause her pain. His cock slipped farther into her channel and she sighed.

"God, Lib, you're so hot you burn me. So perfect. I could spend days inside of you." Her pussy fluttered around him in response to his words, but he still held back, not allowing himself to slide farther into her.

Suddenly, without thinking, she thrust her

hips up and forced him deeper. He sucked in a sharp breath. "Easy, baby, I don't want to hurt you."

A whimper escaped as the need to have him possess her completely drove her to madness. Why the lack of something that never bothered her before suddenly drove her to the brink of screaming, she didn't know. She wanted all of him, was coming undone from her wanting. "Please, Mason, please."

"What, baby? Tell me."

"I need more," she begged as her lips pressed into his chest.

"I don't want to hurt you, Liberty. You're too small."

She wanted to shriek. She wasn't a child. Usually so very even keeled and levelheaded, an unfamiliar temper grabbed hold of her. Her feet flattened on the bed, spreading her knees beside his hips, and she tried to yank him into her, immediately regretting the action. Not because he hurt her. On the contrary, the additional inch she gained was splendid. It was the way his body tensed.

She surprised him by not listening and his disappointment in her unprecedented disobedience was like an intrusive presence between them. It was as if he depended on her consistent submissiveness as much as she depended on his control. It was wrong to suddenly try to change the dynamic they had cultivated for the last five years.

Her shame at disappointing him was a living thing that took hold of her and wouldn't let go. Her body flagged as her guilt became too heavy. Her knees collapsed slowly into his thighs and passivity overcame her as Mason stilled.

He was breathing hard, a sheen of perspiration working over his toned shoulders and chest. He looked at her and she was too overcome with regret to meet his gaze.

"Liberty, look at me." The commanding tone was something that couldn't be ignored. Her eyes met his as a lump formed in her throat. He gazed down at her and frowned. "Stop. Whatever you're thinking, stop."

Her lashes fluttered, fighting back tears. She wanted to apologize for acting like a pushy brat, but if she uttered one word she would cry. If she cried while he was making love to her he would be repulsed and never want to touch her again. Her times of tears and sex ended long ago—or so she thought. Her breathing trembled in her chest as she tried to hold it together.

He caught a glimpse of her struggle and quickly processed it. Something changed in his expression. There was a sharpness, some keen awareness in his eyes that hadn't been there a moment ago.

"Arms above your head," he commanded. She did as he told her, not wanting to forget her place again. It was a quick lesson, how wrong it felt for her to attempt to be the aggressor. It spoiled any end rewards.

"I'm in charge," he whispered with undeniable authority.

Her pussy clenched. She loved when he asserted his strength and power. Such a contrary desire to her once biggest fears. Trust and love had a way of transforming frightening characteristics into something altogether different.

Every decision she made was controlled by her compulsions to remain in control, but when it came to Mason, he had the power to take away her control, demand her surrender in a way that quieted even her greatest demons. He was a man, her man, and he was strong and kind, and fiercely protective of her just as she needed him to be.

When he did or said things that displayed the control he held over himself and others it drove her wild. "I decide, Libby. That's how it has to be. That's how you need it, is it not?"

"Yes."

"Trust me to know what you need, Liberty. Always trust me." She nodded. "Good. Now open your legs for me." Her thighs slowly opened. "That's my girl."

Mason braced his strong arms beside her shoulders and took one slow stroke deeper into her core. Liberty sighed in much needed relief. He was physically negotiating with her, but also keenly observing her, as if he knew her body and soul better than she knew herself.

She trusted that at the first sign of discomfort he would retreat. Liberty was determined not to show weakness. She was a woman in her own right. She may have idiosyncrasies and needs that others would never understand, but she was no weakling. Not when it came to giving her man what he needed. Not when it came to surrendering her body to her husband.

He began to thrust slowly. It was a display of such self-possession, such self-discipline. She couldn't help but admire him as it was a chore to keep herself balanced and in check. But not Mason. Mason was always in complete control of himself. Seeing him embrace his powerful husbandly rights was erotic and immeasurably intoxicating.

"I'm going to go deeper, Liberty, and you're going to take it. Do you understand?"

"Yes."

"Do you need to feel me in you?"

"Yes, Mason, please."

"Then let me give you what you need." He thrust inside of her and her head reflexively fell back into the bedding as a moan of fulfillment escaped from some deep hidden corner of her being.

"Is this what you need?" He forced himself deeper, stretching her sex and spreading her thighs with the breadth of his hips.

"Yes!"

His hips moved faster. His strokes were smooth, but he pressed harder as if he, too, was reaching to meet that inner part of her soul.

"Do you feel how your body clings to mine?

How, no matter how tight, you instinctively accommodate me, your husband?"

"Yes!"

"That's what I am, Liberty. I'm your husband and you're my wife. There's to be no shame between us." He said this and she heard it for the comforting vow that it was.

There had always been that unspoken give and take between them that worked for reasons she didn't dare examine too carefully, but they'd never discussed it. Mason voicing what they were to each other was encouraging. His words baptized her, validated the assumptions of their love already in her head.

"I am your wife," she affirmed.

"*My wife!* Mine." He pressed deeper and the scratch of his pubic bone pressed against her newly shaven pussy as their pelvises kissed. "Tell me who you belong to."

"You, Mason, I belong to you!"

At her words something inside of him broke loose and he fucked her in earnest. His hips pummeled into the cradle of her thighs and she knew she would likely be sore by bedtime, but she needed him to continue.

His thick cock stretched her in a way it had never done before. As his thrusts gained force the hard tip of his shaft tapped against her g-spot. With each touch her body throbbed. That inner stimulation combined with the steady friction over her clit was maddening.

Scrape, pulse, flutter, pound, tap, scrape,

pulse, flutter, pound, tap...the crescendo built and she shouted as he grunted with each pound of her flesh. The contracting of her channel combined into a little internal earthquake as her clit pulsed. Their slick bellies glided over one another as her gaze followed the thick cords of his neck working with exertion.

And then he did something that changed everything. Perhaps he didn't even realize he did it. Perhaps he was so lost in the incredible moment his mind surrendered to his body's direction. He shifted his position and with his left hand he firmly gripped her wrists above her head. His authority and strength mentally threw her into absolute bliss and her body shattered in a physical mirroring.

Her pussy clamped down hard on his fat cock and hot jets of semen filled her channel. Mason roared and threw his head back.

It wasn't making love. It was fucking. But to Liberty, it was one of the most beautiful, extraordinary, and freeing moments of her life.

Mason collapsed on top of her, careful not to crush her. He panted into her damp shoulder. As his grip loosened on her wrists something inside of her unraveled, as if his hold had been keeping her reality at bay and now it was coming back.

All too soon she remembered the trail of watermarks in the foyer and the scent of chlorine that would permeate the sheets. Mason would have to hurry to make it to the hospital on time for his shift and she sympathized with the rush that would taint his evening. Unnecessarily, she dreaded it for him, but he would handle it in stride.

He'd probably eat from a vending machine rather than take the time to visit the cafeteria, so she would have to make him something quickly while he showered. That way he could at least have a shot at something nutritious.

"I feel a gorgeous woman in my arms, but I'm afraid her mind's gone somewhere else in the house," he mumbled, lips pressing into her hair. "Where are you? Mopping?"

She laughed with dry sarcasm. "Ha-ha. For your information I was mentally making you a sandwich, smarty-pants. You're going to be late and I don't want you to skip dinner."

He purposefully poked her with his softening cock still buried deep inside of her. "I won't be late and even if I was I wouldn't care. One day I plan to teach you the true meaning of post-coital bliss."

"I know what it means," she argued.

"Perhaps, but I'll make it my own personal goal in life to make you enjoy it. One day, Libby, I plan on loving you so long and so well, you'll sleep for days and never have to worry about scattered papers or shoes dropped in random disarray rather than properly placed in parallel perfection." He laughed and she didn't mind. It was true. He knew her better than anyone. There was no use denying it.

He kissed her softly then pecked her on the nose. She gave him a persnickety smile.

"Yes, Mrs. Davis, I believe that's my new goal, to one day have you kicking off your shoes at the idea of making love to me and never looking back to where they fall."

CHAPTER 3

*W*hen Mason came down the steps he smirked at the telltale streaks of fading wetness and detected the lemony fragrance Libby favored when it came to cleaning their home. His sneaky little wife had somehow found the time to mop the foyer while he showered. He found her in the kitchen folding over the top of a brown paper lunch bag. She must've snuck into one of the other bathrooms to grab a quick shower.

Her hair was a halo of wild golden curls, the way he loved it. She despised the disheveled natural state of her ringlets, but he found the look beautiful and sexy, all the more appealing for its rareness.

Legs clad in a short pair of old denim cutoffs and a loose, ivory light knit sweater that hung off of one creamy white shoulder she looked adorable. Her nipples poked against the material —braless.

She smiled at him. "Here's your dinner. All you'll need to buy is a drink. Try not to get something with too much sugar."

"Is my birthday the cause of your sudden concern for my health? Are you worried about my mortality?" he teased, as he hugged her from behind and placed a kiss upon her soft exposed neck.

"I am always concerned. This is nothing new."

"Don't you trust me to make good choices?"

She laughed. "For me, yes. For yourself, not so much. If I left it up to you, you'd have the world convinced the four food groups were coffee, candy, soda, and apple pie."

"At least one is a fruit." He squeezed her, not wanting to let her go. Maybe he should retire.

"Hardly."

"Thank you for taking such good care of me," he whispered against her shoulder.

She turned in his arms and looked into his eyes. "That's my job. I love you and I love doing it."

"I love you, too." He kissed her nose and she handed him his lunch. "I'm scheduled to get off around five. So long as there are no early morning emergencies I should be home by six." If he were lucky the evening would pass in a flash.

He'd worked the same shift for years. Every week was the same. He needed to keep his routine to keep life stable and predictable for Liberty. Unfortunately, there were those nights that patients needed him to stay several extra hours and, as a trauma surgeon, if he was needed he didn't have time to call his wife and announce he would be late. He hated those nights, knowing she worried and struggled with the change in routine.

On nights like that he usually returned early morning, the sound of her fingers pounding across the grand piano greeting him from all the way in the garage. He could always tell when Libby hadn't slept, when she'd been awake waiting and worrying for him.

With one final kiss he told her he loved her and she escorted him to the door. Her mouth pressed into his and he poured all of his gratitude and passion into the gesture, savoring the moment as if he could carry it with him until morning. Reluctantly he pulled away.

"Oh, Lib, I noticed my brown loafers were a little scuffed. If you have time could you see if you could buff them out for me?"

She smiled. This was another part of their routine. Liberty needed to constantly feel needed and necessary. It was difficult to do that when he was occupied at work. He made a habit of dropping small hints about ways she could please him in his absence. This usually did wonders for balancing her moods.

His shoes were fine, but, regardless of their untarnished state, he would likely return to not just one shining pair of brown loafers but a closet full of perfectly polished gleaming shoes displayed as if they were being privately gifted to the prince of England himself.

He kissed her one last time and she followed him to the foyer. Pulling his coat off the hanger she held it out to him. After sliding it over his shoulders she latched each button in a way that portrayed her utter devotion.

"I'll be back soon." He pinched her chin affectionately and headed to the garage.

As he backed out of the garage, he took one last glimpse at his gorgeous wife standing in the doorway before focusing on turning the car and pulling out of the drive. She stood at the door, a statue of beauty and salutation, until his car turned and the vision faded.

~

SEAN HAD his doubts that the mansion he'd been parked outside of actually belonged to Mase, but when a Mercedes hummed by and zipped onto the main road he was certain he'd found the place. Shit, Mase had really done well for himself. He'd fit in around here like a hand full of sore thumbs.

The stale scent of travel clung to him as he appraised the five or so coffee cups littering the cab of his truck and his old gym bag sitting beside him. Maybe he should just go.

Mase hadn't called him back, he was married to the girl with the sweet voice that answered the phone, had his Mercedes, and was finally a doctor. He'd done everything he set out to do. Well, mostly. Some things had changed, but time couldn't be undone. Perhaps this whole trip was a waste.

He looked back to where Mase's car had vanished. The sun was setting and pink hues filled the expansive seascape beyond the tall North Carolina dunes. They really lived in the middle of nowhere. There were other homes nearby, but they were all so damn big they seemed spread miles apart. Didn't he get lonely out here?

Sean remembered the sweet voice on the phone. *No, probably not.* Mase had his wife to keep him company.

He wondered what the woman who earned Mase's future was like. Would she be a fair blonde like him or brunette? Would she actually appear feminine at all? When one spent a chunk of their life loving men, he couldn't understand finding much appeal in a feminine woman. It would be like growing up on Italian food all your life and suddenly switching to Chinese.

Were they happy? Did he love her? He had so many questions. Things he would probably never know the answers to, like how often Mase fucked his wife, and if there was an underlying tension between them that would never go away?

His friend sure lived in a big showy house. Sean bet if there was tension in their marriage, they were probably superficial enough to never let it show. For all he knew, *Doctor* Davis might be nothing like the Mase he used to know. Sure as fuck, the cornerstone of who Sean was had been traded in and switched up.

A sick aching dread filled the pit of his stomach as he worried that Mase might have all together forgotten about him. No. He'd never be able to completely erase him from his mind. Not after what they shared. Sure, it had been thirteen years since Sean walked away, but they had two years of history prior to that. No matter how much things might have changed, there was no way Mase could have wiped those two years of his life from his memory.

Sean scrubbed his hands roughly over his face. He badly needed a shave and a bed. He'd been driving for fucking days and hadn't seen a hotel since he crossed the border. There was a town just over the bridge, but it looked to be mostly rental properties, not the kind of place you just walked into and filled a vacancy. The idea of sleeping in his truck didn't appeal.

He looked into the rearview mirror again. Where was Mase heading? Would he be back soon or was he gone for the night? Maybe this whole trip was a waste and he should just keep moving. But what if he left and Mase came right back and they just missed each other, never knowing if his presence would be a welcomed one or not?

Coming so close to his past after all these years and missing the opportunity to face down his greatest regret would be enough to drive him insane. Before all else, he and Mase had been friends. What was to say they couldn't still be friends? That was all they could be if his boy was married now. Jesus, what if they had kids?

Sean started his truck. He had to get out of there. He should've never come. But as he pulled onto the apron of the drive so he could turn around and go back the way he came, a shadow moving across the large front window of the enormous house caught his eye. He wanted a face to put with the voice he'd heard the night before, a face to identify the owner of Mase's heart.

Before he realized what he was doing he was already too far up the drive to turn back unnoticed. He'd just act like he didn't know Mase was out. Maybe the little wife could tell him if he was coming right back.

He recognized for a brief second that he wanted Mase's wife to be fat and ugly, maybe have a ridiculously large wart on her face. He told himself he had the maturity of a toddler and needed to grow up.

As he stepped out of his truck and slammed the heavy door he paused. Music was playing loudly from inside the home. Beautiful music, not the shit that was on the radio nowadays. This was piano and it reverberated from the house. He didn't recognize the song, but whatever it was it was lovely. He could hear the emotion pouring into every chord as if the artist was happy, but somehow alone. There was turmoil in the melody, but also hope, promise.

By the time he reached the front step, lined with impeccable landscaping and an array of plants whose names he probably would never be able to pronounce, he realized he couldn't only hear the music, but feel it as well. It was pumping from within the house so hard that it vibrated the soles of his feet.

Taking a solidifying breath, Sean rang the bell. The music abruptly stopped. Unless someone was standing poised with a remote pointed to the stereo, he suspected that music wasn't recorded, but being played by a real person. Was Mase's wife a musician?

The door opened and he froze. His mind blanked and filled with numbers and calculations. Thirteen years. If Mase moved on right away he could have had a child in that time, but she would be no older that eleven or twelve. This beauty in front of him, although appearing very young, was no child. She also bore no resemblance to Mase. Fuck, was this the missus?

"Can I help you?"

That voice. He recognized that voice. "Mrs. Davis?"

"Yes."

He swallowed thickly. "I'm Sean O'Malley. Is your husband home?"

~

Liberty couldn't help but step back. The stranger standing on her porch was enormous and no one she'd seen before. He didn't look like a solicitor, but for some reason a curious, self-preserving instinct awakened inside of her. She had the sense that this man could harm her, in more than just a physical sense. A foreboding impression unnerved her. His presence signified the one thing she never learned to manage. Change.

The disquiet thrumming through her veins was palpable. This man was more than just a stranger passing by. She held the door securely in a position so she could shut it quickly if need be. "Can I help you?"

The man shifted awkwardly on enormous booted feet and rooted his hands farther into his pockets. The sun had set and, like most Carolina nights on the coast, the temperature had dropped significantly. He wore a threadbare white T and was likely cold. However, that threadbare T did nothing to hide his enormous arms, corded with muscle and decorated with some sort of tattoo peeking past the cuff.

"Mrs. Davis?"

Her searching eyes jerked from his thick arms to his face. How did he know her name? "Yes."

His gaze moved over her as if analyzing her as she'd been analyzing him. Who the hell was this guy and how dare he look at her and make her feel as if she somehow didn't measure up to his expectations? She pressed the door closed a little more and braced her bare foot behind it.

He cleared his throat. "I'm Sean O'Malley. Is your husband home?"

Sean O'Malley? Sean O'Malley? Why did that name sound familiar? "You called last night."

"Yes, I'm the man that called."

She didn't want to admit Mason was out, let alone that he wouldn't return until morning. Not to this towering pile of muscle and tattooed flesh, but she couldn't lie and then fail to produce her husband. "He can't come to the door right now. Can I pass along a message?"

He frowned at her as if he knew she was lying. She stood a little taller, daring him to challenge her. He most likely found her attempt to intimidate him with her five foot stature next to his probably six and a half foot build laughable. Something seemed to click in his mind as his expression softened.

He held his hands out as if in peaceful surrender. "Uh, I know you probably don't know who I am, but I'm an old friend of Mase's. We went to Duke together."

Her shoulders sagged with slight relief, but she wasn't wholly convinced this guy wasn't out to do her family harm. As a doctor, anyone could look up Mason's records and see where he went to school.

"When? He's never mentioned you." She probably shouldn't have said that. It seemed to poke a sensitive nerve. If this was in fact her husband's friend, she'd just said something incredibly rude.

"Thirteen years ago. He lived at Brier House with me. We were in the same fraternity. I played football there, but hurt my knee junior year and my grades weren't enough to keep me in. I ended up leaving when I was twenty-one and finishing up at State back in Arizona."

Libby supposed the slight lilt to his accent was what someone from Arizona would sound like. She eyed him critically. He looked about Mase's age, maybe a few years younger. He definitely could have been an athlete. Even under his loose fitting jeans she could detect heavily muscled thighs.

He smiled kindly, exposing a mouth full of perfectly straight pearl white teeth. Wow, that must have been some popular fraternity. His grin softened his hazel eyes and upgraded him from attractive to gorgeous. A big hand ran through his dirty blonde hair causing it to stand on end and distract Libby.

"Look, Mrs. Davis, I assure you, your husband and I were friends, very good friends. I've been driving for days and I'm in need of a hotel and a bed. Do you know when a better time to stop by might be? I hate to be a pest, but I'm kind of just runnin' on empty right now and didn't want to miss the opportunity to see how he was doing after all these years."

She sighed. The sense of unease she first felt in his presence fading slightly. His forbidding appearance was rendered merely unfamiliar and therefore somewhat less alarming. Slowly acknowledging her total fear might have been misplaced she sensed he was genuine. "Okay, Mr. O'Malley—"

"Sean."

"Sean," she amended. "I'll be honest. Mason isn't home right now. Didn't he return your call yesterday morning? I gave him your message."

"He never called."

That was strange. She pursed her lips. Yesterday had been a complete disaster and that was probably why Mason neglected to tell her that this man was actually his friend from college. She wanted to believe him, and if what he said were true, Mason would expect her to be hospitable to his old friend. She didn't want to disappoint her husband. Her teeth pressed into her lower lip as she considered her options.

"You say you've been driving a while?"

"Over fourteen hours. You see, my dad just passed away and I took off right after the funeral. I really don't have anywhere to be at the moment and somehow wound up here. It only made sense to see if I could locate Mase."

"Oh, I'm so sorry for your loss."

"It's really okay, but thank you."

"Um, can you…can you excuse me for just a minute? I just need to check something. Just one minute please." She held up her finger as she stepped back. When he nodded she shut the door and quietly latched the chain.

She turned and ran into the kitchen, her bare feet smacking quietly across the cool tile floor.

Mason's familiar words played through her mind. *When we're unsure what to do, we ask for help, and our problems immediately feel smaller and easier to solve.*

Picking the cordless phone up off the counter, she pressed speed dial one as she walked into the formal living room and spied on their visitor from behind the heavy satin drapes. Her finger ran through a slight drift of gray dust marring the windowpanes and she made a mental note that cleaning the windows once a week was not enough in the fall.

The phone rang and clicked over to voicemail. "Hello, you have reached the voicemail of Dr. Mason Davis. I'm unable to take your call right now, but please leave a message and I'll return your call as soon as possible. If this is an emergency and you need to reach me, please contact Faith Baptist Hospital, extension two-two-nine."

When the phone beeped Libby said, "Babe, it's me. Um, there's someone here for you and he says he's an old friend from Duke. He seems to know a lot about you and I don't think he's lying. His name's Sean O'Malley. He's the man who called Friday night. Well, he's kind of without a place to go. He drove here all the way from Arizona or somewhere out west and needs a place to stay. I don't know what to do. He says his father just passed and I can't help but feel sorry for him. If he's a friend of yours I think, under the circumstances, you'd want me to welcome him into our home." She pressed her lips together and then mumbled, "God, I hope that's what you would want." She sighed. "I'm going to let him in and offer him something to eat. Please call me as soon as you get this."

When she returned to the door Sean was standing back and gazing toward the soffits. He appeared to be admiring the exterior of their home. It was really getting chilly. She could have called the hospital, but if Mason wasn't answering the phone it was because he was likely with a patient and that was more important than her needing approval. Maybe.

"Um, Sean?"

"Yes."

He looked at her with those piercing hazel eyes and her thoughts scattered like autumn leaves in the wake of a sudden gale. She shook her head and tried to focus. "Um, Mase is going to call back any minute. Would you like to come in? Could I fix you something to eat?"

He stilled for a moment as if considering if the offer was a good idea or not. "Uh, sure. Thank you, Mrs. Davis."

"You can call me Libby."

"Libby?"

"Yeah, it's short for Liberty, like the bell."

He laughed. "Cute. Thank you, Libby."

She stepped back and let him enter their home with one last hope that she wasn't making a mistake. As he stepped past her she looked up at his hulking size and admitted that if she was, she was a dead woman.

~

As Sean crossed the threshold an ominous chill crested his shoulders as though he were crossing into a secret place he might never escape from unscathed. So many insecurities came rushing to the surface. His father's taunting voice intruded on his calm. Stifling the unwanted memories, he focused on the woman in front of him.

Mase's wife wasn't beastly. As a matter of fact, she was perhaps one of the most adorable females he ever laid eyes on.

She was a little thing and he had the unusual urge to lecture her about inviting a strange man, twice her size, into her home when Mase wasn't around. What was she thinking?

He agreed to come in only because he had the sudden ridiculous fear that some other beggar might come knocking and feed her a line of bullshit and trusting Libby might end up inviting someone truly dangerous into her home. Oddly, something about her tapped into his protective instincts. This little woman needed someone to keep an eye on her.

The house entrance was ri-god-damn-diculous. He let out a slow whistle that echoed all the way up to the thirty-foot ceilings. It was homey, but also sort of like a museum. Nothing seemed out of place. Maybe the missus just finished cleaning.

"The kitchen's this way," she announced and he followed.

She only came up to his midsection, not even reaching his chest. Her feet were bare and her toes were painted pink. Girlie. She wore cute frayed daisy dukes and a sweater that hung precariously low over her one arm. Her bare shoulder hinted she had nothing underneath. Wild golden curls bounced with each step. Kudos to Mase for at least finding a woman with a bangin' body. If he were going to switch teams, he clearly made out in the draft.

Impressions of white and open space teased his peripheral vision as he followed. He was too busy sizing up his old friend's wife to truly take in the house. He was sure it was what American dreams were made of if Mase's knack to adhere to a goal was still as sharp as it once had been.

If anything, his boy had an incredible ability for sticking to his guns and keeping his word. He promised one day he would have an easy life with a good partner and nice home. Sean had no doubt he walked into just that.

Libby stopped and Sean plowed right into her. *Nice.* His hands reflexively grabbed her shoulders so he didn't knock her down and hoped he didn't trample her feet. "I'm so sorry."

She quickly extricated herself from his grip and turned to face him. She took a step back and smiled, but he could tell he made her incredibly uncomfortable. *Nice move, bonehead.*

"I wasn't looking where we were going. I hope I didn't step on your feet."

She looked down at her feet and back at him.

Her hand held a cordless phone he hadn't noticed earlier and she tapped it against her thigh nervously.

"Maybe I should go," he suggested. "Thank you for the hospitality, but maybe it would be best if you just tell Mase I stopped by—"

"No!" she said sharply, as if the idea of him leaving was more frightening than the idea of him staying. She softened. "I mean, no, please stay. My husband would want you to stay. Let me make you something to eat. Why don't you have a seat at the counter?"

She seemed a bit jumpy, so he nodded and began to pull out one of the three stools tucked under the marble countertop. This kitchen was like something out of the rich and famous.

"Not that one!"

Sean froze. What just happened?

He didn't move, but looked at her from the corner of his eye for clarification. She took a deep breath and, in a more controlled voice, said, "Not that stool. That one's Mason's. I think you would be happier on the third stool."

She smiled as if the third stool was the best stool in the whole world and surely sitting there would bring him great rewards. *Okaaaay.* He didn't give a shit if he sat on the fucking floor at this point. He was so tired he could literally weep.

He sat and she began to pull items down from cabinets she could barely reach. More than once he caught himself admiring the creamy slice of her ass that peeked out past the hem of her shorts when she went up on her tiptoes. A gentleman would offer to help, but something had him hesitating. Plus, he liked watching her.

He was a people person. He liked sitting back and learning people not by what they claimed they were about, but by how they actually acted.

She made fast work of making two turkey sandwiches for him. He found it curious the way she made them, one step at a time, almost mechanically. Her lips silently counted: one, two, three, slices of turkey then did the same for the next.

She placed one piece of Swiss on top of the meat and used a knife to carefully cut off the two inches that hung over the edge. Doing the same to the other, she lined the discarded pieces beside the bread and aligned two more slices of cheese. Her fingers squared them up and sliced the two pieces so they were exactly the same size as the slice below.

Frowning at the effort she put into feeding him, he wondered why she didn't just cut one identical piece to the—*Why are you turning sandwich making into a math problem?* Just throw it all on there.

As soon as the cheese spectacle was done she grabbed the remaining scraps and moved to the sink. She dropped them down the drain and turned the water on so hot steam rose from the stainless basin. What a waste. He would've eaten those pieces.

He was about to tell her so, but was cut off from speaking when the roar of the garbage disposal clicked on. He was going to say something when it clicked off, but then it clicked on again. And off. And on once more. It was beginning to sound like Morse code and he forgot what he wanted to say.

She moved back to the sandwiches and made an X with mustard then placed a dot inside two of the triangular mustarded off sections and a line in the other two. She did the exact same thing to the other slice of bread.

His mouth hung open in confusion by the time she held slices of lettuce at eye level and carefully tore away edges until they were as identical as they could get. Mason's wife was definitely a weird bird.

She smiled to herself when she finally seemed satisfied with the green leaves. The manicured roughage was strategically centered on the sandwich. The scraps went into the disposal. The same Morse code was applied for what seemed to be proper grinding.

She didn't talk while she worked. She was so focused Sean didn't know how she could have managed a conversation. It was like she was in another place and had forgotten he was watching her.

The two sandwiches were sliced diagonally and organized like a pinwheel on a plate. She poured a glass of juice from the fridge and opened a drawer to retrieve a perfectly folded white linen napkin.

He sat back thinking she would hand the plate to him, but she turned and disappeared into some closet on the far wall. She returned with a glass jar filled with pretzel sticks. After twisting off the metal lid and retrieving four perfect pretzels and throwing away a broken one, she laid each stick between each sandwich slice.

Out of a bowl organized so nicely he mistook it for a decoration, she carefully selected an orange and placed it by the plate. She went to the closet and came back with another orange to replace the one she just removed.

As full lips silently counted out six oranges he noted her tongue was a deep shade of pink. She methodically cut the fruit into six even slices and placed them in a small glass bowl so they resembled a star or a flower or some shit. He wanted to tell her she didn't have to go through all that trouble, but he was sort of interested to see what she would do next. She stepped back and eyed her creations and nodded, apparently satisfied.

He leaned back as Libby carried the plate, bowl, napkin, and cup over to where he sat and adjusted each item until the napkin was perfectly straight, the cup directly above it, the bowl exactly parallel from the cup to the left of the plate, and the plate turned so that the straight edges of the sandwiches formed a cross rather than an X.

Maybe she's a chef.

"*Bon appetit!*"

He was speechless. "Uh, thank you. It looks great."

She beamed at him. Mase's wife really had a stunning face. She was more cute than glamorous, bright blue eyes with soft blonde lashes, pink full lips, and a pert little nose. She looked like an all American girl, but also like no one he'd ever seen before. He took a bite and shut his eyes as he groaned.

"This is delicious," he said with a full mouth.

She nodded happily and cleaned the counter where she'd made his dinner. He ate in silence and continued to study her. The cleanup was as much of a production as the preparation.

The woman seemed to have a method for everything, the way she swept up the crumbs, the way she disposed of things, and washed the dishes. He winced when he noticed how red her hands were after washing the cutting board under steaming hot water, but she didn't seem to notice. She also filled a spray bottle with piping hot water and used it to clean the counter after she bleached it. The clinical scent of disinfectant was so strong it permeated his nostrils and tainted the flavor of his lunch, but he was still grateful for the meal.

Afraid she'd burn her hands again, he offered to wash his own dishes, but that had the effect of a record skidding to a stop in the middle of a party. He realized immediately he'd overstepped and quickly muttered that she never mind.

What the fuck kind of girl did Mase marry? Was this like some sort of Stepford shit?

After they were finished in the kitchen she invited him into what appeared to be the living room. He'd never realized there were so many variables of the color white. The carpets were white. The walls were white. The furniture, the trim, it was all colorless. There was even a painting on the wall of a naked woman's back with only a white sheet covering her finer parts —*Oh shit, not a naked woman, a naked Mrs. Davis.*

He looked away and feared he might have actually blushed.

She obviously caught him. "Mason had that commissioned for our one year anniversary. He insisted we hang it in here. It used to embarrass me, but he loves it so I've gotten over it."

"How long have you been married?"

"Five years."

"Were you together a long while before that?"

She laughed. "Oh, no. We only met about two months before we were married."

Two months! What the fuck? Did Mase realized she had some seriously goofy quirks before the wedding or was that something he learned after the "I do's". He realized she was staring at him. "What? I'm sorry, did you say something?"

"No." She shook her head. "It's just...you...you have a piece of hair sticking...I'm sorry, it's nothing. It was rude of me to stare."

"Oh, this?" He forked his fingers through his hair knowing it was just going to spike out the way it wanted anyway. "There's really no rhyme or reason to it."

Her blue eyes widened as he sent his hair into more disarray. Shit, should he not have done that? The scene from the movie *Rain Man* when Dustin Hoffman lost it over something Tom Cruise did ran through his mind, but Rain Man was autistic. Was that what was going on with Mase's wife? Nah, that didn't seem like the right diagnoses either.

A large grandfather clock in the corner of the room chimed, announcing it was nine o'clock. "Mason will be calling any minute unless he's in surgery. He always calls between nine and nine fifteen on Sundays to say goodnight."

God, Sean hoped it was sooner rather than later.

Two seconds later the phone rang in her hand and she smiled. "Hello? Hi, babe. Yeah. Yes. No, I'm fine. I'm sure. Okay." She held the phone out. "He wants to speak to you."

Sean carefully took the phone from her. The faint scent of flowers around her was amplified as he brought it to his ear. Her sweet fragrance clung to the phone. "Hello?"

"What are you doing there?"

"I'm good. How are you?"

Mase sighed into the phone. "I'm sorry about your father. I'm assuming he passed."

"Tuesday." The mixed emotions that always accompanied the mention of his father's passing slid through his mind, making no more sense to him than they had the day before.

"Guess he lasted a little longer than you expected. Sorry, that was uncalled for. Sean, you can't be there."

"I just wanted to see how you were."

"I get that, but my life doesn't allow for unplanned visitors. Especially visitors my wife has no idea about."

"Yeah, funny thing, that." Although Sean hadn't had many long-term relationships, Mason was married. How could he have never mentioned him to his wife?

Mase scoffed then whispered into the phone, "Of all people, you cannot hold my privacy against me. Besides, it isn't for the reason you think. It's complicated. It isn't good for you to be there with her right now. She had no way of knowing you were coming. I..." There was a sharp beep in the background. "Fuck, I'm being paged. Listen, do me a favor, is...is she okay? Liberty handles things...I know you have no point of reference, but is she acting normal to you?"

Sean hesitated. "Uh..."

"Is she upset or doing anything dangerous? Did you see her do anything you thought maybe wasn't a good idea?"

"Um, one," he hedged, very aware of Liberty standing beside him.

"One what? One thing? What?"

He forced a cough and mumbled, "Hand." He didn't want Liberty to know that they were talking about her right in front of her. Funny, thirteen years and Mase talked to him as if they'd spoken every day for the past decade.

"Fuck. Did she burn them? Was she cleaning?"

"Yeah."

"God damn it. All right, look, I gotta go see about this patient. I'm going to see if they can find one of the other doctors to cover my shift. As soon as someone gets here I'll be home. I know this doesn't make sense, but if she starts doing something you think she shouldn't, ask her for a glass of red wine and accidentally spill it."

"What?"

"Just, please. I have to go. They're paging me again. Let me speak to Libby real quick."

He passed the phone back to Libby and she smiled. "Hello. Okay. I thought you would. Okay. Me too. What?" Her smile briefly faltered. She looked down at her hands and he could tell she was upset. Her head nodded and she sniffled. "Mmhm. I know. I know. I promise. Always. I love you too."

She hung up the phone and looked at Sean. Was that accusation he saw in her gaze? Or perhaps resignation. Or maybe, he was just being paranoid.

"We would like it if you stayed. If you get your things I can show you where the guestroom is and you can get settled."

"Libby, are you okay?" He hated that Mase asked him about her behavior then went right ahead and lectured her. She obviously figured out he told on her. Why the fuck would he do that? Talk about awkward situations.

"What do you mean?"

"I mean your hands—"

"Oh." She looked down at her hands again much like she had when on the phone with Mase. "Sometimes..." She shook her head. "It's something I do when I'm nervous. Mason gets upset, but it's like I feel myself going somewhere I don't want to go and I need to, I don't know, bring myself back, force myself to feel that I'm still here. Please don't tell him."

Too late. Hadn't Mase told her he knew? Sean was sure that was why she looked so guilty before she said goodbye to him. "I...what did he say to you before he hung up?" He had no right to ask, but really wanted to know.

Libby smiled and her cheeks turned a pretty shade of pink. She lowered her lashes and admitted, "He asked if I was being a good girl and told me I was to take good care of myself while he was gone. He's very protective of me and worries. He asked if I would do that for him and then told me he loved me. I should have told him, but I knew he was getting paged and I didn't want him to be distracted when a patient needed him." She then looked up at him and steadfastly said, "I'll tell him the truth tomorrow. I promise. But right now he needs to work."

The bizarre faith Sean had in her honesty surprised him. There was something quite genuine about Liberty. Perhaps it was in her eyes, or the tone she used when giving him her word. Either way, Sean believed her for some reason—believed she would tell Mason what she'd done—which astounded him since he usually didn't trust anyone to keep their promises.

This woman was a lot of things, but definitely not *Rain Man*. She was smart and nurturing and he could already tell she had a heart that was built for loving others with a fierceness that was meant to be treasured.

The next few hours passed without incident. If Sean hadn't witnessed the entire episode that had unwound in the kitchen he would never think there was anything quirky about Libby. She showed him his room and then said she had to do something with shoes.

The shower he took refreshed him enough to wait up for Mase. When he did finally sleep, he had no doubt he was going to sleep like the dead. His bones were already aching for rest. It was only his unsettled mind and desire to see Mason that kept him upright.

Libby told him which room was 'the entertainment room'. He supposed that was what rich folk called the living room. He expected they'd watch some TV there or something, but when he came out of his room the chiming echo of the piano filled the home once more. It was a different song from earlier, but equally beautiful.

He followed the sound of music down the stairs and just before the first landing he realized where the music was coming from. Across the foyer was a large open room with nothing but a white piano set before the large window.

He stared in awe as Libby's fingers worked over the keys. Her eyes were closed and what she was doing wasn't what he'd describe as simply playing an instrument. No. It was too natural, too meant to be. It was as if she and that large piano were one. She was a woman making love to the instrument and it was breathtaking.

He sat on the step in the foyer for over an hour just listening to her play. He didn't want to be anywhere but there. When the front door softly clicked open he turned, forgetting where he was. His heart seized as his eyes met the dark brown stare he had gazed at a million times before. How was it that Mason still looked exactly the same? If anything he had gotten more handsome.

Mase smiled. "Hey you."

"Hey," Sean said in a hoarse whisper, his voice and confidence escaping him.

Mase tilted his head toward the other room. "How long has she been playing?"

"Pretty much since after she hung up with you."

"Good. You look good. How's life been?"

"Fuckin' sucks."

"That why you're here?" So like Mase to be out in the open in every way possible.

Sean shook his head sadly. "No. I guess I'm here because it's the one thing I said I would do when that bastard died and I didn't want to break my word. I see you kept your word too. She's something spectacular, man."

Mase looked toward his wife who still played without realizing she had an audience. "She is that." The affection in his voice plucked at a jealous chord buried somewhere in Sean's heart. "You couldn't have expected me to wait. I told you I wouldn't."

"I know. I'll be out of here in the morning."

Mase's eyes met his, the familiar edge of accusation in their dark depths. "You can stay. No one asked you to leave. No matter what, Sean, you'll always be someone I consider my friend."

"Mase—"

"Stay." Sean had always been helpless against that commanding tone in his voice. "For at least a little while."

He hesitated for a moment, knowing if he agreed to stay and be a voyeur of Mason and Liberty's perfect world it would likely be the most torturous experience of his life. He sighed. He was his own worst enemy. "Yes. Okay. I'll stay."

CHAPTER 4

*M*ason hung up his coat and placed his keys on the table by the door. His stomach had been in knots since he received Libby's message saying that Sean was at the house. The last thing he ever expected was for him to come to their home. Complicated didn't begin to explain the situation. And to see him now...

One would think thirteen years would age a person. Well, Sean had definitely aged, but in a way that agreed with him more than anything else. Mason ignored the jolt of familiar longing.

He still had a full head of light brown hair naturally streaked with various shades of blonde. His eyes weren't as bright as they once were, but still riveting as hell. The small creases in the corners only made him seem softer. He'd certainly grown into himself. Seeing the man who was no longer a boy brought back pain Mason had long ago buried. He wasn't sure he was ready to deal with such memories, but he also wasn't ready to watch him walk out of his life again.

He turned and Sean stood from the step. "I'll let you two talk. I gotta get some sleep. See you in the morning?" Sean said from the landing just as the piano stopped playing.

Mason sensed Libby approaching. Without taking his eyes off Sean he held his hand out to his left and said, "In the morning."

Libby's small hand, warm from playing, filled his. Sean's gaze moved over their intertwined fingers. The soft weight of Liberty's head on his arm was a welcome one. He glanced away from his old friend to kiss the top of her head and when he looked back to Sean there was something in his expression that made Mason so sad for him and angry with him at the same time.

"Are you going to bed, Sean?" Libby asked.

Sean looked to his wife and Mason held his breath. There was no way of predicting how the two would interact, but he wouldn't tolerate any kind of disrespect to his wife in their home or anywhere else. If Sean was carrying any old baggage he better have checked it at the door.

"I am. Thank you so much for everything, Liberty. You're a gracious host along with many other fine qualities. I can see why Mase chose you."

Mason let out a sigh of relief and pulled Liberty closer to his side. Interesting that Sean phrased his pairing with Liberty as a choice. To

Mason's way of thinking, Sean removed any sense of choice the moment he walked out on him thirteen years ago.

Recalling the sharp stab of rejection he suffered the moment Sean actually pulled away, Mason nodded a final goodnight. Seeing Sean leave thirteen years ago, actually watching him drive away forever had been a blade slicing through his heart that left wounds too large to ever fully heal.

Liberty's voice and soft laughter brought him back to the present. "It'll be fun having one of Mason's old college friends here for a visit. We don't get out much and I don't think I've ever met anyone from that time in his life." She smiled cheekily. "I bet you could tell me all sorts of things about my husband I never would've been able to pry out of him. I can't wait to trade stories."

Sean looked speechless and Mason had to laugh. He looked down at Libby, shamelessly teasing her for her ever curious nature. "Fraternal brothers share a loyalty that cannot be betrayed, Lib. It would take some seriously persuasive tactics to break that bond. But I will tell you, Sean is a sucker for apple pie. Maybe you should make another one and see if you can get him to talk."

She snorted at his obvious self-serving motive and playfully swatted him on the stomach. "Oh no, Mr. I Ate a Pie in Two Days. I'm not falling for that. Birthday's over—"

"I don't like pie anyway," Sean added. "But for chocolate cake I'll tell you whatever you want to know."

"Still a choc-a-holic, I see," Mason teased.

"Still obsessed with pie?"

There was a moment where no one spoke, a split second, perhaps a tad more. Sean was likely remembering the same moment in time that filled Mason's mind. Soft echoes of laughter colored the memory sepia in his mind. Naked limbs tangled around one another bathed in sweet, sticky smears of chocolate, other confections forming a muddy paste, making their hard bodies slick and delicious. The vision snagged on one specific image of Sean's gaze hooking his own as their laughter fell away like the weightless snow that had been coming down outside their apartment. He still remembered his exact thought in that moment when Sean stared at him.

I will never stop wanting you.

He turned in Sean's direction and sensed that he was there in his mind too. Thankfully, Libby broke the fleeting trance by cheering, "Finally, someone else who loves chocolate! Tomorrow night I'm going to make lava cakes!"

Mason shook away the images of his broken past and scoffed. "You have some nerve commenting on my diet. Those lava things you make are way worse than an innocent apple pie!"

"A slice is innocent. An empty pie dish in the

sink the morning after it was baked is a trace of a deviant."

"I'll show you deviant," he teased as he leaned down and tickled her belly and quickly kissed her neck.

Liberty yelped and then, just as she turned away, mindful of their audience, her eyes met his and energy surged between them. So potent, he might as well have been punched in the gut. He caught his breath on a near gasp.

If he and Libby had been alone he would have kissed her right then and there and perhaps made love to her in the foyer. Memories of their morning still fresh in his mind. He turned back to Sean and saw the same longing in his eyes.

Sean cleared his throat and the spell was broken. "I'll see you two in the a.m."

"Goodnight, Sean," Libby called as he already started walking away.

The rush of guilt that cut through Mason in that moment was something new and not at all pleasant, but the guilt was quickly replaced with defensiveness. He had no reason to feel uncomfortable for kissing his wife in his own home. And if Sean was uncomfortable with the way Mason was living his life, well, that was his own damn fault.

$\sim$

LIBERTY CLIMBED into bed just as Mason entered their bedroom after locking up the house. When he began removing his clothing she sat up, a ripple disturbing her tranquil mood.

"What is it?"

"You didn't hit the dimmer switch," she reminded him, knowing Mason always turned on the timed dimmer after locking up the house and before coming into bed. It was their routine.

"What if we left the lights on for a while?"

"But…then they'll be on when we fall asleep. We'll have to get out of bed to turn them off and then…I just think you…I mean, I think it would be best if we did things the way we always do." She tried not to sound panicked, but why wasn't he doing what he always did?

He sighed and sat down on the bed. "Talk to me about today, Libby."

Heat rushed to her face and she looked away from him. "Why?"

"What happened when Sean came here?"

"I told him you couldn't come to the door."

"Good girl. Then what?"

"Well, he told me how far he had come and how you two used to be friends in college and that his dad had just passed and I couldn't just send him away. I thought, if he were telling me the truth, you would have wanted me to invite him in, but I wasn't sure so I called you, but you weren't there. I didn't know what to do. I only wanted to do what you would have asked. I didn't want to disappoint you."

"You didn't disappoint me." He looked at her with such an understanding about how hard that decision had been for her that her tension immediately eased. Giving her leg a squeeze through the blankets, he said, "You have better instincts then you give yourself credit for, Lib. You would have known if Sean was a stranger lying to you. Try to trust yourself."

She looked down at her hands and nodded. Mason always promoted her autonomy. It was she who chose to be dependent on his final decisions. It was laughable how much she mentally remained a child. Sometimes she could be so pathetic.

"Tell me what happened next," Mason said, as if purposely trying to detour her self-deprecating thoughts that were probably written across her face.

"I made him something to eat."

"Did he say anything to upset you?"

"No, of course not. He was perfectly polite."

"So you weren't upset at all?"

"Why are you asking this?"

"I just imagine that it was difficult for you to have an unexpected visitor suddenly come to the house and then to have him inform you he was a friend of mine, a friend we've never discussed. Was it?"

She didn't answer. It hurt that Mason rarely spoke to her about his friendships from that part of his life. At the same time she feared he hadn't omitted Sean's presence in his past so much as her own crap overshadowed the moments for such little anecdotes. Five years seemed like an eternity, but it was amazing how many things could still go unattended when things were far from perfect. She'd do better from now on.

"Liberty, look at me."

Slowly she raised her gaze. He didn't appear angry, only concerned.

"Baby, don't hide from me. Remember what happens when you do? We're past that stage. Now, do you want to tell me what upset you?"

Her resolution to be a better wife took a backseat as she played back that afternoon's moments of weakness. Words jumbled in her throat. She wanted to let them out, but her brain refused to tell her muscles to move. Mason waited patiently for her to find the strength.

She sighed. "He sat in your seat."

"Is that all?"

God, she was a horrible person. "His plate," she whispered.

"What about it?"

"There was mustard on it."

"Oh, honey, you know you can't let yourself get upset about that kind of stuff."

"I know." He was right and she was disgusted with herself.

It had been over a year since she let something so inconsequential upset her. Mason ate every day and she tolerated his entitlement to do so without the rules she placed upon herself and her own precise approach to dining.

Years ago, watching others eat without any form of order would have tied her stomach in knots. She'd gotten past that. It was impossible to live with another person and worry about such nonsense, but sometimes, around new people, it still bothered her. Obsessing over such things gave her the same agonizing constriction in her stomach and throat she got when unsuccessfully trying to thread a needle.

Mason softly massaged her toes through the covers. "We have no control over what others do, remember? Only when someone's hurting someone else can we tell them to change what they're doing. The only thing you can do in a situation that's making you uncomfortable, where no one is being harmed and it would be wrong for you to interfere, is walk away. Liberty, you cannot wash away other's imperfections any more than you can wash away your own."

She blinked. A tear fell to her lap, the tiny drop making a dark circle on her otherwise flawless nightclothes. "I know."

"If you think this will be a problem while Sean is staying here, I'll either ask him to leave or have the hot water heater adjusted again."

She looked at him and quickly said, "No. I'll behave better. I promise. If the water isn't hot I won't be able to clean the counters and the floors the way they should be."

"Okay, but you have to give me your word that you won't burn yourself. If you're bothered, walk away. If that doesn't help, come find me, go to the piano room, or take a swim, but you aren't to harm yourself. Do you understand?"

"Yes. I promise. Are you disappointed?"

"No. We all make mistakes, Lib. I know you're already upset with yourself. It's over now. Do you understand?" He gave her a pointed look. "Over. I'm not upset and there's no reason to feel guilty or to beat yourself up over it. I just wanted to make sure you were okay."

"I am."

"Now, are you okay with Sean being here?"

"Will he stay for thirteen days?"

He laughed and then gave a comical sigh. "Ah, Libby, you do have a reason for everything, don't you? Is that thirteen days for the thirteen years since he and I last saw each other?"

She tilted up her chin and took great pleasure in informing him that he was wrong. "No, that would be silly."

"Then why thirteen?"

"Because he arrived on a Sunday and it's now late and already Monday. A proper visit should be two weeks, but day one is over."

"And who says a proper visit should be two weeks, might I ask?"

She rolled her eyes at him. Taking on an air of hauteur, she crossed her arms over her chest and informed him, "All sophisticated people know a proper visit is two weeks. I can't help it if you don't know these things."

"Liberty?" Rather than answer she looked down her nose at him and tried not to laugh. When he seemed convinced he had her attention he said, "I love you."

What was it about him, about the way he always accepted her without condition that made her continuously fall more and more in love with him each day? She let her arms drop and met his gaze head-on. "I love you, too."

He turned and climbed across the bed until he was directly in front of her. His lips kissed her nose and he whispered, "Lie back."

"But..." She'd already begun doing what he asked and then hesitated. This wasn't right. "It's Sunday...and the lights..."

"Yes, it's Sunday and your husband has come home from work early and would like to make love to you. He's also decided his wife's beauty is too great to waste on the darkness. Now, do as your husband asked and lie back."

Her body fell back to the mattress. Anticipation bubbled low in her belly.

"Hands above your head," he instructed. She did as he told her. "Good girl. Now, these adorable little shorts must come off, I'm afraid."

He was acting so playful she laughed. Mason slid her silk bottoms over her legs and tossed them over his shoulder. They landed just to the left of the long dresser. She'd put them in the hamper as soon as they were finished whatever he had in store.

"How do you feel? Are we okay?" His expression was only momentarily serious, but he expected an honest answer.

She had to think why he was asking. She'd been so caught up in anticipating whatever he was planning she forgot about her apprehension. Selfless pride fluttered in her chest as she noted how quickly the unordinary conditions in which they were about to make love had slipped her mind. Her lips tugged with a smile. "I'm okay."

"Good. Spread your legs, Libby. Let me see how beautiful my wife is."

She slowly did as he asked. Her face flushed when he looked directly at her sex.

"You're enjoying this," he commented as he swept a finger through the slit of her folds, coming back with a glistening fingertip, and holding it up for her to view.

Liberty didn't know if she should feel embarrassed or aroused. She supposed she was experiencing a combination of both. The two emotions blended into a potent cocktail that gave her the same tipsy sensation she got when drunk.

Mason climbed into the space between her legs, pants still on, and braced his arms just outside of her breasts. He caged her in, making her feel so completely feminine that her arousal increased.

"What would you say, Liberty, if I told you I was tired of making love to my beautiful wife like a married minister, only on Fridays and Wednesdays and only ever in the dark? Would you be opposed to me changing things? I know you like to have an idea of what to expect, but I've been doing some thinking, and I think it's time we stopped being so damn predictable in bed."

Her heart raced as she considered everything he was asking. While it excited her and met many hidden desires, it also terrified her, stirring her deepest fears.

"I also think, as strange as this may sound, that when we're fucking it's the *only time* you actually favor spontaneity," he continued. "I think you want to be taken by surprise. I think when we make love, not like we've been doing for the past five years, but the way we did yesterday, whatever it is inside of you that tells you everything has to be perfect, goes quiet. Your body somehow knows it's better to simply let it happen, to feel, and you, in turn, surrender your control. Yesterday at the pool I watched you, Lib. I watched you come undone and it was the sexiest fucking thing I have ever saw in my entire life."

His spot on explanation for everything she'd been feeling of late astounded her. How could he have made such quick sense of things she was trying to comprehend for months? No one had ever known her mind so completely to the degree that Mason did. She wanted to cry, to shout, *Yes! That's what I want!*

She breathed heavily. Mason slowly leaned down, easing closer to her lips, but never taking his gaze off of her. A wild gleam filled his eyes and ever so slowly he licked across her bottom lip. A moan escaped before she could stop it.

"Is that what you want, Liberty? Do you want your husband to fuck you until you can't think anymore? Until all the noise, the memories, the need for perfection is silent and all you can think about is your heartbeat throbbing in your pussy, screaming in your ears, followed by the symphony of white noise as you come?"

It was too much. Each word created an image so erotic and desirable her pussy was already clenching, begging for him to make good on all his provocative promises.

"Yes," she admitted breathlessly.

"Then that's what you're going to get."

His mouth crashed down on hers, as her body seemed to get electrocuted back to life. The hard bulge at the crotch of his pants pressed into the cradle of her sex as he began to roughly grind himself against her softness. His arm slipped under her back and he raised her upper body off the bed.

"Hold onto my shoulders," he ordered against her lips then returned to ravishing her mouth.

She held on as he pulled her upward. His hands lifted her as he fumbled with his belt buckle and rolled to his back. Her knees came down on the mattress at either side of his hips and she was suddenly straddling him. He kept one arm firmly behind her back as his other hand held his cock and glided it through the moisture weeping from her folds.

"I want you to fuck me, Liberty. Just like this. I want you to fuck me until you come." He was breathing hard into the curve of her neck as he held himself beneath her, the tip of his erection already probing her sex. "Now, Liberty."

She impaled herself on his cock and screamed at the delicious shock of pleasure. He stretched her channel, still tender from that morning. Her spine arched and her head fell back. There was a sharp tug at her scalp as Mason gripped a fistful of her hair. She was riding him, but he was in complete control, completely dominant. She imagined how they must have appeared and a surge of cream coated his hard cock as she bobbed up and down on it and sobbed out her pleasure.

He cradled her ass in the strong grip of his other hand as he began thrusting his hips off the bed. The effect was even deeper penetration. With every thrust he grunted and she cried out in response, over and over, and soon the bed-springs were mimicking her cries.

SEAN LAY in the unfamiliar hotel-like bed, arm folded over his eyes, and tried not to hear the sounds of pleasure echoing through the house from down the hall. He was strongly considering packing his shit up and leaving, but he was pretty sure a house like this came complete with a security system that would rival Fort Knox. The last thing he needed to do was interrupt them by tripping some alarm while trying to creep out.

How on earth did he convince himself coming here was a good idea?

The moans built in tempo and volume until finally Liberty's scream of pleasure was followed by a crescendo of shouts as they both reached their finish. Yeah, he knew what that was like, but he wasn't going to allow himself to think about that.

He was here now, so he might as well make the best of it. Remembering Mase the way he was, expecting him to be who he used to be, would only wind up hurting everyone. It was clear, by the way he looked at his wife, that his college days were only a chapter of self-examination that led to discovering his true nature.

Following the eruption of climaxing cries, there was only the muffled drone of voices here and there and then nothing but blissful silence. He hoped he would finally be able to get some sleep, but his brain wouldn't shut off.

Mason's lips, mason's thighs, his strong hands, flashes of his body and what his body was capable of played through his mind. Yet with every vision came the interruption of softer counterparts. Lily-white skin, soft, dainty shoulders, pale pink nipples, his mind accounted for what he didn't know.

Images collided as bodies writhed under a fog of woven fantasies no good hearted person would entertain. He needed to get out of there. It seemed in one short week he'd lost his father and Mason all over again.

True, he'd given up Mason years ago, but hearing him make love to his sweet wife, seeing him gaze into her eyes with such unguarded affection, it made the loss so much more pronounced. New wounds appeared where old scars had hardly healed.

Sean was torturing himself when all he wanted was some form of closure, a closure he'd never been able to find since the day he walked away from the one person he'd given his heart to, the one person who'd ever truly loved him without condition.

He was breaking with every tick of the clock, every blink of his eye, and every beat of his heart. Yet he couldn't make himself rise and walk out that door. He was here and something cried out inside of him to stay.

∾

PRESS, *pull, squeeze. Press, pull, squeeze.* Libby was kneading dough for biscuits on the marble counter when two firm hands grabbed her by the hips. She jumped and then smelled Mason's aftershave as he pressed his soft lips into her neck.

"Good morning," he said as he nibbled her shoulder.

Liberty smiled as a chill worked up her spine. "Good morning. Did you sleep well?"

"Amazing. Only problem was I went to bed with a gorgeous woman and when I woke up this morning she was gone. Have you seen her?"

She chuckled. His hands wrapped around her waist and traveled upwards until he cupped her breasts through her fitted T-shirt. She gazed down at her fingers covered in flour and sticky dough. A sprinkling of flour flurried to the floor. She couldn't see where it landed, but knew it was there.

"What are you making?" He plucked at her hardening nipples and she sagged into his hold and sighed.

She swallowed. "Sausage and biscuits."

"Mmm. Have I ever told you how much I love your biscuits?" He cupped her breasts suggestively.

His erection nudged against the back of her thin eyelet skirt. "Mason, we have a guest in the house."

His hand traveled down low and then back up, under her shirt. His warm fingertips coasting over the soft skin of her belly made her body shiver and a yearning for him began to fill her tummy. "Don't worry. Sean's always been a sound sleeper."

"I have dough all over my hands," she whined, playfulness masking how much the mess truly bothered her.

"Then you'd better keep them on the counter." He reached up and placed one palm flat on the cool marble surface, then the other. More powder fell to the ground, this time sprinkling the edge of the lower cabinets. "God, I love it when you wear skirts."

Cool air touched the flesh of her backside as he flipped up her skirt and all thoughts of flour dusting her clean floors temporarily vanished. "Mason! We're in the kitchen!"

"I know." His hand slid beneath her silk panties and over the cheek of her ass. The thin strap pulled away from her hip as his hand nudged its way to her front and cupped her sex. "This..." He rubbed the smooth surface of her pussy. "I love."

Her weight pressed into her palms balanced on the lip of the counter as her body warmed. Mason's foot tapped at the inside of her ankles and she widened her stance. He leaned into her so that she was somewhat hunched over the messy surface as he rubbed his cock up and down the cleft of her ass. Her panties and his sweats seemed almost inconsequential.

This new, aggressive side of her husband spoke to some baser part of her and couldn't be ignored. It was like robbing Peter to pay Paul. Her compulsion eased just enough to let him in the result of her surrender was her sweet reward.

Sex—the way they'd been having it lately—brought a flash of silence and peace to her that she'd been chasing for years. Something so coveted shouldn't be overlooked, so she savored the continued presence of her husband's libido, allowed it to enhance her own.

She could trade a dusting of flour for those few seconds of peace. She could stomach putting off her routine a few minutes for those luxurious seconds of utter tranquility and stillness within her mind. She only hoped the price was not more than the profit in the end. It was a gamble with her sanity, forcing herself to relax long enough to reap the benefits of what she coveted most, an unbroken moment of perfect serenity.

He moved his hand the slightest degree and the tip of his index finger pressed, not into her slit, but right under the hood and onto her throbbing clit. Her body jerked at the sensation.

"I want to make you come in the kitchen, Liberty. And when I eat your biscuits, I'm going to remember that you came while making them." He whispered into her neck as he licked and kissed her flesh.

His finger softly flicked up and down as his other palm pressed into her abdomen, holding her against him, the slight restraint working to amplify every twitch and brush of his body against hers.

Someone cleared their throat and Mason stilled. Mortification ran through Liberty like ice water through her veins.

Mason's softly whispered, "Fuck." And she knew she hadn't imagined the sound.

He slowly removed his hand from her panties and from under her shirt. The cool weight of linen over her rear replaced the warmth of his body as he stepped back. Although he was no longer touching her intimately, he still used his form to shelter her from Sean's view and she was grateful for that.

"You gonna be okay?" her husband whispered.

Her body was totally aroused, but he wasn't asking about the state of her body. He was asking if this was going to ruin her day and, in turn, totally alter the course of his. She'd already had one episode that week. She refused to have another. Her head tipped in a tight nod and he pressed a brief kiss to her neck and stepped further back then turned.

"Sleep okay, Sean?"

"Uh, yeah. I didn't mean to…"

Mason shook his head at Sean and their guest thankfully dropped it. "Breakfast should be ready soon. What do you say I give you a tour of the house? About thirty minutes sound good, Lib?"

She bit her lip hard and nodded, unable to face them. When their retreating footsteps faded into the foyer she sagged with relief. This was exactly why kitchens were meant for cooking and not much else!

CHAPTER 5

*S*ean followed silently behind Mason as he led the way through the echoing foyer and up the floating staircase, each step a suspended plank providing an airiness to the space that Sean considered quite fitting with the simplistic style and clean lines of the house. It struck him as odd, how some parts of the house seemed so warm and others so cold.

Some rooms, like the guestroom he stayed in, were furnished in warm wood tones and plush fabrics that combined shades of sea green and robin's egg blue to perfection while others were so monochromatically done he felt as though he should be wearing a hospital gown and preparing for a medical procedure.

The dark stained steps gave way to pristine white carpet running through the second floor hall. There wasn't a spec of lint on the rug, nor a footprint, or stain, or smudge anywhere. This wasn't a cream color rug in the white family either. No, this was pure ass white. Maybe it was brand new or something.

They turned into a small nook with an inset door. Mason opened it and Sean followed him inside and froze. *Holy fucking shit.* They were standing in a guy palace.

Heavy leather club chairs faced a seventy-inch LED flat screen. Behind them was a red felt top pool table that, by the looks of the detailed undercarriage, was custom made. A large oak desk, equally detailed, sat off to the right. The room was large enough that furniture could sit cockeyed in the middle of different areas and still look organized, creating airy sections without walls in one generous space. But it was the back of the room that had him drooling.

The entire back wall was covered with top shelf liquors beautifully displayed in front of the mirrored back. Overhead racks in the cabinets dangled snifters and goblets and martini glasses of all kinds of shapes and sizes. In front of the wall was a twenty-foot brass railed saloon style bar fitted with ten leather stools, each complete with brass grommets. The taps peeking over the top of the polished wood showed all names of expensive imports.

"Jesus Christ, you've turned into James Bond. Either that or I've just entered the bat cave."

"This is my office, or study, as Lib likes to call it. This is one of my domains in the house. You're welcome in here whenever you'd like while you're our guest."

Sean didn't know if he should say something about what he'd walked into in the kitchen. Mase's tone was clipped. His words were friendly, but his mannerisms clearly showed he would rather be fucking his wife right now than giving him a tour.

Sean walked over to the bar and ran a hand over the smooth top. "This is really nice, Mase. You must be a kick ass surgeon."

"I do all right."

"All right in this economy doesn't reflect this. Dude, I'm paying you a compliment. Take it. This is fucking beautiful."

A little of the hostility left Mase's expression. "Thank you. Come on, I'll show you something you'll like even more."

Sean smiled, a little more at ease now that they were talking and Mase was acting more like himself again. He followed him down the hall and to a nondescript door. "What's this?"

"It doesn't look fancy from here, but that's because it's soundproof." Mason opened the door and stepped into a dark space. There was no echo to the room and the air felt a few degrees cooler than the rest of the house. Their footsteps were muffled by the flat, sponge-like carpet and the silent darkness made him extremely aware of their proximity.

"Shut the door and just bear with me for a

sec," Mase said as he picked something up off a nearby piece of furniture.

Sean shut the door and was bombarded with Mase's memorable and suddenly familiar scent. Realizing he'd misplaced this memory, he quickly seized it and cataloged it back in a pleasant part of his mind where it belonged.

As shameless as a kleptomaniac, Sean inhaled Mason's deep scent, stealing it, without requiring any rational cause, for himself. Nostalgic emotions tickled the peripheral of his mind at the familiar spice of *Ralph Lauren* cologne and *Ivory* soap. Mason smelled exactly the same. He was suddenly self-conscious of his breathing, but before he could develop a complex, a roar of sound circled the room scaring the piss out of him.

It was the boot up sound to an HD system just before a movie begins. A soft amber glow streamed from recessed lighting in the carpet and dispelled the darkness. The return of his sight caused his keen sense of smell to ebb. If he thought the television in the study was huge than this movie theater sized screen in front of him was mammoth. An antique style popcorn maker and six leather recliners, complete with cup holders and massage remotes, were the only other furniture in the room.

The screen slowly lit and the lights dimmed as soft percussions began to play a slow beat over the Bose sound system surrounding them. He knew those cymbals.

The Paramount Pictures mountain appeared

on the screen just as the first bell tolled and the beat picked up. "Shut. The fuck. Up."

Mase laughed. "I thought you'd like this."

Tom Cruise's name faded onto the screen, expanding about a foot per letter and Sean was pretty sure he had a boner. The whole spiel about the navy finding the top percentile of pilots played on the display and Sean and Mase both recited it without reading a word. They had it all memorized. It was something every guy knew.

When they reached the last line they were each smiling, recollections of reciting the litany of words a hundred times before, played through his mind. "Today, the Navy calls it Fighter Weapon School. The Flyers call it..." They waited for the screen to change and the gong to bang then roared, *"Top Gun!"*

What a couple of assholes they were, but no matter how old a guy, if he had nuts, he still got a rush when you heard the intro to *Top Gun*.

The whistle of the wind blowing over the aircraft carrier was a work of theatric art on the sound system as it sung with the percussions. When the radio instructed the pilot he felt like he was in the fucking cockpit. In that moment he was Goose and Mase was Mav.

His body literally vibrated with the bass shaking the room. The jet fuel burning out the back of the plane on the runway bellowed as though it was right next to his head. The floor shook with the treble and then...*fuckin' A*, they were headin' to the danger zone.

As Kenny Logins rocked out *Highway to the Danger Zone* a nostalgic rush of adrenaline zipped up Sean's spine and he smiled genuinely for the first time in a long time. This was the shit he'd been missing for the past thirteen years. Perfect Mase, always doing as he should when required, was still perfectly okay with just goofing off and being a regular guy for the fun of it.

"What do you think?" Mase yelled over the roar of the jets taking off. The bass was so alive Sean could swear his hair was blowing back.

"What do I think? Are you crazy? This shit's insane! I love it!"

"Ready for this?"

He hit a button on the universal remote and a light came on along the right wall. Suddenly a mantel began to rise from out of the floor. Thirty seconds later they were facing a wall of back to back DVDs. There must have been over two thousand.

"Shut. Up." Sean walked over to the display. It was out of this world. The disks were organized by genre and then alphabetically. They even had color coded stickers on the spines of the cases to identify them.

Mase lowered the TV so he didn't have to shout. "Just so you know the sound won't work if the door is open. It's all wired to function only when the room is set for optimal performance." As he spoke he randomly pulled about a dozen DVDs from the shelf and just as randomly slipped them back into different slots. "You can help yourself to whatever you feel like watching and if you want popcorn all you have to do is hit the switch and fresh kernels will be popped and buttered for you in no time."

Sean was speechless. What was there to say, really? This was probably the coolest room he ever set foot in. Mase knew he would love it. He didn't have to tell him, but he would anyway.

As he opened his mouth to do just that Mase grabbed another stack of movies. "Dude, what the fuck are you doing?"

Mase stilled as if he was doing something out of habit and hadn't realized that mixing up a perfectly organized display was weird. "Uh, I do it for Libby. She sometimes runs out of things to keep her busy and she likes to organize stuff. I'll tell her I noticed some cases were out of place this week when I sense her getting restless and she'll come in here and feel better when she's done."

Sean didn't want to overstep, but he had to ask. "What's the deal with her? I'm not trying to be a smartass," he quickly assured him. "I just don't understand."

Mase put the last case away and shifted uncomfortably. "Liberty's special. I'm not really sure how to explain it. Medically, it's called OCD, but it's more than that. She has compulsions to make everything perfect, or what's considered perfect in her mind. She sometimes becomes obsessed with details and if she's having a really hard time coping, she gets upset. You'll see her do things that'll raise your eyebrows and then you get used to it and forget she has a clinical disorder and chalk it up to just being quirky. It's easy to forget she has it. I've been living with her for so long, I just kind of adjusted my own routines to help balance hers. So long as I don't stray too far from our usual routine we don't have much of a problem and it's smooth sailing."

"Isn't there, like, medicine she can take for that?"

Mase chuckled. "Like I said, it's complicated. There are medicines, but one of Libby's quirks is that she has a very hard time swallowing pills. She can get them down, but then she freaks herself out because she feels like they're stuck in her throat. She'll continuously touch her throat until she's covered in hives from irritating her skin. Plus, if she goes off the meds her issues return and as far as coping, she's then out of practice. All she's doing is numbing out a part of who she is. We'd rather see her work through it."

"We?"

"Yeah, me and Libby. She's aware she has it. The level of which she suffers from the disorder is extremely overwhelming to her at times."

"Did you know she was like that before you married her?"

Mase laughed. "What's that supposed to mean? You think I wouldn't have married her if I knew she had imperfections? Gee, thanks."

"No, I just…Liberty told me you two got married, like, a month after you met."

Mase didn't appear offended and continued to smile. "You guys talked about that? Actually, it was two months. And yes, I knew she had it the night I met her. It's kind of what brought us together."

"How do you mean?"

Mase looked at his watch. "Another time. It's been twenty-seven minutes. I told her we'd be back in thirty. Let's not keep her waiting." The mantel returned to the floor and the screen went dark. They shut off the lights and headed back downstairs. Libby was placing three glasses of orange juice directly above three perfectly folded napkins just as they entered the dining room.

She smiled when she saw them come in. "Perfect timing."

∾

BECAUSE SUNDAY WAS Mason's nightshift period, he was essentially off Monday unless he got called in, which, by the sound of it, rarely happened. If Sean's intrusion that morning upset Liberty, she failed to show it. Breakfast was outstanding. Sean couldn't recall the last time he was so well fed.

After breakfast she busied herself with tidying up the kitchen and Sean and Mason returned to the entertainment room to digest and watch the remainder of *Top Gun.* There was little talking, but that was fine. When the movie was over Liberty was again playing the piano.

The afternoon seemed to progress without incident. After lunch they spent a good part of the afternoon playing cards and small talking. No heavy topics were discussed and Sean got the chance to play voyeur and see the inside workings of Mason and Libby's relationship he imagined most people didn't see.

There was no denying Liberty's appeal. She was one hundred percent feminine, but in a more adorable way than a femme fatale way. When she laughed she did so openly and her laugh was one that inspired the smiles. She was what Sean would call a cotton kind of girl. She looked good in natural fibers, wore them well, and anything over processed or weighted in detail would only detract from her natural beauty.

Her frame was small and Mason frequently held onto her, pulling her to his lap, tucking her under his arm. These were actions men, no matter how reserved, tended to do with petite women. She opened up sides of Mase he would have never been able to fabricate in his own mind.

Mase was always an even keeled kind of guy, even back in his twenties, but he was softer with Liberty. Sean had a difficult time reconciling the cries of ecstasy he overheard the night before with the chaste handling he observed throughout the day. Even that morning, he had known simply by the energy of the room that he walked in on a private moment, but he couldn't imagine the two of them experiencing the intense dynamic he and Mase had shared years ago.

"Last card."

Sean looked up as Liberty called out her status. Shit. He was losing his shirt in this match. Time to put on his game face. Crazy Eights was something he had known how to play since he was a child and he wasn't too fond of losing, no matter how cute Liberty was when she won. He slammed down a deuce. "We'll see."

"Oh, not nice, Mr. O'Malley." She pouted and picked up two cards.

"All is fair in love and cards," he informed her.

Mase laughed. "You'll see Sean is a cut throat gamer, Lib. I can't believe you won two hands already." He threw down a three, causing Sean to miss his turn and bring it back to Libby. "I doubt he'll lose gracefully again at this point. My boy's a terrible loser."

Sean's heartbeat stuttered, as his eyes shot to Mase's while Libby evaluated her hand. Had he realized what he said? Yes. The look in his eyes told him he caught the old endearment, however, it also told him it was a slip.

"There. Of course, I'm now holding suits that have already been used. I can't believe you put a two on me."

They stayed locked in a stare a moment longer and then Mason turned away to take his turn. Every time Mase did that, looked at him like that and then tore his gaze away, it felt like he was tearing away a layer of flesh with it.

Sean tried to sound light, as if nothing had distracted him. "Believe it. Cuteness will only get you so far in cards, my dear. I plan on cleaning the floor with you."

A few minutes later Sean was down to his last card and Libby had a fist full of them. He watched as she struggled to find the perfect order in her dainty hand. His mind strayed, wondering if she preferred to line them up by color, suit, or number. Any unknowing onlooker would see no difference in the way she organized her hand from any other person, but after what Mase told him earlier Sean found himself searching for signs of her Obsessive Compulsive Disorder. He was right, the longer one was around her, the more used to it one became and the harder it was to see.

"I'm out."

His gaze shot from Liberty to Mase. "Son of a bitch. I didn't even realize you were close."

"That's because my strategy was to let my beautiful wife distract you. See how well my diabolical plan worked? Shall I do my maniacal laugh? *Muahaha!*"

Although Liberty only laughed at her husband's joke, Sean was incredibly self-conscious of how transparent he'd become. As always, Mason, no matter how unobservant he appeared, missed nothing.

Sean had been intently watching Libby, maybe even ogling her at times, but for him to scrutinize this part of Mase's current life…it was mind boggling in so many ways. He hoped Mase wasn't pissed he was analyzing. He would have to be less obvious. Really, he should stop, but she fascinated him.

"Indeed," Sean admitted. "Try not to be so beautiful next time, Liberty. I may be a terrible loser, but Mason is an even worse winner. If he wins this hand it'll be unbearable and I'll have to go to a hotel just to avoid his obnoxious gloating."

She laughed. "You're as much of a sweet talker as Mason. You two must've driven the girls crazy on campus. I can just imagine the traffic through your frat house. Tell me, Sean, did Mason constantly have a tie hanging from his doorknob or some other symbol for 'Do Not Disturb'?"

"Are you asking if I was a whore in college?" Mase asked, pretending to be completely appalled by her insinuation.

"Yes," Liberty answered unrepentantly. She looked back at him. "Well, Sean, was he? Was Mason the campus man whore?"

Sean busied himself with shuffling the deck and dealing out the next hand. How to answer such a question? Finally he said, "Uh, actually no. I mean we only met my sophomore year. Mase was already onto his masters by then, so I have no idea how he spent his time while earning his undergraduate, but during the two years I knew him I can only recall him ever going out with one person."

"Ah," she said as if she'd just been given a

valuable clue to a puzzle. "An old flame. What was her name? Was she pretty? Mason never tells me any of the juicy parts of his past."

Sean cleared his throat and looked up at Mason. He should've kept his mouth shut. Mason only looked amused at the pickle Sean put himself in.

Thankfully, Mase asked for coffee and Liberty's focus was pulled to solely meeting her husband's needs. She disregarded their conversation and stood, excusing herself to immediately go make a fresh pot.

After she left the room Mason looked at him. "That would have been an interesting explanation to hear. Do me a favor and try not to go there again."

His words were reproving, but his tone was light. They looked at each other for a long sobering moment. "Why didn't you ever tell her?" he finally asked quietly. "She's your wife."

"I would have, but there never seemed to be the perfect moment. That would be a long conversation and believe it or not, we have plenty of stuff to keep us busy. I guess it just never came up."

Sean only half believed him. He wondered if shame was partly to blame for Mase's secretiveness.

"Don't look at me like that, Sean. I was never ashamed of what we had. That was you."

"Mase—"

Mason held up his hand to halt protests.

"Don't. The past is the past and there's no changing it. We both know why things didn't work out. Unfortunately, it took thirteen more years of you living with your bigoted old man's abuse to realize how asinine your stance on the entire situation was. Did you ever get the closure you were searching for?"

A hoarse, "No," was all he could manage.

"Well," Mase looked at him sadly. "Then I'm sorry for that. I'm sorry for a lot of things."

"Me too."

The sound of the door being nudged open stifled any further conversation on the topic, as Liberty carried in a tray laden with three Danishes and three cups of steaming coffee.

LATER THAT EVENING, Sean had a life changing experience. He learned what a Lava Cake was. Liberty told him any chocolate lover needed to be well versed in the incredible healing powers of such a dessert and she hadn't lied.

The piping hot, cake-like brownie sat on top of cold vanilla ice cream and was bathed in hot fudge and covered in crushed nuts. Upon tasting such an orgasmic concoction the first words out of his mouth were, "Oh my God, marry me." She laughed, but he was dead serious. "Forget Mason. You and I can run away and live on a lava island and eat nothing but this for the rest of our lives."

Liberty smiled adorably, her cheeks a deep shade of pink.

Mason shoved him. "Get your own wife."

"Quiet, apple pie boy. Libby, go pack your stuff."

Sean ate every last bite and was more than tempted to lick the bowl. By the time he was finished he was falling into a chocolate coma. It was indeed a beautiful thing.

"Have you ever been married?" Liberty asked after dinner when they settled into the living room to loaf and watch some TV.

"Me? No. I don't think I'm the marrying type." He only ever loved one person and in that case marriage was out of the question—at least back then it had been.

She tilted her head, causing her blond ringlets to bounce and settle back into place. "Why's that?"

"I guess I just have unusual tastes. I'm very particular about what I want. No one's ever really suited me enough to make that type of commitment."

It wasn't a lie as much as an omission of detail. He avoided Mason's stare.

"I believe there's someone perfect out there for everyone. I mean, if I could find Mason...I'm sure you'll someday find a woman who completes you."

Mason cleared his throat meaningfully. "Lib, don't pressure him. Not everyone wants a long-term partner in life."

Thirteen years ago, Sean would have agreed with him. Now, he wasn't so sure. Lonely was a long road and he'd been on it for a while.

Liberty turned back to him and asked, "Do you date? Mason works with some lovely women. And most of them are doctors, too."

"Lib," Mason warned, but Sean smiled, telling him it was all right.

"I've dated. Even had some longer relationships. As easygoing as I seem on the outside, I can be quite different when involved with someone intimately. I don't think I'm an easy person to please."

"I don't believe it. I can't imagine you being anything but easygoing."

"You'd be surprised," he muttered, again avoiding Mase's gaze.

~

"HAVE you asked Sean about staying for the next twelve days?" Liberty asked as Mason removed his clothing and climbed into bed.

"No, but I will tomorrow. He seems to really like you."

"I'm glad. I like him too. I sense that he's sad, though. Do you get that feeling? I wonder if it's because he just lost his father."

There was something peculiar about Sean. Sometimes she caught such a desperate look of longing in his eyes she wanted to weep. She wondered if he were simply mourning the loss of his father or if it was something more.

Mason rolled to his side and she faced him. The lights were still on. He, again, didn't hit the dimmer, but Liberty was only mildly bothered. Her mind quietly reconciling itself with the lack of consequence that followed last evening's illuminated interlude. He reached over and twirled one of her curls around his finger.

"I think Sean's lost a great number of things in his life, some things because of his own stupidity, and others due to no fault of his own. He has a lot of regrets, but I doubt losing his father is one of them."

"Why do you think that?"

"Mr. O'Malley was a mean old bastard. When Sean was younger he used to beat him and his mother. Sean's always feared one day he'd grow into his father and that's probably why he's never allowed himself to get too close to any woman."

She shook her head. For as intimidating as Sean appeared, she was certain he was nothing more than a gentle giant. "Do you think Sean is capable of hurting a woman like that? I can't imagine him doing that. He just doesn't strike me as someone capable of being cruel."

"No, I don't think he could hit a woman or a child, but I'm not him. I do know that for Sean to get close to a partner they need to be strong, otherwise he'll avoid all possibility of intimacy."

"He *is* a big guy," Libby added, imagining his enormous biceps.

Mason released her curls and trailed a finger over her collarbone and down to the shallow valley between her breasts. "Liberty?"

She lowered her lashes. "Yes."

"I want to talk to you about the way we've been recently, intimacy wise, I mean. Do you feel like it's improved our relationship?"

Greed had the ability to spoil many things that were near perfection. She'd learned long ago that tolerance and temperance were sometimes worth more than perfection. Benevolence was safe.

She thought carefully about how to answer Mason, momentarily seeing herself as a teenage girl cowering at her mother's table, KarLyn's cruel words cutting her down with the grace of a hacking ax.

"You can be such a greedy brat, Liberty. It's not enough that you're an only child, doted on without the distraction of other siblings. No, you're not satisfied until you have everyone scrambling about, working to right the ridiculous drama you create. Nobody likes a liar. That's what you are, you know, a little liar.

"I will not let your filth affect my happiness! You should be ashamed of yourself. What have I done to deserve such a petulant, dishonest child? What is this thirst in you to see your family so unhappy? Greedy and spoiled rotten, that's what you are. Now get away from me. I don't want to see you again until you're

ready to speak the truth. I'm done listening to your lies."

LIBERTY LOOKED into Mason's eyes. "I'm very happy with our marriage, Mason. I have no complaints."

"I understand that, but even good things can be improved. There is no denying that the last two times we've made love things have been a little more...intense. I'm not sure what caused this, but it seems to be working for both of us. I need to know if I'm right. Do you like the way it's been?"

She blushed. Greed could so easily lead to destruction. Her fears battled with her desires. Mason was not her mother. He loved her. She gave the slightest nod and he smiled.

"Is that a yes?"

She smiled back at him shyly. "Do you like it?"

"Yes. I always enjoy being intimate with you, but recently...I don't know. Something's changed. It's like we've tapped into something that was locked up before. I feel this incredible rush when you surrender to me and let me have control."

"You've always had the control, Mason. You know I don't want it in that department. As much as I come off like a control freak, I'm really not. I know I'm sick. It controls me, not the other way around. But...you're stronger than *it* and with you, when you're in control, I feel... better.

What's inside of me isn't my friend. It's an intruder I wish would go away. You're my husband and I love you and trust you with every part of my life. I'll gladly give you control, because while I'm not strong enough to make it go away, you are."

"You're stronger than you think, Libby. Just look how far you've come since the night we met."

She hated thinking about that night. True, it had brought her to Mason, but it was an ugly memory and always made her feel dirty.

I can't wash it off...

The filth that seeped from her pores that night clung to her like tar and there was no removing it no matter how hard she tried. An uncomfortable noise left her throat and Mason quickly apologized for stirring her demons. "Sorry. Don't think about it. Let's get back to what I was saying. I've been thinking that whatever this new energy is between us in the bedroom, I want to experiment with it, see how far we can take it. What do you think about that?"

"What do you mean by how far?" She welcomed the distraction his suggestions stimulated inside of her, chasing the shadows of her past away.

"I mean, I've always sort of handled you with kid gloves. In the beginning, I think that was necessary and the only way for our relationship to work in order to progress intimately and build a foundation of trust. But I think we've moved past that preliminary stage. We're solid, Lib. We have great communication and we're always honest with each other. I have no doubt that our relationship can sustain a little pressure. Is this something you'd like to experiment with?"

She thought about the last few times they made love. Something had certainly changed between them. Sunday, after Mason left for work, was the first time in weeks she hadn't secretly masturbated.

Her moods seemed all together lighter and that needy ache had subsided. It was still there, but it was somewhat pacified. A heady satisfaction accompanied their recent sessions of love-making that had been absent in all their past encounters. She didn't want to go back to the way things were, lights out, gentle petting, tender kisses. She would still enjoy making slow love from time to time, but right now her body craved something more intense, slightly frightening yet safe, because it was with Mason.

"Would I be able to change my mind if I said yes?"

"Of course. You'll always have a choice. There will always be a place for you to catch your breath. All you need to do is tell me you need to regroup and then we'll stop and discuss what's happening. Worst case scenario, we go back to the way things were. I have no complaints about how things were. I'm just wondering if they could be better."

She considered his words and then agreed. "Okay."

A slow smile curled his lips. "Good. That pleases me, Libby."

His praise was an aphrodisiac. Her belly tightened and her sex tickled. She really did love the way he handled their marriage.

Allowing him to be the man, to be the head of the household in all matters, gave them each very clear roles. She could trust Mason with everything and that was very freeing. To him, her submission was a gift, but to her, him taking control of the things she couldn't, was an even bigger gift.

"Is there anything specific I can do?" she asked.

"Yes. Before we jump into this, let's discuss some limits. I want you to be completely clear on what I'm asking of you and I want you to be honest with me if something makes you uncomfortable. I'm not saying I'll automatically take it off the table, but we'll definitely take some time to evaluate why something touches a nerve and then decide if it would be wiser to move ahead or take a different course. Okay?"

She nodded and he continued, "I'm done making love to you only on Fridays and Wednesday. You're my wife and as my wife I want full access to you. If I feel like fucking in the middle of a Thursday afternoon, then I want to do just that. And from now on the lights will be on. I like watching you when you're at the peak of your pleasure. I feel like we connect on an emotional level we were missing before when the lights were always off. I want to be in control, Liberty. I know you say you're okay with that, but I want you to understand that when I say control I mean complete control.

"I decide how and where we make love and you'll give me your complete submission unless you feel it's leading you into a bad place. At that point you'll tell me and we'll take a minute to breathe like I said. I'm going to push your limits, Lib. I had all intentions of fucking you in the kitchen this morning and would have if Sean hadn't walked in. There's no place in this house or on your body that's off limits. Can you handle that?"

Her mouth was completely dry and her pussy was sopping wet. Where was this side of him coming from? Everything he said was intimidating and a little frightening, but also erotic.

As she listed each demand her anticipation grew. Her heart raced as if she were on a roller coaster that just climbed up the steep ramp and she was waiting for that unpredictable 'click' just before it let go.

She swallowed and rasped, "I can handle that."

He nodded, a pleased expression on his face. "There are things we've never done, Lib, things that some women might find repulsive. There's no shame between us. I don't want boundaries. I'll tell you now and I'll remind you every chance I get. You're a gorgeous woman and I enjoy looking at you and seeing you as God intended you to be. Our bodies are our own and we wouldn't have been given the ability to do certain things if they were completely wrong. I'll never humiliate you or purposefully cause you harm, but I will do my best to push down any unnecessary walls between us and take you to a place where all you can do is feel how incredible sex can be."

He cupped his palm along the side of her face and told her, "You're my wife and I love you. I'd give up everything for you and give my own life to protect you from getting hurt. I need to know that you trust me to know what's safe and where your limits lie."

"I trust you, Mason."

"Good. I may add some additional expectations as we proceed, but for right now, that's about it. There is one more thing, though. The third floor is yours. That guestroom will be the one place in the house you can go that stops everything until you're ready to continue. If you feel overwhelmed and need to hit the brakes, you go there. I won't cross that threshold unless you ask me to. No matter what. I'm giving you that space so that you always know that, in the end, you're the one with all the power. You're the one with the final say."

He appeared to have said everything he intended to say at that point and now he waited for her to accept his request. He was basically asking if she would agree to try this sort of dynamic, and once she agreed, he would cease to ask again. At that point she would have already signed her X on the dotted line and handed him her complete acquiescence.

It was a big choice to make, a choice she probably should consider carefully. Any normal woman would have, but she'd never really been normal by society's measuring stick.

She had needs other women didn't. Mason provided her with a life where she didn't need to make excuses or explain herself. He accepted her. He wanted this as much as she did, so there should be no shame in her acceptance.

His domination would be a gift, a relief, and she was eager to receive it.

"I agree."

CHAPTER 6

*T*he atmosphere changed the moment she accepted his edict. Something animalistic glimmered in the deep set pupils of his eyes and she tried not to tremble as his smile grew into something somewhat devious. She wondered if that was the look the devil gave those after contracting a soul. That's what she'd basically promised her husband, her soul.

"Stand up."

His tone was soft, but there was a definite command in his voice she wasn't going to question. Her fingers slowly pushed the covers aside and climbed out of bed. She knew she was safe and had nothing to fear, but she couldn't help the way her body trembled in response.

"From now on, I want you coming to bed in nothing but your wedding rings unless instructed otherwise. Why don't you take off that gown and put it away?"

He worded it as a suggestion, but Liberty heard it for the command it was. She silently slid the silk gown off of her shoulders and stepped out of it. Her nipples pulled tight when the cool air hit her flesh.

Slowly walking it over to her dresser, her hands neatly folded it, and tucked it into a drawer. She returned to stand at the side of the bed to wait for his next instruction. Her thighs pressed together to keep her arousal from slipping down her legs.

"Good girl." He sat up and pulled the duvet and sheet down to the foot of the bed. "Now I want you to lie down on your back."

She did as he asked and waited, the cool central air a weightless blanket upon her naked skin. He climbed on top of her and straddled her hips. The fully erect weight of his cock tapped on her belly, doubling her arousal. Her body was pinned beneath him and that excited her more, for reasons she wasn't yet prepared to evaluate.

"Arms above your head."

She complied. The motion caused her spine to extend and her ribs to slightly protrude. Her slight breasts fell flat and heat rushed up her neck to the sensitive points of her ears. When she laid like this she self-consciously felt like a boy, flat chested and small.

Mason's large hands reached for her diminutive breasts. His fingers found her tight nipples and he proceeded to roll them between his thumb and index finger. She moaned when he applied a bit more pressure than she was accustomed to.

"You like when I pinch them," he observed accurately. "You have beautiful breasts, Liberty. I know you think they're small, but I think they're perfect. Sweet and tender. I love sucking on your tight nipples. You're so sensitive here. Perfect."

Liberty arched beneath him as he played with her breasts a while longer, tugging and tweaking the delicate tips, and she began to fidget and squirm beneath him, but she didn't move her arms. Her hips were still pinned between his muscular thighs. When he sat back on his heels he took his cock into his fist and slowly pumped his hand over the smooth flesh.

She'd never seen him touch himself before and found it mesmerizing. Her eyes focused on the firm way he gripped his flesh. His touch was much harder than she ever dared to touch him. His fist squeezed and the plump head of his cock produced a small pearl of moisture. His thumb ran over the drop as he continued to touch himself even as he watched her.

"Do you ever touch yourself when I'm not around, Liberty?"

She looked at him and felt a fire burning under her cheeks, too embarrassed to answer. But her blush must have given her away. No wonder she sucked at cards.

"Really?" he said, raising his eyebrows in amusement. "How often?"

She swallowed. Should she lie? He would know if she did.

"Answer the question, Liberty."

She glanced down to where he was still fondling himself then back to his face. "I never used to, but recently I've had this urge... I've been doing it a lot lately."

"How often?" he repeated. His hand was moving slowly, but pumping somewhat forcefully.

"Sometimes three times a day."

He stilled. He obviously hadn't expected that answer. He quickly recovered and went back to jerking himself off. "Well, I've clearly been shirking some of my responsibilities. My apologies. From now on, though, you won't touch yourself unless I tell you to. If you have an urge, you'll tell me, and I'll satisfy it. Do you understand?"

"Yes, Mason."

"Where do you go to masturbate?"

"I usually come up here. Sometimes I do it in the bathtub and once I did it on the third floor."

"When you're in the tub do you use the shower attachment?"

She stopped breathing for a moment. Why had she never thought to do that? Now she wanted to, but he just told her she wasn't allowed to touch herself anymore without permission. Damn it. "No."

"Do you come?"

It was titillating to hear him use such crass

words. She knew all those words and used them sometimes herself, but they never really used them together, during times of intimacy. "Yes."

"And how do you touch yourself? Do you rub your little pink clit until you climax or do you stick those pretty painted fingers inside of your pussy?"

Her heartbeat thundered. "Usually I just touch…I don't usually finger myself."

"Why not?"

"It's faster the other way."

"So you're doing it solely for the release not the experience?"

"I guess so," she admitted, never really thinking about her purpose.

"Do you fantasize while you're doing it?"

"Yes."

He gave her a hard look and waited. "Who do you think about?"

She almost smiled at the hint of jealousy in his voice. He was very territorial in regards to her and that was something she liked. "You."

"Are you sure?"

"Yes. As a matter of fact, last Friday, an hour before you came home I was masturbating right here and as I came I screamed your name."

His nostrils flared as he looked at her through darkening eyes. "Let me explain something to you, Liberty. You are my wife. Your body belongs to me so long as you're willing to agree to this."

He released his cock and leaned forward. He cupped his hands over her breasts and drew them together. "These are my tits and that's my pussy. The one thing I can't demand of you is your mind, but I won't tolerate another man filling your fantasies. Do you understand?"

"Yes, Mason."

"Good." He climbed off of her and stood up, taking a pillow with him. "Come here, please." He stood in the center of the room where a small seating area was arranged. His hands dropped the plush ivory pillow onto the white carpet at his feet. She stood before him and waited.

Without preamble he swooped down and kissed her hard and passionately. His tongue pressed past her lips and forced its way to the back of her mouth. His palm held the back of her head and his fingers knotted in her curls and she moaned. When he pulled away she was dazed and ready to comply with whatever he wanted.

"On your knees, please," he suddenly said.

She looked down to the pillow at their feet and then back up to him. He raised an eyebrow and waited. She dropped down to kneel on the pillow.

"Eyes up here."

Liberty gazed up at him. Excitement danced in her belly, as if it were a jostled beehive holding a hundred hornets dying to break free. She was kneeling, but also sitting back on her calves. His erection poked upward toward his smooth muscled belly.

"We're going to be doing a lot of new things, Liberty. I plan on touching, tasting, fucking, and marking every part of you. Your body's mine and I won't have a wife who feels she needs to sneak off and masturbate in order to be satisfied. Tonight I want to show you how to properly satisfy your husband."

He took himself in hand again. "Up."

She lifted her bottom off her heels and was suddenly at eye level with his thick cock. She understood what he wanted and had no problem offering it. She'd wanted to do this to him many times before, but was always afraid to ask and he never expressed interest. As she raised her bottom off her calves, blood rushed into her lower legs and she swayed slightly.

His hand gently passed over the top of her head, pressing her coiled bangs back. Her unruly curls sprang forward as his hand smoothed behind her hair and came around the base of her neck until he was cupping her jaw.

He looked down at her with such love and admiration. A surge of pride bathed her senses. She sat a little taller.

"So beautiful. I want you to make me come, Liberty. Will you do that?"

She swallowed and nodded, hoping she could do this for him. Another pearl of precum gathered at the tip of his cock. Holding her jaw still with one hand and his cock in his other, he leaned forward and traced the smooth dewy tip across her lips, painting them with iridescent moisture.

"Open for me."

She opened and he placed the large, weighty head of his cock on her lower lip. His feet stepped out, widening his stance and he released her jaw so he could hold his hands behind his back. He was leaving his pleasure completely up to her and she wanted nothing more in that moment then to make him come. He gazed down at her and gave one final nod. That was all the encouragement she needed.

Her mouth closed over him and she swallowed as much of his length as she could manage. It wasn't that Mason was abnormally long. The issue was that he was very wide. Her lips stretched to accommodate his girth and her hand came up to help her center her motions. Her fingers wrapped around the thick root of him, but her thumb still didn't touch her fingers.

Her head bobbed over him, her hand accommodating the flesh she couldn't take. He grunted and rocked his hips forward. Moisture gathered at her tongue as she made small twisting pulls at his tip that he seemed to like.

"That's it, baby, suck my cock."

His encouragement caused a surge of moisture to trickle down her thighs. She moaned over him and the vibration of her vocalization sent him to his toes.

"Jesus," he rasped as his hand suddenly came from behind his back and grabbed onto her hair. "That's it. Fast like that. Let me feel how hard you can suck me."

Her saliva seeped past her lips and onto her

hand. She pumped her fist over him faster and faster. The prickle of his grip in her hair had her picking up speed. Something about him guiding her motions caused her to grow more enthusiastic with each motion.

She slurped back the extra wetness and the back of her throat convulsively swallowed, which caused her soft palate to press down on his engorged head. He seemed to really enjoy that. When he poked the back of her throat again his grip tightened and he held her there for a moment as he groaned, long and loud.

His grip relaxed and she continued to move her wet mouth over him. Her palm gripped his thickly muscled thighs and as she became more comfortable with the position and allowed him to take over.

Mason fucked her mouth hard. Never going too deep or holding himself at the back of her throat too long, but controlling her movements all the same.

An inspired thought struck her as he quickly pumped his hips and thrust her head up and down on his cock. Her left hand reached up and found his sac, lifting the weight into her palm and fondling. His knees shook and his cock swelled as it beat over her tongue. They were both moaning and panting with each thrust. His sac drew up tight and suddenly he released her hair and ripped his cock from her mouth with a pop. She freed her hold and looked up at him.

"Lean back on your palms," he instructed

quickly as he began to jerk himself off with quick, hard yanks of his fist.

Her bottom lowered to her heels and she arched backwards, placing her palms behind her on the plush carpet. He pointed his cock at her tits just as the first warm ribbon of semen shot across her breasts. The act was both jarring and incredibly erotic. She felt claimed in a way she would never have dreamed of.

He grunted as the last bit of warm liquid hit her nipple and trickled toward her belly. With one final groan of pleasure he released himself and shivered. When he looked down at her she was suddenly self-conscious.

"God, you look beautiful with my mark on you." All insecurity faded away and she flushed with pride. He lowered himself to the carpet and kissed her lovingly. "Lie back. Let me take care of my beautiful wife."

He eased her onto the floor and kissed her again, softly and reverently. His hands went to her breasts and came in contact with the fluid he'd left there. He chuckled over her mouth and then dragged his fingers through the trails of come, gathering the mess and smearing it over the flesh of her belly and down toward her sex.

"My wife," he said as he kissed her. "My tits." His palm cupped her sex slipping two wet fingers into her channel. "My pussy."

She moaned and he forced the fingers deeper. He'd never been this aggressive with her. He filled her needy pussy with his digits and proceeded to pump them in and out as she writhed and moaned.

His mouth traveled down her throat and to her breast, latched onto her nipple and suckled hard. She cried out in pleasure and realized he might be tasting his own release, yet it didn't seem to bother him.

He licked from one breast to the other as his fingers fucked her hard. Her knees fell open and his tongue moved across her ribs and down her tummy. He was like a man possessed and her body reveled at his overwhelming touch as though he was in ten places at once. He was everywhere. Inside her pussy, on her breasts, she was in his mouth, under his tongue, beneath his hand.

When his fingers pulled out of her channel she moaned, but then gasped as he yanked her body and lifted her by her thighs to his mouth. She would have marks there as evidence of his intense need for her. His tongue pierced her folds and fucked her with languid yet probing licks.

It was too much. Just as she grew used to the intrusion he switched it up and licked at her folds from a different angle.

Never in her life had she imagined her husband in this light. He was doing things to her she would have never suspected him capable of doing, completely and utterly focused on only her pleasure.

The animalistic edge to his touch was beyond

liberating. She spared no time or thought to how raw and uncivilized their actions might appear to a more sophisticated outside world. Here there was only pleasure and she was prepared to take as much as her husband was willing to give.

When he pulled back and licked from the tight pucker of her ass all the way to her clit she almost came out of her skin. He laughed at her reaction then fed his thumb into the lowest part of her sex so that he could rest his fingers over her taint. Her legs draped over his shoulders and her back barely touched the floor.

His mouth hovered over her clit as his thumb made shallow, purposeful dips into her sex. Each breath he took fanned the bundle of nerves peeking past her flesh and she wanted so badly for him to take her clit in his mouth.

"And for the record," he whispered over her clit as one of his fingers gently circled the rosette of her ass. "This is my ass too."

His mouth crashed down and he sucked her clit between his lips, pulling relentlessly. She screamed and came in a hard rush of spasms. He continued to torment her, sucking hard and flicking with his tongue as his thumb jammed in and out of her cunt with force. She trembled and cried out, her nerves splintering into a thousand pieces.

"I can't take any more," she shouted, trying to pull her pelvis away from his mouth.

His arm wrapped tightly around her waist and he held her there. "Yes, you can."

She screamed as he moved his hand so that his thumb was replaced with two fingers. He lowered her body back to the carpet and continued to suck hard on her clit. She twitched and convulsed, a multitude of sensations and emotions combating for space in her mind. It was too much at once. She wanted it to stop yet wanted it to go on forever.

His fingers pressed deep inside of her and suddenly she climaxed again. He praised her as he licked up her juices, but he didn't release her. On and on he fucked her with his mouth and fingers until she lost count of how many times she came.

When he finally released her she was unaware of anything other than her throbbing pussy. Her clit seemed to have a heartbeat of its own and every few seconds her insides would flutter with an aftershock from coming too many times. She might still be experiencing aftershocks tomorrow, sporadically delayed jolt of ecstasy trembling through her veins.

Mason laid his cheek on her belly and panted. They must have both fallen asleep on the floor for a while, because the next thing she knew she was freezing and Mason was carrying her back to the bed. He covered her and rather than laying on his back like he usually did, he pulled her tightly to his side.

She smiled in the now dark room. So far, she had no regrets.

~

WHEN SHE WOKE up around five the following morning she was still in his arms. She tried to carefully slip out from beneath the weight of his arm, but he grunted and tightened his hold on her. Her mind panicked for a moment.

She needed to get up and shower so that she could make breakfast and mop the foyer before the house was awake. It was what she did. She didn't want to disturb him, but the urge to go about her business as usual was nagging and making it hard to breathe with each passing second.

Her fingers tried to pry open his grip, but he was actually fighting her.

"No." The stern, grumbled order caused her to freeze.

She licked her lips and tried not to get alarmed. After a moment, she calmly said, "Mason, honey, I need to start breakfast. I can't sleep as late as you do."

His voice was muffled in the pillows. "I'm awake now."

"Well, I have things to do. Let me up and I'll let you get back to sleep."

"No. I'm not ready to let you go. You're warm."

She was glad he wanted to spend time with her, but she needed to get moving. She was already fifteen minutes behind schedule. If the floor didn't get done it would have twice as much dirt and dust on it tomorrow because she wouldn't be able to get to it in the middle of the day with people constantly walking through. Then tomorrow it would take twice as long to clean and she would know that extra grime was there so she would have to forgo the mop and get down on her hands and knees and do it with a sponge and bucket.

She didn't want to disappoint him, but she needed to draw the line. She had responsibilities.

"Mason, I need to get up. Ouch!" He pinched her nipple. "Hey, that hurt."

Frustrated and a little upset, she began to struggle to sit up. He pulled his face out from the pillow and easily flattened her into the mattress and subdued her struggles. He leaned down and kissed her. At first she protested, but then his persistent mouth wiped away all irritation.

"Good morning, Liberty."

She pursed her lips and frowned at him.

"Is that anyway to greet your husband in the morning? I said, good morning, Liberty."

"Good morning," she grumbled.

"Well, someone got up on the wrong side of the bed today."

"No, someone can't seem to get out of bed today."

"Hmm. Well, let's see if I can make it worth your while to stay."

"Mason, I have chores—"

His firm cock nudged against her sex, cutting

off her train of thought. "My rules, Liberty, remember?"

Her lips pressed together. She needed to mop the floor. She was now twenty-three minutes behind schedule. He breached the entrance of her sex and moved the head of his erection up and down over her swollen lips and slit. Her stupid, traitorous body bloomed like a slick flower for him and her moisture coated the tip of his cock.

He seated himself and moaned. "There, now isn't that better?"

She struggled with wanting to move against him and the need to continue her protests. Now she wasn't sure if she wanted to mop or have sex. He slowly pulled himself out and thrust back into her. Yeah, she would just have to wake up extra early tomorrow. Because there was no way she was leaving this bed now.

Without being asked to do so, she raised her arms above her head and laced her fingers together. Mason smiled. "Ah, there's my girl." She smiled back at him and found herself forgetting about chores and time and focusing only on her husband.

CHAPTER 7

*S*ean entered the quiet kitchen and wondered where everyone was. Did they go out? It was almost nine o'clock and Liberty said she would see him at breakfast in the morning. The day before, she'd gotten up obscenely early. Didn't she always do that?

His stomach growled and he frowned at the immaculate, state of the art kitchen and considered peeking behind some of the custom cabinets to see if he could score a bowl of Captain Crunch.

At the counter he noticed the Cuisinart coffee pot sitting open with fresh ground coffee already waiting in the crisp new filter. He gazed over his shoulder and to the door. With a shrug he shut the trap and hit start. Moments later the aroma of freshly brewing coffee filled the air accompanied by the happy perking sounds coming from the machine. The presence of noise in the house other than his own breathing made him feel a little more relaxed.

Moving to the cabinets, he began scavenging for food. The first few cabinets he opened were filled with meticulously organized dishes, glasses, and bowls. He noticed a pattern of one upturned dish for every type. *Weird.*

The cups were all lined up as if on a grid, perfectly spaced from every angle. But then the last glass on the left was always upside down. He wanted a drink, but wasn't sure if he should take the odd cup out or go for one of the more uniformly stacked ones. After realizing he'd stood there for almost a minute debating something so stupid, he rolled his eyes and grabbed any old glass. Liberty was having an effect on him.

He filled the glass at the faucet and chugged it. When he was done he placed it on the counter and continued to scavenge for food. There was plenty of it. Problem was, it was all in forms he didn't know how to use.

Clear glass jars were filled with various white powders. Sean could identify the flour and sugar, but other than that he had no idea what they were. There were tons of them. It almost looked like he was snooping in a culinary meth lab or underground coke kitchen.

He pulled one small jar of white stuff down to get a closer look and was relieved to find a label on the top claiming it baking powder. The rest were also labeled. Who knew there were so many variations of flour and sweeteners and sugars? Made no difference anyway, he didn't have a damn clue how to make things with ingredients like that.

He moved to another cabinet that looked similar to the white one, but this one was filled with jars of various dried beans. The next one was much the same, but with smaller jars of spices. He was growing frustrated and hungrier by the minute. By the time he reached the pasta cabinet he'd seen enough. He slammed the cabinet and didn't even get the satisfaction of hearing it slam. *Stupid dove tail jointing.*

"What the fuck?" He ran his fingers through his hair and groaned. "Where's all the food?"

A slow creak in the distance caused him to still. Was that them? Were they home? He walked to the foyer and didn't see any signs of them. Then he heard a noise again. It came from upstairs. When it came again he identified it and groaned.

Not again. Female cries that only a woman being thoroughly fucked could make filtered to his ears. Over and over, louder and louder Liberty's cries echoed through the house and he could almost feel each tight thrust of Mase's cock. He certainly could hear the rhythm his boy was keeping.

His mind wandered and he imagined how they would look like fucking. Was Liberty an on top kind of girl or a doggy style one? Mase was definitely a man who liked to be in charge. It had been one of the things they struggled with in their own relationship. Two alpha males.

The vision that filled his head as her cries of ecstasy filled the house was so real it knocked the breath out of him. In his mind he saw Libby getting fucked, but it wasn't Mason's hands that held onto her hips. They were his.

Through his mind's eye he followed the narrow column of her spine until he saw nothing but blond curls bouncing with each thrust. His fantasy traveled farther and he saw Mason wearing nothing but an expression of pure rapture as he fed his wife his fat cock.

Sean shook his head and stumbled back as if the vision was a living thing that grabbed hold of him. Just as his head returned to reality he heard Mason's deep voice shout and Liberty's accompanying cry and knew they had finished. He turned and went into the kitchen. He was leaving today.

~

MASON FOLLOWED Liberty down the steps after they shared a long shower. When she reached the landing her steps faltered and a look of panic intruded on her otherwise serene expression. "Lib?"

"Someone's made the coffee. Sean made the coffee."

She made to bolt, but he snagged her hand

LYDIA MICHAELS

and kept her from leaving his side. "Hey, look at me. It's just coffee. Sean knows how to make coffee. He's probably done it a million times. Besides, all he had to do was turn it on. Now, we talked about this. Nothing's different. We're just starting the day a little later. Look at it this way, now you have one less thing to do to catch up."

She hesitated and then nodded. Mason realized his greedy libido was already costing her. He just hoped she could keep a grip on herself and make it through the day without any major setbacks.

Cursing under his breath he realized it was Tuesday and he had to be at the hospital by eleven, he acknowledged it was a shit day to fuck with her routine.

They walked down the steps in silence and headed toward the kitchen from where the warm scent of coffee was flowing. When they walked into the room nothing appeared out of place other than the presence of the massive man in jeans and a tight T-shirt sitting at the counter scowling at them over a mug.

"Morning," Sean greeted, none too cheery.

"Good morning," Mason replied.

Beside him Liberty made a grunt of distress and quickly untangled their hands and went to the coffee pot. She took the pot out and dumped it down the drain and followed it with the still steaming soggy grounds. She ran the garbage disposal six times. Not the best sign. Sean looked

156

concerned, but Mason just shook his head and gave him a signal to ignore her.

He took his seat on the stool he usually occupied and watched as Libby scoured the counter and proceeded to brew a fresh pot of coffee. He could tell she was upset, but waited for her to find level ground.

When she opened the cabinet to pull down the mugs and found one already missing another sound of panic left her throat. Sean shot him another look of concern and then guiltily glanced down at his cup.

Fuck. Mason was going to have to do something. He couldn't leave her like this and he doubted she would be over it by the time he left. He looked at the clock and mentally cursed again. Less than an hour and a half before he had to leave. Maybe he should just call out. But he left early on Sunday. He couldn't keep doing this.

Sean cleared his throat as Libby proceeded to make breakfast. "Uh, look, I was thinking. Maybe it would be best if I headed out today. You guys have been great to put me up and I really appreciate it, but maybe—" Whatever he was going to say was cut off by the sound of a pan slamming down on the counter.

That was it. Mason looked at Sean. "Living room. Now." To his wife he said, "Liberty, enough. I'll deal with it. Remember your promise the other day. Those are my hands too. We'll be back in ten minutes."

He silently led Sean out of the kitchen, but

they didn't make it to the living room. Once in the foyer Sean turned on him. "Dude, *what* the fuck? What are you handling? Look, I'm sorry. Thank you for your hospitality, but I really can't deal with this. Your wife's great, but I obviously did something to piss her off. I'm just gonna go."

Before he could turn away Mason grabbed a fistful of his shirt and dragged him into the living room and quietly shut the French doors. "You can't go."

"What? Why?"

"Because you need to stay for twelve more days or she'll lose it."

"What's in twelve more days?"

"Nothing, it's just how long she expects you to stay. Besides, I need to go to work in an hour and I need you to stay with her. She's having a bad day and I can't call out again."

Sean held up his palms. "What? No, dude, I don't know enough about what she has. I gotta get out of here—"

Mason instantly became irate and defensive. He got into Sean's face, hissing, "What she has is a good heart. It's not like she's a fucking leper so stop acting like you can catch it, you prick!" Realizing how badly he just lashed out, he quickly stepped back. "I'm sorry. This isn't your fault. Sorry."

"You sure about that? Would this be happening if I'd never shown up?"

Good point. "It doesn't matter. You're here now, you might as well stay."

"I can't."

Mason shook his head and let out an exasperated breath. "I guess some things don't change. Things get a little too real and you go running. Fine. Go. I'll deal with it."

"Hey, that isn't even a bit fair!"

"No? You show up uninvited and surprise my wife, barging in here when I'm not even home—"

"She invited me in!"

"What else was she supposed to do?" Mason shouted. "You told her we were old friends. Unlike you, my wife puts everyone else's comfort first. After you give her some sob story about losing your father, a father you never even *liked*, I remind you, and how you traveled all this way just to reconnect with an old friend. Well, she felt for you and only wanted to put you at ease. You took advantage of that and you know it!"

"That's not true!"

"No? Then you tell me how it happened."

"I stayed because I felt like she shouldn't be alone. I can't explain it. I was just going to go and she told me to wait. I knew you weren't home and for some reason I couldn't leave."

"Never had a problem leaving before," Mason sneered.

"Oh, will you give it up? It was thirteen years ago. I was moving to a different state and you were going off to medical school to start your internship. I'd just blown out my knee and had no place to live."

"You could have lived with me and you know it."

"*We* weren't there yet. It would have been for all the wrong reasons."

"*You* weren't there yet." Mason accusingly corrected.

"Yeah, well, maybe I wasn't! Big fucking deal. We never would have made it work anyway. I mean, look at you. That was never the lifestyle you wanted. *This is!*"

Mason's chest puffed and his nostrils flared as he said through clenched teeth, "Don't tell me what I wanted. You want to blame anyone, blame yourself. This all has to do with you and your undying need to please your chronically miserable father."

"That's not true. My dad had nothing to do with it."

Mason couldn't listen to another lie. He'd heard enough of them thirteen years ago and he certainly wasn't going to listen to them now. "Then why are you here? You never had his approval. What would introducing him to your gay lover change? You threw away *everything* we could have had and for what? He's dead now, Sean. Dead. Did he ever tell you, just *once*, that he loved you?" Mason's voice cracked with emotion. "Because I was ready to tell you every day for the rest of your life."

Sean looked up at him with such hurt in his eyes. He didn't say a word for several heartbeats and then, "You're right. I'm an idiot. I don't know what I expected to find here, but...You've made your point loud and clear. I missed my chance."

"Sean—"

"No. I'm sorry for barging in and messing up your life again."

He turned to leave and Mason grabbed hold of his arm. Sean turned and just that quickly Mason felt the weight of the connection they once shared. Visions of outdated dreams reintroduced themselves with remembered pain. It could have been him, but he left, leaving Mase floundering in the shambles of a broken heart.

Sean's presence changed nothing about the past, but the pain of watching him leave again was unbearable. Shutting his eyes, he whispered, "I have nothing to offer you, but I want you to stay."

"I have to go, Mase," Sean murmured in a defeated voice.

Mason stepped closer to him, his muscles tight with familiar fear. He hadn't asked for any of this, never wanted the interruption, but this was where they were and he couldn't let him go without getting a say. "Stay, because no matter what, you'll always be welcome in my life."

Sean shook his head and shut his eyes. "I don't belong here, Mason. It hurts to watch you two. I...I can't do it."

Emotion choked him for a moment. Once again his needs came second to Sean's. How could something from so long ago still hurt so much? "This hurts," he quietly admitted. "Is it supposed to still hurt this much?"

"I don't know, but I feel it too. What you and Liberty have is special. I can't compete with that. I don't want to."

It wasn't a competition, yet he understood the confusion. Sean's sudden presence was confusing him too. Speaking the reminder they both seemed to need, he said, "My loyalties are to her."

He scowled. "I never intended to threaten your marriage, Mase."

Then why was he suddenly questioning so much? "Are you sure?"

"Yes," he snapped. "I'm not an asshole." He turned away.

For some reason his fortitude stung. The temptation was there, but maybe, once again, Mason's feelings ran deeper than Sean's. Without thinking he gripped Sean's neck and locked his gaze with his. "Don't go."

Like fuel being ignited by a flame there was a hiss of energy surrounding them and suddenly Sean's mouth was on his, greedily taking what was no longer an option.

Sean locked his fist in Mason's hair and held him. The rough slide of stubble along his jaw abraded his face and Sean was backing him into the wall. He hit the bookcase with a soft thud and Sean pressed the bulk of his form into Mason. He bit at Mason's lips and yanked his head back to suck at his neck.

He roughly reached under his shirt and Mason caught his arm in an iron grip. "No."

Sean stilled and pressed his forehead into Mason's shoulder as he breathed heavily.

"This can't happen," Mason rasped. "I want you to stay, but it can't be like this. I won't do that to her. I love her, Sean."

Sean stepped away and turned. He ran his hand over his head and gripped the back of his neck while he released a tense breath. "Fuck," he whispered. "I didn't mean for that to happen. I swear, I don't want to interfere in your relationship."

"I know. This is just new and we were both a little heated." He took a step back and released his hold of his arm.

"What'll happen if I don't stay as long as she expects?"

"It'll be like this morning and the other day, only maybe worse. She wants you here. I want you here. I'm asking you to stay."

Sean turned back to him and blew out a slow breath. "All right. I'll stay, but do me a favor."

"Anything."

"Put a lid on it in the bedroom. Last thing I need to hear is you fucking your wife."

~

MASON AND SEAN walked into the dining room just as Liberty placed three glasses of orange juice on the table, oatmeal, one cup in each bowl, three cut strawberries making nine perfect slices and three blueberries forming an isosceles triangle in between.

"Looks great! Thanks, Liberty," Sean said as he took his seat.

Mason came over and squeezed her shoulder. "You okay, babe?" She gently nudged him off of her and mumbled a reply that could be taken as a yes or no. She didn't want to talk about the uneasy nervousness barely banked inside of her at the moment.

They sat down and began to eat. "Wow, this is outstanding. I don't think I ever had oatmeal that didn't come from a paper packet." Sean seemed awfully chatty. Liberty didn't feel like talking, but mumbled a thank you.

"Liberty," Mason said and waited for her to look at him. When she met his gaze he continued. "In about an hour I have to—"

"I know what your schedule is, Mason." He raised his brow at her clipped tone, but she didn't care. Everything was wrong and falling apart faster than she could fix it. "And I suppose you'll be leaving as well, Sean?"

Sean, clearly caught off guard, paused before shoveling a large bite of oatmeal into his mouth and looked over to Mason.

Her husband cleared his throat. "Sean's decided to stay with us up until the Sunday following this one. Isn't that great, Lib?"

She looked at Mason and back to Sean. "I thought you wanted to leave."

"Only if you want me to go, Liberty. I don't want to interfere with your...life. What would you prefer?"

"Stay." She looked over to Mason and saw that he still agreed. "You should stay for a proper visit. Mason and I would enjoy that."

"Then that's what I'll do."

"Sean has some stuff he needs to take care of for about an hour. I told him to make himself at home and assured him he wouldn't be disturbed in my office while he makes his calls. That'll give you enough time to do the floor without worrying about tracks being left on it, won't it?"

It was practically immoral how much joy she felt at knowing she would be able to do the floors before lunch. "That would work." They always were done before breakfast, but if she did them late it would be best to do them before lunch.

Mason's hand settled over hers, stilling her fingers and she realized she'd been unconsciously folding her napkin only to unfold it and refold it again. He brushed his thumb over her wedding band and smiled apologetically.

She smiled, realizing he regretted much of how their day began. Her hands clasped on her lap so she would stop fidgeting.

"And I noticed that some of the DVDs are out of order in the entertainment room. Do you think you could straighten that out for me?" he asked softly.

"Sure."

They finished eating and Liberty stood to

clear the dishes and take them into the kitchen. She immediately set out to wash them, and as she reached for the faucet she paused.

Don't.

The sound of the kitchen door swinging open startled her and she quickly turned on the water at the coldest possible setting.

"Thanks for breakfast, Lib. It was spectacular as everything else you cook," Sean said as he tentatively placed his arm around her shoulders. Her mind retreated as her body craved the blanketing weight of his heavy arm. He leaned close, the scent of his clothing filling her senses, and whispered, "Are you sure you're okay with me staying?"

He'd never touched her. He smelled nice. Right. The way Sean should smell. She nodded tightly and reached for one of the bowls from breakfast.

"One of these times I'm going to do the dishes for you. Give you a chance to take a break and relax for a change."

No.

She should tell him that wouldn't work, but he was just trying to be nice. But he couldn't do the dishes, because he might not move the sponge in clockwise motions and the—*Stop it!* She slammed down another bowl and Sean jumped, pulling his arm off of her.

Just then Mason walked into the kitchen. "What's going on?"

Sean stepped back. "Nothing. I just told Libby

one of these days I would do the dishes for her so she could relax. I only meant it as a thank you for all her delicious cooking."

"Lib?" Mason walked over to where she stood with her palms braced on the lip of the sink as the water rushed from the faucet. He reached over and shut off the valve, but before he did he slipped a finger under the flow to test the temperature. "Do you want me to call out, Liberty?"

"No."

"What would make this better? Tell me and I'll do it."

She looked at the dishes still needing to be done and then at the time. Mason had thirty minutes before he had to leave. He needed a lunch. *Banana, sliced in half and then thirds per half forming six pieces. One cup of Greek yogurt. Thirty-six clusters of granola for topping. Two egg salad sandwiches made from three eggs and three teaspoons of mayonnaise. Six... Fuck, fuck, fuck, fuck, fuck...*she tried not to think it. Tried to leave it at five fucks.

Fuck!

"I have to make your lunch." She pushed past them and left the dishes undone.

She found her small pot and filled it with six cups of water. Then she turned the dial on the stove to six, knowing she needed it to be on high for the eggs to boil, but needing it set at six for six minutes before she could do that.

Fifteen minutes to hard boil an egg. Twenty-eight minutes until Mason leaves. Six minutes to start the pot. That leaves only seven minutes to cool them and make the egg salad and the rest of his lunch. Seven minutes wouldn't work.

She anxiously watched the clock, needing another minute to pass so that she would have a remainder of six. As soon as the minutes changed she set into motion.

Pulling out all of her supplies, she lined them up on the counter. Sean asked Mason something, but she was too focused on what she was doing to make out his question. Once everything was set out she turned and moved to finish the dishes.

~

SEAN FOLLOWED Mason out of the kitchen. "Come on. I have to get ready for work. Follow me so I can tell you what's going to happen."

Sean followed him up the steps. "Yeah, that would probably be a huge help. And what exactly will I be doing in your man cave for an hour when you leave?"

They walked into Mason and Liberty's bedroom and Sean froze. This was so not a place he needed to be. He looked at the bed and imagined what he'd heard that morning.

Mason's fingers snapped in front of his face. "Focus! She's having a really bad day and it's my fault because I wouldn't let her out of bed this morning. I really need you to keep an eye on her for the next nine hours while I'm out. It doesn't matter what you do in my study. Watch a movie, play pool, read a book, I don't care. She just needs to wash the foyer floor without anyone around to walk on it."

"Why don't you just tell her to forget about it?"

"Don't you get it? I could give a fuck if the floor was mopped more than once a year. She needs to do it. It helps her. She sets up these standards for herself and if they don't get done in accordance with what she determines is a timely manner she gets upset. You give her one hour. That's it. Then you find her and you don't leave her alone for the rest of the day. Can you do that?"

He watched as Mason stared back at him with one leg in his pants and one leg out, waiting for an answer.

"Hello?"

Sean jerked his gaze away. "What? Yes. Sure."

"Are you sure? Because if you can't do it then I'll call out. She needs someone with her when she gets like this, but you can't make it like you're babysitting her."

"How often does this happen?"

"It used to happen a lot more frequently than it does now. She's just having a bad couple of days and I shouldn't have interrupted her schedule this morning." He paused from tying his tie and Sean could tell he really felt guilty about causing Liberty stress.

"What if I do something that sets her off? You

saw how pissed she got when I offered to do the dishes. I was just trying to be helpful."

"She knows that. Believe me, she *knows* that. I would almost guarantee her frustration at that moment wasn't with you, but with herself. She needs to do things a certain way. She probably appreciated the offer, but made herself sick over the fact that you wouldn't do the dishes exactly as she sees fit. You can't take it personally. Like I said, she just needs to do certain things a certain way. Just go with it and try to get her mind away from things that might set her off and onto something a little more fun. If you distract her long enough, she's okay."

"Okay. Keep my mouth shut and try to have fun. Got it."

Mason looked at his watch. "And remember, one hour, no more, no less."

"Got it." They started walking out the door and Sean stopped him. "Dude, you got a cell phone number in case anything goes wrong so I can get ahold of you?"

"Yeah, that's a good idea."

LIBERTY USED the tongs to place the eggs inside of a glass bowl resting in the basin of the sink and ran ice-cold water from the tap over them. Tiny bubbles formed on the hot shells. She glanced to the door then back to the bowl as the cold water began to flow over the rim and into the drain. Mason was still upstairs. She submerged her hands into the cold water and grabbed hold of two still scalding eggs, moaning until the pain eased and the cold water soothed the burn.

The door eased open and Mason walked in. He came over to the sink and kissed her. Again he shut off the tap after casually testing the temperature. When he felt the coldness of it he smiled at her.

He already knew she was having a shitty day. He was stressing. She could see it in his eyes.

"Mmm, egg salad. Yum. What else do I get?"

The eggs were now chilled so she carried them to the cutting board and began to peel and dice them. "A banana and granola yogurt."

"Sounds great." He was only trying to fill time with words so he could watch her to get a bead on her emotions.

She tossed the chopped egg into a bowl and faced him. *Four minutes left.*

"Mason, I'll be fine. I'm already cleaned up from breakfast. It'll take me no time to clean up from making your lunch. While Sean is getting his stuff done I'll take care of the floors and then all I need to do is feed him lunch, check the rooms, make his bed, fix the DVDs, and run to the store."

She continued to mix the eggs then divide the salad into halves. Three scoops from each half on two sandwiches making six total. Mason saw her do this, and would know she was compensating, but there was nothing else she could do at this point.

"What do you need at the store? It's Tuesday."

"We don't have the right laundry detergent."

"What's wrong with our detergent?"

"Nothing, but Sean uses a different one. I think it's *All* but it might be *Gain.* I'm not sure. I'll have to smell them to be sure."

"You could ask him."

"Then he'll feel like an inconvenience. No. I'll figure it out on my own. My point is I'll be fine." She placed the last of his lunch into the bag and neatly folded the top. "Here you go."

Mason smiled at her, but it didn't reach his eyes. "I'll call you on my break."

She walked him to the door and waited as he gathered his belongings. He kissed her goodbye and she waited as he pulled out of the drive. When his car disappeared she shut the door and went to clean up the kitchen, warring with the shards of disquiet that lingered.

LIBERTY WIPED THE COUNTERS, horizontal patterns for afternoon unlike the vertical design she used in the evenings and the circular pattern she employed in the morning. After preparing a small garden salad for lunch she carried the scraps to the garbage disposal and dropped them down the center drain.

She hit the switch and turned the faucet on

hot. *One, two, three. One, two, three.* A sense of completion was triggered by the second count of three. She was getting it together.

Shutting the faucet off, she ignoring the compulsion to touch the scalding flow of water, when her houseguest emerged from the other room. The foyer had been mopped and had plenty of time to dry without traffic to mark its pristine appearance.

"Hey," Sean said as he came to sit on his stool at the counter. He seemed a bit uncomfortable and unsure, which Liberty knew was her fault.

She was fighting her demons hard this morning and she refused to let them win. She was in control. She could handle herself. She just needed to focus her energy on being productive and not on the obstacles that got in her way.

"Hi. Did you finish everything you needed to get done?" She placed his glass three inches and forty-five degrees to the upper right corner of his napkin and moved to sit down on the stool next to him.

"Uh, yeah. Thanks for giving me some time."

"I suppose you had to call out of work."

"Well, I have a lot of personal time that's built up over the years, so I told them after my father's funeral I would be out for awhile. They have a new temp filling in for me."

"This is probably something I should've already asked, but...what is it you do, Sean?"

"I'm a physical therapist at a clinic down in Dallas."

"Dallas, not somewhere in Arizona?"

"No, definitely not Arizona. I haven't lived there since college. That's where my dad was, so I suppose it's home, but... I didn't need to be there."

"You didn't get along with your father." It wasn't a question. Mason told her as much.

"No. My dad was a military man who never could see past his militant ways."

"And your mom?"

"She died when I was sixteen."

"I'm sorry. Do you have any siblings?"

"No, it's just me."

"Me too. I never even knew my real father. My mother and I don't speak."

Sean looked at her as he chewed a bite of his salad. His full lips closed over the fork and his sharp hazel eyes analyzed her. Something had changed.

Sean had seen her begin to fall apart and hadn't remarked on it or treated her in any significantly different manner. Not like some people. Maybe he understood. Maybe he had his own demons. She wasn't as uncomfortable as she normally would have been under someone's scrutiny and she didn't understand why. For some reason she was relaxed around Sean.

She assumed he would ask more about her family, but he didn't. She was relieved. Maybe he got it, like Mason. She appreciated his sensitivity.

"Mason said you have to go to the store later?"

"Yes," Liberty answered. "I have a few things to pick up. I shouldn't be gone long."

"Mind if I tag along?"

"Not at all, but don't feel like you have to. I'll be fine."

"I need to pick up a few things if I'm going to be here for a while."

She smiled. Glad he decided to stay. Placing her fork on the edge of her plate she said, "If you would rather just make a list I could pick up whatever you need. You're our guest after all."

He put his fork down on his empty plate and faced her. Their thighs touched and she didn't move away from the contact, not wanting to offend him. "Libby, are you trying to get rid of me?"

"What? No." She suddenly smiled, noticing the teasing creases in the corner of his eyes. "I just didn't want you to feel like you have to do chores while you're here. I usually take care of that stuff."

"I noticed. Mason's very lucky to have a wife who knows how to really take care of a man."

Heat spread in her chest at his complimentary words. Usually only Mason's praise had that effect on her. "Thank you, Sean."

They looked at each other a moment longer and Sean stood. "What would you like me to do before we go?"

"Um…" She suddenly felt disoriented. Where had her mind drifted off? "If you just want to get yourself ready I should have this cleaned up and be ready to go in about fifteen minutes."

"Okay, sounds good."

After Liberty tidied up the kitchen she ran up to her bedroom and found her gold slippers with three stones over the toe. Gazing in the mirror, she fussed with her disorderly curls. She was still smiling when she left her room and almost crashed into Sean.

He caught her by the shoulders and a small jolt of electricity snapped through her as he steadied her and stepped back. "Hey, ready?"

Liberty felt suddenly flustered. She shook her head. "Sure. Would you like to drive? Mason usually does when we go shopping together."

"Ah, do you really want to sit in my dirty truck?"

"No, silly, we'll take the Escalade."

They went down to the foyer and Liberty handed Sean the keys to the Cadillac.

"Are you sure? I'm not on your insurance policy."

"It's okay. I trust you."

She held the door as Sean stepped onto the porch then turned to lock it behind them. He was already in the garage by the time she caught up. He was waiting by the passenger side of the Escalade holding the door for her. "Your chariot awaits, milady."

She smiled and stepped up on the footboard. Sean shut the door and came around to the driver side. After he adjusted the mirrors and seat settings they were on their way. On the drive to the store they talked about North Carolina and Libby pointed out various tourist traps and trendy places to visit.

"What made you guys move here?"

"I needed to get away from my mother and Mason wanted the same. He doesn't much care for my mother, but sometimes we visit his family. Probably not as often as we should."

"But why the Carolina's?"

"It's beautiful, quiet, free. You should see when the wild horses cross. It's breathtaking. We came here on our honeymoon and I wanted to come back. Mason applied for a transfer as soon as we returned. It took about six months, but that was fine because we had to wait for the house to be built. We drove back and forth every other weekend to check on its progress."

"Mase certainly has made a living for himself."

"Yes, but he isn't snobby about it. He does a lot for charity. Last month he spearheaded a fundraiser for one of his patients who lost her husband and medical coverage all in one month and then was diagnosed with cancer. He raised forty thousand dollars for her, ten of which he donated himself."

"Oh, I wasn't making an accusation, just an observation. I know Mason can be quite generous."

They pulled into the superstore parking lot and Sean told her to wait until he came around.

As he helped her down from the cab another quiver ran up her spine when his strong hands grasped her hips. What was wrong with her? It was disconcerting to have such a reaction to her husband's friend. When he released her she was flustered once more.

"I'll go grab a cart," she quickly said and brushed past him hoping he didn't notice the flush she could feel crawling up her neck.

Sean followed closely behind her and perused the aisles much like any man did, taking note of common household items and frowning as if he'd never noticed such things before. Liberty led them to the detergent aisle and casually began picking up small bottles of laundry detergent and sniffing the liquid.

"Are you looking for one particular kind?" Sean asked as he sniffed bottles alongside of her.

"No, there's a specific kind I need, but I'm not sure who makes it."

"This one's nice. *Lavender blossom.*"

Libby paused before scenting the next bottle and looked at him. "Oh…do you like that one? If you like that one best that's the one I'll get."

"No, it's your call. I was just saying it smells nice. Girlie, but nice."

She frowned. Did he want the kind he usually used or something else? "Well, maybe you should pick."

He put the bottle back after tightening the lid. "I don't care. Soap's soap. Besides, it isn't my place to tell you what to buy."

She pursed her lips. Maybe it should be his place. If he could just decide and tell her what to do she would feel a lot better. She tapped her fingers at her thigh impatiently. "I think you should pick."

Sean frowned at her then looked back at the never ending shelf full of choices. He seemed to reach a decision in his mind. He leaned close to her and she stopped breathing. His unique scent muddled her thoughts and her heart raced as he brought his face to the curve of her shoulder and her neck, inhaling deeply.

Heat radiated from his skin. When he spoke, his breath fanned over her hair sending small wisps sweeping across her exposed skin. "You smell nice. What kind do you use?"

Libby swallowed. Her throat was suddenly very, very dry. Sean straightened to his full height, seemingly unaffected by what just happened. Had anything happened? Or was she simply overreacting? She was struck dumb for a moment then uttered, "But that isn't your kind."

He looked at her and laughed. "Is that what this is? Libby, I don't have a kind. I'm a bachelor. I use whatever I grab. This is the longest I have ever stood in a soap aisle. Just pick whatever you'd like and it'll be fine. I definitely trust a woman's choice over mine." He laughed. "I'm lucky my clothes don't get washed in floor cleaner considering how much thought I put into reading labels. Please, don't go out of your way. Just get what you always do."

"But…"

He looked at her, seeming to understand her struggle as silly as she knew it was. Then he did exactly what she needed him to do. "Get what you always buy. That's what I want. Find it and put it in the cart, Liberty."

His instructions cut off her indecisive thoughts as an urge to do exactly as he said kicked in. She turned and found the bottle of detergent she usually used and placed it in the cart. Gazing up at him, he slid the list out of her hands and read it. "Okay, looks like we need paper towels. We'll get them next."

They went through the list much the same way until they found the last item. Sean instructed her on what to do and she followed his command, feeling lighter because of his guidance. When they reached the end of the list he said, "Now you need to find something pretty for yourself to put in the cart."

"It doesn't say that."

"Yes it does. It says Liberty will select something pretty for herself which Sean, the house guest, will purchase for her."

"Sean—"

"Liberty, let me buy you something nice as a thank you for putting me up. Please. It would make me happy."

She debated for a minute. "Okay, but something small."

They walked around the store, meandering in and out of aisles. Sean would pick up random items and play with them. It was slightly embarrassing, but more humorous than anything else.

Sean had a very youthful quality about him that seemed contagious. It was easy to laugh with him, to play. When they reached the toy aisle, which they had no business being in, Sean decided they needed to have an all-out light saber duel.

He made swishing sound effects as he slowly sliced the glowing saber through the air around her. "Choose your weapon and I shall show you what a true Jedi can do."

She fought a smile and gave him a look that said he was being a child, but picked up a light saber anyway. Pressing the button with her thumb, the wand glowed red as opposed to his bright blue one.

"Ah, a rebel!" He made a sound effect and clashed his sword against hers and began to circle her. "Aren't you a little short for a storm trooper?"

She scoffed and tried to jab him with her saber, but he deflected the motion and again made a clashing sound.

"The force is strong with this one!"

She laughed and wished she knew lines from the movie. She'd only seen Star Wars a few times. Sean quickly twisted and swatted her on the butt with his saber. She jumped and he laughed. It had been a mock joust, but it came fast and swift, leaving a bit of a sting in its wake.

"Hey!" Liberty parried his next move and hit

him in the leg with her saber. She wasn't as graceful as he. "Now I must destroy you," she warned, trying to sound as if she knew the lines.

"I find your lack of faith disturbing." He swatted her butt again, this time a bit harder. A thrill rushed over her.

She laughed and swung back, this time connecting with *his* behind. He quickly moved and pivoted on his large feet. The battle continued and their voices grew louder as their imaginations took flight.

In one clumsy swing, Liberty accidentally knocked over a small display of action figures. They clattered to the floor and made an embarrassingly loud racket that attracted the attention of nearby shoppers who gave them disapproving looks. Liberty sensed her cheeks turning as red as her saber and went to clean up the mess.

Suddenly an employee entered the aisle and frowned at them. "Excuse me, but unless you intend on purchasing those items I'm going to have to ask you to return them to the shelf."

Mortified, she quickly moved to put the toy light saber back when Sean grabbed her and swung her into his grip. Her back pressed against his warm front and his muscular arm wrapped around her shoulders just above her breasts.

What was he doing? They were going to get thrown out.

"She's part of the Rebel Alliance and a traitor. Take her away!"

Her stare shot over her shoulder at him, outraged, but when she recognized the glimmer of humor in his eyes her nervousness transcended to laughter. Let them kick them out. They were just having some fun. She smiled and looked back at the store clerk and said, "My apologies, but you know how uncivilized a wookie can be."

Sean tipped his head back as deep laughter came bellowing out of his mouth followed by a noteworthy impression of Chewbacca's howl. She fell into hysterics and the clerk rolled his eyes and walked away. Apparently they scared him off.

Sean looked down at her for a moment and said, "I think there's a naughty streak in you, little Liberty." Their laughter faded away and they stared at each other. The moment seemed to get heavier by the second and finally Liberty looked away, the intimacy of their shared gaze producing an unnamable reaction inside of her.

She extricated herself from his grip, moving to pick up the toys she knocked over. When she stood she found Sean waiting at the cart that now had two light sabers sticking out of it. "Are we buying them?"

"Yes," he said as if it made perfect sense.

The checkout process was uneventful, although Liberty found herself wrestling with vagrant feelings that continued all the way to the car and on the drive home. Sean was uncharacteristically silent.

∾

SEAN STEPPED out of the luxury shower and onto the earth toned tiled floor, rubbing away the drops of water from his skin. When he finished drying, he tossed his towel in the hamper. The sultry steam of the bathroom subdued the chilled central air filling the sleeping quarters of the guestroom.

He looked around the room as he brushed his teeth. It reminded him of a cave or some Chinese hut. Everything was stone and separated with rice paper dividers. There was a fireplace in the bathroom filled with various tapered candles and a medieval looking tray hanging from the ceiling like a chandelier housing various pillar candles. He rinsed his mouth out and wiped his face on the hand towel.

As he opened the door he caught a flash of white out of the corner of his eye and turned. A white linen sheet parachuted over his bed and Liberty's startled shriek reached his ears just as her form came into view. She gasped when she saw him and quickly covered her eyes.

"Shit!" Sean turned around offering a clear shot of his naked ass rather than his cash and prizes. He focused on the juxtaposed sinks he could still see through the bathroom door, but his vision filled with the image of Liberty's shocked expression.

"Oh my gosh! I'm so sorry! I thought you would have taken longer. I just wanted to freshen up your sheets and make your bed."

Sean actually felt himself flush. "Uh, that's

okay. It's my fault. Um...do you mind just step-ping out for a sec so I can put on some pants? Then you can do whatever you need to do."

Her soft retreating footsteps were followed by the click of the door closing. *Fuck.* He hoped this didn't mess up her mood. They had a good few hours with no incidents as far as he could tell. Cursing, he quickly drew on a pair of jeans pulled from his bag and walked to the door. He opened it and found Liberty standing there, face beet red, wringing her hands.

"I'm decent. You can come back in."

She looked up at him then quickly looked away. She made the bed with practiced speed and avoided making eye contact. Sean on the other hand couldn't tear his eyes away from her as she worked. As soon as the bed was made he wanted to toss her down on it and mess it right back up.

Whoa! What the fuck?

"I have to go practice. I'll see you downstairs," she mumbled as she swiftly left the room.

Blindsided by his unprecedented thought, he let her escape without objection. What the hell was wrong with him? So. Many. Things.

Piano cords drifted to the second floor as he gripped the back of his neck and exhaled roughly. This was not good.

It didn't mean anything. She saw you naked and you were just reacting to the adrenaline. It was a simple case of misinterpreted biology. Yes! What the fuck are you talking about?

He shook his head and groaned. He needed to

get a handle on his shit. First, this morning, he'd been totally out of line putting his lips on Mason. Now, he was fantasizing about fucking his wife. Clearly he wasn't getting enough sleep.

He spent the next hour wandering around the house listening to Liberty play the piano. At first the melody sounded frantic, but by the end of the hour she seemed to have calmed sufficiently and fell into a soothing tempo that climbed up and down the keys in soft brushing strokes that filled the house in a sort of melodic lullaby.

Sean found himself standing by the poolroom when the music slowly faded away. The conclusion of her playing was so perfectly graceful he almost didn't realize she stopped. He stared through the glass wall at the flat surface of blue water laid out before him.

The narrow rectangular pool fit between lines of white marble columns. Seamless ivory tile made up the floor wrapping around the perimeter. A glass wall across the room showed the fading afternoon sunshine and tall dunes concealing the ocean in the distance.

On either side of the pool were two square cots made of whitewashed wood and squared off foam mattresses dressed in flat snowy linens with a heavy bath sheet folded neatly at each foot. Although the house was a cool sixty-five degrees he could feel the heat penetrating the glass from the other side, see the quivering beads of condensation in the crevices and seams of the glass.

"Did you want to go for a swim?"

Sean started at the sound of Liberty's soft voice. He turned. She was barefoot and had removed her yellow cardigan. Her small breasts filled out the top of her white tank top and he could make out the petite shape of her nipples behind the fabric. *Puckered tight and not brown. Pink. Perhaps the same color one would find in the center of a nectarine.*

Fuck. He was such a piece of classless shit. This was Mason's *wife.* Checking her out was a betrayal to Mason on so many levels he winced. But Liberty's image stuck in his head. He couldn't shake the vision. Why was she affecting him like that? She was married. *To your ex lover!*

He slowly opened his eyes. She wore a bright turquoise beaded necklace that intensified the blue of her eyes. "I don't have a suit," he rasped.

"I can loan you one of Mason's. I'm sure he wouldn't mind sharing."

He would if he knew what I wanted to borrow.

Jesus, maybe he *needed* to submerge himself in a pool of cool water. Before he could answer Liberty said, "I'll go get you one and bring it to your room."

"What are you going to do?" he wondered.

She giggled. "I'm going to join you."

About ten minutes later he was standing on the opposite side of the glass in a pair of borrowed shorts waiting for Liberty. The room was warm and smelled slightly of chlorine. He flinched when music flooded the space. *Ain't No*

Sunshine by Bill Withers began to whine from hidden speakers, but there was no sign of Libby.

The slide of a door caught his attention, a small entrance he somehow missed. Liberty emerged holding a fluffy white towel and wearing a loose fitting button down made out of some kind of girlie net material that wasn't quite lace. Sean swallowed hard.

Her thighs were slender yet delicately muscled. Her chaotic halo of curls was clipped high on her head and the few anarchic tendrils that refused to stay with the others curled down the long column of her neck.

She tossed her towel on one of the cots and smiled. "You didn't have to wait for me."

She pulled the cover up over her head and revealed a form-fitting white suit. It was one piece and simple, but there was a chunk missing just below her left breast down to her lower left hip. The soft curve exposed her feminine little belly button. A vision flashed through his mind of him dipping his tongue into that tiny crevice and tickling her as she writhed beneath him.

God damn it!

He turned away.

"Are you coming?" Liberty said from the steps of the pool.

He nearly choked at her choice of words. *Practically!*

The sound of water sloshing drew his attention. She stepped deeper into the pool and softly dove into the shallow end. Sean turned fully, just in time to catch the slope of her ass peeking up over the surface and then disappearing under the water. Before she had time to emerge he walked to the deep end and dropped his large body into the water, allowing himself to sink right to the bottom.

Unfortunately it wasn't cold, so the hard on he was suddenly sporting didn't shrivel to an unnoticeable state. What the fuck was going on with him? He kissed Mason that morning and now he was getting a boner over his wife. Maybe he should take a trip into town later on and see if he could find someone to take the edge off his suddenly raging libido for a bit.

Sean swam through the smooth water in an attempt to sooth his overheated body as he made his way to the shallow end. His lungs tightened and he pierced the surface, rubbing the droplets from his face. Liberty was across from him, back to the wall of the pool, elbows resting on the rim, breasts thrust forward, hard pink nipples showing through the white of her suit.

Christ!

Not even thinking, he warned, "Better watch the way you look at me, little girl."

The comment clearly caught her off guard. She straightened and quickly disappeared under the water. The song changed from the sultry rhythm of *Ain't No Sunshine* to the climbing rattles and pulses of Marvin Gaye's *Heard it Through the Grapevine*. Sean lowered his shoulders into the water and took up a similar position to the one Liberty had held.

She popped up in the center of the deep end and watched him silently as she treaded water. What game was she playing? She was flirting with him. Did she realize that?

She removed the barrette from her hair, her eyes now appearing enormous. The slow building pulse of the music put him in a playful mood and Liberty seemed to want to play as well.

He smiled slowly. She watched him as he began to cover his eyes. "I'll count." He fully covered his eyes and leisurely counted to ten. By five she seemed to catch on when splashes caught his ears as she stealthily moved through the water.

When he reached ten he uncovered his eyes, but kept them closed. "Marco?"

"Polo." She was in the deep end.

He dove under the water and swam until his palm made contact with the far wall. Breaking through the surface he called, "Marco?"

She giggled from some distance away. "Polo."

He smiled. He wouldn't lose her again. Using his hands to guide him he tugged his body along the wall. "Marco?"

"Polo," she sung back, closer, but on the move.

The song changed again and Barry White began to sing *Never Gonna Give You Up*. The faster beat had his heart pounding or so he told himself. He became a predator, closing in on his prey. Just when he thought he had her she dove under the water with the grace of a mermaid and escaped him.

Sean recalled learning about mermaids in a mythology class at Duke. They were said to be sirens of the sea, capable of enchanting sailors to walk right off the decks of their ships. Their song and beauty could enthrall even the most devoted man and seduce him straight to his death.

He imagined Mason as Poseidon, the great king of the sea, and Liberty as Amphitrite, his lovely queen. That left him as Odysseus, the one lured to a great demise by the siren. But he was not going down.

His competitive nature crept in and it became imperative that he catch her. He needed a new strategy. He dove under the water and swam from one end to the other. When he immerged he only listened. Without calling Marco he dove back under and went to where he heard her excited breathing. As close as he could tell, he swam to her and stood.

She was outsmarting him. "Marco?" he growled.

She was silent and then, her breath warm on his back, she whispered, "Polo."

Sean turned with the speed of a wild animal and grabbed hold. She yelped and laughed as he pulled her slick body against his. She was so petite. Her legs floated out from under her as he held her in his grasp. His cock swelled as her pert bottom pressed against his lower body.

Laughter faded and she stilled, not in a panicked way, but in the way a woman melts into a man's care when she submits. Subdued under his strong hold in a display of beautiful, natural surrender, combined with the speed he was able to gentle her only added to his arousal.

The water settled and their echoed breathing filled the air. The rumble of Barry White's voice faded away as the song droned to an end. His palm lay flat against her soft abdomen as his other arm banded around her midriff. He wanted to reach up to her breasts. He wanted to grind himself into her.

Her small fingers gripped the bulk of his forearm, tiny pink nails pressing into his skin, and he could feel each breath as it filled her lungs. "I gotch'you," he said in a hoarse voice.

"What now?" she whispered.

What now? Excellent question. Sean breathed in her scent mixed with a touch of chlorine. What was he doing? Mason was his friend, his ex-lover. His common sense seemed to be muffled, because that certainly wasn't the part of him that spoke. "What do you want?"

His fingertips moved slightly and the edge of her suit surrounding her soft, exposed belly greeted his touch. His fingertips pressed under the wet material clinging to her skin and the prick of her nipples pressed into his arm. His cock swelled further in response.

"Sean?" She spoke his name more as a pleading breath than a warning.

"Mm-hm?"

"We can't."

"I know."

Her arms fell away as she seemed to yield a bit more in his grasp. He held her buoyant, inconsequential weight. His hand moved slowly upward and he cupped the curve of her breast. His wrist twisted and his thumb found the small point, lightly brushing over it once. She probably was outraged. She should have been, but rather than push him away, she moaned and another rush of blood flooded his cock.

Sean reached for her other nipple and touched it in the same way, but this time adding a tight pinch. Her bottom pressed into his pelvis as her chest eased forward to fill his hand. He leaned down and pressed his mouth to the curve of her shoulder, brushing his lips over her soft, damp skin and wiping away the clean droplets that clung there.

"No," she whispered with little conviction.

"No," he repeated in agreement. The large humid room seemed hollow, their breath an echo, altogether too loud. He shut his eyes and inhaled her scent then released her. She stood, but didn't move away. Goose bumps scattered over her narrow shoulders. He stepped back.

"Go, Liberty."

She turned and looked at him, confusion showing in her big blue eyes. Her lower lip quivered. He was a bastard.

"Go. Now," he barked and she quickly turned and waded to the steps.

He glared as she climbed out of the pool and gathered her towel around her shivering body. Just as she seemed ready to turn and face him again he guzzled a breath of air and dove under the surface like the coward he was. He held his breath as long as he could and when he emerged she was gone.

CHAPTER 8

*F*ilthy. Her mother was right. She was a filthy whore, a temptress, a pervert. Liberty's skin still tingled from the nearly scalding shower she'd taken after leaving the pool. A deep rosy blush seemed burned into her flesh, yet it did nothing to relieve or excoriate the putrid grime running through her veins. She was disgusting.

Why had she allowed Sean to touch her? He was Mason's friend, a guest in their home. She needed to tell Mason what happened, but feared he would rage at Sean. She couldn't allow that to happen. Nothing would've happened if she weren't such a dirty girl.

The pan heated and she spread her palm wide over the copper base. Hotter and hotter the metal grew until her breath hissed through her teeth and her arm trembled. A sharp ache shot through her flesh, stabbing her somewhere inside where her pain receptors lay. Liberty jerked her arm away from the stove and cradled her abused palm to her chest as tears stung her eyes.

She took a shuddering breath and moved to pour a splash of olive oil into the searing pan and then dropped three fillets of tilapia where her hand had recently been. She mixed the spring salad and moved to slice the mangos for the salsa. Her fingers worked in fast, rote motions that allowed her mind to wander, capably ignoring the stinging palm of her burned hand.

She couldn't tell Mason, she decided. Would Sean? Her husband was extremely possessive when it came to her and he always made her safety his highest priority. Liberty knew she wasn't in any danger from Sean. They had just gotten carried away. Like before, she wondered if her mind was exaggerating what had actually happened.

Her mind went back to a different time, a different place. She lay in the bed of her childhood home, staring as the moon played in the shadows of the curtains and knickknacks along the sill. She still could recall her heart jolting in her small chest at the sound of the knob turning. He always appeared so calm and patient at first. The way he touched her hair and ran a finger down her cheek was the act of a caring dad, but he wasn't her dad.

Her gut twisted as she recalled one evening in particular when Eric had awoken her.

. . .

"You okay, cupcake? I heard you crying."

She hadn't been crying. She had been sound asleep and woken up from a peaceful dream by the feel of her stepfather's hand rubbing her leg through her bed covers. At first she trusted him.

Liberty could never recall the exact moment that Eric transcended from good guy to bad guy, but she knew that by the time of this particular memory she was clear on the sort of monster he was. Her jaw locked as she cringed under his touch.

How well he played the role of a concerned loving parent, so ready to take on the responsibilities of dad for the fatherless child. He was no father. He was a predator and he was smarter. One thousand trapped screams rested in her chest night after night as his visits became more frequent. She wanted to let them all out.

LIBERTY'S MIND jumped to the day she confessed her fears to her mother, the repulsed look in her mother's eyes as she judged her and called her a liar and a whore. Liberty had been grounded to her room for two weeks that summer, a room that should have been her sanctuary, but had turned into nothing more than a torture chamber. That was when her childhood crumbled.

It was those two weeks that she learned things no child should know and she was changed forever. That was when she started to burn herself. The pain outside sometimes

equaled the pain within, sometimes took her away and helped her pretend.

Only the evidence of real pain seemed to hold the power to balance her out. She needed to see it, feel it, know it existed, and it had to be strong enough to distract her from all the other hurt inside.

Later that summer she tried locking her door. When school started she had come home to find the lock gone. Her stepfather made sure she understood she would never lock him out again.

A piercing beep rent the air and Liberty jolted back to the present. She turned and opened the oven where a sheet spread with brightly colored summer squash roasted. Without thinking she reached in to pull the grilled vegetables out of the oven and hissed, jerking back as her fingers made contact with the hot metal.

"*Shit!*" she hissed, as the pan clattered down.

Her pain was her least worry. She examined the tips of her fingers and prayed the damage wasn't too bad. Mason would think she did it on purpose. She grabbed an oven mitt with her other hand and pulled the squash out of the oven, sitting the sizzling cookie sheet on the countertop and rushing to the sink to treat her burn with cold water.

The pain faded and she tried not to panic. Her gaze shot to the clock. Mason would be home in a few minutes. Her scalded fingers trembled as she turned the water off and on three more times then examined the damage. Not too bad. A little pink, a little puffy.

She needed to get a hold of herself. She couldn't go back to her past. Her life was in the present. It had to be.

When dinner was prepared she set the table and rushed upstairs to freshen up. She inspected the rooms after her shower. Sean was in Mason's study with the door closed.

Sitting at her vanity she twisted and pinned her blond curls high on her head, exposing the long line of her neck. No earrings today. Her white linen pants hid her figure up to her hips where they fitted to her waist. She threw on a loose fitting black cowl neck blouse to drape in voluminous folds.

She fought the urge to run to the third floor and hide in shame. On her way back downstairs she quickly passed the now empty study and stepped back to inspect the room. Magazines were out of place and the remote control wasn't perpendicular to Mason's chair. Liberty fixed the items and shut the door, opening and closing it twice more before turning away.

When she reached the foyer she stood on the third tile, nine feet exactly and folded her hands. Her thumb fondled her burned fingers and she pressed into the pain. The sharp throb the pressure eased her anxiety and helped her focus, helped her pretend that nothing untoward had happened.

But the sound of Mason's Mercedes pulling

up the drive had her heart racing. She needed to calm down. The garage door closed and she took a deep breath. The knob clicked and for a moment in time she saw her stepfather, Eric, walking toward her.

Her mind shook away the frightening image of the ghost of her past and smiled with trembling lips as her husband stepped through the door.

Mason smiled. "Hey, beautiful, how was your day?"

"Good. How was yours?"

He dropped his newspaper on the side table and removed his coat. When he turned he smiled at her again. "How about a kiss?"

Liberty released her hold on herself and went to him. Mason looked down at her with loving eyes and cupped the side of her face with gentle hands. "I missed you," he whispered as his soft lips pressed into hers. Smiling, he tenderly licked at her mouth and some of her tension washed away. "Did you have fun playing with Sean today?"

Liberty tensed. Images of Sean's large hand dwarfing her breast played through her mind. Mason pulled back and looked down at her, obviously catching her reaction. "Liberty?"

She fumbled trying to find a reply. "I made grilled tilapia with mango salsa."

"Sounds perfect. Do I have time to change?"

"Of course." She took his coat and hung it in the closet. After she gathered his papers she turned and froze. Sean stood at the top of the high stairs watching them. His eyes seemed to be on her, but also watching Mason. Would he tell?

"Hey, Sean. Enjoy your day?" Mason called as he moved up the stairs.

Sean's body relaxed as he looked toward her husband. The release of Sean's gaze catapulted her into action and she fled to the kitchen. She didn't need to hear his reply.

Dinner was quiet. Mason held up most of the conversation while she and Sean only offered abrupt, one or two word replies. After she cleared the table she brought out coffee for the boys and excused herself to go clean up the dishes. When she returned to the dining room Mason and Sean were both laughing and leaning back in their chairs, seeming at ease.

Mason's gaze found hers and he smiled. "You all done, baby?" She nodded. "What do you say we watch a movie? Sean, you want to join us?"

Sean hesitated a moment and sat up. "Ah, you know, I think I'm gonna hit the sack if you don't mind, but you two have fun."

"You sure?" Mason asked.

"Yeah. I'll see you two in the morning."

When they made their way upstairs Liberty turned and noticed Sean's door was tightly closed. Mason accepted the hand that she offered him, the hand that didn't bear evidence of her earlier perfidy, and led her to the entertainment room.

She curled up on a recliner as Mason set up

the movie. It was a sci-fi flick and Liberty wasn't really much of a fan of that genre so she began to daydream.

Halfway through the movie Mason touched her cheek. "Do you want to go to bed, Lib?"

"The movie's not over."

"Yeah, but you aren't watching it. Where are you?"

"I was just thinking."

"About what?" he asked softly, no longer watching the screen, his attention solely on her.

"Things I shouldn't be thinking of."

"I'm sorry you had a difficult day, Lib. That was my fault. I shouldn't have made you stay in bed."

"I wanted to stay. I...I hate that something I enjoyed...can be taken away like that." She frowned as she tried to find the words to explain how much she hated what she had.

"Shh. Don't worry. I get it. You don't need to explain it to me. We'll try to be a little more proactive in the future, that's all. Try to avoid situations that can backfire. It's over. Don't stress yourself out."

She nodded, knowing he was right, but there were other things on her mind as well. She wished she could shut off her brain.

He tugged her hand. "Come here. Let me hold you. You seem tense."

Liberty climbed off of her leather recliner and walked over to Mason. She stood before him, filling the space between his knees. He reached for her hand and pulled her to his lap, situating her limbs until she lay with her head on his chest, legs draped to the side and hip pressed into his abdomen. His fingers went to her neck and toyed with the curls that had fallen loose from her clip.

His touch traced gentle circles over her skin and lightly massaged some of the tension out of her shoulders. Liberty let the stresses of the day wash away as her husband's palms moved over her neck, shoulders, and back.

His hands coasted under her arms and found her breasts. Strong palms cupped them through her light blouse and toyed with the mounds until her nipples formed hard points under his gentle touch. She leaned into him and soon her blouse was being pulled over her shoulders and tossed onto the floor.

"That's it, baby, let me take care of you." His gentle words were her undoing. Making a sound of distress, she cowered from his touch. "Lib? What's wrong?"

God, it hurt. She never wanted to disappoint him and now she'd done something irrevocable that might destroy his generous trust. Breathing rapidly, she glanced at her lap and confessed, "Something happened today."

He tensed, his hand slowly moving to hers and turning over her palm. When he saw the slight discoloration he sighed. "This is my fault—"

"No, Mason. It's mine. I did something very stupid and I hate—"

"I have to tell you something."

"—knowing that my mother was right about me."

He stilled. His brow creased as his tone turned serious. "Liberty, your mother was *not* right about you."

Her vision blurred. "You don't understand."

"I don't care what happened today. You are not to believe your mother's accusations. We've been through this."

A tear fell to her lap. In a small voice she rasped, "I think I have a crush on your friend."

The room stilled in utter silence as neither of them seemed to breathe. "You...you have feelings for Sean?"

"No. I don't know. I don't want to feel the things I'm feeling but—"

"Shh...take a breath."

She drew in a large gulp of air as he rubbed a hand in circles at her back.

"Start at the beginning. When did you start feeling these things?"

She exhaled roughly, the pressure in her chest constricting another degree. "Today. We were shopping and goofing off and just having fun, but then when we came home everything seemed different."

"Different how?"

"Like...the energy changed."

His brow remained tense, as he appeared to be picturing the two of them. Slowly, he said, "Sean can be a very captivating man. He has a way of making a person feel like they're the center of the universe."

"I don't want to be the center of anyone's world but yours." She softly confessed, her voice laden with tears as he pulled her close. "I'm sorry. I don't know what's wrong with me."

"Hey. Look at me." He gently turned her chin and wiped away a tear. "There is *nothing* wrong with you. Our bodies react to different people and circumstances in different ways."

Her stomach clenched with unbearable guilt and she moaned. "Please stop making excuses for me. Mason... I let him touch me."

His muscles tensed as his Adam's apple slowly shifted. In a gravely whisper, he echoed, "Sean touched you?"

"We were in the pool, playing Marco Polo. He was *It* and when he grabbed me—"

"An innocent game, Liberty."

"It wasn't innocent. We both knew we were doing something wrong and that we had to stop."

"Did you?"

"Yes. He told me to get away from him and I left."

Some of his tension appeared to fade. "Did he kiss you?"

"No, he touched me." She lifted his hand and held it to her breast. "Here, through my suit."

Gazing away he let his hand slide to a resting position.

"I'm so sorry, Mason—"

"Stop." His commanding tone silenced her.

"You do not have to apologize. Sometimes… sometimes a moment can get away from us. It's clear you never intended for this to happen. We all make mistakes, Liberty."

"It won't happen again."

He studied her for a long moment. "What if it did?"

"What? I won't let it."

"Take the guilt away for a moment, Lib. What do you feel about Sean?"

"I…like him. He's your friend."

"Are you attracted to him?"

Her mouth pursed as her brow tightened.

"No guilt. Just honesty."

She bit her lip. "Yes."

"I don't want you punishing yourself for sincere feelings, feelings you have no control over."

"But my actions—"

"Sometimes our actions aren't as bad as they seem. I trust you and I'm actually…okay with what happened."

Her eyes widened with shock. "You are?"

He drew in a long breath. "Yes. With any other man I'd be livid, but… I don't know how to explain it. I don't feel angry or betrayed. Everything will work out, but first I have to tell you something, something that might change—"

"Oh, Mason." Her relief was so acute, so all encompassing, she couldn't think of anything else at the moment. Her hands cupped his face as she pressed her lips to his, cutting off anymore talk. "I love you. I'm so lucky to have such an accepting husband."

He hesitated only a second and then kissed her back, his hands hauling her tight to his body. But as he pulled away she saw hesitation in his gaze.

His gaze drifted to the floor. "Liberty, we need to talk about something."

Her fingers rode over his shoulders as she pressed her lips to his throat. "Can it wait until tomorrow? Please? I want you so much right now. I need you, Mason." Her lips closed around his ear as she whispered, "I need my husband."

His face turned as he abruptly cut off her begging with a penetrating kiss. His hands rolled down her spine as he tugged at her clothes and she crawled over his lap. His lips caressed her shoulders and his tongue found that sensitive spot at the curve of her neck. Her head rested on his arm as his fingers fondled her breasts through the slight material of her lace bra. His hand drifted over her belly and stopped just between her legs.

Their mouths explored of each other. Licking and nipping, tasting and loving one another. Her skin began to heat and she found herself tugging at Mason's clothing. His fingers wrapped around her wrist, a gentle but unbreakable hold as he pulled her hand away. "No. Let me pleasure you."

She was frustrated for only a moment and then surrendered to his command. He plucked at the ties of her linen pants until they came undone. With a soft nudge he helped her stand and step out of them. She stood before him in nothing but her bra and panties, quivering, awaiting his next move.

Mason leaned forward and kissed her soft tummy. His tongue licked slowly over her hip as his thumbs fit under the elastic and drew the fabric of her panties downward. Her sex was hot and swollen, the cool air of the room soothing.

"Step out," he whispered as her panties fell to her ankles. He sat back a moment to study her and her fingers began to twitch at her sides. Leaning forward, Mason gently licked the tip of her clit budding out from the hood of her sex. Her lashes lowered as she sighed. His lips, rather than kissing her sex, dragged over her smooth mound and back to her sensitized belly. His teeth nipped at her hips.

His large hands slid to her sides and with slow, controlled ease, glided up to her rib cage until her breasts rested in the V of his thumbs and index fingers. He paused there for a moment looking at her hard nipples pressing through the silk of her bra then moved on, coasting over the sensitive tips of her breasts.

Slowly pulling the straps down her arms, his hot mouth closed over one turgid nipple, sucking gently at first and then hard. With every pull of his mouth he stole a piece of her soul.

"What do you need, Liberty?"

Unable to form an answer, she moaned.

His hand went to the apex of her thighs and

she jolted, her spine stiffening, as he surprised her by plunging one finger deep inside her wet folds. She could barely register the invasion before he removed his digit and sat back, resting his jaw in the curve between his thumb and forefinger. He watched her, completely at ease and in complete command.

"Do you want to get fucked, Liberty?"

She tried not to wince at his crude words. They were wrong, but excited her on some level. Yes, she wanted Mason inside of her. Her skin prickled with need.

"Answer me."

She looked into his eyes. He was serious and she reminded herself of all she'd promised the night before. He was in charge. "Yes, Mason."

"Yes, Mason, what?"

"Yes, Mason, I want you to fuck me."

The corner of his lip turned up and she knew he was pleased. "How would you like to be fucked, Liberty?"

"Hard."

His eyes burned with lust, pupils dilating, followed by the brief flare of his nostrils, and his expression sobered. "Go up to our room and I'll be there in a minute."

She leaned down to gather her clothes.

"Leave them."

"But Sean—"

"Sean's asleep. Do as I say." He stood and turned off the entertainment system. She paused for a moment, slightly unsure. "Liberty."

At the commanding tone of his voice her body sprang into action. She turned the knob and blinked as the soft hall lighting disturbed her eyes. Looking left then right, she relaxed once she saw the hallway was empty and Sean's bedroom door was still closed. Her bare feet stepped into the hall and moved toward their bedroom.

Mason grabbed her arm when she was only halfway there and spun her. Her back crashed into the cool wall and his mouth came down on hers. His tongue pressed past her lips and he kissed her fiercely. She moaned and raised her knee to hook over his hip. The bulge of his cock jammed against her sex. She would leave a wet mark on his pants, but she ground herself against him anyway.

"Undo my pants, Liberty."

Her fingers went to the waist of his pants and released the button. She quickly lowered the zipper and his cock sprang free. Without being told her fingers wrapped around his thickness and her thumb ran over the wet tip. He caught her wrist and stilled her movements.

"You have to ask."

"Can I touch you?" She was mad with lust and needed to feel him. Surely he could grant her that.

"With your mouth." He looked into her eyes, his own eyes pools of dark lust. "Still want to touch me?"

"Yes."

"On your knees."

She dropped to her knees so fast she would probably have bruises there. Her mouth found his thick cock and sucked him deep to the back of her throat. He groaned, rocking to the balls of his feet. She quickly untangled her arms from her bra and reached for his hips, but he was faster. He grabbed her hands and pinned them against the wall, over her head, in one large hand.

"Your mouth feels incredible on my cock, Liberty. Take me deeper. I know you can."

She shut her eyes and felt her shoulders tighten as she leaned forward. Her mouth stretched over his hot flesh and she moved her tongue along the underside of his shaft.

"Deeper," he commanded and she leaned into him as far as her position allowed. The way he held her arms she could only reach so far. He spread his feet apart, lowering himself another inch. His hand went to the back of her head and sifted through her curls.

She would have felt the wall there had he not used his hand as a buffer. As it were, the new placement of his hand allowed him to thrust deeper into her mouth.

She moaned as he filled mouth. Her eyes watered as his flesh pressed farther toward the back of her throat. "That's it, baby. Take all of me. Just like that."

When the smooth head of his engorged cock pressed against the soft pallet of her throat he held himself there. Liberty started to panic as she realized with him that deep she couldn't breathe.

Tightness gripped her chest and her eyes burned. He pulled himself back and air flooded into her lungs.

He looked down at her, his thumb reaching below her ear to trace the gentle curve of her extended jaw. "Feel that, baby? That's you taking all of me. I'm going to do that again, but this time I want you to relax. When you feel me at the back of your throat I want you to swallow so I can feel your hot mouth constricting my cock."

She waited as he slowly fed his cock down the back of her throat. Taking one last breath of air she felt him reach the deepest point and she swallowed. Mason groaned long and hard then retreated. He did this a few more times and Liberty grew more comfortable with it, knowing he would never hold himself there for more than a couple seconds.

Mason moaned and panted, he said dirty things to her that should have been offensive, but only enflamed her lust more. His thrusts became frantic and his grip in her hair tightened. He forced himself in and out and Liberty couldn't tell if he was thrusting his hips toward her or jerking her head down on his cock. Either way, she understood that his control was slipping and he was now literally fucking her mouth and she loved it, loved being able to do this to him, to pleasure him so intensely that he lost a bit of his command.

His cock suddenly ripped from her mouth. She panted and looked up at him in surprise. He pointed to the soft white runner. "On your hands and knees."

Liberty crawled to the center of the carpet as he tossed off his shirt and knelt behind her. His thighs nudged her legs farther apart as his hard cock, still wet with her saliva, fell into the crease of her ass. She stared straight ahead as he rubbed himself up and down the seam there. The tip of his cock paused, resting over the tight rosette of her ass.

"I'm going to fuck you here one day, Liberty, one day soon."

Shivers racked her body as anticipation of that day heated her blood.

"But tonight I need to feel your tight pussy wrapping around my cock, holding me like a tight little fist." His hand slid up her spine and over her shoulder. He pressed her toward the carpet. "Rest your head on your arms."

Her shoulders lowered as he lined his cock up with her wet opening. He chuckled. "It seems my wife loves sucking me off. You're soaking wet." He teased her, swirling the tip of his engorged cock at the rim of her opening, and she moaned. Fingers gripped her hips and he suddenly slammed home.

He filled her in such a delicious rush of force she screamed out. She asked him to fuck her hard and it seemed that was exactly what he intended to do. He pounded into her sex so hard she couldn't help the cry of pleasure that punctuated each forceful thrust.

Filled and hot, her body reveled in the extreme bliss of being thoroughly taken by her husband, being owned by him and him alone. His possession was the most invigorating, comforting thing she had ever experienced.

∼

SEAN AWOKE with a start when he heard someone scream. He'd been sleeping fitfully, dreaming of Liberty, well, Liberty and Mase. Frowning into the darkness, he accepted how much staying here with the two of them was costing him. His cock was semi-erect, which for the last few days seemed to be the norm.

A deep grunt caught his ear and he turned to face the door in the dark. It sounded as if someone were out in the hall. He listened and when he heard a thud he decided to investigate. Carefully navigating through the dark to the door of his bedroom he noticed the hall lights were still on. Glancing at the digital clock on his nightstand he realized he hadn't slept that long. It was only eleven-thirty.

Sean opened the door and the sounds that awoken him were amplified without the barrier of walls. His eyes went wide at the vision that greeted him. A naked Liberty, on her knees, head low, blond curls spilling over her arms and onto the white carpet as her shoulders jolted and her voice cried out in pleasure with each hard thrust Mason pounded into her from behind.

Jesus fucking Christ!

Her long spine trailed to a perfectly shaped ass. The backdrop to said ass was two beautifully cut hips and a toned abdomen thrusting forcefully against her. Sean's eyes traveled up the well-muscled torso, noticing every rivulet of sweat that trickled over Mason's hard abs. Sean's cock suddenly slammed to full attention.

Mason's pecs were as sculpted as ever. His lungs expanded in his chest as he fucked his wife hard. Sean couldn't look away. His eyes molested the other man's body all the way up to the thick cords of his neck. When he reached his face he froze.

Mason, pounding his wife hard, was looking right at him. He tipped his chin up in acknowledgement, a trickle of sweat working its way over the curve of his strong jaw, as he increased his pace and nailed Liberty harder.

Sean looked down at Liberty. She seemed to love it. Sean then looked down at the huge bulge under his briefs. He loved it too.

Mason paused and Liberty let out a protesting moan. Sean watched as Mase slowly reached for his wife's shoulder and leaned down to her ear, softly whispering, but Sean heard every word.

"Liberty, we're being watched."

Liberty stiffened and slowly raised her head. Her deep blue eyes, now the color of stormy skies, found Sean's immediately. Her cheeks flushed and she nervously licked her lips.

Looking back in Mason's eyes, Sean knew he was too far gone with lust to be thinking clearly. He was being completely driven by the eroticism of the moment. He'd always been a bit of an exhibitionist.

Mason gently pulled Liberty up by the shoulders and kissed and licked her neck as he held her up for inspection. Her arms crossed over her breasts and Sean could see where Mason's fat cock filled her slick pussy. She was shaven smooth and her folds glistened with arousal. The vein on Mason's cock bulged and curved to remain inside of her in this upward position.

She panted and gazed seductively at him. By the look of things, she found the idea of being watched erotic as well, but also struggled with it, as a hint of panic infused her stare. Knowing Mason, he wouldn't allow her to hold any shame in moments of intimacy.

Mason's hands went to Liberty's and he gently eased them away from her breasts. He used one hand to circle her wrists and pull her arms down. "Show Sean your pretty tits, Liberty."

Liberty responded to his direction. It was a beautiful display of submission, one that Sean found intoxicating. His cock lengthened a little more and he reached down to adjust himself. His ex still seemed to follow a dominant no shame policy.

Mason slid his hands under her arms and guided her limbs around his neck. The caress caused a tickle of chills to chase over Liberty's flesh and Sean could actually see her nipples ruche a bit more. They were beautiful, small, tight, and, as he already knew, deep pink. He swallowed.

Mason's fingers went to those perfectly puckered nipples and pinched them between his fingers. Liberty moaned long and deep. Her head fell back on Mason's shoulder and her eyes shut. She was drunk on passion, totally gone. Sean had never imagined Liberty appearing so free and unrestrained. It was beautiful.

Mason played a while longer with her breasts, still seated deep inside of her, then he whispered, "Liberty." Her eyes opened only into drowsy slits. "What if I told you I wanted Sean to suck on your pretty nipples?"

She moaned.

"Would you do that for me? I know you'll enjoy it. Sean has such a nice mouth, don't you think?"

Liberty arched, her cunt sliding down further over Mason's slick cock as he held her to him. "Is that a yes?"

"Yes, Mason."

Mason looked back to him and raised an eyebrow as if to ask what Sean thought about that. Sean shook his head. He couldn't. Liberty was Mason's wife! He'd already been tempted by her beauty once. He couldn't allow himself to do this. But oh, he wanted to.

His cock throbbed and he touched himself again through his briefs. Mason's eyes zeroed in on the movement and Sean watched as he thrust one long stroke deep into Liberty's pussy. She cried out and writhed in his arms.

Sean was frozen in place. This was wrong.

"Come here, Sean."

The command in Mason's voice both excited and irritated him. He was weak when Mason used such a tone with him, and yet control had been something they each battled for in their relationship. Two alpha males, each struggling to be on top. Sean usually wound up being in control, requiring Mason's complete trust and surrender. Trust he had forsaken the minute he walked away from their relationship. He took a step forward and halted.

Mason pacified his whimpering wife, who was teetering on what was sure to be an explosive orgasm, by ramming his cock into her a few times as he waited for Sean. Mase's uncivilized grunt that followed each thrust enlightened him to just how sweet Libby's tight pussy was. Mase cupped and plumped her breasts as if offering them to his friend.

"Tell Sean what I want. What you want to give me, Liberty."

Her head slowly tilted forward from where she'd been lolling on his shoulder. Lustful blue eyes stared into his. "Help me please my husband, Sean. Please come touch my breasts."

She asked so prettily he found himself moving forward. Mase smiled slowly at his progress. His hands coasted over her breasts and up the length of her arms, unlatching them from around his neck as he held them out to the side. She looked like a pagan sacrifice upon a cross and Mason was offering her to him.

Sean dropped to his knees. He could smell the scent of her arousal dripping down Mason's cock and heavy sac. God, he wanted to lick it up, but he was only invited to play with these pretty tits. His fingers were actually shaking as his hand slowly reached for her. A breath away from her heated flesh, he paused. He looked into Mason's gaze and the other man grinned.

"Touch her, Sean. Help me pleasure her. I want to make her come, but not yet. First I want her begging for it."

Sean pushed out a shaky breath and tried to make his heartbeat slow. He stretched forward and slowly ran the tips of his fingers over the soft curve of Liberty's breast. She sighed, and Sean reveled in giving her what she needed.

His thumb traveled down the upturned slope of her breast and pinched hard over that small, cherry tip. Liberty hissed in a breath through her teeth and looked at him in question.

"Sean isn't as gentle as I am, Liberty. Do you still want him to touch you?"

He waited. He wasn't a gentle lover, thus his preference of male companionship. Well, one male in particular. He'd done a lot of experimenting in his younger days and traveled through different scenes, only to surrender to the idea that he would likely always be a loner.

"What do you want, Mason? If it pleases you, it pleases me."

"I want Sean to suck those pretty tits."

Sean waited as Liberty looked up at him, so God damn beautiful he wanted to take her and run away with her. "Please suck my breasts, Sean." Je-sus-Christ. There was no refusing a request like that.

His weight rested on his knees as he leaned in and inhaled the soft, clean scent of her skin. His tongue extended and flicked over one nipple. Liberty gasped and arched, begging for more.

Mason pulled her arms tighter to her side, which caused her chest to expand toward his mouth. "Sean's in charge of your pleasure, Liberty. Only me and Sean."

Sean looked up at Mason and he nodded. That was all the permission he needed. His large palm went around Liberty's slender waist and flattened against her back, bringing her front to his mouth. The heat of Mason's chest scorched the back of his hand and familiar smells of long ago clouded his mind. He pulled the tip of Liberty's breast into his mouth and sucked the bud hard between his lips, adding the slight pressure of his teeth.

She cried out and her body moved as Mason pumped inside of her, twice, hard. "Prettiest, pert nipples you've ever seen, aren't they, Sean?"

He groaned his admiration. "They sure are. So tight and pink. Makes me want to stretch her breasts tight around my cock and fuck her tits."

He sucked the other nipple into his mouth and sat back to admire the two wet tips. They were slightly redder than they'd been. Mason released her arms and they fell to her sides. His hand fed through the space over her hip and traveled down to the delta of her pussy.

"And here, Sean, look here. See how she keeps herself so smooth and pretty for me."

Sean grunted in agreement. "Very beautiful."

"Liberty, how would you feel about Sean licking that sweet clit of yours while I fuck your pussy nice, slow, and deep?" She began to pant and moan. "I think that's a yes. What do you think, Sean?"

"Let's see." Sean took the tip of his finger and swirled it over her breasts and down her narrow torso. She was so soft and delicate, hanging by a thread on the verge of complete ecstasy. His finger eased over her smooth mound and he noticed the tiny tip of her clit peeking past her flesh stretched taut over Mason's wide cock. God, he wanted them both.

His finger pressed over her clit as if he was flicking a switch and she jerked in Mason's hold.

"Can you take it, Liberty? If it's too much, we'll stop," Mason whispered. She breathed hard and Sean flicked and toyed with her clit again. "Tell me, Liberty. Should we stop?"

"No!" she answered almost frantically.

"Do you want to feel Sean's mouth on you there?"

"Yes, please."

"Then ask him nice."

Sean saw the battle she faced to simply open her eyes and form words. When she looked at him breath slipped past her pouty, full lips earning a trickle of come from his cock.

The tip of her pink tongue licked over the full curve of her lower lip and she swallowed. "Sean, will you please lick my pussy?"

"Gladly."

He dove to the floor and fastened his mouth around that little bud and she screamed. He gripped her delicate hips then slid his palms back to hold Mase's tight ass as he slowly thrust his cock deep inside of her. Liberty cried as Sean licked her clit and Mason fucked her tight cunt.

Unable to help himself, he extended his tongue and licked a firm line from the top of Mason's sac, up the wide base of his cock and planted his tongue deep under Liberty's hood just over her clit. Mason jerked and groaned in pleasure as Liberty convulsed and thrashed as the beginnings of an intense orgasm took hold of her reflexes.

"Hold her, Mase."

Mason wrapped his arms around his wife and clutched her tightly to him. His broad fingers plucked and pinched her nipples as Sean made a feast out of her pussy and Mason's cock. His hands traveled over Mase's firm ass and gripped him hard. The three of them became a trifecta of frenzied need and lust.

He pulled her bud deep between his lips. Her

heartbeat pulsed through her flesh, pattering rapidly on his tongue. She shouted obscenities and half-words, insisting he and Mase never stop. Her hands suddenly knotted in Sean's hair and gripped him hard, the pinch of pain practically making him come in his shorts.

Sean's fingers found the cleft of Mason's ass and separated his flesh while he ate at Libby's pussy. He found the tight knot of his ass and applied mild pressure.

"Fuck!" Mason shouted and proceeded to ride his wife hard. She shook and screamed as her orgasm peaked and she bathed Sean's tongue in her sweet honey.

"Take her," Mase grunted and Sean sat up, gathering Libby in his arms. God, she felt perfect there.

He moved his legs out from under him and eased himself onto his back, pulling Libby with him. Mason fell on top of them and Sean held her in his arms as Mason fucked her hard. The slap of his balls against Sean's cock covered by only his briefs threw him into overdrive.

He began to thrust his hips upward, below the two of them, his sheltered dick pressing into Liberty's soft stomach. Her face pressed into his shoulder as Sean's eyes stared intently into the gaze of a lover he had once known by heart.

His hand reached around to Mason's ass again and he grabbed a handful of firm flesh. His fingers dug in and Mase shouted as he filled Liberty with his release.

The three of them cried out as if they were all experiencing Mase's orgasm. Mase collapsed on top of them, but quickly rolled to the side, pulling Liberty with him.

Reality hit Sean's conscience with a sobering slap. What the fuck had he just done? He breathed hard, as did Mase and Liberty, but no one uttered a word.

The weight in his chest only mildly eased as Mason gathered his wife in his arms and kissed her tenderly, praising her. She clung to him as she caught her breath.

Sean was the first to recover, it seemed. He made to sit up, wanting nothing more in that moment then to leave the couple and return to his own private room. But Liberty, with her cheek resting on Mase's chest, opened her eyes, and placed a small hand on Sean's bicep. It actually hurt. The yearning he felt at the sight of her dainty hand holding him there physically hurt.

He looked at her and waited, but she said nothing—nothing, yet everything all at the same time. She smiled softly as if telling him thank you.

Sean frowned. What they'd done was wrong. If only she knew how he'd touched her husband she wouldn't be thanking him. And if Mason knew of his behavior in the pool he'd be knocking him out.

With her taste still on his tongue he forced a reassuring smile and stood from the floor. Mase called his name in a questioning tone, but Sean didn't stop. He went straight to his room, stepped inside with alacrity, and shut the door.

~

ABOUT TWENTY MINUTES LATER, as he was settling back into bed, he heard the knob turn. Mason's form filled the doorframe, silhouetted against the soft glow of the hall light. "You asleep?"

"No."

"Can I come in?"

"Your house."

Mason stepped over the threshold and softly shut the door. He walked to the bed and Sean prayed he wouldn't come too close.

"Where's Libby?"

"She's sleeping." Mase sat down on the edge of the bed. He'd put sweats on and his knee brushed Sean's thigh through the covers. "Are you okay with what just happened?"

"Are you?"

"It depends. If you can handle it, then yes."

"And what about Libby?" Sean felt protective of her in ways he couldn't explain. Never before had he felt such a need to shelter a woman.

"Liberty will be okay so long as you don't freak her out."

"Me? Correct me if I'm wrong, but you allowed another man to touch your wife tonight. If I'm right in my assumption, this is new territory to y'all."

"Not just any man. *You.* I trust you, and Libby

likes you. She trusts me. But you're right, this is new to us."

"Why?"

"Why what? Why have we never had a threesome before?"

"No," Sean snapped. "Why now, all of a sudden? Why with me?"

"Like I said, I trust you."

"With your wife?"

"Yes, with my wife," Mason agreed calmly.

"You haven't seen me in thirteen years, Mase. For all you know I could have turned into a complete scum bag."

"You didn't," Mason said with complete confidence and unjustified conviction.

Sean scoffed. "How the fuck do you know?"

Mason looked at him with steel in his eyes. "Because I know. I know you, Sean. You can't hide who you are from me. You never could. She told me what happened in the pool today. You liked women long before you started liking men."

Sean stiffened. He'd never liked men. Only Mason. And what happened in the pool was an oversight.

"Relax. I'm not going to run out and buy you a rainbow flag, but you really should get over that. It's all just labels. You are who you are no matter what you label it."

"Are you upset about the pool?"

Mase shifted his jaw. "I'm surprised, but after thinking about it, no, I'm not upset. Like I said, Liberty likes you."

"She said that?"

He chuckled. "Yes. As a matter of fact, she admitted she was attracted to you."

His mind boggled at such an open and honest relationship where a wife could admit to liking another man. But beyond his confusion, was deep pride. She liked him. *Him.*

Sean pressed his lips together and took a deep breath. "What happens now?"

"Well, if you aren't planning to run away scared then I'm not really sure. We'll have to play things out and see. I can tell you what *can't* happen though. Under no circumstances are you allowed to act like *nothing* happened. If you stay, you acknowledge the fact that tonight happened. Liberty's fragile and has a lot of demons in her past. She won't be able to deal with you pretending nothing happened. It'll stir up old memories she doesn't need right now. I won't allow her to feel ashamed."

"So what, you want me to bring it up at breakfast tomorrow? 'Gee, Libby, this French toast is delicious. By the way, so is your pussy.' *What the fuck, man?* I can't do that!"

"Don't be an idiot. I'm just saying...be casual about it. How would you act with a lover the next morning?"

"I'm usually out by sunrise."

Mason pursed his lips. "I'm not surprised."

"Don't," Sean warned. He didn't need another lecture about his inability to commit to even short term affairs. Sighing, he tried to think of how he would act with a woman the morning after. "I don't know. I guess I would be a little affectionate. Knowing me I'd probably try to hit it one more time before I sent her home."

"Okay, then be like that with Libby, affectionate, but no hitting it."

Sean was shocked. "Are you serious?"

"Very. I'll tell her I'm okay with this—for now —so long as we all remain honest with each other and you don't fuck my wife without my permission."

Sean's eyes went wide. "Dude, do you hear yourself? Fuck your wife? You're out of your mind! You two took vows—"

"If you can't handle this then I'll help you pack. But if you're going to sit here and act like you aren't interested, I'm going to tell you you're full of shit. It was my cock you were licking a half hour ago."

Sean gritted his teeth and fought the urge to punch him in the face. "I'll stay."

"Good. I'll talk to Libby in the morning." He stood. "Oh, and one more thing. On the third floor is another guestroom. Under no circumstances are you allowed in that room unless Liberty invites you. Understand?"

"What's up there?"

"Nothing. That's just her space. She knows she can go there and catch her breath if things overwhelm her. Promise me you won't go up there unless she invites you."

"Okay, I promise."

"Good." He turned toward the door.

"Wait," Sean hastily called and Mase stilled, glancing back. Sean felt his gaze even through the darkness of the room. "What about us? Do you expect this shit to go on and your wife not to notice that another man's hand on your ass throws you into orgasm?"

His sigh echoed in the darkness. He came back to the bed and lowered himself to sit on the edge of the mattress. Sean jerked in surprise at the brush of Mason's knuckles over his rough jaw and couldn't stop himself from leaning into the caress.

"I need to tell her. I'm just trying to find the right moment. I almost told her tonight, but the opportunity slipped away from me. I don't know what the next week will bring, but I know I loved being with both of you tonight. Liberty loved it too. And I'm pretty positive you were enjoying yourself. I think we should just see what happens. However, as much as I'm in control of my wife's pleasure, I'm usually aware of what she wants and doesn't want. The moment she changes her mind or objects, everything stops and it's over. I don't need her to say it out loud. I'll be able to tell."

Sean caught his wrist. "Where does this leave me?"

Mason sighed. "I don't know. I don't want to hurt you any more than I want to hurt Libby. If you think I'm being selfish, tell me, and we'll call it quits."

"I don't want to quit."

"Neither do I," Mason whispered back.

Sean tugged him closer and pressed his forehead to Mase's. "I've missed you. I'm not gonna lie. I want you."

Mase shut his eyes and pressed his lips together. "She's my wife, Sean. If it doesn't include her, it doesn't happen."

Sean placed Mase's palm on his chest. "Nothing stops the way I feel. Just feelings, that's all I'm telling you. I just need you to know. Right here, that's where you are, my boy."

"Fuck," Mason quietly swore and turned away, his hand gripping Sean's tightly. "I've never broken my vows to her. You change that and I don't want this to be a secret we keep."

"So tell her. After tonight, I can't imagine she'd be that shocked." Sensing this was killing him, he pulled him into a hug. "Come here."

Mason went easily, resting his head against his shoulder. It was clear how heavy of a burden this was for him. "I don't want to hurt her."

"We'll figure it out. Tomorrow we'll talk and everything will work out some way or another."

"What if it doesn't? What if it's too much for her and you have to go. I don't want you to go, Sean."

He didn't want to leave either. It had never been more apparent how much Mason put everyone else's needs before his own. If it was too much, his friend would do everything in his power to reestablish a stable environment for his wife and Sean would be fucked.

He wasn't ready to let go. Easing back, he pulled Mase to his chest. "Let me just hold you for a minute."

Soft hair tickled his chin as he held him. The silence stretched and soon Mason's hand found his stomach where it made gentle whorls over his skin. He pressed his lips to Mason's head and he turned, eyes glimmering in the dark with so many questions hidden in their depths.

His strong hand wrapped around Sean's neck as his thumb traced the sharp line of his jaw. The blankets shifted as Mase leaned forward and traced his lips over his. It was too much temptation. He gripped the back of his head and slanted his mouth over his, deepening the kiss.

They bit at each other's lips as Sean's cock lengthened. Mason lowered his body, dragging his hips against him and Sean realized, he too, was hard. The weight was so familiar, amplifying everything he'd forsaken when he walked away thirteen years ago. A sharp pain sliced through his heart and he fought the urge to break down and cry. "I'm sorry," he whispered against Mason's beating pulse.

"I forget how to do this," Mason confessed, pain and so much regret lacing his voice.

Sean reached for his hand, pulling it from his neck, placing it between his legs. "I'll never be able to stop you from touching me. But you don't have to." In this instance he needed Mason to be in control. If he chose to stop, they'd stop.

Mason broke the kiss and turned, breathing hard into the hard curve of Sean's shoulder. He said nothing, but reached into Sean's briefs and pulled out his cock, slowly running his hand up and down the length as he squeezed. As wonderful as Mason's body and touch felt, fairness and fidelity tainted the bulk of what they were feeling. He ran his hand over the back of Mase's head tenderly and held him as he stroked.

Mason's hand moved faster, jerking and pulling on Sean's hard cock without looking at him or what he was doing, only feeling, likely remembering how it was. Memories came hurtling back. The moment was so intense they each seemed to have trouble breathing through it.

Sean kissed the side of his head. "Remember how good it was? How many nights we went without sleep just to be with each other?"

Mason's grip tightened as he tugged harder, faster. Sean's balls drew up tight. "I'm gonna come if you keep that up," he quietly warned. Mason only provoked him farther by moving even faster.

They were each breathing heavily. His toes tingled and jolts of electricity buzzed up his spine. Sean's cock swelled and pulsed under his firm grip as hot come spilled over his hand. It was such an all-encompassing release, one he'd longed for, one only Mason could provide. Tears prickled his eyes.

Mase slowed and eased his grip. Sean's head hummed with pleasure as his heart pounded in his chest. He quickly turned and rolled himself on top of Mase.

There were tears in his old lover's eyes. "Don't cry, Mase. Please. Your life is beautiful. Don't let the past confuse you. I wasn't strong enough to be what you needed. Libby is. I'll stay, but not if it hurts either of you." He leaned down and softly kissed him.

Mason slowly gave over his mouth. They became reacquainted with each other's taste and feel. When they pulled apart Mason whispered, "I doubt I'll ever stop loving you."

Sean looked into his soft brown eyes. "I know. Me too."

CHAPTER 9

*S*ean came downstairs to a delicious scent that sent his imagination on a wild tail-spin of hunger and unleashed his raw lust for Libby's cooking. As he entered the dining room he found Mason reading the paper, already dressed for work, but no food in sight.

"Hey," he greeted as he took a seat and poured himself a cup of coffee from the carafe sitting on the table. His eyes couldn't seem to pick a place to focus so he busied himself with doctoring up his coffee.

"Good morning."

"Did you sleep well?" Sean asked, the quiet clack of his spoon tapping the mug as he stirred.

With a shuffle of papers, Mason gazed back at him, a knowing look in his eyes. "What do you think?"

He didn't know what to think. His mind was in a spin-bin. "How is she?"

"She's good."

How could he be so casual about this? "And you?"

Mase paused, his eyes finally lifting from the paper. "I'm...good." He grinned and his chest tightened. God, he missed that smile. "I plan on telling her everything tonight."

It was a relief to hear all their cards would soon be on the table, but at the same time his gut was unsettled with worry. This could blow up in their faces at any minute. "Did she say anything?"

"I spoke to her early this morning and so long as you remember what I said last night, everything should be fine."

"Yeah, about that," Sean said, sipped his coffee. God damn, but everything that woman made tasted perfect. "What exactly do you expect me to do?"

"I told you. Just act like you would with any other partner you spent the night with."

A frustrated sound crept from the back of his throat. He put his mug down. Leaning forward he whispered, "But that's the thing, Mase, she isn't my partner. She's my ex- partner's wife."

Mase sighed and folded the paper and tossed it aside. "Right. I'm your ex-partner and she's my wife and this morning my wife confessed to being attracted to my old college friend, who, guess what, is also you. Now that we have everyone labeled correctly can we move on?"

"No," he hissed. "I know you just *loooove* to break my balls about my labels, but this isn't about that. This is about you loaning out your wife. That's fucked up."

Mason glared at him, his eyes suddenly cold and serious. "I'm not *loaning* out Liberty. I'm inviting you to join us as we explore some things. Don't make it into something it's not. She isn't my property, but my partner, my helpmate. I love that woman more than anything else in this world. I think we've hit on something that...I haven't worked it all out yet, but my gut is telling me to go with it. But Sean, make no mistake, she's her own person. That being said, she's also *my* wife. Mine. So long as we're both in agreement that you two can...*play*, then I don't see the harm. It's consensual and I won't allow her to feel shame about her desires. We're all entitled to our own proclivities. I've spent years helping her accept hers. If you can't, then maybe you should bow out gracefully. But don't judge her or me, especially when I'm quite aware of *your* tastes."

"Okay fine, but it's a lot different saying something is okay and then being right in the fucking moment and living it. You could change your mind the second you see some other dude pawing your wife."

"Not with you."

"You're so sure?" Sean sneered.

The door from the kitchen opened and Sean blanked his expression, repressing his hostility for the moment. Liberty entered the dining room carrying plates, linen napkins, and three glasses of orange juice on a tray.

"Completely," Mason said, picking his paper up again and putting an end to further discussion.

"Good morning, Sean," Liberty said, almost melodiously as she laid out the plates in what was clearly a proscribed manner and lined up the folded napkins.

Sean was fuming at Mase's arrogance. What did he know? Suddenly, he had an idea. Sean stood up before Liberty could place the last glass neatly above his napkin.

"Good morning, little Liberty." He blocked her from the table, crowded her smaller form with his much larger one. Imposing on her personal space, he inched closer. She looked up at him, confusion shining in her bright blue eyes. Her soft white-blond curls danced as she tipped her head back to meet his gaze.

"Sean?"

Sean tucked a stray curl behind her ear only to have the insolent coil spring back out of line. With shaky fingers, Libby reached for the curl and forced it into place.

"I like it down," Sean said in a husky whisper and was rewarded with the softest pink tinge darkening her cheeks. Like a sunset, her cheeks had various shade of warmth, each one beautiful, each one rewarding.

Her golden lashes fluttered. "So does Mason. It's a nightmare. I don't know why I even bother keeping it long." Her fingers fluttered at the edge of one unruly ringlet.

Mason put down his paper and Sean figured he finally got his attention. Good. He smiled down at Liberty and slowly reached for the clip in her hair. He carefully pressed the spring on the contraption, causing its hold to loosen, and all of her spirals came tumbling down.

Her chest rose and fell as her breath quickened. Her nipples were straining against the thin fabric of her cotton shirt. He tossed the clip on the table and reached over her shoulders, lifting the weight of her hair into his hands and savoring the silken feel of it springing and wrapping around his fingers. Liberty's lashes lowered creating small purple shadows on her ivory skin.

He leaned down and held his mouth a mere inch away from hers. The heat of her sweet breath teased his lips. He may have had his mouth on her most intimate parts last night, but he had yet to kiss her.

And she had a mouth made to drive men mad. Her pouty lower lip was plump, the kind a man could bite into, but it was her upper lip that was so unique. Two full peaks, beautiful like the ties of a bow, it was almost feline like. She had a mouth that celebrities paid fortunes to emulate. He leaned in and coasted his lips over hers, barely a brush—a test.

Soft. Warm. He barely touched her, but fuck, she felt incredible. He could sense her trembling but, like a good girl, she waited. "I'm going to kiss you, Liberty. Is that what you want?"

The sound of Mason's chair creaked behind

them. Would this be the moment Mason wised the fuck up? Liberty trembled in his grip. He cupped the back of her head and traced his thumb along the graceful line of her jaw until it landed on her lower lip. Her sharp pink tongue crept out and his dick pulsed at the sight.

Sean tipped the pad of his thumb into her mouth and those succulent lips instinctively closed over his digit. She gave a gentle suck as she shut her eyes and sighed. Sean groaned. She was so fucking sexy. Her beauty came naturally. She didn't even have to try.

He slowly withdrew his thumb and leaned in. His kiss was firm at first. Not invading, but in charge. She would know the kind of man he was by the way he kissed, the kind of lover, because at this point there was no doubt in his mind that he *would* have her. Stupid Mason for allowing him this ecstasy. Only a eunuch could refuse an offer so sweet.

He wasn't one to pussy foot around. His hand slid down her back and cupped her ass and he kept his other hand steadily at the side of her jaw. In one smooth movement he opened his mouth over hers and pressed her lips apart. She moaned and he sunk his tongue into the heat of her mouth, stealing her flavor, memorizing her soft touch.

He kissed her deeply, leaving his imprint on her, making sure she could think of nothing but him. He demanded full attention and would settle for nothing less.

While one hand rested softly over his chest her other hand trembled, still holding the glass of orange juice. She probably felt his heart racing beneath the wall of his chest. She did this to him and he couldn't recall ever feeling so exhilarated at the mere idea of kissing a woman.

Taking one final sweep of her soft tongue as it timidly toyed with his, Sean drew his lips together and concluded the kiss. It was difficult not to keep going back for more. His lips closed and his cock twitched. Breaking their kiss into nips and licks, he savored her to the last drop. Finally he pulled himself away and breathed, "Mornin'."

Stepping back with a self-satisfied grin, he plopped into his chair and took a swig of coffee. He gave Mason a 'how do ya like them apples' look.

Liberty mumbled something and set his glass down then left the room to bring in breakfast. Mase's eyes were fixed on the table, his fingers slowly tracing over the folded pages of the paper. Sean couldn't read his expression, but it hinted at being caught off guard.

He leaned back and arrogantly sighed. "Still okay with me touching your wife?"

Mase didn't move or even blink. "Yes." His words were one hundred and ten percent certain.

It was Sean's turn to be surprised. He turned to Mason and frowned. "Seriously? Mason, do you even—"

Mason held a hand up, silencing his criticism.

He pointed to the table where his gaze was still locked. Sean turned his head. It took him a moment to grasp what he was supposed to be seeing, but once he saw it, he matched Mase's shock. He knew it was huge. On the table, set right by the edge, far away and more to the left of the napkin than anything else, sat Sean's glass of orange juice.

They each stared at the glass resting outside of its "proper" place. Turning to each other in silence, their eyes communicated how novel her mix up was. Even after only a few days, Sean knew it was a big deal.

Was this because of the kiss? Had he distracted her? What did this mean? Sean feared it would end in a meltdown like the morning before, or worse. He wasn't really sure about all this obsessive compulsive stuff or what exactly brought it on or set Liberty off, but he was damn sure the next time he got around a computer he would look it up.

Before they could comment out loud on the glass, Liberty returned with a tray full of food. Her cheeks were flushed a radiant shade of burnt sienna. Sean wanted her. She was flustered, but in a good way. The hint of a smile played at the corners of her mouth. She set out the food and Mase sent him a look. Sean acknowledged the look and decided not to move the glass for some time, just in case.

They ate in relative silence. Sean caught Liberty glancing at Mase, and when her husband caught her glance he reassuringly returned it with a smile. As she turned her bashful grin to him, he realized how much control she actually had, despite her condition. She was the wheel that steered the ship. He was a goner.

∼

LIBERTY WAS DRYING off the dishes as Sean entered the kitchen, his hair still damp from a shower. With Mason at work, she wasn't quite sure what the day would bring. As she placed the last of the silverware in the drawer she glanced at Sean, excitement churning inside her belly.

"So, what's on the agenda today?"

Liberty had to think. It was unlike her to be so scatterbrained. "Um, well, it's Wednesday, so Mason will be home for dinner. I usually just putter around on Wednesdays once my chores are done." After drying off the plates she opened the cabinet and winced.

"Hey, what was that?"

"What was what?" She stood on her toes and slid a plate on the stack.

"You made a face. Did I say something wrong?"

"Oh, no, it's just my back. I must have slept at a weird angle." She placed another plate on the stack and a nerve pinched. She sucked in a breath as a precise stab of pain lanced just beneath her shoulders.

"You did it again." The sound of Sean's stool

scraping across the floor filled the kitchen. "Where does it hurt?"

"It's nothing, really. I just need to work it out."

"Did you take anything?"

"I can't take pills." She hated swallowing pills. It never felt like they landed in the right place. Her arm reached up to place the last plate on the stack and the motion sent a searing sting slicing up her shoulder and into her neck. Sean made an exasperated sound and shut the cabinet for her.

The heat from his broad body penetrated her clothing and she froze. His strong hands closed gently around her shoulder, his right palm glided down her spine. "Where does it hurt? Here?"

She winced. "Yeah."

"Ooh, you got a knot."

He began rubbing and kneading out the kinks and she sighed. For someone so large he sure had a gentle touch. Her weight leaned into him and shut her eyes.

"Tell you what. Why don't you let me give you a massage?"

Liberty straightened and poorly masked the sharp pinching pain that came with the motion. "Don't be silly. It's nothing. I'm sure once I get moving it'll work itself out."

"Or put more pressure on the nerve and do more damage. Seriously, Liberty, let me give you a massage. I'm a physical therapist. I do it all the time for my clients. I'll be completely pro-fessional."

Liberty sighed. She didn't want her back to

hurt worse. It already was pinching more than it had been an hour ago. "Fine. Where should I sit?"

"Oh no," Sean said and smiled. "You're getting the full treatment. Go upstairs, put on a robe, and meet me in my room in about ten minutes. I just gotta go get my things out of my truck."

"A robe?"

"Yes. Don't worry. I've seen it all before. You have to be naked so that I can do it right."

Her mind screamed mayday. Mason said that he wanted her to let herself go with Sean, do what her body wanted, but this was all very, very new. After he'd kissed her this morning *in front of her husband*, Liberty wasn't sure what to make of their relationship.

Being intimate with Sean seemed oddly right, but also unfamiliar, and therefore wrong on some level. Mason appeared pleased with the way things had gone last night and this morning. His only request was that there be no intercourse. So what did that mean?

"Libby?"

"Huh?"

"Relax. It's just a massage. I just want to help your back. Go put on a robe." She looked at him for a moment and then he crossed his arms and gave her a stern expression and said, "Go." There was no arguing with that kind of direction. Liberty turned and went to change.

∾

SEAN SMILED as he watched Liberty scamper out of the room. She left three glasses on the counter. Interesting. He slipped them into the cabinet and flipped the last one as he remembered the way she kept them.

After getting his bag from his truck he headed to his room. Tossing the sheet aside, he fluffed the comforter over the bed and smoothed the surface. In the bathroom he found a large towel and laid it in the center of the mattress. He folded some hand towels to replace the pillows and set out his oils on the bedside table.

When everything was set he grabbed the sheet and dimmed the lights. Soft gray sunshine filtered past the shades casting the room in a somber glow. There was a soft knock at the door. His body pulsed in a surge of misplaced excitement.

You're just helping her back. Chill.

He opened the door and found a timid looking Liberty on the other side in an oversized white terrycloth robe. God, was there anything she didn't look good in?

"Come on in."

She stepped through the door and looked around. "I would have made the bed for you."

"No," he reminded. "Your back's messed up. I wouldn't have let you." She frowned at him. He raised an eyebrow and held up the sheet. "Drop the robe."

Eyes big, she turned to face him. "But…"

"Do we really need to go through this again?

LYDIA MICHAELS

Where's the brave girl I saw last night? She had no problem being naked."

Her blush traveled down the length of her throat to the tops of her breasts, disappearing behind the thick lapels. He winked at her, which only seemed to fluster her more. Cutting her a break he held up the sheet and turned his head. The muffled thud of the robe hitting the carpet was the prerequisite to her yanking the sheet out of his hands. When he turned back she stood before him like a Grecian Goddess wrapped in white.

He swallowed. "Go lay on the bed," he rasped. "Make sure the sheet doesn't get tucked under your body."

She moved to the bed, collecting the discarded robe on the way and carefully placing it on a chair before situating herself as he instructed. Sean found it amusing how she struggled to keep her modesty while untangling the sheet from under her limbs. When she settled, he stepped over to the bed.

He needed to slow his pulse. The sight of her on his bed did crazy things to his psyche. *Down boy.*

Sean folded down the sheet, exposing her narrow shoulders and the narrow line of her spine. Her skin was made of satin and cream. How did girls always manage to be so soft? He left her bottom covered and selected his favorite oil.

Rubbing the oil between his fingers, he

246

warmed his hands. Sean climbed onto the bed and straddled her small form, careful not to put any weight on her lower back. When he first touched the sensitive area she flinched.

"Relax. It's just oil. Shut your eyes and try to unwind."

She appeared to forcibly try to unclench her muscles. Thankfully, once he rubbed the warm oil over her shoulders and down her back much of the tension visibly eased. He worked in slow strokes, massaging the deep tissue, and working out knots and kinks along the way. One of his large hands covered the span of her waist.

Carefully shifting his position, he rubbed over her narrow thighs and spent extra time at the backs of her knees. Her ankles were extraordinarily delicate. Discovering she was ticklish on her side and at her feet brought him inexplicable joy. He only mildly tormented her, but later, when she was feeling better, he intended to really tease her.

He massaged her body for well over an hour, removing the sheet little by little, exposing more of her ivory flesh one inch at a time. As his fingers drifted over her satin skin he always kept contact, never removing his touch completely as he worked.

Soon, she was merely a sighing form of putty. His hands coasted over the soft curve of her calves, the petite arches of her feet. He caressed and memorized the shape of her thighs and the firmness of her backside. He made love to her fingers and toes and pulled and applied pressure to every nerve, joint, and muscle. He never enjoyed giving a massage so much.

As he neared the end of the rub down, he scooted down the bed and knelt between her legs, easing her legs apart to accommodate his bulk.

His palms glided up her limbs, over the backs of her knees, as his thumbs worked the firm muscles of her gluteus. Shifting the sheet slightly so he could better reach her upper thighs, his motions stilled at the unexpected flash of moist pink folds.

Motherfucker, she was drenched. Kneading her ass, his eyes glued to her tight passage. His thumbs traveled closer and closer to her entrance and she softly moaned with each tender press. Her hips slowly undulated, dragging and pressing it into the bedding. She was obviously aroused.

Sean folded the sheet up another inch, exposing her entire bottom. His mouth went completely dry as he set his sights on the perfect rosette snugly set in between the two succulent globes of her ass. He wondered if she was a virgin there and fought the urge to lean forward and take a bite of her heated flesh.

His thumbs worked inward, creeping toward the cleft of her ass. A slow glide of iridescent honey worked its way from her pussy onto the sheet. He shifted uncomfortably, trying to ignore the raging hard on he was contending with. The

pad of his thumb crested her buttocks and accidentally came into contact with her tight little
asshole. Liberty moaned low and long into the
mattress.

Sean stilled. What to do? He sat back on his
heels for a moment and she moaned in objection.
Fuck.

"Sean?"

"Yeah." His voice was rougher than gravel on
sandpaper.

"Why'd you stop?"

Her needy tone enchanted him. What should
he do? What would Mason want him to do? He
knew what he wanted to do, but that was out of
the question. Clearing his throat, he finally asked,
"Do you want me to keep going?"

Her pert little butt swayed seductively before
his eyes. "Your hands are like heaven."

He swallowed down a hard lump of desire. If
he touched her again he couldn't be held responsible for what happened next. Reaching for the
bottle of oil, he rubbed some more into his
hands. Trying to be somewhat professional, he
focused on her lower back. The farther he leaned
in the more the intoxicating scent of her arousal
penetrated his senses. Soft, sweet, succulent
flesh...

"Ouch!" she squeaked. "Did you just bite me?"

Sean cleared his throat. "I might have."

She giggled. "You like to play rough don't you,
Sean?"

"Oh, you have no idea," he grumbled as he

moved his hands over her ass and leaned in low to take a long inhale of her sweet, tangy sex.

"Mason's always afraid I'll break."

The mention of Mason did odd things to Sean. Touching another man's wife provoked a dirty feeling inside of him, yet he'd been given permission. He held onto the secret of their past, knowing he and Liberty had more in common than she realized. "He just doesn't want to hurt you. He would never forgive himself if he caused you pain."

"Sometimes pain isn't always a bad thing."

Sean's head kicked up and his fingers stilled. *Well, well, well.* "And what do you know about pain, little Liberty?"

Her voice was slow and drowsy as he continued to massage her flesh. "I know that there's bad pain and then there's good pain."

"And what's good pain?"

"The kind that stings for a moment, but then gives way to a soft burn that spreads across your flesh like a blanket, slowly transcending all the hurt into deep pleasure. That's the good kind. Like when Mason's kissing my breasts and he suddenly bites the tips. It stings for a moment, but then this warm heat spreads through me and everything becomes a little more sensitized and every lick feels like it's left by a hundred fiery tongues."

Sean made slow circles and worked his thumbs into her crease. "Are you saying you enjoy a little pleasure that burns?" He gently placed his thumb on the tiny rosette of her ass.

She stilled and gasped.

He massaged the small bit of flesh. "I agree, sometimes a little nip of pain can give way to a nirvana of pleasure." The oily tip of his thumb nudged her tight opening and she made a small sound of distress in the back of her throat. "Are you asking me to show you what I'm referring to?" He pressed the broad tip of his thumb a bit farther until he met the resistance of her tissue and waited for her answer.

Liberty was completely submissive whether she knew it about herself or not. The memory of her surrender with him and Mase sent him into total dominant male mode. "Answer me."

"I...I don't know."

"Has Mason ever fucked you here, Liberty? Fingered your tight little hole while he played at your pussy?"

She gasped a breathless, "No."

"Do you trust me to decide for you? To bring you pleasure without causing you real pain?"

Her shoulders flexed as her breath quickened. She was thinking. He held his thumb partially seated in her ass and waited. Finally, she nodded.

"Is that a yes, Liberty?"

"Yes," she moaned, her tone grudgingly surrendering to her need.

Still conflicted about his friend's request to touch his wife, but not fuck her, he considered the blurry line he was about to cross.

His motions seemed to be two steps ahead of his conscience. "Good girl," he rasped, reaching for the bottle of oil.

Wet, slick drizzles ran down her lower back and ass. It trickled to the towel beneath her and into her crevices. He removed his thumb and smeared the oil into her skin, directing it to her puckered hole. His fingers lubricated the area, making firm massaging strokes followed by shallow dips.

Liberty was squirming beneath him, growing impatient for his touch. "Before Mase, have you ever had a cock up your ass, Liberty?"

She stilled.

"Answer me."

"No."

"A finger? A dildo?"

"No."

"I didn't think so. The trick is to relax into it. Feel my finger? It feels huge, but it's nothing compared to a cock. Mason's cock is wide. If you ever intend on taking your husband there you'll need to build up a tolerance for anal play. Would you like me to help you with that? Help you so that you can better please Mason?"

"Yes, please."

"Relax. I'm going to squirt some oil into your hole. It'll feel wet, but it'll make it easier when I penetrate you the first time."

He picked up the small bottle of oil and flipped the cap. He spread her cheeks wide and made a V with his fingers to hold them out of the way. Lining the small nozzle up with her hole, he squeezed. Liberty made an uncomfortable sound.

"Still okay?"

"Yes."

"Good." He lubed up his index finger. There were two ways to go about this. He was more a rip the Band-Aid right off kind of guy though. He brought a knee to the side of her hip and draped his other leg over the backs of her thighs. He lined his oily finger up with her hole and touched down. "Ready?"

"Mm-hm."

Sean pressed forward and slid the digit all the way to the top knuckle with one fast press. Crying out, her shoulders lifted off the bed. Prepared for her shock, he gently pressed her to the mattress. "Don't fight it. Relax. Feel the burn fade into pleasure."

Making tight swirls in her passage with the tip of his finger, he did what he personally found pleasurable, hoping to get her to a point beyond the burn. She took hissing, hard breaths through her clenched teeth as her muscles fisted around his finger. Adjusting his position, he moved between her thighs and slowly lifted his hand off of her back. Like a good little sub she didn't try to move again.

With his free hand he reached to her wet pussy and tickled her folds as he extracted the finger wedged in her ass. "Feel the pain subsiding? You wanted it out, but now you want it back, don't you?"

She groaned.

"That's it. Let your frustration out." He removed his finger until only the very tip remained then pressed deep again. Her shoulders pulled together like butterfly wings as he withdrew and thrust the finger, finding his rhythm.

His other hand swirled the juices dripping from her cunt. Finding the hard nub of her clit, he roughly flicked it. Liberty jolted at the contact. His finger pumped in and out of her ass and she panted and moaned with each thrust. "Look at how beautifully you surrender. You would do anything to please Mason, wouldn't you, baby?"

"Mmmm," she moaned in agreement.

"I wonder if you can take more, Liberty. What would it be like to someday have a cock where my finger is and have another one here?"

Ramming two fingers into her pussy, he fucked her in tandem with both hands. She sobbed out her pleasure, forging onto her knees. Sean moved his fingers faster, the one in her ass pumping in quick shallow thrusts. His knuckles knocked against her supple ass while the fingers wedged in her pussy reached for her G-spot and tickled that inner bundle of nerves.

Her cries matched his quick rhythm as he licked the soft flesh of her ass juggling with each pump of his fist. "When I tell you to, you're going to come for me, Liberty. I want you to drench my hand when I give you permission."

He stretched his fingers deep inside of her

sex, hooked the digits, and pressed firmly into her G-spot. She practically howled.

"Now, Liberty. Come now!" He bit down into the juicy curve of her ass as her cream bathed his knuckles and fingers as she contracted like a vise around him. Her sobs filled the room. She was so beautiful when she relinquished all control. Just watching her come was enough to make him blow his load.

Withdrawing both hands he slid lower, dropping his back to the mattress. Yanking her trembling thighs apart, he fastened his mouth to her sex and drank as though she were a holy offering.

Holding her tight hips over his face as she cried out he licked and sucked at the lips of her pussy as she continued to come against his mouth. He couldn't get enough of her. Like an animal, he bathed her with his tongue, cleaning away every last drop of her pleasure. She was so frantic in her release, without his support she likely would have collapsed.

He flipped her to her back and climbed up her small body, all boundaries forgotten. His mouth crashed down on hers as her hands knotted in his hair and scratched at his shoulders. Her thigh hooked over his hip and he grabbed her wrists, pinning them over her head as he ravaged her sweet mouth.

"Taste yourself on me. See how delicious you are?"

Her tongue darted out and licked across his lips as she moaned, savoring her own flavor.

Knowing his eyes were as mad with the lust reflected in her stormy blue ones, he pit that plump lower lip and sucked it between his own. God, he wanted to tear off his clothes and shove his cock so deep she would taste his come.

Her legs wrapped around his hips and he ground himself into her. *Do not* fuck *her!* He kissed down her neck and bit at her jaw and shoulders. When he reached her tits he unapologetically sucked a tip hard into his mouth. She gasped, but he was relentless. He licked the underside of her breast and sucked there as well, needing to mark her pale flesh.

"Please, Sean, please!"

His tongue flicked over her hard nipple. "Tell me what you need."

"You! I need you!"

Down her quivering belly he kissed, wrenching her thighs open. Lining his thumbs up with her folds he held her open and fucked her with his tongue again, making sharp stabbing motions. It wasn't enough. He wanted to use his cock.

"Please! More, I need more," she begged.

Sean briefly thought about his promise to Mason and hoped he wasn't breaking any rules. Needing some form of relief, he sat up and quickly undid his pants, shucking them frantically off his legs. Climbing over her, he straddled her hips. Her legs twitched and scissored beneath him. Fisting his cock in his hand, he jerked himself off as he twisted backward with his other hand and reached for her clit.

The forbidden territory, the blurred lines of permission, it all added to the erotic rush of the moment. His scruples objected, but they were both too far gone. This would've never gotten so out of hand if Mason hadn't insisted he play with his wife.

His fingers worked fast and hard, driving her directly into one screaming orgasm after another. He released her abused clit and moved higher on her body.

"Open."

Liberty's eyes went wide. Sean knew he was a lot bigger than Mason when it came to length. Liberty was likely realizing the difference in that moment too.

"Just take as much as you can," he said. She nodded. Sean leaned forward and grasped the top of the headboard as he slowly fed his cock into her hot mouth. Those bee-stung lips wrapped tight around him and he groaned. "Fuck, you feel good."

He thrust into the warm cavern, taking narrow dips, careful not to gag her by going too far. She clawed at his thighs, gripped his hips as if trying to hold him deep.

She was incredible. She moaned around his cock and his balls drew up tight.

"I want your tits." He withdrew from her mouth. "Arms above your head." He scooted down her body until his ass rested just at her ribs. Taking both her breasts in his hands he plumped them together and fit his dick in between the small mound, loving the tight pull of her flesh. "God, you're beautiful."

He thrust his cock in between the snug crease of her breasts, precum and the remnants of her saliva slicking the close-fitting passage. She was small breasted, but they were perfect. He held her in place with bruising force. His thumb found her nipples and toyed with them. "I'm going to come all over these pretty tits. Is that what you want, Liberty?"

"Yes!"

"I want you to feel me all over you. I want you to taste me!" Faster and faster he fucked her tits and finally he could take no more. He leaned back and grabbed his cock in his hand. "Open your mouth."

He needed come, oh God, had he ever needed anything so desperately? Her body rocked as his fist pumped hard over his flesh and the first hot ribbons of come shot across her breasts and neck. Another shot tore from his cock and fell right on her tongue.

"Swallow it." She did and the sight blew his ever lovin' mind.

As he squeezed out the last drop and panted. Leaning down, he kissed her reverently, tasting his own salty flavor upon her lips. "You are," he breathed, "the most amazing woman I have ever met in my entire life. Never have I seen a woman come so beautifully or surrender so gracefully. You're incredible."

She smiled and he couldn't help but kiss her again.

As his heart rate slowed and they each caught their breath, Sean pulled the covers up over them and held Liberty tight by his side. For as much as he fought Mason's opinion that it was okay to be with his wife, it was worse now that he was lying with her. An intimate betrayal.

There was something so personal about holding her after they both shared incredible orgasms. It was wrong and he had no business holding another man's wife in such a way, but if anyone tried to take her away from him in that moment he'd snap their arm off like a rabid dog.

CHAPTER 10

*M*ason pulled into the garage and tucked his keys in his pocket as he collected the paper from the passenger seat. He'd been anxious all day, worrying about Libby and Sean. Turning the knob, he breathed a sigh of relief as his eyes set on her. Beautiful. Perfect. His heart thundered with a sweet melodic beat that played only for his Liberty.

"Hey, baby. How was your day?"

"Good. How was yours?" Her smile faltered only a second before her blue eyes fully focused on him.

"Long. How about a kiss?"

She walked to him and leaned up on her tiptoes. His mouth crested over hers triggering a nostalgic spark. She smelled like Sean.

"Were you a good girl today?" he asked against her lush lips. Liberty tipped her head down as a blush stole over her cheeks. He tipped up her chin. "Lib?"

"I...I did what we talked about?" A deep breath pulled into his lungs. His nostrils flared as a smile formed on his face and his cock lengthened.

"Really? Well, you'll have to tell me all about it. Did you enjoy yourself?" He couldn't explain the rush of excitement that came from imagining Liberty and Sean touching and playing with each other.

Liberty nodded. "Dinner's ready."

"Do I have time to change?"

"Of course."

Maintaining their scripted routine, Mason's sharp senses were on the lookout for any atypical behavior. The placement of the glass that morning had shocked him and amplified his belief that having Sean there was a good thing.

He went upstairs to change. As he left his room in a much more comfortable pair of track pants he saw Sean exiting his own room. "Hey."

Sean froze and he laughed. He looked like a bandit caught in the guard's spotlight. Put a black and white striped shirt on him and a mask and he'd be looking at a cartoon.

"Hey," Sean answered tightly, eyes darting to the floor.

Mason wondered if he was fighting a losing battle, trying to get Sean to accept this. "Relax. Lib already told me."

"She did?" His discomfort with the circumstances was obvious in the way he foisted his hands in his pockets and averted his gaze.

"Well, not in detail, but she said you two had a nice time together. I filled in the blanks. Was the feeling not mutual?"

Sean looked away and squeezed the back of his neck. "Oh no, it was mutual. I, however, think you're nuts."

"Why? You planning on stealing my wife?" he teased.

"Tempted," Sean joked, but Mason picked up on the serious undertone to his words.

He tilted his head and thought for a moment. No matter Sean's trepidation, Mason knew him and believed wholeheartedly he could trust him. Finally he said, "You wouldn't do that."

Sean laughed, but it wasn't a nice sound. "I wouldn't be so sure. Still want me as your houseguest?"

"Yes. I know you, Sean. I know who you are deep down, under all that cynicism. You'd never be able to live with yourself if you betrayed me. And that's beside the point. Liberty and I share something the two of us honor above all else. She'll never leave me."

"Put enough pressure on even the strongest structure and it will crack, Mase. You're taking an awfully big gamble here."

Perhaps, but his instinct said to keep at it. There was a reason it seemed so crucial to open up the gates of their relationship and let him in. Not just any man. Sean. No matter how bizarre and wrong the situation might appear, something about it seemed very right. "Anything involving love involves risk."

He waited for Sean to meet his gaze. When he did, Mason knew he had made his point. *Yes, even you, you stubborn ass. I even love you.*

Dinner was peaceful. As always, Liberty's cooking was outstanding. He took her hand and ran his thumb over the top of her fingers and she smiled trustingly. "So tell me what you did today."

She flushed a delicate shade of pink. "Sean gave me a massage."

A massage? Huh, not what he expected, but he could see how that could lead to something else. Sean interrupted his thoughts. "Liberty hurt her back."

Mason's easy expression shifted to a frown. Liberty had a bad habit of ignoring her needs and jeopardizing her health when she thought something else held a higher priority. More times than not, the items she placed at the top of her list were unnecessary and insignificant compared to her wellbeing. "You did? How?"

"I don't know. I guess I slept wrong. The massage helped. I'm only a little sore now."

His protective instincts kicked into gear. Had Sean fooled around with her knowing she didn't feel well? He took a deep breath and forced himself to relax. Sean wasn't an idiot. He would've considered her needs and wellbeing.

He was being a control freak and needed to

relax. If they were going to do this he was going to have to remind himself to truly trust everyone involved. He wouldn't be able to micromanage every encounter they shared.

"If your back's still bothering you I want you to go take a long bath and go to bed early."

She gave him a mutinous glare. He enjoyed those random moments when she fought back. It kept him from becoming complacent by her agreeable ways.

"I need to clean up from dinner."

"That's fine, but after the kitchen's done I don't want you doing anything else."

She pursed her lips, but he'd earned her agreement. "What are you two going to do?"

Mason glanced at Sean who had been observing the byplay quietly and trying to appear uninterested. "I think Sean and I'll hang out in the study and do some catching up."

LATER THAT EVENING Mason found himself sitting at the bar drinking an imported lager across from Sean. "So how did he go?" he asked, not needing to clarify he was asking about Sean's old man. His passing was the event that had catapulted them back into each other's lives, leaving his death never too far from either of their minds.

"Heart attack. It was the middle of the night. Lisa was with him. She called me. I drove there.

The funeral was Tuesday. Wednesday I left and headed here."

"How'd you know where to find me?"

"The Internet is a wonderful tool."

Mason nodded. "I'm sorry."

"Don't be. You, more than anyone, know what a dick he was. It was nothing like losing my mom."

"How's Lisa doing?" Last Mason heard Sean and his father's girlfriend had a fairly decent relationship.

"She's all right. She's young. I hope she doesn't mourn him too long. I'd like to see her find a decent guy. She deserves some peace after putting up with my old man for so long."

They each sipped their beer silently until Sean finally said, "Tell me about Liberty."

"What do you want to know?"

"I want to know why she's the way she is. I'm not going to even pretend I know the tiniest bit about what she has."

Mason sighed. "She didn't have an easy childhood. Her mother's a cunt, plain and simple. All of her life she told Liberty she wasn't good enough. It didn't matter what she did, how well she behaved, how good she did in school, KarLyn was never pleased with her daughter.

"When she was about ten, her mother remarried a man named Eric. To hear Liberty tell it, she loved the idea of finally having a father. However, Eric was more of a monster than any-

LYDIA MICHAELS

thing else. He showed his true colors around the time she hit puberty. It started then."

"It?"

Mason's stomach knotted, bile slowly rising. "Yeah, late night visits to her room. Hugging her a little too long. Accidentally walking in on her without knocking. When Libby started to get uncomfortable she told her mom, but KarLyn just blew her off and told her she was being dramatic. She made Liberty feel like there was something wrong with her for even thinking such a thing, told her only a disturbed child with an overactive sexual imagination would concoct such nonsense. And then she did the worse thing she could have ever done."

"What?"

"KarLyn told Eric."

Sean looked away and Mason saw his fists clenching. "How long did this go on? Couldn't she have told a teacher or something?"

Mason shook his head. "When I say KarLyn was a cunt, it's only because I don't know a more vile insult. She was by far the biggest bitch I've ever come across in my life. I met Liberty when she was twenty-one, just before her twenty-second birthday, and by that point the obsessive need to earn her mother's nonexistent approval had manifested itself so deep in her psyche she was already a prisoner to her disorder."

He ran his thumb down the cool side of his glass. "Obsessive Compulsive Disorder can be triggered by lots of different things. For Liberty, it was her mother's desire to have a doll rather than a child. She expected her daughter to be a certain way and her standards were more than absurd. Liberty was punished for so many ridiculous shortcomings that any normal parent would see as regular, human limits. She would make herself sick trying to earn her mother's praise. But when KarLyn found a new plaything, Eric, and stopped acknowledging her daughter completely. The problem was, she'd been conditioned to require her mother's approval above all else. It was an impossible goal and nothing to do with Liberty."

"Where's the bitch now?" Sean growled.

Mason chuckled, appreciating his friend's protective instincts concerning Libby. "She lives in Florida and never contacts Libby. I don't want Liberty to contact her either and she's more than fine with that. I think telling Liberty to cease contact with KarLyn, taking away her choice, was something she prayed for."

Sean grumbled an expletive and took a sip of his beer.

"OCD stems from anxiety. Her mother planted those seeds. Eric added to the problem, nurturing her need to be accepted in a way that benefited his own twisted cravings. Once he earned Libby's trust and broke it by abusing her, she started to hurt herself."

"How?"

"She feels a need to burn herself when she struggles with guilt, to equalize or replace the pain. In her mind I think it's a way of washing away the immorality. A lot of times she uses scalding water. She's never done it badly enough to leave obvious scars, but she's done some serious damage to her soft tissue in the past. The twisted part is that Libby's condition's considered ego dystonic, which means she's aware that what she's doing isn't normal and that awareness only adds to her stress and anxiety. It further fucks up her need to be perfect."

"Did you know all this when you met her? I mean about OCD and stuff. You seem to be pretty knowledgeable."

"I studied it in passing during college a few times. I knew enough to recognize it. The first time I met Liberty she was in the middle of a complete breakdown, so I realized right away what was going on."

Sean's fingers flipped a thin coaster back and forth on the lacquered bar top. "How'd you meet?"

"I'd been working at St. Mary's. I had a patient rushed in who fell off a train platform. It was Eric. When the train came he didn't die right away. He was mangled, and I knew as soon as they wheeled him in he wasn't going to make it.

"KarLyn had been hysterical and I think I actually felt bad for her. Of course, that was before I knew what a fucking bitch she was. I remember seeing a small girl standing a few feet behind her looking pale and lost. Her eyes were huge and I thought she was a teenager. She looked so young.

"When Eric died it was my job to inform the family. That's when I realized the girl was with KarLyn. I couldn't take my eyes off her. She looked like she was about to break. As I told them the bad news I was watching the girl so intently that I missed the change in her mother's demeanor. All of a sudden the woman turned and cracked her across the cheek, knocking her clean off her feet. I was so shocked I couldn't move for a second." Mason absently noted how tense Sean had become, much like a mountain lion preparing to hunt.

"KarLyn began to scream at the girl, degrade her with no concern for those in clear earshot. That was when I realized Liberty was her daughter. She accused her of causing the accident. Of bringing so much stress to Eric's life that he was distracted and therefore not paying attention to where he was going. She called her a whore and a hundred other cruel things. I eventually had to get an orderly in there to restrain the bitch before she beat her daughter again. Liberty slipped away in the chaos and when the waiting room was quiet I couldn't find her.

"Finally, I located her in a family bathroom on the third floor. I don't know what made me check in there but thank God I did. She was hysterical and her flesh was burned up to her elbows. She'd been scrubbing herself raw for forty-five minutes. She was so beside herself she didn't even hear me enter the restroom. The moment I touched her shoulder she turned around swinging. Detaining her, I wrapped my arms around her and she suddenly broke.

"She sobbed violently and I held her. There was no one nearby to help. I realized she wasn't a teenager, but a young woman, hiding under loose clothing that disguised her femininity and shape. I sat on the floor rocking her for a long time as she simply fell apart."

"Jesus," Sean hissed. "Was she upset that fucking pervert died?"

"No. She was upset because she wished it. Remember how I told you, no matter what, you had to acknowledge what you and Liberty shared?"

Sean nodded. "Yeah."

"Well, that's because Eric never did. He would creep into her room like a ghost, harm her, leaving scars on the inside that no one could see and only she could feel, and then he would act perfectly normal the next day. When her own mother didn't believe her she began to doubt her sanity. She held a horrible secret for years, causing her exorbitant guilt and shame. She doubted her reality and questioned her stability."

"Has she ever talked to someone professionally about this?"

"Yes, she has an incredible therapist by the name of Dr. Young who helped her make sense of her past. We still see her from time to time, but for the most part, once Libby left that unhealthy environment, cut off her mother, and was surrounded by people who loved and accepted her, she started making breakthroughs.

She has a nice relationship with my sister and my mom adores her. Believe it or not, what Eric did was nothing compared to her mother's refusal to believe her. KarLyn sided with a man who preyed on her daughter. Eric's dead and can never hurt Libby again, but she'll always know her mother is never going to believe her and will probably blame her for the rest of her miserable life."

Sean blew out a long breath. "Fuck. That's a lot of shit for one woman to deal with in a lifetime. And Liberty's young, man. Christ, I don't know how she handles all those demons."

"She's amazing and a lot stronger than she gives herself credit for being. She has setbacks, but we work through them. I've only ever had to call Dr. Young once when she went into crisis mode and that was eleven months ago because her mother called. I've since blocked KarLyn's number and had my attorney contact her with legal threats of what would happen if she tried contacting Liberty again."

"What about the other day?"

"What about it?"

Sean shook his head. "I saw Liberty scald her hands while making me lunch and then the day before when she was all jumpy and shit."

"That's nothing. We can deal with that. I talked to her about the water incident. She knows it's a choice. I told her if she chooses to harm herself again I'd adjust the hot water heater. She doesn't want to do these things, so I believe she'll try her best to make better choices. She also hates feeling as though she's disappointing me. I only care about her safety and happiness though. I understand we all have our own crosses to bear and sometimes we stumble. But more than anything else, Libby's honest with me. She may use avoidance at times, but if I ask the right question she'll give me an honest answer. I don't accept lies between us."

"But don't you think what we're doing could end in a disaster for her?"

Mason thought for several moments. "Here's what I think. Because of Libby's past, she's taken longer than most to accept herself as a sexual being and not link her urges with shame or guilt. I want to encourage her to explore this side of herself. I would never allow a man other than you to touch my wife. For some reason you're different. And there's something else that I know you can help me achieve."

Sean looked uneasy. "What?"

"You have an edge, Sean. I remember the way you were as a lover. I know the kind of things you enjoy and I believe you're responsible enough to know how to incorporate certain things into sex without risking anyone's safety."

He frowned. "Tell me you aren't suggesting what I think you are? Mase, how the fuck is that going to help a woman like Liberty? That could seriously fuck her up! I mean, she's been through enough." He began to stand and Mason grabbed his arm.

His gaze was absolutely serious. "Wait. Think about it. There's something about the pain that eases her. When she loses the battle to her OCD she has incredible guilt. The guilt triggers the need to punish herself. The physical pain exorcises the emotional pain. I know she has it under control for the most part, but don't think I don't know she sneaks in subtle ways to hurt herself here and there. It's like cutting. It's all part of the spectrum of self-mutilation as a form of relief. It's tied to self-loathing and creates a pain that's real, opposed to the ones we can't see. What if we could give her that relief, but in a safe and controlled way?" His voice broke. "What if…what if I could do that for her? Maybe she'd finally be okay with who she is and stop harming herself."

He hated that there were certain things he couldn't fix for his wife. His teeth ground together as he fought the urge to get in his car, drive to Florida, and shoot KarLyn in her cold-blooded heart. He blinked hard and tried to center his emotions and cool the rage burning inside of him.

Looking down, he pleaded, "She isn't as fragile as she seems. I know I treat her like glass sometimes, but I'm working on it. I know she's strong. I don't want her to still be battling these demons when she's thirty or forty years old. We could help. I know we can and we can do it in a safe way."

"But there's no guarantee on her emotional safety."

"Do you know what it's like to watch someone you love suffer and know that there's nothing you can do to help? It's an awful, impotent feeling. I think pushing her, using an edge, erotic intensity can relieve some of the pressures she applies to her daily life. I don't know enough to risk it on my own, but you do."

Sean pressed his face into his palms and slid his fingers through his hair, grabbing a tight fistful of his golden locks. He growled. "I don't know."

"Please," Mason begged. "For me. For Liberty. Please help me help my wife."

Sean sighed, eyes tight with hesitance. "Okay."

LIBERTY AWOKE to warmth moving over her thigh and down between her legs. Her belly pressed into the bedding as the mattress dipped. She moaned and stretched as Mason's lips pressed into the soft curve of her neck.

"Good morning," he whispered, punctuating his words with a nudge of his hard cock against her behind.

She opened her eyes and saw that it was still dark out. Veined shadows touched the glass windows as tree branches segmented moonlight. The low glow of the bathroom light made it possible to see. Her eyes adjusted to the dimness. "What time is it?"

"Early." His fingers traced over her folds and

his other hand coasted up to her breasts. "I've decided that if I want to play with my wife in the morning I have to start waking up earlier. She's a very busy woman, you know."

Liberty giggled as he rolled her to her side and draped her leg over his thigh, his fingers delving into her moistening sex.

He bit at her shoulder. "How's your back?"

"Much better. The bath really helped I think."

"Good." He gathered her arousal on the tips of his fingers and glided his way up to her clit. The thumb and forefinger of his other hand plucked at her nipples and she arched in his grip. "We have a busy day today," he whispered over her flesh.

"We do?"

"Mm-hm." Mason slid his cock along her folds, not quite penetrating, but exciting her all the same. "We're going to take a trip into town and then I think we'll hit the beach for a few hours. I was thinking rather than cooking tonight, we could order a pizza. Give my wife the night off. What do you think about that?"

"Sounds wonderful," she sighed.

"I'll show you wonderful." He suddenly flipped her to her back and covered her front.

His mouth crashed over hers in an impatient and demanding kiss as he fit himself between her thighs. Her shoulders and spine pressed into the bedding as she purred against his mouth.

"Show me what I want," he whispered.

Raising her arms above her head, she laced her fingers.

Mason smiled. "Beautiful." He grabbed her hips and yanked her closer to him. Leaning up on his knees he dragged his cock against the mouth of her sex. "I love you."

Her heart fluttered and she smiled. It was a lovely way to be awakened. "I love you, too."

He drove into her fast and hard. She moaned and luxuriated in the way he filled her. The need pouring off of him was so reassuring. He took her as if his survival depended on it. Relentlessly, he pounded into her. The bed rocked hard against the wall and she cried out with each thrust.

When something caught Mason's attention to the left she followed his gaze and sucked in a breath. Sean was standing in the doorway of their bedroom watching them. Excitement needled her spine.

A slow, devious smile crept across Mason's lips. "We have an audience."

She looked back at Sean where he casually leaned against the jamb of the door, arms loosely crossed over his bare chest, making no effort to hide the fact that he was observing them. In only a pair of fitted black briefs Liberty could see his huge erection filling the tight front panel of his shorts.

"Eyes on me, Liberty. When it's my cock inside you, your eyes remain on me."

At the sound of Mason's demanding voice she

locked her gaze with his dark, lust filled eyes. His cock slammed deep and she sucked in a breath.

He held himself, their pelvises kissing, breath mingling. "What do you want, Lib?"

His cock prodded, pressing at every angle of her channel. She moaned.

"Should I tell Sean to join us?"

Us. Liberty suddenly had a vision of Mason and Sean kissing. What would that be like? Her pussy fluttered and Mason groaned, obviously feeling her body's reaction to his words.

"Oh, I think you like that idea," he said then requested over his shoulder to Sean, "Care to join us?" He pushed his hands and lifted his chest, leaving her front more exposed to Sean's view.

Sean's expression was unreadable. He appeared in complete control and it was a little intimidating. There was no trace of the easygoing guy she'd played Star Wars against.

He slowly walked to the bed and Liberty finally understood the meaning of swagger. Casually, he reached down and flicked one of her nipples. Sensation shot from her breast and knotted deliciously in her belly. The idea that Mason watched Sean's bold affection only excited her more.

"Are you enjoying your morning, little Liberty?"

Breathless with anticipation, she struggled to find accurate words for the emotions tunneling through her.

"Answer Sean, Liberty." Mason, again, pressed deep into her sex.

"Yes."

"Good," they simultaneously replied, leaving her overwhelmed and slightly outnumbered.

"Why don't you turn her over," Sean suggested.

"Because I'm rather enjoying her like this."

Liberty waited as they hit a stalemate. They were both very dominant men. Again she wondered if they were to kiss and touch, who would come out on top and in control. Those thoughts sent her sex into a spasm of pulsing excitement around Mason's cock.

Mason gazed down at her, his lashes low, eyes smoldering. "And I think she's enjoying it as well, aren't you, Lib?"

"Yes, Mason."

He smiled. "I think Sean's feeling left out. Do you think you could help him with that?"

When their gazes met Sean's it burned through her all the way to her womb. "What do you say, Libby?"

"Okay."

Sean's nostrils flared. He kept his eyes on her as he slid his briefs off of his legs. One knee at a time, he climbed onto the bed. His thighs were so muscular. She again was taken aback by the size of him. He was huge *everywhere.*

His large fist stroked his fully erect cock as he settled on his knees beside her shoulders. His finger reached out and trailed over her flesh from her ear to her nipple. She shivered and Mason's grip on her hips tightened.

Suddenly insecure about the situation, she glanced at Mason, but he wasn't watching her. His lazy gaze was glued to Sean as he slowly fed his wide cock into her with a long, languid stroke. Sean, however, was focused on her mouth.

Mason sat further back and Sean climbed on top of her, settling over her waist. The added weight was marvelously confining. Again, she was excited by their unabashed nearness to each other. Sean's body held her in place as Mason, now out of view, continued to fuck her.

Unable to slide into her husband with Sean on top of her added a whole new layer of emotion to what was happening. She was being taken. She was surrendering to her husband and Sean, trusting them to take care of her and see to her pleasure.

Sean leaned forward. "I want that pretty mouth of yours wrapped around my cock again."

Her sex twitched as her neck heated. If Mason hadn't pieced together what they'd done, he knew now. Her breasts barely jiggled. Sean's body pinned her in place, yet, behind him, her sex was being fucked hard. Mason was picking up speed. He seemed to be growing harder inside of her since Sean joined them. She couldn't help the small hiccups of pleasure that escaped her throat.

She licked her lips as Sean leaned forward. A

small dewdrop of come gathered at the dark tip of his cock and her mouth watered, but he continued to hold himself back, taunting her.

She extended her neck and licked the pearl of moisture away. He groaned and tipped his head back. Languidly glancing over his shoulder, he said, "Does she not have the prettiest mouth you've ever seen?"

"It'd be prettier with your cock in it."

Taken aback by her husband's comment, her mind went somewhere else for a moment, somewhere decadent. The broad head of Sean's cock brushed over her lips, jolting her back to the present. She opened and he forced his way inside.

Her eyes watered at the first touch to the back of her throat, but once Sean found his rhythm she adjusted to the intrusion. He pumped quickly in and out and she realized she really didn't have to do much. It was a good thing, too, because having two cocks in her body at once made it awfully difficult to concentrate. Mason was moving with slow, deep thrusts, while Sean was pumping with rapid quick dips.

Suddenly he stilled. She couldn't see Sean's face, only the dewy muscles of his abdomen flexing above her.

"Stay there," she heard Mason command. Liberty waited, breathing hard through her nose, not knowing what to expect. Sean let out a deep guttural groan and his cock twitched over her tongue. What was happening?

"Now slow," Mason said and Sean slowly slid deeper in her mouth.

Her husband was seated deep inside of her, filling her to the hilt, but barely moving aside for small jolts here and there. Sean's large body blocked her view and she was certain she was missing something. It had the same effect as being blindfolded.

"Fuck," Sean grunted as his cock twitched again.

"Liberty," Mason said from behind Sean. "Sean is going to come and I want you to swallow every last drop. Can you do that? If not, he'll pull out and come on your tits."

Her heart and mind raced. There was something so incredibly erotic about Mason being so attuned to not only her, but Sean. He was an enormously muscled man, yet Mason seemed to hold an authority over him she couldn't fathom. He wouldn't have suggested such a thing if he didn't want it.

She'd had never swallowed before and hoped it wasn't like swallowing pills, because in that moment she wanted to be everything they asked and needed. She moaned, expressing her eager agreement as best she could in her position.

"Is that a yes?" Mason asked. "Turn your face away from Sean if you don't think you can handle it."

She moved her tongue, creating a tight suctioning grip as Sean groaned and cursed. "I think she's okay with it, Mase." He sounded as if he was struggling to hold off his orgasm.

"Good. Go deep, Sean."

Sean eased himself deep into the back of her throat and his entire body tightened above her. His cock swelled and pulsed rapidly over her tongue. He cried out, his voice hoarse and strained, but what he called out in extremis wasn't about her. "Fuck, Mase, *fuck!*"

The first shot of hot come hit the back of her throat. Her eyes watered and she focused hard on getting it down. Her throat convulsively swallowed as another splash slid down her back. The warm release was gone so fast she barely tasted it.

Sean pulled out and quivered. He seemed like he'd just gone through the wringer both emotionally and physically. Lifting his leg over her chest, Mason eased back and Sean collapsed beside her.

Liberty frowned. As much as she would have loved to take responsibility for his blissful state, she didn't think she could. Even if she had some unknown natural talent when it came to giving head, she knew she wasn't that good.

Before she could contemplate what happened, Mason thrust hard and fast. Now, with her mouth no longer occupied, her chest no longer constricted, she fell back into the moment and sobbed out her pleasure.

Mason was like a mad man, pumping into her with such delicious force she could barely keep up. Something set him off. Was it her sucking Sean's dick?

She was vaguely aware of Sean still catching his breath and staring at the ceiling when Mason called out that he was about to come. With one final press forward, he sunk into her, melding their pelvises together as his grip on her hips tightened. She hadn't even realized until that moment that his hands had been elsewhere for a time. Heat filled her as his body shook with the force of his intense orgasm.

When he finished he fell to her other side. Sean kissed one side of her neck while Mason kissed the other and, again, she wished they would meet in the middle and kiss each other.

Mason's body pulled from hers with a slick tug, but before she could lament his withdrawal fingers were playing at her clit. It took her a moment to discern whose hand was touching her. It was Sean.

She wondered if he was aware that Mason didn't use condoms and his juices were now mixed with her own. Before she could say something Sean shifted and asked, "Did you think we would just take our own pleasure and not see to yours?"

Quickly angling toward the bottom of the bed, his mouth fastened over her sex and she moaned at the sudden contact to her sensitized sex. He was drinking in both of them, overwhelming her with a potent level of eroticism she'd never experienced.

"Shh," Mason said as he kissed her. The pleasure, the trill, the taboo desires were all too much. Her husband cupped her face as he whispered against her mouth. "It's okay. Let Sean take care of you. I want him to."

Her senses were being assaulted from so many angles she couldn't relax. An abyss of pleasure swirled around her, threatening to swallow her whole. She turned her face from Mason and broke the kiss, only to be pulled back to his mouth.

"Tell me what his mouth feels like, Lib. Is he licking you long and hard or sucking on your tight clit?"

She whimpered. "Sucking…he's sucking me."

"And is he touching you anywhere else?"

Just then Sean's large finger slid between her swollen folds, filling her sex. "Yes!"

"He has such big hands, doesn't he? Almost as big as his cock."

Her sex muddled mind tried to tell her something, but the thought fluttered away like a feather lost on a breeze. She moaned and Mason's fingers began to cup and pull at her breasts.

"How would you like to feel that big cock inside of you?"

She was going to come. She opened her mouth to answer, but only sobbed incoherent cries as Sean brought her to an intense, rapid orgasm. As the waves subsided, Sean continued to lick and kiss at her flesh. The sharp pinch of his teeth on the soft flesh of her thigh made her jerk and shiver.

Sean eased away and the mattress dipped with the loss of his weight. Mason held her as she came down from her incredible high. She looked for Sean, but Mason stilled her. "Shh, he'll be right back."

She relaxed in his hold as he caressed and kissed her softly. When he looked toward the door she sensed Sean's return.

"Ready?" Mason asked.

Ready for what? There couldn't possibly be more. She looked to Sean and he nodded.

Mason shifted positions on the bed so that he was sitting up with his back to the headboard, cushioned by the pillows. He pulled her into the V of his thighs so that her back pressed against his front. Sean stood at the foot of the bed and gazed at her as he rolled on a condom.

Her sex thrummed as heat swirled low in her belly and her heart raced. She wanted him. Mason, for some reason wanted her to have him. It was all so confusing, but she was too tempted to think of reasons why she shouldn't allow this to happen.

Mason slid his hands under her legs, gripping the underside of her thighs. Her knees bent and pulled apart, baring her most intimate parts to Sean.

Without asking, Sean climbed onto the bed and settled on top of her. He gently ran the backs of his knuckles down her cheek and smiled softly. "I'll try to be gentle, Libby."

She nodded.

The feel of another man's penis touching her there was jarring. Mason kissed her neck and whispered words of assurance while telling her how happy she made him and how beautiful she was.

The heat of Sean's cock seared her slit. His palm pressed into the mattress as he breached her tight folds with slow, shallow probing motions.

Once partially inside, he held himself there for a moment. The surreal awareness of having another man inside of her was too much for her mind to grasp. He looked into her eyes, making her quite mindful that it was not her husband filling her, and thrust himself to the hilt.

She couldn't stifle the gasp that burned through her lungs. Sean was much longer than Mason. He touched on nerves that weren't used to being reached. Although Mason was wider, Sean was practically in her womb. He adjusted his position and suddenly it felt as though the head of his cock was kissing her G-spot.

He seemed to be completely aware of where he was inside of her and what he was doing to her. He looked into her eyes as the side of his mouth kicked up in a self-satisfied smirk. He rotated his hips and she moaned as the wiry hair at the root of his cock abraded her swollen clit.

Mason's mouth nipped at her neck. His

breath filled her ear sending shivers down her spine. "He's big, isn't he, Lib? Is he filling you up? Can you feel him sinking deep inside of you where all those exciting nerves are?"

It boggled her mind that Mason could so easily talk about another man's penis, especially while inside of her, but at the same time, every word he said drove her arousal up another notch. She moaned her agreement, incapable of forming words while her senses were under such an all-encompassing attack of pleasure.

Sean fit his arms under her knees as Mason released her legs and moved his hands up to her breasts. She was scooted lower as Sean positioned her calves on his shoulders. Her body folded and Mason's hand slid to her sex. Her heart thundered in her chest the closer her husband's hand drew to Sean's cock, but he didn't touch the other man.

Instead, he found her clit. Just as he started to rub the tight bud, Sean pressed in deeper and rapture surged from both the inside and outside of her sex. The pressure escalated and she fought back the pleasure. Her body pulled tighter than it ever had, reflexively jerking and thrashing in Mason's hold.

"Hold her still," Sean gritted out and Mason's arm banded over her chest, trapping her arms.

"It's too much!" she cried, torn between the comforting feeling of being held and possessed by two men and a feeling of shame and helplessness. Sean gave a tight, hard thrust, tapping her G-spot again and cutting off her words.

"Give into it, baby," Mason soothed by her ear as he gently rubbed her clit. "Let it wash over you. Nothing will happen if you surrender to it. I've got you. I'm here. I want you to let go. No one will blame you for taking what you deserve."

She breathed hard and shut her eyes. Everything felt different. There was so much intensity coming from every angle she wasn't sure what was happening, if what she was feeling was normal.

"Do you like my cock deep in your pussy, Libby?"

She looked up at Sean and tried to concentrate. She nodded.

"And you liked it in your mouth too, didn't you?"

"Yes." She couldn't decide if she needed to burst into orgasm or burst into tears. Whatever they were doing to her was overwhelming every nerve of her body. Her body felt too full, as if she would suddenly lose control of herself. She fought to hold onto that thread, that last bit of control she simply couldn't surrender for fear of becoming all the horrid things her mother accused her of being.

"Do you trust me, Libby?" Sean asked. "Do you trust me to never hurt or humiliate you? To know what'll bring you pleasure? Do you trust, not just Mason, but me to possess you in ways you've never imagined possible?"

She squeezed her eyes tight. He was demanding too much. They both were. She began to panic. Pleasure intensified until it bordered on pain. Sweet delicious hints of agony blurred the peripheral of her mind and she wanted it no matter how much letting go frightened her. If she let go now she would break. She tried to chase away her oncoming orgasm and bring back her senses, but she was too far gone.

"Do you trust us?" Mason demanded as he pulled back her pussy and she felt him further expose her hard clit. His fingers were so close to Sean's cock it was distracting. "Do you trust my decision to trust Sean with the most important person in my life, you, my wife, Liberty? Tell us you trust us both and we'll let you come and make it all go away."

"Yes!" she shouted, unable to take any more. "I trust you both!"

Mason pinched her clit hard and rubbed the sensitive flesh rapidly just as Sean pressed forward and wedged his cock as far as it could possibly go, putting incredible pressure on her G-spot. Something snapped inside.

Her control slipped and her body released as she came on a hard, feral shout of animal lust. Her sex contracted around Sean's cock as her body sucked him deeper. The inside of her nerves pulsed outward to Mason's fingers where he held her and stimulated her orgasm higher and higher. She screamed, her eyes opening wide, as her climax left her body in a wash of fluid that drenched Sean's lower abdomen.

"Fuck, she's clamping down like a vise!" Sean gritted out as he began to pump into her, stretching her, as she shrank around him.

She didn't know what was happening but there seemed to be no stopping it. She screamed again. Mason finally freed her clit and wrapped his arms around her reassuringly. Sean's cock swelled inside the fluttering, quaking walls of her sex as he came. She'd forgotten he'd worn a condom until that moment.

Releasing her legs, he collapsed on top of her as his chest heaved. Their bodies pressed together, trapping the warm sticky evidence of her passion. Breath sawed in and out of her and Mason continued to praise and kiss her. She was still twitching from severe aftershocks.

Licking her dry lips, she turned to find Mason and whimpered, needing reassurance. That wasn't normal. Her insecurities crept in as she faced him.

He opened his eyes and smiled at her, but then frowned when he seemed to realize her apprehension. "What is it, Lib?"

"What did I do?"

His lip twitched and she could see he was trying to hide his amusement. She tried to push away from him but between the two of them there was nowhere to go. Humiliation burned through her euphoria.

"Shh." He kissed her. "You had an orgasm, that's what you did. A very intense orgasm."

"But I…"

"I know. It happens. It's a result of putting pressure on your G-spot and building it up. When that happens the climax comes in a rush and there tends to be more fluid than with a typical orgasm. It's perfectly normal and you were beautiful."

Relief washed over her. Sean curled his large body against her back and she was again sandwiched between the two of them.

"What time is it?" The need to build distance between indulgence and the pleasure she gained from structure quickly crept in—a defense mechanism she leaned on whenever overwhelmed. She pushed for a bit of distance, reached for her 'normal' self.

But then Mase reassured her, "You have about twenty minutes until you usually get out of bed, baby. Try to rest here with us for a bit."

Us.

Her mind savored the concept. Her body felt light and her thoughts quieted. Her body was calm and oddly at peace. She shut her eyes and snuggled deeper into the heat coming off the two strong bodies surrounding her and finally, she was able to relax.

CHAPTER 11

They took the Escalade into town. Mason drove and Sean sat in the back. They wouldn't tell her where they were heading so Liberty decided to play twenty questions.

"Have I been there before?"

"No," Mason answered, smirking behind the wheel.

"Is it a store?"

"Yes."

"Do they sell food?"

"No." Her husband laughed.

Sean leaned forward. "Well, now that isn't necessarily true, Mase. They carry edibles." He laughed as well and Liberty pursed her lips.

"Edibles? Like candy?"

"Sort of," Sean said and they both chuckled again as she frowned.

Crossing her arms over her chest, she pretended to pout.

"Now, don't get upset, little Libby," Sean said, reaching forward again, this time to yank on one of her curls. "It's more fun if it's a surprise."

She ignored them both. A while later she asked, "Do they sell clothes?" And they both groaned.

"We're here," Mason announced as he pulled into a strip mall and she stared out the windshield. It occurred to her that Sean also wouldn't know exactly where they were going and this was likely her husband's idea.

She looked at the line of stores as they parked. "Are we just shopping? Or did you have a particular store in mind?"

"A particular one," Mason said as he climbed out of the car.

He walked around the front of the SUV, but the door opened before he rounded the fender. "Come on, girlie," Sean said as he held out a hand to help her down.

Her neck heated. They were in public and she wasn't expecting him to be so publicly affectionate or chivalrous in her husband's presence. Recalling the other day when they went grocery shopping, she realized he was like that in public with her even before they slept together.

As they walked to the stores Mason held her hand and Sean placed his palm on the small of her back. Initially, she very self-conscious of people staring, but in actuality, no one seemed to notice them.

They passed a few clothing boutiques and

LYDIA MICHAELS

then approached a door lined with black paper. The sign on the door said OPEN. She glanced to the glass window, also blacked out, and read the name, *Frisk!*

"What is this place?"

"Come on," they said simultaneously as they shuffled her through the door. She frowned. It looked like a video store at first sight. Then she noticed the pictures on the DVD covers. "These are dirty movies!" she hissed.

Sean chuckled and Mason said, "I know."

Momentarily mesmerized by the nude poses on the covers lining the display, her pulse quickened and her panties moistened. She looked over both her shoulders. The only other person in the store was a large man behind the counter. He was chewing on a straw and wore wide rainbow suspenders over the bulging stomach peeking past the waistband of his pants.

"Why are we here?" she whispered.

"We're shopping," Mason whispered back, clearly mocking her.

She looked to Sean for assistance, but he looked away and said, "Come on."

She followed them past three racks of pornography. There were displays of magazines, condoms, and erotic romance novels dispersed throughout. Blood rushing to the surface of her cheeks as she was suddenly embarrassed to be openly standing in such a place. Mason and Sean disappeared through a doorway hidden by a beaded curtain and she paused. A large hand reached out through the beads and tugged her to the other side.

Colors collided and she tried to take in everything she was seeing. Sean and Mason observed her. Her mouth hung open as she slowly turned. Dildos, vibrators, costumes, cuffs, whips, and things she didn't even know the names of hung from every square inch of each wall.

Two racks stood in the center. Stepping forward, her hand reached to touch a long chain hanging from a spoke. Two feathery fuzz balls dangled from each end. Was it a necklace?

"They're clamps," Sean said, coming to stand beside her. He picked up the chain and she noticed rhinestones attached to the black feathery parts.

"Clamps?"

"Yeah," he held the fuzzy parts up to his chest. "Nipple clamps."

Liberty's eyes went wide. Who would want a clamp on their nipple? Mason laughed and put his arm around her shoulder. "Come over here, baby. Don't let Sean freak you out. What do you think of these?"

She looked at the rows and rows of vibrators. Her eyes caught on a small silver one she recognized. She reached for it.

"Do you like that one?"

"It's awfully small," Sean commented and Mason scowled at him.

"Would you like me to buy that for you, Lib?" Mason asked. She retracted her hand and looked down. Mason waited a moment then pulled the package off the wall. He quickly read the back. "If you like this one I'll get it for you."

Crap. She sighed and mumbled, "I already have it."

Sean snorted and Mason stilled. "Come again?"

She let out a frustrated breath and faced him. "I already own that vibrator."

Her husband's eyebrows practically disappeared in his hairline. "You do? Oh, okay."

Sean was cracking up. Mason put the package back on the wall and faced her again. "Do you have any other toys I should know about?"

"No."

"And how did you manage to procure that one?"

"I ordered it out of a beauty magazine."

"They sell this stuff in beauty magazines?"

"Well, yes and no. They call them 'massagers' in the magazine, but everyone knows what they really are."

"Okay then." Mason turned and she wasn't sure if she'd upset him.

"I've only had it for three months."

Mason pinched the bridge of his nose and shut his eyes. She turned to see where Sean disappeared. He was on the other side of the room, his arms laden with items. He removed a white lab coat from the wall. When he saw her watching him he paused. "What?"

"Are you buying all that stuff?"

Mason walked over and peeked at his collection. "Anal beads, really?"

"What? I like them."

Liberty wondered if he liked using them on women or women using them on him. Mason took the lab coat from him and hung it back on the wall. "If you want to play doctor I have about two dozen of these at home."

"Oh, that's right. Cool!"

"Doctor?" She frowned.

Sean held a large rubber dildo that had a spiraled covering and antennae sticking out one end and a thin rod curving out from the other side. She crinkled her nose when she noticed a scrap of hot pink lace draped over his arm. "Who's the thong for?"

He scoffed. *"You."*

"I don't like thongs."

"You'll like this one."

He moved to stand in front of a display with studded collars, lots of leather, and whips. She scoffed back. "Don't even think of buying something on that wall and using it on me. I'm not into that."

Growing impatient, Sean sighed and turned to face her. He looked at her and she fought the urge to fidget under his scrutiny. "Then why are your nipples hard?"

She gazed down. *Damn it!* "Well, we're in a sex room. It's a little hard not to notice."

"Liberty," Mason called from the other side of the room. He held a satin sash and was checking out a long peacock feather. His collection seemed a lot less intimidating than Sean's so she went over there.

"Sean's a pervert," she whispered as soon as she neared her husband.

"Don't judge, Libby. If he was the only one who enjoyed those things then they wouldn't sell them at every adult store. Try to be open-minded. Besides, you'll hurt his feelings. He can hear you."

She turned back to look at Sean. He was smiling and held a fringy leather thing in his hand. An evil gleam crept in his eyes and he whipped it against his thigh.

She groaned. "He's taunting me."

"He's playing with you," Mason corrected, then a little louder he said, "Sean, behave yourself. You're scaring Liberty." He held up the feather. "What do you think of this?"

"It's a feather."

"I'm aware of what it is."

She shrugged. "Other than making center-pieces I'm not sure what you can do with it."

Mason stepped behind her and trailed the satin sash over her exposed collarbone as she shivered. The heat from his body crept through the barrier of her clothing and she melted into him.

In a thick, low voice he asked, "What if I blindfolded you and tied you down with these satin sashes then used the feather to tickle and torment you? You'd never know where I was or what to expect. I could spend hours pleasuring you and you would be helpless to stop me, completely at my mercy."

Chills ran up her spine. Her sex pulsed with excitement and her nipples were hard once more.

"You like that idea, don't you, baby? Being completely helpless and under my command. That turns me on, the idea of having you naked and at my disposal to play with, tease, fuck, and titillate. We could make it a game. How many times can two men make a woman come in one evening? I bet if we brought home some of these toys we'd really have a good time. What do you say, Lib? Do you want to submit to two men and see how many times and how hard we can make you come?"

She was having a hard time catching her breath. Images of the two of them touching and taking her while she was tethered and helpless filled her imagination. What was wrong with her that she found the idea of being tied down so completely erotic?

Mason pressed his body into her back, his erection digging into her side. There might be something wrong with her for liking the idea of being bound, but Mason *really* seemed to like the idea too. "Okay."

He growled and leaned down to suck the side of her neck. His hands cupped her aching breasts through her shirt. She leaned into him and wanted him to take her right then and there. He pulled away all too soon and said, "Sean, go check out. Here's my *AmEx*."

The beads rattled as Sean's footsteps retreated from the room. Mason's mouth was back on her neck, his hands now gathering the linen of her skirt.

Her needy body seemed heavier and oh so wet as Mason's hand delved beneath her panties and landed right on her sex. She gasped. They were in a store! "Mason—"

"Shh, no one's in here. The cashier's busy helping Sean. He'll keep him busy until we're finished. Spread your legs for me, baby."

Her heart raced. Someone could walk in at any moment. There was something terrifying and exhilarating about possibly being caught. Her feet stepped farther apart and her thighs separated. Mason groaned in approval.

His finger slipped into her sex and gathered some of her cream, pulling it back to her clit and rubbing tight little circles as he kissed her neck and nibbled her ear. As his tongue licked the sensitive slope of her shoulder, her body rocketed into full out arousal. When he pinched a nipple through her shirt she moaned.

"Shh, we have to be quiet."

She bit her lip. Pressure built deep in her belly as her knees trembled. "Mason," she whispered. "I'm going to come."

"I know." He continued to rub her clit and she whimpered.

"I don't know how to be quiet."

His hand left her breast as his other hand worked faster, harder. Her body tensed. She squeaked and suddenly Mason's hand was over her mouth, her breath echoing off the tops of his fingers. Fear, excitement, and a welcomed sense of forbidden pleasure had her eyes opening wide. "Come for me, Liberty."

Her orgasm broke over her and Mason's hand trapped her cries in the back of her throat. Her body trembled as he cupped his palm between her legs. Chills traveled over her shoulders and to her scalp. He kissed her neck and slowly removed his hand from her mouth.

"Beautiful."

Liberty sighed, her head lolling to his shoulder. "Mason?"

"Yes, baby?"

"Can we go home now?"

∿

AFTER RETURNING from town they enjoyed a quick lunch and changed for the beach. Sean and Mason carried the bags and towels over the high dunes, which always reminded Liberty of great big tortoise shells turned to sip off the coast. They settled their belongings and the guys took off for the water once they were sure she was comfortable.

Liberty loved autumn in the Outer Banks when all the summer tourists fluttered home to heed the upcoming winter and hurricane season.

The beaches were bare but still warm. The ocean was perfect for fishing right from the surf and the temperature dropped just enough for cozy sweatshirts and bonfires at night. Turning her head to the left, she kept her eyes closed against the sun as its warm rays heated her skin. She was nervous in a delicious way about what would happen once they returned to the house. She was glad that Mason decided they would order pizza tonight because she was completely distracted and, for once, preparing a meal was the farthest thing from her mind.

Her husband's deep laugh had her opening her eyes. Her head lifted and she squinted against the white beams of sunlight, drawing her hand up to act as a visor. There, in the water, Sean tackled Mason. He jumped up, palms firmly planted on his shoulders, keeping his muscular arms stiff and rocketed himself into the air, forcing Mason to topple over. Mason shot back through the surface, his hair streaming an arc of crystal droplets against the blue backdrop of the horizon as he threw himself at Sean and knocked the larger man down.

It was amusing, how men of all ages never stopped horsing around like boys. Something caught Liberty's eye and she shifted to get a better view. What had she just seen? A change, but she wasn't sure what it was, perhaps a slight alteration in Mason's posture or a familiar, meaningful tilt of his head. Whatever it was it was subtle, but Liberty recognized it. It triggered a sexual stirring inside of her like a green light triggered the impulse to go, but she was all the way over here and Mason wasn't looking at her. He was looking at Sean.

Sean laughed and dove under the water. He resurfaced several yards away and at a much deeper point. Mason followed and it became too much of a strain on her eyes to continue watching them. They bobbed in the distance, the water cloaking their bodies to their shoulders. Their heads were close together, two black dots winking in and out of view like a mirage. It seemed they were discussing something. Her stomach quivered at the idea that they were likely discussing her.

She turned her head and rested her cheek on the blanket, facing the dunes. Her hearing muffled and she let the slow washing sounds of the waves soothe her. She must have drifted off, because the next thing she knew cool droplets of salt water were jarring her awake.

"You sleeping, Lib?"

She turned at her husband's voice. He was drying himself off. "Where's Sean?"

"He walked back to the house. You about ready to do the same?"

"What time is it?"

"Four. Your shoulders are getting a little pink. I think you've had enough sun for the day."

Four. How long had she been sleeping? She stretched and gathered her belongings. Shaking the sand off the blanket and folded it, she handed it to Mason who then helped her slide her arms into her cover up. After he tied the belt at the waist he gently kissed her nose and smiled down at her.

"Are you hungry?"

"Not really, but if you and Sean want to eat that's fine with me."

His eyes blazed and his nostrils flared. In a hoarse voice he said, "Come on."

The cool air of the house blanketed her sun kissed skin and goose bumps scattered over her breasts and shoulders. "Go upstairs and shower, Lib."

Mason's expression was shuttered, but determined. A shiver of excitement tickled her heart followed by a twinge of nervousness. She nodded and silently headed up to her room.

The warm water of the shower revived her sleepy head. She'd definitely gotten a little more sun than she intended that afternoon. After she washed all the salt water from her skin and sand from her hair she dried herself off and methodically applied lotion to her tender flesh. Shaking out her damp curls, she slipped into her ivory robe.

The silk hem tickled her upper thighs as she stepped into the bedroom she froze. Mason and Sean stood on the opposite sides of the bed, both clad in only a pair of fitted jeans. They each showered and their hair was still wet. The duvet had been stripped off the bed and on the sheet sat a pile of satin sashes, the same sashes Mason showed her earlier that morning in the adult store.

"Come here, Liberty."

She hesitated only a moment, heart racing, then did as her husband asked, walking slowly and trying to keep her gaze on both men. Sean stood, watching her, with his hands clasped behind his back.

Mason reached down and quickly tugged the tie of her robe open. "I want to play with you, Liberty. How do you feel about that?"

How did she feel? She felt a lot of different emotions in that moment, anxiety, thrilling excitement, arousal, nervousness. Her flesh was alive as if it buzzed on her bones, electrical charges arcing within her the closer she came to Mason's touch. "Okay."

He smiled. "Sean's going to play with us."

She nodded her acknowledgement of this.

"Good girl. Sean, hand me a sash."

Sean leaned down and slid a silky tie off of the sheet with a satin hiss. The others remained coiled in the center of the bed, but soon they'd all be put to use. Mason slid her robe off her shoulders as it puddled on the floor in a soft heap. "Let me see your hands, Lib."

She held her hands out in front of her, palms up. Mason drew first the right then the left up to his mouth and gently kissed the backs of her fingers. He placed her wrists together, forming an X with her wrists and wound the soft material around her skin. He tied the knot expertly and ran his finger under the material to test the give and make sure her circulation wasn't being affected. Sean came over and did the same. Her nipples were hard and tight from the simple touch of his hands at her wrists.

Mason stepped back and sat on the upholstered chair in the corner. He lifted his legs and rested them on the stuffed ottoman as he leaned back, trusting her in Sean's care. Scrutinizing her, his fingers steepled, as if contemplating the next step. "Liberty, I want you to kiss Sean."

Obviously he was maintaining control of the situation. She turned to face Sean and found him watching her. His pupils were huge, leaving only a smoky rim of hazel showing against the dark pools. How this lighthearted man could naturally trade jovialness for intensity was beyond her. She supposed this was what he meant when he said he was a tough partner to please.

Her confidence wavered. What if she couldn't please him?

She glanced at Mason, his expression equally intense. Sean closed in like a great predator, blocking her view of her husband. Gazing into his eyes, she couldn't stop the shiver of excitement when the backs of his knuckles scraped her breast. He pinched her nipple and she gasped.

"Your husband asked you to kiss me, Libby."

Her entire body shook with the intensity of the moment. This wasn't what normal married couples did. She knew it was wrong. Her mother's remembered words trespassed on the moment.

"You will always be treated like a whore, because you're too weak to say no. Every time a man touches you, he'll use you, because that's all you deserve. Girls who act like little sluts get treated that way. You can't blame a man for taking what you dangle in his face."

"Liberty." The snap in Mason's voice had her jerking her eyes to the left. She quickly buried the cruel memories skipping through her mind. "You will think *only* of pleasure. Yours, Sean's, and mine. I don't want anything else filling your mind. There's no shame here. Do you understand?"

She gave a stiff nod. "Yes, Mason."

"Good. Now, I want you to kiss Sean."

She swallowed and looked up at the other man. He was very tall and would have to meet her halfway. She lifted her tethered hands and gently placed them on the center of his tanned, muscled chest. The heat from his skin seared her palms. He looked at her, but didn't bend.

Realizing he wasn't going to help her, she leaned up on her tiptoes and placed a soft kiss on the hard line of his jaw. Beneath the stubble his scent was intensified. Her lips pressed into him and his slow intake of breath caused his chest to rise beneath her touch.

She grew flustered. Why wasn't he meeting her halfway? It was as if he was deliberately being difficult. Suddenly he stepped back and her bound hands dropped to her waist. She lowered her eyes. She hadn't done as Mason wanted.

Looking back at her husband, there was no censure in his expression. "Talk to me, Liberty."

"I can't reach."

"What do we do when we need help?"

She looked at him and blinked. "Ask for it."

He nodded and she looked back at Sean. She stepped close to him again. "Please help me kiss you, Sean."

The straight line of his mouth twitched with the start of a smile. He took a slow step toward her. "You ask so pretty, little Liberty."

With their thighs flush against one another, his arms reached out to steady her, taking her upper arms in a strong but gentle grip. He leaned down slowly with complete control. His nose teased hers in a soft Eskimo kiss and then his tongue traced the trembling pout of her lower lip.

Her muscles contracted as her knees tightened and her belly trembled with excitement. She let out a shaky breath and his mouth took that opportunity to slant over hers. His hot tongue pressed between her lips, wasting no time, as he pillaged her mouth. She moaned and he growled. Her tongue dueled but then backed off, passively allowing him to control the pace and pressure of the kiss.

She jerked as she felt the press of the cool wall against her back. Had she moved? It would appear so. The moment pulled her away on a tide of anticipation. Her body reacted, wanting more.

"Enough." The sound of Mason's voice had her heavy eyes opening.

As Sean's soft mouth sucked her lips in a slow release from the intense connection, his gaze burned into her and she shivered. So close. He pulled away but didn't leave the intimate space. His breath teased her wet lips as he slowly nudged the weight of his denim clad erection into her belly.

Sharp pleasure pierced her nipple and she turned to find Mason standing beside her, his hand cupping her breast. "Do you like it when Sean touches you, Liberty?"

She should say no. A good wife would say no. She looked into her husband's gaze and knew she couldn't lie. "Yes."

"Good."

Somehow she understood, in this realm, Mason didn't want a good wife. He wanted this, the three of them together. He was so calm, yet as her eyes dropped to his waist he was obviously affected.

Stripping off his pants, Mason's heavy, dark erection rose up along his thigh. His hand traced down her arms and gently took her tied wrists into his grip. Raising her hands above her head, Sean lifted her hips as Mason fit her tied wrists over the pewter sconce on the wall. When her toes touched back down on the floor she was trapped, tied to a hook she wouldn't be able to escape without assistance.

Her body stretched, nipples lifting, as her small breasts leveled into her chest, leaving only small, taught mounds tipped in delicate pink buds. Sean's large palms framed her ribcage and his thumbs played at her sensitized tips. "Beautiful."

Mason stepped back and, as if they were one, Sean's hands pulled away. Incredible vulnerability and exposure awakened her to their every caress. It was as if her body catalogued each touch, her instincts on high alert, yet her mind craved the helplessness. They each stood before her and looked over her extended body. Her flesh heated all the way to the tips of her breasts.

"Tell me what you want, Liberty," Mason whispered.

She looked at the two beautiful men before her. Her husband's trim, sculpted body was darker than Sean's. He was narrower than the hulking man to his left. Where Sean's coloring was more bronzed from the sun Mason's held a natural olive tone.

Sean's rigid washboard stomach cut hard lines into his waist. There wasn't an ounce of fat on him. His large arms were worked to a point of perfection, where Mason, again, seemed more naturally toned. Her husband was muscled as a result of active living, but Sean had honed his body to a point of pride. Tattoos decorated his flesh, drawing attention to all his dedicated effort.

Strength and command, that's what they were, Mason holding all the power and authority, while Sean was might and force. Should a crack formed in Sean's veneer it would be like releasing bottled lighting trapped for too many years.

There was something peculiar about the way her husband could bare himself in front of this man. Her mind flashed to the two of them playing in the ocean, memories of subtle glances over breakfast, soft touches that seemed natural. She frowned. Was she reading too much into their relationship? Or was she truly seeing something special between them, something that went beyond friendship?

Her breath came in quick shallow pulls of excitement. She wanted it to be the latter. She wanted them to love each other, but she also didn't want to upset Mason or offend Sean by insinuating anything.

She tilted her head as she watched them. Sean's gaze followed hers as she looked down at Mason's erection. Mason looked down at himself then back to her.

"Tell me what you want," he repeated.

Liberty turned to Sean and saw a glimmer of understanding in his eyes. There was no revulsion or shock. If anything she saw his lip twitch in what she assumed was satisfaction. Her throat swallowed convulsively. She couldn't.

Sean suddenly stepped forward and looked her in the eye. He tucked a stray curl behind her ear and whispered, "Seems little Liberty can't find her voice. I think I'd like to help her with that."

Mason's low chuckle met her ears and Sean continued, "Perhaps when you find your voice you can tell us what it is you're thinking that's put that naughty gleam in those pretty blue eyes."

He dropped to his knees and forced her thighs apart. She assumed it was the wetness coating the inside of her thighs that made him growl just as he pierced her folds with his tongue, his broad shoulders wedging between her legs and relieving some of the pressure on her back.

She screamed and his hot mouth licked her pussy, his tongue penetrating her with deep, quick strokes. He shouldered his way under her knees and suddenly she was hanging over his mouth, body suspended against the wall, feet far off the ground. Her head fell back and she cried out. He was bringing her to orgasm faster than her mind could comprehend.

Her moans collided in a broken rhythm of high pitched need. Her pulse accelerated, plowing toward her release. Almost. She was going to come then suddenly he stopped. She groaned and panted.

Mason's mouth kissed and licked up the underside of her arm and she shivered. It was too much. She needed to come.

"Are you ready to talk, love?"

She shut her eyes and breathed. Mason's mouth worked up to her elbow and he bit down on her flesh. Her back arched against the wall as her nipples pressed forward, begging for attention. Sean's hard breath beat against her pussy. She wanted someone to touch her, play with her, and make her come.

And then they both stepped away. The sudden absence of their heat was a tactile punishment that drew a growl of frustration from deep within. Mason went to his nightstand and opened his drawer. Her eyes bulged when she saw what he retrieved.

Sean smiled as Mason displayed an enormous rubber dildo. It was longer than Sean and wider that her husband. "You won't have us until you tell us what you want, Liberty, and I know you have something quite specific in your mind. I can see it in your eyes."

Mason handed the dildo to Sean and went over to the chair. He slid the ottoman across the floor, wedging the low piece of furniture between her calves, forcing her thighs to spread. He left her there, spread and hanging, and returned back to sit on the chair in the corner.

Sean approached, holding the dildo in his hand. He casually stepped over the ottoman, straddling it, and lowered his body until he was seated in front of her. He leaned forward and breathed deeply. His fingers feathered over her damp flesh, not quite titillating her, but...

opening her. It was difficult to see exactly what he was doing from her position against the wall. His head tilted toward her spread thighs and he seemed to be concentrating very hard on what he was doing.

The cool touch of rubber to her flesh was firm and foreign. The dildo lacked the heat of a real man. She trembled as Sean rubbed the toy over her flesh, allowing her juices to coat and lubricate it.

"Do you want to tell us what you want, Libby?" he asked as he slowly twisted the wide head at the mouth of her sex, carefully fitting her body to what was bound to stretch her. She was so over sensitized she could barely remember what she had wanted, what she was too shy to voice.

"No?"

He nudged the fat rubber cock into her pussy, only slightly penetrating, but showing her that it would indeed stretch her. She grunted at the intrusion, but her body reflexively softened around the tip.

"Okay then," Sean said as he leaned forward and gently kissed her tummy. "Deep breath."

Liberty filled her lungs and as soon as the enormous dildo pressed into her channel she exhaled in a rush. It stretched her outer lips and pulled along her moist inner folds. The moment it passed the point she was accustomed to being penetrated her body bowed.

Tight. She was incredibly tight. She breathed fast as Sean pulled the cock out, only to screw it right back in, taking it a little further. Liberty's flesh moistened and beads of perspiration trickled down her spine.

"What do you think, Mase? She's got about half of it. You think she could take more?"

Half! Liberty was sure she had more than that inside of her. She'd never felt so full. Good grief, it didn't seem possible for her to fit another inch.

"That's up to her," Mason said from his seat in the corner. "Liberty?"

Her eyes blinked. The look he sent her was so intense it caused her sex to flutter around the phallic toy stuffed inside of her. She moaned. She was going to come.

"Oh, no you don't," Sean said and suddenly the dildo pulled from her clenching sex leaving her body empty and alive with longing. He held up the dildo coated in her cream and her mouth opened in shock as he licked the rubber cock like a popsicle. He looked her in the eyes and smiled around the dildo as he took it deep in his mouth, cleaning away her arousal.

She threw her head back and moaned, turned on beyond belief.

"Does that turn you on, Liberty?"

She panted and he returned the dildo to her opening. Very quietly he whispered, "Do you like watching me suck cock?"

Mason leaned forward and she knew he missed what Sean asked. She gazed down at Sean and back to her husband. Sean might be all right with that, but she didn't think if Mason would be.

"Ask him," Sean whispered again.

Liberty shook her head. She was depraved to want such a thing. She couldn't ask that of her husband. That was going too far, even if the idea was completely erotic.

The dildo shoved deep inside of her as Sean demanded her full attention. "Ask him, Liberty. He won't be angry. Trust me."

What made him so certain? Did he know her husband better than she did? They had a past she knew nothing about, but he was *her* husband. Sean clucked his tongue and shook his head, appearing disappointed in her inability to vocalize her desires.

Her indecisiveness shattered on a gasp as Sean apparently lost his patience. The next thing she knew she was being fucked. There was no gentle easing into it. Sean pumped his hand fast, stabbing the rubber cock into her slick channel to her G-spot. She remembered what had happened before when he had applied pressure like that.

"Mason," he barked as natural reflexes threatened her control. She was, again, barreling toward an explosive climax. Suddenly her husband was beside her.

"Did you upset Sean, Liberty? What did he ask you?"

She shook her head, unable to admit what he'd asked. The cock filled her and stopped, held deep inside her body. She twitched and moaned. Her body sagged with need. "Please let me come." Mason tilted his head, as if evaluating her, trying to read her. He leaned in and slowly pressed a kiss onto her dry lips. "I love you, Liberty. Love you more than I've ever loved another."

Before she could process his words he was turning away. Her mouth opened and her eyes went wide as he tapped Sean's chin, turning the other man's head toward his body. Sean looked up at Mason and Liberty, again, noticed something more than simple friendship in his gaze.

Her husband's hand caressed Sean's cheek, his thumb catching on his lower lip and dipping into the moistness of his mouth. Sean's eyes closed. She was mesmerized. While she should have been furious at the sight of her husband's hands lovingly caressing someone else, she couldn't seem to find the anger. Her gaze clung to their movements like a thief, stealing their pleasure and making it her own.

Mason stepped closer and spread his legs. His hand slid to the back of Sean's neck and Sean allowed his head to fall back. As his mouth opened, Liberty watched in stunned silence, as Mason fed his cock past the other man's lips.

Her vagina clenched on the toy as if Mason were filling her at the same time he stuffed Sean's mouth with his flesh. There was something practiced about the movement, familiar, and done with ease.

All three of them moaned at once. Mason's hand tightened in Sean's hair as he forced his cock deep down the other man's throat. Sean peeked at her under his golden lashes and gave the dildo a subtle thrust. The sensation of the toy filling her and the sight of Mason, now rapidly fucking Sean's mouth had her flying into an orgasm she was unprepared for. She screamed and jerked her arms against the ties.

Her cries mixed with Mason's moans of pleasure and Sean's grunts. The cock twisted inside of her channel, prodding, and thrusting, all a mixture of sensation causing a continuum of pleasure that drove one orgasm into another.

Sean ripped his mouth from Mason's cock and sealed it over her clit. She screamed again and again as she came on his tongue. A starburst of colors exploded behind her eyes as her mind suddenly blanked. White noise, heartbeats, tingles racing over every square inch of flesh, she fell into some sort of space lost in time. She was being lifted away.

Strong hands massaged the tired muscles in her arms and shoulders, and then the soft bedding pressed into her back. She just needed to rest a moment. Just rest. It was the most peaceful place her mind ever visited and she wondered why she'd never known it before.

~

LIBERTY'S MIND came awake to the soft deep rumbles of masculine whispers. Her body was cocooned in warmth.

"You have to tell her."

"I have no intention of keeping it from her."

"Do you think she'll be all right with it?" She could hear the worry in Sean's voice. "I don't want to do anything that'll upset her, Mase."

"I wouldn't allow that anyway. I told you, she's first no matter what."

"Agreed."

Liberty snuggled into the warm chest in front of her, her mind too drowsy to process their words.

"Hey, baby. You have a nice nap?"

"Mm-hm." She pressed a kiss on Mason's shoulder and his lips pressed into her hair. A warm hand coasted over her hip and Sean's body nestled into her buttocks. He'd removed his pants by the feel of his velvet shaft against her thighs.

Lips pressed into the back of her shoulder as his hands traveled up the curve of her hip and cupped her breast. Her hands had been untied. She should probably be concerned at how little Sean's sense of entitlement bothered her. He touched her as if they'd been lovers before. Strangely, they shared an inexplicable bond, which made his familiarity excusable.

Then there was the way he touched Mason, the ease in which Mason accepted the other man's presence and advances. As she recalled what they'd done, she sucked in a deep breath, her brain finally jolting awake. Her mind was on overload. Everything, as she knew it, had suddenly changed.

Mason slid lower on the bed and licked over her nipple as Sean held her breast out for him. The feel of one man's hand and another man's mouth on her breasts was new and arousing. They touched her with amiable camaraderie. As Sean's mouth kissed her shoulders and nipped at her neck, his hips slowly ground against her. The hot brand of his erection slid along her tailbone.

They needed to talk. She had so many questions, yet the sensation of the two of them loving her so tenderly made it extremely difficult to object. Her fingers sifted through Mason's dark hair as his mouth tugged on her tight nipples, his mouth sucking delicately at an easy pace.

"I want to fuck you, Liberty." She stilled at Sean's dark whisper by her ear.

Mason continued to suckle her breasts as his fingers trailed down her belly and played at the soft tender flesh between her legs. Sean lifted her leg over his hip and fed his cock between her thighs, teasing her slit as his hips ground into her behind.

Her body was exhausted and tender, but so were his motions. His touch was drugging, making it impossible to object. "Just relax. I just need to feel your body holding mine." His hot flesh slid against her moistening sex just as Mason's hands traveled to the same place from the opposite direction. All three of them stilled as they realized the pretzel they'd become.

Slowly, Mason's hand turned under her sex and she felt him take Sean's cock into his hold. She gasped at the vision filling her mind. He seemed tentative at first, his grip slight and slow, there between her legs, over the other man's erection.

Mason looked into her eyes and she watched him as his knuckles grazed her wet sex with each sure pump of Sean's cock. "Do you want this?" he whispered. "If not, say so and it won't happen. But you need to tell me before we go any further, Liberty."

Her husband was jerking off another man. The other man's cock was rubbing against her flesh as her husband fisted him. What the hell was happening?

She focused on her husband's eyes, saw the desire there. Sean's body was tense and waiting behind her. It seemed they all wanted this. She smiled lovingly at Mason and whispered, "I want this."

She felt, as well as heard, both their sighs of relief. Mason pressed his forehead to her shoulder and sighed. She faintly heard him whisper, "Thank you." But utterance was so quiet she might have imagined it.

Sean rolled to his back, easing her weight onto his chest. He lifted her arms and held her to him. His hands found her breasts and cupped and plucked at them as his knees fit between her own and drew her thighs slightly apart.

Mason rotated to the foot of the bed and adjusted her footing. Sean's legs spread wider as Mason planted her feet flat outside of Sean's muscular thighs. She was completely exposed. The length and heat of Sean's flesh radiated into the hot opening of her pussy. Mason climbed between their legs.

She jolted at the feel of his finger trailing from her clit, between the creamy folds of her flesh, and down to the tight bud of her ass. Sean hold tightened and she realized she was again restrained. The heat of Mason's tongue flattened along her flesh as he took one long lick. She moaned and Sean's fingers tightened over her nipples.

The gentle kiss of Mason's mouth left her body and was replaced with the soft brush of his hair over her naked lips. Sean's body tightened beneath her as he sucked in a hard breath. She realized then, that Mason had taken Sean in his mouth. Her body lifted as Sean's hips bucked beneath her as he forced himself deeper in Mason's throat.

The idea that her husband had another man's cock in his mouth made her suddenly crazy with desire. She wanted to watch the act. She tried to move, but Sean's hold on her nipples tightened almost to the point of pain and she stilled.

"Stay," he commanded and her body fell back into his hold, submitting to his demands.

Mason pulled away from Sean's cock and the wet tip tapped against her opening. Her husband licked at her sex and the mixture of his mouth, Sean's cock, and her pussy all tangled into one knot of sensation as Mason expertly pleasure them both. She'd never known him to be so un-inhibited before.

Their moans echoed through the bedroom. Mason's mouth became more aggressive as Sean's body seemed to swell and tense beneath her. Her nipples felt bruised and what had, at some point stung her flesh, her body now craved. She wanted the rough clasp of Sean's fingers to continue pinching and pulling at the sore tips of her breasts.

While Sean's left hand continued to tease and torment her breasts his right hand glided down her belly and found her clit. He began to rub in slow circles as the heat of Mason's mouth pulled away. The loss was very real, causing her body to jerk in protest. There was movement, the sound of a drawer opening and closing, and then the easy weight of Mason climbing back between their legs.

Sean's fingers formed a V, opening her flesh wide and exposing her clit. Mason's mouth latched and she was suddenly coming hard and fast. She knew it was partly due to the stimu-lating contact, but she credited the mental image of her husband licking over her flesh and another man's fingers, dewy with her cream, for the rapid spin of her body's release.

Her empty sex fluttered and contracted, wanting more. As the waves of pleasure subsided, Mason sat back on his knees and she heard the sound of foil tearing. "Turn her."

Sean did as Mason asked and she was shifted, straddling Sean's hips as he kissed her passionately. Mason took hold of her hips and pulled her lower on Sean's torso until the tip of his latex covered cock lined up with her sex. It was as if they were one. Sean's body supported her as Mason's hands guided her onto Sean's cock.

The tip pressed in and she instinctively sat up to settle her body over his. "Slow," Mason said, still holding her hips.

He held her as she breathed and lowered herself onto Sean's long cock. She was sore, but needed him inside of her. Once she seated herself comfortably, taking all of his length, Mason nudged her shoulders forward.

"Lean down. Let Sean hold you."

Liberty lowered herself onto Sean's chest as he slowly pumped his hips, filling her. He wrapped his arms around her and kissed her temple. "You feel so goddamn good wrapped around my cock, Libby. Makes it hard to hold onto my control."

She moaned as he rotated his hips. There was a click and then cool liquid was being drizzled over her bottom. She stilled and Sean's hands rubbed lovingly over her back.

"Relax, baby. Mason knows what he's doing. Just enjoy." Slightly distracted by Sean's use of her husband's endearment for her, she started when Mason's fingers massaged the oil into the puckered flesh of her rectum. Sean continued to rub his hands over her back as he offered soothing words and she settled.

She was still very new to being touched back there. It was pleasant, but also scary. She recalled the tight pinch that came with penetration at her back entrance, but she also remembered the slow burn of pleasure that flooded her body once the shock of intrusion eased.

Mason's fingers worked over her bottom, coating his digits and her hole, making slow shallow dips past the tight muscles. She moaned and settled into Sean's hold as he slowly fucked her. The cap of the oil snapped open again and Mason moved, but not where she could feel him.

Sean stilled and sucked in a shuddering breath, his neck extending and his muscles tightening. He grunted and relaxed. His cock fluttered and pulsed deep inside of her. She looked at him curiously.

Sean's glazed eyes stared through smoky hazel pools of lust. In a hoarse voice he mumbled, "You'll love it, Liberty, the feel of being penetrated there. Such possession, such an exchange of trust," he grunted again and his hips drove up into her as if by reflex. "He's always gentle." Was he speaking from experience?

Mason's mouth kissed along her raised bottom and chills ran up her spine. "Hold her for me, Sean."

Sean's hands moved to her ass and gripped her cheeks, spreading her open. Her breath came faster as anticipation bordered on fear. "Shh, relax. He won't fuck you there until you're ready. He's just going to insert a small vibrator."

"A vibrator?"

Sean grunted and there was a sudden trembling running through the walls of her sex, radiating from Sean's length. "Yes, just like the one he just shoved in me." His eyes closed and his breath grew choppy. "Lay your head on my shoulder, baby, and let him have control."

Liberty lowered her head and felt the cool tip of the vibrator nudge the tight opening of her anus. Mason's palm flattened on her lower back, stilling her jerky movements. "Deep breath, Liberty. Then let it out slowly."

She breathed in and as she let the breath out the vibrator pressed past her taut muscle and deep within her back entrance, deeper than anything else had ever been. She whimpered at the intrusion. It was uncomfortable. It was as if there was something wedged up her ass, which there was.

Sean's lips kissed her forehead as his arms tightened around her. She felt extremely tight. Stuffed. Sean's cock filled her sex and pulsed from the vibrations traveling through his back channel. The narrow barrier of her anatomy was taut against the large cock and the vibrator now wedged snugly in her bottom.

There was a slight twist and then buzzing

filled her ears as it shook her entire being from the within. "Oh God!" She felt her muscles immediately move to climax.

"Relax," they both said at once and suddenly the vibrator was moving, but there was no stopping her release.

It trembled as Mason pulled it slowly back and slid it in again. His weight rocked the bed as he did the same thing with the vibrator filling Sean to judge by the way his cock leapt and pulsed within her. Her orgasm steadily ripped through her, unending. She was so aware of and apart from her body at the same time.

Sean's hips lifted as he began to fuck her slow and deep, as if each thrust ended with an enunciated punch to her womb. Dear God, she was going to shatter into a million pieces. Her clit throbbed over Sean's gliding pelvis.

Repetitive cries provoked by each thrust escaped her mouth. It was smooth, but rough. There was a bite of pain that deliciously followed each throb of pleasure. Her orgasm rolled from one into the next. Suddenly the buzzing sound sped up and her ass seemed to light on fire. Her climax tripled, blanketing her and all thoughts fled her mind. Her legs drew up tight and Sean yelled out a curse. She felt his release filling the condom as her pussy clamped forcefully around him.

Her body throbbed, convulsed, and contracted over and over again. Sean's neck was taut with columns of thickly corded muscle. His grip on her tightened and she was grateful for his secure hold. She was flying out of control. When the last jolt of pleasure rocketed through her, her muscles gave out and she collapsed like a puddle of flesh and bones onto Sean. He shook in concert.

The vibrator slowly retracted from her ass and she imagined Sean was feeling the same as he grunted. She was rolled gently onto her back, but was too tired to open her eyes. Sean pulled himself out of her and lay next to her, panting. She peeked at him through her lashes and he clumsily reached for her and reassuringly squeezed her hand.

"Our boy doesn't seem to be finished yet," he mumbled.

She tilted her chin and saw Mason kneeling at the foot of the bed, his fist slowly stroking over the dark flesh of his cock. Despite everything they had done since returning from the beach, Mason had yet to come. She slowly pulled herself into a sitting position and faced her husband. Looking up at him she softly asked, "Can I make you come, Mason?"

His nostrils flared. "Come here, baby. Let me feel those lush lips wrapped around my cock."

She crawled to the edge of the bed and wasted no time taking him into her mouth as she swallowed him to the back of her throat. His hand knotted in her curls as he pumped his hips. She closed her eyes and reveled in his aggressive passion. He was so powerful, so loving, and so controlled.

Suddenly cool lips touched her cheek and her eyes opened. Sean was kneeling beside her. She turned and Mason's cock slipped from her mouth. Sean claimed her lips with a deeply carnal kiss that left her breathless. As he pulled away she panted and sucked in a deep breath as she watched him take Mason deep in his mouth.

Mason gripped Sean's hair in a fist that was much harsher than he would ever use on her. Fascinated, she watched as he rammed his cock down Sean's throat almost as if he wanted to punish him.

Sean's eyes closed, shadows of golden lashes leaving dark crescents over his cheeks as they hollowed over Mason's cock. He looked so at peace, pleasuring her husband, like he'd waited an eternity to be permitted to do so. It wasn't something she would have guessed a man like Sean to be into, but he clearly was.

Mason withdrew with a pop from Sean's glossy lips and faced her. She looked at him and he tenderly caressed her cheek down to her jaw. With the slight pressure on her chin, she opened and he slowly fed his cock into her mouth.

He was gentle. There was none of the aggressive thrusting she witnessed between him and Sean. She licked over his flesh. Pulled and kissed him and when he had had enough he gently touched her cheek and she released him. Sean was there a moment later taking him deep again.

Without thinking she leaned in, not wanting to be left out, and pressed an open mouthed kiss to the base of Mason's cock.

Sean's eyes opened and he released Mason. His mouth found hers in a searing tangle of lips and tongues and then Mason was probing between both their lips. They kissed and licked over his hard flesh and she watched, amazed, as Mason's control buckled.

Sean grabbed her and bodily dragged her back onto the mattress. She wasn't sure what was happening. Had she done something wrong? Mason's eyes were crazed with lust as they zeroed in on her pussy.

Sean stood up and climbed off the bed, but not before his hand snaked out and grabbed the bottle of lube. He walked behind her husband and roughly pressed him forward with a shove. Mason's hands caught his weight as he collapsed over her.

The sound of foil tearing again rent the air and Mason's gaze found hers. Her husband looked at her, eyes glazed with desire and something she'd never seen in him before. Guilt?

"Tell him to stop, Liberty, and he will."

Unable to speak, she slowly shook her head. Mason's nostrils flared and she watched Sean climb behind him. The sound of oil escaping the bottle filled the air as Sean's hands worked over Mason's ass. His gaze met hers over her husband's, daring her to object. She barely nodded and Sean looked down. Mason's muscles bunching as he sucked in a deep breath. She knew—in that breath—Sean's cock was now deep inside of him.

Her mouth fell open in utter shock. It was incredible. To Liberty it was like seeing the alpha wolf being toppled and claimed by the next in line. Sean was suddenly dominating Mason, who was *always* in complete control. Her body throbbed as she watched Sean take her husband, somehow knowing he would give no quarter.

He gripped Mason's hips in an iron hold and slammed his cock deep. Mason grunted and took the pleasure Sean gave. His knuckles tightened in the bed linens and Liberty watched, completely aroused.

"Eat your wife's pretty pussy," Sean demanded. "Eat it until she's screaming and her come is running down your throat."

She was suddenly being dragged down the bed by her ankles, legs spread wide, and then Mason's mouth was making a meal of her. She twisted and tried to escape the intense onslaught of pleasure. It was too much, too soon. Mason's breath beat out of him, smacking hotly against the wet lips of her sex with each hard thrust of Sean's cock. She barely had time to process the new position. Mason was relentless. His body jerked and his rough jaw scraped against her tenderized flesh as Sean pounded into him from behind.

"Lick her up, Mase. You keep her satisfied until I've had my fill."

There was something fierce and commanding in Sean's voice, an intensity she'd never heard before. Mason was suddenly the submissive one doing Sean's bidding and here in the mix of it all was herself, completely under their command, a slave to their desires.

Hard, fast thrusts rocked the bed. Her husband's ragged cries roared into her sex as he licked and nipped and sucked. She was coming and coming over and over without a break. She feared she might pass out. Her voice cried out words that were intended to slow him down, but she was robbed of speech as another orgasm washed over her.

She suddenly screamed and trembled, Mason's fingers digging into her flesh, holding her in place, when suddenly Sean's bellow, followed by her husband's sob of pleasure, collided with her own.

"On her belly!" Sean grunted and Mason's mouth was suddenly gone as he rose to his knees. Sean's heavily muscled arm banded around Mason, his fist gripping her husband's cock and tugging roughly. Warm hot jets of his come splattered over her soft, quivering tummy and ran down her sides.

Sean's mouth latched onto Mason's neck before he turned and kissed him hard. Liberty wanted to watch them, but her body simply gave out, and a blanket of peace washed over her, swallowing her whole and everything faded to black.

CHAPTER 12

*S*ean awoke to the sound of jazz, his body wonderfully sore. Was he in a dream? He stretched and opened his eyes. He was alone. Memories of the previous night came rushing back to him and his cock swelled. Where were Mase and Libby?

The sound of running water had him looking around. He stood and walked on wobbly legs to the bathroom. The scent of Mason's soap laced the steamy air. He quietly washed his face and cleaned himself up. When the water stopped he leaned a hip on the counter and waited. Mason stepped out of the shower, reached for a towel and froze.

Their gazes locked and he was pleased to see Mase's cock stiffen. "Where's Libby?"

"She's making breakfast." He tied the towel around his waist. The material tented and gaped over his erection.

"Can I help you with that?"

Mase looked down and then back to Sean. His damp chest rose and fell as he drew in a deep breath. He seemed uncertain.

Many times the night before, they awakened and stared awkwardly through the silence, both seeming to wonder if it had all been a dream. It was as if they'd finally broken down the walls and boundaries. He would be lying if he said he wasn't concerned about where that left things in the light of day. He needed to know before he faced Libby.

Mase broke eye contact and strode to the sink. He reached for his shaving cream and Sean caught his hand. Mase still wouldn't look at him.

"Don't." The word fell from Mason's lips like a guillotine. Sean gritted his teeth and released him.

"Is that how it's going to be?"

He shut off the water and faced him. "I have to go to work. I haven't had a chance to talk to Liberty today. I don't know how things are going to be until I talk to her."

"And what about me, Mase? Do I get a say in any of this?"

"You know I have to put her first."

"And what if she says she likes the way things are going?"

"Then we go from there."

He was right, but Sean was still aggravated that he had no choice in the matter. He felt... used.

What if last night was all there would ever be? Part of him believed it was worth it, but another part hated knowing what he would never have again. The thought of being rejected by Mason and Libby, while the two of them still had one another, left a gaping void in his heart that vied with the one he'd tolerated since leaving Mase the first time. A cacophony of emotion bubbled up inside of him, desire, hurt, fear...love.

Unable to mask his hurt, he snapped, "If you want another cock to fuck your wife, use a vibrator. I'm not a fucking toy." He turned abruptly. "I'm out of here."

Before he could storm out of the bathroom, Mason pinned him to the wall, and hissed, "I know you aren't a fucking toy! How could you even say something like that?"

He pushed his hands off of him. "Because that's what it feels like."

"Bullshit. You know why I have to be careful with her. I can't jump into anything."

"And last night when your cock was in my mouth and five minutes after that when mine was up your ass, what was that if not jumping?"

His boy looked down as if ashamed.

"Whatever." Sean shoved him away and stormed into the bathroom.

"Stop!" At the commanding tone in Mason's voice Sean stilled. He waited, his eyes glued to the rumpled bedding that still reeked of sex. He couldn't turn to face him.

He sensed him stepping closer. "I...I'm not

sure I really thought this through." The uncertainty, the tentativeness in Mason's voice was in direct contrast to his former autocratic tone.

Part of Sean's heart dropped into the soles of his feet. He knew this would happen. He knew he shouldn't have agreed to any of this. Sighing, he tightly nodded. "Enough said. I'll get my shit and be out of here before you get back from work."

"No," Mason snapped, panic in his voice. The weight of Mason's palm on his shoulder was a balm to his confused heart. "I just...I wasn't prepared for all these emotions to come back. I...I shouldn't be having these feelings. She's my wife and I love her."

"You asked for this!"

"I asked for it for her. I feel like I'm taking more from it than she is and that was never my intention."

"I got it. Loud and clear," he gritted.

"You don't understand, Sean—"

"No need to spell it out. Like I said, just let me get a shower and grab my stuff."

"I don't want you to leave!"

Sean spun on him. *"Then what the fuck do you want, Mason?"*

Suddenly toppled back onto the bed, Mase's mouth crashed against his. He gripped Mason's damp hair in a tight fist and rolled on top of him only to be forced to roll over again. Mase's towel fell away and the heat of their cocks struck like matches against tinder, burning hotly. Mase's mouth kissed down his throat and bit at his shoulder.

Sean was taken in an iron grip as Mase pulled hard on his cock. His hand touched blindly on the bottle of lube left tangled in the sheets. "Here."

Mase took it and quickly filled his palm with oil, stroking his flesh until it gleamed hot and polished. He backed off the bed and Sean rolled to his stomach, planting his feet firmly on the floor. Mason wasted no time. Sean's feet were kicked apart and Mase's cock nudging at his hole. Their breathing was the only sound for a split second and then his rectum stretched around Mase's wide cock.

It had been years since anyone had fucked him there. Thirteen to be exact. Never had he wanted another man the way he wanted Mase. He'd be a lying fool to deny that he loved the man. The prickle of tears and an unfamiliar tightness in his throat were the prelude to Mase filling him in one fast, solid thrust. Forgotten sensations wracked his mind and thrilled his body.

Once seated deep inside, he didn't take Sean hard as he expected he would. Rather, he gentled his hold and seemed to fold himself over his body, blanketing him, caressing him, making love to him. Slow and deep, Mason poured his heart and soul into each stroke.

This was what Sean had been afraid of, loving two people at once. While a short affair with consulting adults was all well and good, emotions and pasts made things altogether messy. The sudden awareness of his feelings for Liberty exacerbated everything.

Mason's lips pressed into his back as he whispered endearments over his flesh. "I don't know if I can lose you again. I wasn't expecting to feel so much for you. I thought I was over you."

"I'm sorry," he rasped. Sean was so sorry for so many things. Mase probably suspected he was apologizing for complicating their lives by showing up, but in truth he was sorry for lacking the courage Mase deserved from him thirteen years ago. He was sorry and ashamed that he couldn't stand up to his father, a man who had never loved him, when Mason had never done *anything* but love him. And now...now he had fallen in love with his wife as well.

Mason's voice was ragged. "I didn't expect it to hurt like this. I can't seem to accept you leaving again."

At that, Sean pulled away and Mase let him go. He turned and kneeled on the bed, facing his boy. Pain stitched into his heart at the sight of tears running down his face. With a gentle hand he wiped away the salty drops, cupping his beautiful face, and kissed him.

"I should have never left, Mason. I was a fool. I knew it the moment I left, I know it now, and I will know it when I'm an old man leaving this world with no one to love me."

"I love you."

"I love you, too, but it isn't enough anymore. You have Liberty and your life's with her. All this pain, it's my fault. It'll always be my fault and I'm so sorry. Tell me what to do and I'll do it. You want me to go? I'll go."

Mason shook his head. "I don't want you to go."

"Then ask me to stay and I'm yours. Libby's too. We could make it work, I think. She's sweet and giving and..." What was he saying? What was he suggesting? The hope that showed in Mase's eyes wasn't fair to any of them. Mase was right. They couldn't make these decisions without Liberty.

He was having an affair with a married man, a man whose wife he cared deeply. What they were currently doing suddenly materialized as very different from what the three of them shared the previous night.

Today there were intimacies that had remained closeted up until now. There was an entire plane of emotions laced with a complex past that Liberty had no idea about. It wasn't fair to discuss these things without her there.

He hated the sense that he was somehow betraying her at the moment. Suddenly, he realized he'd never touch Mase again without her acceptance. Sean wanted her acceptance as much as he wanted Mason's. He loved them both.

Staggered by the realization, he looked at Mason, finally understanding the pain and fear, the incredible agony of loving someone that you might never have again.

He cupped his palm over the rough edge of Mason's jaw and smiled sadly. "We have to stop."

～

LIBERTY STUMBLED back from the bedroom door and dropped the pile of linens onto the white carpet. What had she just witnessed? That wasn't lust, as she assumed the night before. It was love, love rooted in a foundation she knew nothing about, love that stood apart from her and Mason's.

The pain etched on Mason's face told her he was breaking apart, torn in two directions. Her husband was in love with Sean. How could she have been so stupid? She never saw even the slightest evidence of Mason finding other men attractive until she witnessed him with Sean.

There was more than arousal fueling those desires that had come in to play in the past few days. But this was bigger than that. This was a history that had been hidden from her. She felt foolish and betrayed, and at the same time terrified she would be cast aside.

Biting her knuckles to stifle a sob, she quickly turned and rushed down the hall until she gained the stairs. Her frantic steps didn't stop until her feet crossed the threshold of the guest room on the third floor. Looking back at the empty hallway, she quietly closed the door and turned the key.

Liberty's body staggered backward until she hit the wall with a thud. Her spine slid down the surface, her bottom landing on the hard floor. She stared around the perfect room, seeking comfort in its precise display.

Whitewashed wood floors gleamed without the slightest fleck of dust. Pristine ivory carpet fit the square room with perfectly measured angles. The thick button upholstery of the white headboard delineated the various monochromatic throw pillows.

Everything was clean and perfect and pure. From the glossy white framed mirror to the chic crystal chandelier, to the Irish lace curtains filtering in the white rays of sunshine, there wasn't a single impure mark. Then her eyes landed on the immaculate mantel painted a pale shade of eggshell. There, centered like a gaping sore, was the black fireplace. A stain upon an angel's wings. *She* was that stain.

She looked at her white linen pants and examined her pale polished toes. No matter how hard she tried to wash out her boldness, it remained, that same blackness seeping from her pores.

Three tiers of metal, three crystal beads, three shiny bulbs, three dressed windows, three round pillows, three white sconces, one chipped toenail.

She shouted, her voice hoarse as she reached for an object to throw, an object that wasn't there. Her fingers went to her one imperfect toe. She slid the tip of her fingernail under the scale of hard polish and chipped away the remainder until there was nothing but natural peach showing through. Nine perfectly painted toes, one misfit.

Looking down at the mess she made, she quickly stood. She wouldn't get on her hands and knees to clean up those microscopic flecks of chipped paint. *No!*

Whirling around, she marched into the bathroom of the guest room and froze. Under a curtain of draped gossamer, sat a porcelain claw tub. Her heart beat hard in her chest. Her shoulders trembled.

No, no, no, no, no... She fisted her hair and pulled. *No!*

Her eyes molested the white curves of the tub, its purifying purpose seducing her demons without effort. One drop, one turn of the wrist, and the water could flow. She could take off her clothes and climb into the scalding water, immerse her filthy soul, and wash it all away. A taste of serenity, a baptism that would cleanse her of the devil's fingerprints. The pain would be so good. Images of patchy pink flesh played in her mind as shivers twitched her limbs. She could make the hurt go away. She could own it, control it...*nine perfect toes.*

She took a staggering step forward and halted. Sharp pain buried itself inside of every nerve as some part of her refused to go to the tub. The long gold spigot called to her. She could almost hear the tight, releasing moan as her fingers turned the brass knob free.

Her ears could summon the sound of water rushing through the pipes, beating back gravity with its force, the soft flush of liquid breaking past the faucet and slowly pooling, filling the curves of the tub. Her eyes fell closed and her head rolled to one shoulder as she imagined the steam on her face, her curls tightening and moistening in the sultry, hot haze coming off the water and caressing her dewy skin, consuming her flesh. She moaned.

Her hands tightened into fists. *One imperfect toe. Three lovers, one imperfect third.* She didn't fit. She and Mason had always been two, three seemed to be better, but now she would be forgotten, a pawn for pleasure in a game of deceit. They weren't three. They were two and she was one.

Her fist smacked against her thigh hard. And then harder.

Again!

She struck the tender flesh under the linen of her pants until her muscles throbbed and she vaguely recognized the beginnings of a bruise forming along her thigh. Far away in the distance she heard someone call her name, but she couldn't answer.

Don't go near the tub. Don't cross the street without looking both ways. Don't walk alone after dark. Don't be a whore. Don't go near the tub.

She wouldn't do this to herself. She wouldn't do this to Mason.

Punch. Punch. Punch.

She thought of Dr. Young. Saw the woman's number written on the notepad downstairs by the fridge. Knew the number, imagined dialing it, but couldn't move her feet to get there. She didn't trust herself to move in the right direction. The bath was still calling her, tempting her.

Abruptly, she stopped her self-abuse.

Two dozen thumps, eight sets of three, and her thigh muscle was screaming for mercy, but that wasn't why she stopped. It was the pattern that fulfilled, won out over the tub. With shaking hands she brought her fingers to the tender flesh of her other wrist and pinched until tears stung her eyes—*two, four, six*. There. Conquered. She would deal with it later.

Trembling fingers wiped at her cheeks, brushed over her hair, and straightened her clothes. On a deep breath she forced her body to turn away and walk out of the bathroom. She slammed the door behind her and moved to the bed, shoving it like a bulwark against the door. Her breath came fast and she stared at the white carpet, her feet traveling over the snowy surface to the puddles of white sunshine over the glistening wood floors. Then her eyes touched on two large feet on the other side of the now opened door and she gasped.

Mason stood, watching her, his expression wrecked with dismay.

~

MASON'S BODY quaked with relief when Liberty emerged from the bathroom and slammed the door. He'd given her his word that he wouldn't cross the threshold and enter her sanctuary without a clear invitation, yet even from his self-imposed exile in the hall he witnessed her internal struggle, saw her fighting back her demons, and knew he would break his word if she harmed herself.

He waited, seeing the effort it took for her to collect herself as she sat on the edge of the bed. This was his fault. He knew he fucked up before he saw the linens dumped carelessly in the hall.

The game was over. He pushed her too far and he would never forgive himself if he sent her back to the dangerous place they'd spent the last five years escaping.

She seemed to catch her breath. The weight of Sean's eyes on him from down the hall pulled at his heart like a thousand hooks, but his focus remained on his wife, where it was needed most.

The same selfish side of him that had gotten them into this predicament wanted to call to his boy, ask for his support in helping their girl. But he wasn't his boy and she wasn't *their* girl. She was his wife and Sean was supposed to be a guest in their house. Liberty's home.

She was supposed to be safe here. He never imagined she'd evoke his promise regarding the third floor when the entire house was intended to be her sanctuary, yet there she sat, unreachable, yet only ten feet away.

Her body stiffened as she noticed him standing there. He hated the way her blue irises shimmered under unshed tears. Tears he caused.

"Please let me in, Liberty," he begged, his heart on the brink of shattering.

"You love him."

Not a question. Mason looked down, unable to meet her gaze. He could feel her determination, sense her need to know the truth.

"How long?" she suddenly asked.

Not understanding, he looked at her and asked, "How long what?"

"How long has this been going on? Was this whole thing a set-up? Have you been sleeping with him throughout our entire marriage?"

He took a step forward and halted. "Oh, God, baby, no." He wanted to go to her but also didn't want to break another vow. "Liberty, I've never cheated on you—"

"I *saw* you."

"What you saw should have never happened. I swear to you, I haven't seen or talked to Sean in thirteen years. Yes, we used to be lovers in college and I should've told you. I wanted to. The other night I tried, but the opportunity slipped away and—"

"It would be one thing," she said, now looking toward the wall, "if it was the physical closeness that bothered me, but it's not. What I cannot comprehend is how my husband can look at another person with such unrefined love in his eyes, such need, such emotional longing, and I never even knew this ghost of your past existed." She laughed harshly. "I have to admit, if I'd been aware of the history you two shared I might've been more cautious about agreeing to invite him into our bed. I didn't realize he was my competition."

"There's *no* competition," he said fiercely.

"Isn't there? You love him, Mason. You're lying to me and yourself if you deny it."

"I love you too."

She nodded. "I know you do. And I actually take partial responsibility for my ignorance. I'm quite demanding of your time. Our marriage has always revolved around my needs, my illness. If I wasn't so messed up we would've probably discussed this a long time ago, but with all my issues, there simply wasn't time, was there? My hurt feelings are just another result of my selfishness. My mother was right. You should have never married me."

Her words sliced through him like a searing blade. He couldn't take anymore. He entered the room and fell to his knees before her. His trembling hands took her cold fingers and brought them to his lips.

"No, Lib, don't ever think that. You're my wife and I love you. Do you think *I'm* perfect? Because I'm not! There are days that I hate myself and can barely look at myself in the mirror. You heal me. None of us are perfect. Don't ever think you take more from this marriage than I do. You give so much of yourself. You've spoiled me and I'd never be able to make it through the day without knowing you're there for me."

A tear landed on his hand with a silent splash. She shook her head. "Don't you see, Mason? Our marriage is already crowded, with you, me, *and* my sickness. I've allowed it to become a living thing between us, an unwelcome guest in our home, a monster we harbor. Why would you want all this chaos when you could have Sean? Because no matter how hard I try, I'll never be perfect."

God, she was destroying him and she didn't know it. He squeezed his eyes tight and shook his head, gripping her small hands harder. "I don't want perfection. I want you, Liberty. You, with all your quirks, and needs, and compulsions are what make my world right. It doesn't matter what's typical here, only that we're perfectly happy, because I assure your there is no such thing as simply perfect."

She suddenly sobbed, her shoulders quaking. "I wanted to be better. I thought…I thought by now I would've been. You've tried so hard to fix me."

He pulled her into his arms, her body sliding from the bed into his lap. He rocked her as she cried. "No, baby, no. It was never my intention to fix you, only support you when you need it as you support me. You aren't broken. You're you and I love you, all of you. Please understand that."

Why had he pushed her? Why had he allowed his past into his present? His emotions were so jumbled. While he loved Sean, *that* was now perfectly clear, he'd also invited a serpent into their home. He'd never forgive himself for misleading her.

Silently, he rocked her for uncountable minutes and her tears eventually waned as her breathing slowed. "Please come downstairs, Liberty. We'll work all this out. I swear it. I'll tell Sean he's to go and—"

"*No!*" She fought his grip on her.

"No? I thought—"

"This involves him as much as it involves you and me. He just lost his father and found you again. I don't want to throw him out. He has nowhere to go."

A part of his heart swelled with relief and trembled with trepidation. "Lib, Sean has a place to go—"

"No, Mason. He has shelter, but not a home. A home should be filled with love. Otherwise it's just an emotional prison keeping you apart from the world. He has no family to return to, no partner. I can't let you ask him to leave."

"He may want to leave."

"I'll talk to him," she suggested..

"Liberty, think about what you're saying. No more secrets. No more lies. Sean's someone from my past that I cared about very much. I never expected to feel the same way so many years later, but I do. His presence complicates things and will continue to."

"And you think sending him away will make you stop loving him? Mason, I know how you two feel about each other. I saw it clear as day."

"I'm married. I'm not someone who does this—"

Her hand softly covered his lips, halting his words. "We can't be ashamed of how we feel."

Recognizing his own advice, he shook his head. "This isn't that simple, Lib. Anything that threatens *our* marriage isn't worth sacrificing everything we have."

"Maybe it wouldn't be a sacrifice."

He swallowed and tried to follow her meaning. "What are you saying?"

"I'm saying…if you claim we're partners, belonging to one as much as the other, then I have as much of a right as you do to…" Her words faded away as she blushed.

"Liberty?"

"I want you to be happy, Mason," she rushed the words out. "I can't deny you this. I just…I… Please, don't abandon me."

Her words hit him like a cannon ball in the stomach, buckling his strength. "Oh, sweetheart, I would never—*never*—abandon you. Why would you even think that?"

"Because what you have with Sean, it's apart from me."

"No, Lib, you're the glue that binds me together. There is no you, separate from me. We're one. Sean may have been a part of my past, but you're my future and there's no me without you."

"Why can't we *all* be together."

This was insane. He shook his head. "You come first. You'll always come first."

She sniffled and cupped her palm over his jaw. "I don't see a rewind button in this situation, Mason. If one of us bows out, someone gets hurt. I don't want anyone hurting or resenting their circumstances. We're all here and I think we should cope with it and move on accordingly. I understand why you care so much for Sean. I do. He's very easy to love."

He stilled. Slowly lifting his face, he looked in her eyes and whispered, "Do you love him?"

"Not the way I love you, but I think there're parts of him I love. He's funny and sweet and kind."

She seemed to be remembering something. A secret smile played at the corner of her mouth as she stared unseeingly over his shoulder. He would have given anything to be able to read her mind, but didn't dare ask.

"I believe we could do this, Mason. If we all promise to be honest with each other, I think there's a chance we may find a level of happiness most people can only dream of."

He wanted to believe she was right, but he'd always been a realist. "Liberty, it won't be easy. This isn't simple logistics. It's more than sleeping arrangements and another mouth to feed."

"I'm aware Sean isn't a golden retriever, Mason. He would be a part of our family. Not a pet we play with when it suits us."

He hesitated, unsure how to explain this. He decided honesty was absolutely the best policy. "He may not want to."

"Why?"

"When Sean and I called it quits it was because he couldn't admit to the world he was in love with a man. You're asking him to openly have a relationship with not just another man, but another man and his wife. And think about what this would mean to you. We may not be the most social couple, but eventually people will notice and talk. We could wind up being ostracized."

"I know you think I'm being naive, but so what? Who cares what they think? I've been ostracized my entire life. If anyone has to be concerned, it's you, Mason. You're the one in the public eye. And not to sound like a bitch, but I'm pretty sure when someone needs an emergency operation and you're the only surgeon available they won't care what kind of proclivities you have so long as you can save their life. Let them talk. I'm so over caring about what others think."

He wanted to believe her. He wanted to take her words to the bank, but one never knew what the future would bring. He sat, thinking quietly for a while when she whispered, "Is this something you would want, Mason? Would sharing our home, our bed, our marriage with Sean please you?"

He shut his eyes. *If it were only that easy.*

"It could be."

He didn't realize he'd spoken aloud until he heard the words echo around the room. He looked at his wife, but could think of nothing more to say. Something momentous had happened to her. He got that, but the significance of it eluded his reeling brain. Something changed for Liberty.

"Why don't we ask Sean what he wants instead of deciding for him?"

"Liberty, the only way I'll ever consider this is if you understand that, no matter what, you're first. If this doesn't work, both of us are walking away. You aren't abandoning *me.*"

She smiled a smile that seemed to speak volumes if only Mason could read it. "Okay."

CHAPTER 13

"You want to do what?" Sean sat in Mase's study facing the two of them, sure he hadn't heard them correctly.

"We want you to live with us," Liberty said with such serene calm that Sean had to fight the urge to accept the invitation without question.

"What? Why? For how long?"

Mason looked at Sean. "For as long as it works out."

"Forever." Liberty said, both answering at the same time.

Rather than look to each other for clarity, Mase arched his brow and looked at him. Sean understood the message he was sending. He walked away thirteen years ago and that underlined the fact that he was still odd man out. Good. Sean needed to know Mase was looking out for Liberty before all else.

"Sean, we understand that this isn't a traditional arrangement—"

"You got that right," he said, interrupting Liberty.

Mase leaned forward. "Look, we discussed this and feel that you should stay. Not as our guest, but as part of our family. If you don't want to then we'll understand."

He couldn't wrap his brain around whether he wanted to or not. It was all too strange to comprehend, easier to focus on the two of them, both nuttier than bat shit. "You guys are married," he said, stating the obvious.

"Yes, and as husband and wife we've decided this is something we both want."

At Mase's words Sean turned to Liberty and eyed her suspiciously. "You want this?"

"If it will make Mason happy—"

"Will it make *you* happy?"

Her lips stilled. She thought for a moment. "Yes. Having you here would make me happy."

"What about my job?"

"You could find work here," Mase said.

"How…I don't even know how something like this would work. Where would we sleep?"

"We discussed that. The house has three bedrooms. Each of us will have our own private space. Liberty has the third floor and our room. You have the guestroom."

"I think we should all sleep in the master bedroom, but if we need space there are always other options," Liberty added as if she were simply saying she planned on making a chocolate cake instead of vanilla.

Sean shook his head. This would never work. Visions of each of them walking away, a little older, a little wiser, and a little more broken filled his mind and the predictable guilt of such an end choked him, stifling any impetuous desire to actually attempt what they were suggesting.

"Look," Mase said, but Sean had heard enough.

He stood. "I think you both are nuts."

"Why? Because we aren't afraid to ask for what we want? What will make us happy?" Liberty said.

"You have no idea what you're asking."

"We know perfectly well what we're asking," Mase said.

He narrowed his eyes at the both of them. "You're welcoming another man into your *marriage*! People don't do that for good reason. It won't work. The novelty will wear off and after a while you'll wonder why another man keeps fucking your wife!"

Mason looked at Liberty. She winced at Sean's crude words, but he didn't regret what he said. They needed to understand the reality of what they were asking. People didn't just run off into the sunset like reverse polygamists.

"I've told Liberty everything about our past. There'll be no secrets or lies between us—that means the three of us. If that isn't a commitment you can make than the entire arrangement is off.

But being that we're being truthful with one another, I can honestly say I will no more wonder why you're fucking my wife than she'll wonder why *I'm* fucking *you*."

Sean glared at him with challenge. "That isn't how it works and you know it."

"That's how it worked this morning."

"That was different. If you're talking long term, you know I need more than that. I'm not a bottom."

"I know what you need," Mase said with equal challenge.

"And what about Liberty? Have you told her why I'm single after all this time?"

"I've explained that you have specific likes when it comes to women."

Sean turned to Liberty. She fidgeted under his stare. Pink crested her cheeks and he waited for her to look to Mason for assurance, surprised when she didn't. He was unnerving her, he could tell, but she held his gaze. "I won't tolerate hesitation on your part because you require another man's approval or permission. I won't be second rate to another."

"Of course not, Sean."

"I'm demanding, Liberty, more so than I've already showed you."

"I understand."

He shifted his weight. He wanted to say yes, but was reluctant to trust that this was what they both truly wanted. Sometimes people asked for dumb shit and then realized they were fucked when it was too late to go back.

He turned to Mase. "I'm clean. I had a physical three months ago and haven't been with anyone, aside from you two, since. I'm not wearing rubbers."

Mase slowly smiled and leaned back. He knew he was getting what he wanted. Stupid fuck. Sean still couldn't fathom why he would ask for this. He wanted to show him how asinine this entire idea was.

"Of course not. The three of us will be in a monogamous, committed, consensual relationship. I see no need for condoms."

"Is Liberty on the pill?"

"She can't have children."

Mase's words dropped through the air like a cinderblock, landing with a thud in the pit of his stomach. Sean shut his eyes and immediately regretted his words. He was an insensitive ass.

He turned to Liberty who was staring back at him, chin raised, as if daring him to show pity. Sean understood then and there that this was an issue she'd come to terms with long ago. She was braced for his comment, but it wasn't the time. There was enough to deal with. Avoiding the subject would be an act of mercy she would appreciate, but later, he intended to have a heart to heart with her and apologize for his insensitive intrusion. For now, he needed to make the point they were struggling to see.

He looked at her. "What if I told you I wanted

to fuck you right now, just you and me, while Mason watched?"

She swallowed slowly and nodded.

"I'm selfish, Liberty. I'm not always easygoing. I warned you, but you refuse to see me in that light. I'm greedy and sometimes I want it to be all about me. Sometimes I want it to hurt."

She raised her chin and straightened her shoulders. "Like I told you before, sometimes there's good pain and sometimes there's bad pain. I trust you to know the difference, Sean."

From the corner of his eye Sean saw Mase shift his weight. He kept his focus on Liberty. "I expect complete submission from my women, Liberty."

With more bite than he expected she retorted, "I expect you to only have *one* woman, Sean, so I suppose I'll have to meet your expectations."

He understood her challenge and his cock swelled. "Stand up."

She gracefully rose.

"Take off your clothes and go stand by the pool table."

As she did as he instructed he looked back at Mason. "Tell me to stop and I'll walk out of here, grab my stuff, and never bother you again. Tell me to stay and I'm going right to that table to fuck your wife long and hard while you watch me. You interfere and I'm gone."

Mason crossed one foot over his knee and looked at him from where he sat in the designer leather chair. "Stay."

Sean nodded.

Honey, I'm home!

~

SEAN SLOWLY REMOVED his clothing and draped it over the arm of the chair. Liberty waited, hands clasped at her waist, head bowed submissively, as she stood beside the pool table. The bulk of Sean's muscular thighs rippled just below the heavy weight of his long cock. Mason's body became aroused the moment Sean had looked at him with that determined gleam in his eye.

Slowly, Sean walked over to the pool table. He didn't address Liberty. One by one, he pushed the heavy balls into the pockets, the soft clicks filling the air as they silently traveled over the smooth red felt top of the table to vanish from sight.

Once he cleared the table he stood behind Liberty, but didn't touch her. Mason noticed Sean's proximity to his wife excited her. Her pink nipples pebbled and her stomach quivered as her chest rose and fell. Sean moved slowly around her as if inspecting her. A jolt of pride ran through Mason at how beautifully she waited, complete trust and acceptance as she submitted to Sean's authority.

Sean removed the clip from Liberty's hair and tossed it on the floor, out of the way. She flinched at the sound of the plastic barrette clattering across the hardwood, the sound sharp and startling in the silence. That one misplaced clip would addle her, but she hid her distraction well. She didn't look up and she didn't look to him for reassurance or approval. She only waited for Sean's direction.

There was no disguising the effect she had on Sean. His body was taut with need. He moved her hair, spreading her blond curls over her shoulders almost reverently. Sean's cock jerked as he breathed in the scent of her arousal and Mason's cock mimicked the move. Knowing his wife's sweet fragrance by heart, he, too, loved to breathe it in. Goose bumps crested Liberty's narrow shoulders as her body trembled.

The backs of Sean's fingers ran down the slender curve of her waist from her breast to her hip. "You're very beautiful, Liberty," Sean whispered.

His fingertips coasted over her hip, barely making contact with her flesh and went to the apex of her thighs. "Spread." Liberty obediently widened her stance, but Sean didn't touch her there. "Are you wet, Liberty?"

She slowly nodded.

"I expect an answer."

"Y—yes. I'm wet."

"Who are you speaking to? Mase? I'm a needy man, Libby. I require a certain amount of attention."

"I am speaking to you, Sean. I'm very wet."

"Do you need to be fucked?"

Mason winced at Sean's words. He understood the draw of using such words. They distracted Liberty, broke down her defenses, but hearing Sean speak that way to her definitely would take some adjusting to on his part.

"I want you to fuck me, Sean."

Mason also wanted it. Sean's hands lightly touched the tops of her shoulders and slid slowly down her arms until he reached her wrists and pulled them gently behind her back. The move lifted her tits higher and Mason fought the urge to stand and join them. This was about Sean asserting himself.

"Who's touching you, Liberty?"

"You are, Sean."

"Look at your husband. Do you see any objection in his eyes?"

"No, Sean."

"Does it bother you that he's letting another man touch your body?"

"It pleases me as much as it pleases him."

"And will it please you when I fuck your body hard, taking my pleasure greedily, making your cunt my own private wonderland?"

"Yes, Sean."

Mason's breath caught as Sean suddenly turned her face and kissed her hard on the mouth. Her body tensed and then relaxed in Sean's possessive hold. Becoming so aroused, he undid the top button of his pants to allow his cock room.

When they broke apart they were both panting. Sean shot him a challenging look as if to warn him that after this there would be no going back. Mason nodded.

"Go to the other end of the table, Liberty. I want you to look at your husband as he watches another man fuck you. Know that it isn't his cock inside you. See that he doesn't object to your body being mine to use."

Mason gritted his teeth. Sean was trying to break the two of them, trying to get them to retract their offer. That wasn't going to happen. However, that also didn't mean that, when all was said and done, Mason couldn't break Sean's jaw if he pushed too far.

He wouldn't permit humiliation or disrespect into their relationship. As far as he was concerned humiliation dishonored a person and bred shame. Shame had no place in his marriage, no matter what. She was beautiful and so incredibly natural in her submission. No matter how he tried Sean couldn't pretend to be immune to such grace.

Sean wanted to make this about her apprehension, but his own insecurities were showing. It wouldn't be easy for him to accept that one person loved him, let alone two. His father seeded his trust issues and those issues hadn't waned over the years. It seemed no matter how many promises his boy heard, he could never fully bet his heart and trust another.

That was why Sean played the dominant. It made abandonment less personal. If someone left he could blame it on a difference of needs. It wasn't because of him. It was because of his demands. Funny, that the same insecure bullying bullshit his father used to manipulated him, Sean now applied to himself. Dead and buried, but his words still lived on.

Sean lived by a code his father created, a code that showed no chink in a man's suit of armor. No one was permitted closeness, because they might spot the tiny cracks in his armor. Intimidating others was only a ruse to hide the fact that he was just a scared little boy looking for someone brave enough to love him without conditions.

Sean glided his hands over Liberty's arms and pressed her palms into the soft fabric of the table. Her small breasts hung delicately in her shadow. He ran a hand down her spine and paused. She breathed in, her eyes going wide, and Mason knew Sean was touching the tight little pucker of her ass.

"Perhaps I'll fuck this tight virgin ass of yours. I'm sure since Mase is such a liberal, sharing guy he won't have any objections."

He was wrong. Mason wouldn't let Sean take her ass for the first time. Not because he didn't trust him to be gentle with her, but because he knew Liberty was still testing her trust in Sean. It would add unnecessary stress to a new experience and she'd suffered enough in a life that left her sexually stunted. He'd spent years building up her confidence and courage to try new things. He wouldn't risk Sean setting them back. If that made him a control freak, then so be it.

There was a long moment where the two of them simply stared at each other. A faceoff. Sean asserting his newly found authority over another man's wife and Mason affirming that while he offered the other man his wife he gave up nothing of his own authority. Eventually Sean backed down, but played it off as if it were by choice.

"No, I think I want that hot pussy milking my cock."

Mason relaxed, his faith in his friend's sensibility returning.

Sean took his length in hand. When they'd been a couple, just the two of them, it had always been Sean who was in control. Sure they battled, a steady game of king of the mountain, but in the end, Mason never minded giving Sean power over him. He felt cherished under the other man's control. But when Sean broke his trust something changed in Mason. Sean would eventually understand that they wouldn't fall into the same dynamic, at least not while his trust still needed mending.

His attention was jerked to his wife at the sound of the breath leaving her lungs in a quick feminine moan. He'd finally taken her from behind. The other man's hands didn't hold her. No, they remained planted on the wooden lip of the table, a clear display of Sean's desires to keep his emotions separate from what was happening.

He thrust his hips forward roughly, propelling Liberty's body and jostling her tits. A small grunted mewl escaped her throat with each hard pump of Sean's cock. She took it without complaint. She likely suspected she wouldn't come and Sean would draw out his pleasure, taking from her body without reciprocating, but she surrendered to him anyway.

It was clearly Sean's intention to get that message across. His point was made with each selfish thrust. Sean's hazel eyes stared hard into Mason's.

From his seat in the club chair several feet away, he sensed Sean's anger. His eyes bore into his as he bent over his wife. No doubt this complicated matters. Sean had a hard time walking away from a challenge. He saw it as a sign of weakness. However, Mason knew him well enough to understand that an invitation into a safe, caring relationship would terrify the balls off him.

"Who's fucking you?" Sean grunted as he pummeled her from behind. Liberty took every rough thrust. Her blue eyes burned into his as Sean used her hard.

"You are, Sean," she answered mechanically. Withdraw, thrust, withdraw, thrust, Sean's motions were sure and paced. He obviously intended to stretch her tolerance, milk his pleasure for every drop.

"And where's your husband?"

"Watching us."

"Watching who?"

"You and me, Sean."

"Tell me what he's seeing."

"He's watching his lover fuck his wife."

Mason hid his smile. *Very good, Liberty Bell.*

Sean appeared a bit thrown by her reply. While Mase held no shame in his sexual appetites, Sean still struggled with accepting his own. Her blunt label of lover had shocked Sean, thrown him momentarily off balance. He regained his composure and roughly grabbed Liberty's hips. His pace increased, and Mason could see a bit of his control slipping.

He plowed into her and pressed her shoulders lower on the table. He now yanked her slight form into each thrust. He was being rough, but Liberty could take it. Mason was very aware of his wife's comfort and was an expert in reading her.

Sean panted and grit his teeth, fatigue beginning to take hold. Whatever he was searching for he wasn't finding it. Had he been looking for rejection? Better to have a fast death than face the fear of what he thought inevitable? It was sad how little faith he held in his own appeal. He was actually quite easy to love, yet could never seem to love himself.

Suddenly Sean withdrew from Liberty and released her from his grip. She staggered but quickly righted herself. Mason sat a little straighter. Sean had better tread carefully.

He saw the frustration in Sean's eyes. Sweat

beaded along his brow that crinkled in concentration. He forked his fingers through his golden hair and turned. His dick was iridescent with Liberty's cream.

Liberty covertly looked at him in question as she caught her breath. Without alerting Sean, Mason raised his palm a half inch off the arm of the chair and spread his fingers wide as if to say 'just give him a minute, let's see what he does'.

She nodded ever so slightly and a tiny smirk skated across her lips. *Smart girl.* She knew exactly what was happening here. She understood Sean was trying to alienate himself in a way that left him unaccountable. *Not. Gonna. Happen.*

Like a caged tiger, Sean paced away from Liberty and back. He wouldn't look at Mason. The tension made the air heavy, like a great fog choking one's breath away. Finally seeming to reach some sort of decision, Sean stomped to a spot just in front of Mason.

"Come here, Liberty." She stood and slowly walked toward him. "On your knees."

She gracefully dropped to her knees without objection. No matter how much Sean loved being dominant, Liberty's flawless submission obviously irritated him in that moment. He clearly wanted to break her, make her cry out so that Mason would call halt. If Liberty felt like she was being pushed too hard or too far she would have no problem stopping Sean. Things only continued because she was as determined to prove their acceptance of Sean as much as Mason. They made an unbeatable team and Sean would soon come to accept that.

"Open your mouth wide and suck my cock. You *will* take all of it this time."

Sean's cock was long and thick. Even Mason had a difficult time accommodating him in oral sex. There was no way Liberty would fit all of him without gagging.

She opened her mouth and Sean locked his hands behind him. He was forcing himself to hold back. In the past, Sean would have grabbed a woman's hair and held her to him as he fucked her mouth, but his restraint showed he was still aware of her comfort no matter how much he growled like a beast. Liberty's mouth closed over him.

"Deeper! Suck it all. Don't make me fuck your mouth like I did your cunt."

Her eyes shut and she leaned in. Her dainty fingers wrapped around the outside of Sean's rugged thighs as her head bobbed up and down.

Sean's head tipped back and he grunted. "Yes. That's it. Suck it like you mean it."

She moved faster at his words, and his hips occasionally jerked forward as if beyond their own volition. Mason noticed wetness spiking Liberty's lashes where her eyes pressed tightly closed and knew she was pushing herself. He wanted to tell her she'd done enough and been wonderful, but she would resent his interference. She needed to prove this to herself as much as they both wanted to prove it to Sean.

Mason's gaze crawled over her body as fierce possession took hold of him. Remnants of her arousal slid down the inside of her thighs. They were close enough that he could smell the scent of sex seeping from both their pores. It was intoxicating and he had to fight to remain seated, stay physically apart from what he was forced to witness. He wanted to join them.

The muscles in Sean's tanned neck bunched and corded. His abs trembled as his toes curled over the carpet. He was fighting it.

"Stop," Sean growled.

Liberty froze, Sean's cock balanced on the pillow of her lower lip. Her eyes opened wide and she looked up to him and waited.

"I told you I wanted you to take it all. Now do it. Take me to the back of your throat."

She swallowed. Her pink tongue flicked past her lips. Hardly moving, she nodded. Still looking up at him she slowly closed her mouth over him once more and began taking him deep to the back of her throat.

She moved up and back a few times to slick her way and when she forced herself to take him to the hilt Mason saw her shoulders tense and knew she was struggling, her throat likely working to reject Sean's intrusion. She tried again and her body reflexively jerked away. Her eyes began to tear. She sat back on her knees to catch her breath.

Mason gritted his teeth. Liberty didn't like being unable to do things. He could see this frustrated her. Rather than praise her for trying, Sean shook his head, and cupped her jaw.

"Open," he gently whispered.

She did.

Sean's hips pumped in quick succession over her tongue. He held her face in a way that allowed her little movement or control, but Mason recognized the gentleness of his grip. He was incapable of hurting her, just as Mason knew.

Suddenly he stumbled back. "Lean back. Spread your pussy wide for me." His fist gripped his length and pumped his cock hard. "Wider. I wanna see that little pink hole."

Mason's hands tightened on the arms of the chair at the sound of Sean's crassness. Liberty held herself open and Sean pumped his fist rapidly over his flesh and grunted out his pleasure. The first ribbon of come landed directly on the delta of her pussy.

"Rub it in," Sean demanded.

She blinked, and then comprehended. Her fingers moved over her clit and she rubbed Sean's semen into her sex. The next two shots landed on the flat of her belly.

Sean was breathing heavily and staring at the ceiling. Something shifted in the energy of the room. Liberty wouldn't climax, not because she was being denied, but because something distracted her, something more significant to her than her own comfort. He saw the compassion welling in his wife's eyes. Her fingers slowly stopped moving and returned to her sides. She sat, bathed in another man's come, spread in a position of complete deference.

Sean's breath echoed through the study. He finally looked down and Mason took no pleasure in witnessing Sean's regret in what he'd wrought. His features twisted. Mason knew his conscience battled with shame and his stubbornness insisted he show no regret, but this wasn't a proud moment.

His jaw ticked as he looked down at Liberty who was no longer looking at him, but had lowered her gaze to the floor. Mason's head was angled in her direction, but his eyes strained up at Sean, waiting. Sean's eyes glazed with unshed tears and Mason felt the moment Sean regretted asking for an audience for such a vile display of coldness. Coldness that was artificial when in reality Sean was incapable of intimacy without emotion.

"There," he barked at Mason, the sharp word a racket in the otherwise silent room. The air throbbed with awkwardness. "How does it feel to get your wife back covered in another man's pleasure? Hope you're happy, because after letting me use her like that I sure fuckin' am."

Sean's words were cruel, intended to wound, but there was no mistaking the way his voice cracked at the end of his statement, the last word coming out in a hoarse whisper.

His words were a lie. His lips pressed together and his glassy eyes wavered under damp blond lashes. He suddenly turned and stormed out of the room.

Liberty said not a word. After the door slammed and Sean left, he looked at her and sighed. "Are you okay?"

"He's upset."

"Yes," Mason agreed. "Why don't you go take a shower and a nap? I'll be up soon to lay with you and we'll talk about all this. Sound good?"

She nodded and slowly began to stand. He could tell her muscles were already growing stiff. Standing, he helped her off the floor. Looking into her eyes he gently caressed her cheek with the backs of his fingers. "I love you, Liberty. Sean has some demons of his own to deal with. He'll never disrespect you like that again. I don't need to make that promise, because I guarantee he will."

"I know he didn't do it on purpose. He was trying to make us give up on him. I don't want to give up on him. Do you? He needs someone to love him, Mason."

Mason smiled. His sweet little wife. "No, Lib, I don't want to give up on him. He doesn't have to trust our arrangement from the beginning, but he also cannot abuse it."

It suddenly occurred to him that she may be hiding some sort of shame behind her concern for Sean. He trailed his finger through the moisture coating her tummy. "You were wonderful, Lib. You're such an impressively strong woman. I'm proud of you."

She smiled under his praise and he leaned down to kiss her gently. She sighed and relaxed into his hold. Mason made sure to show complete acceptance of what she'd done. He didn't approve of the cutting words Sean had chosen, but he understood why he tried to be cruel. So did Liberty, thankfully.

He pulled away slowly. "Give me about an hour and I'll be up. Try to get some rest before I get there." She nodded and gathered her belongings then left him alone.

Mason pulled in a hard breath, letting it out on a long sigh. He looked back at the pool table and shook his head. It was going to be a long hour.

CHAPTER 14

*S*ean entered the guestroom and slammed the door. Angrily unzipping the packed duffle bag waiting on his bed, he yanked out a pair of jeans. Unbidden, an image of Liberty flashed in his mind, kneeling before him with blind acceptance in her eyes and his mark on her belly.

"Fuck!"

He threw the duffle off the bed and fisted his hands in his hair. Throwing his ass on the edge of the bed he panicked. He was such a pathetic piece of fucking shit! He needed to think. The door clicked before he had a chance to work out a single fucking thought and Mason's shadow fell over him.

"I'm leaving. I just need to get dressed."

"Where are you going?" The calmness of Mase's voice irritated him to no end.

"Like you fucking care."

"Of course I care."

He scowled at him. "Why? After what I just did, why the fuck would you care?"

"Because I care about you. *We* care about you."

"You're a fucking moron then."

Mase folded his arms over his chest and casually leaned back into the wall. Sean hated the way he looked at him as if he could see right through all his bullshit.

"What did you think would happen, Sean? If you actually were able to break her will, did you think you would be able to just walk away knowing you hurt her?"

"I *did* hurt her," he growled.

Mase shook his head. "She's stronger than you think. You never did get it. After all this time and all your useless chest thumping, you never did figure it out. Submission, trusting someone enough to let them take the reins, is where the real strength lies. Power's easy when it's given without question, with complete trust."

"She should've never trusted me and you shouldn't have trusted me with her."

"I don't regret it."

"Like I said... moron."

"You wouldn't hurt her, Sean. I know you too well to buy into the hardass act. This'll never work if we can't be honest with ourselves and each other. How about you being honest with yourself for once? Because we all see you in there, hiding from the truth, and we love you and accept you the way you are, not the way you were 'expected' to be."

"Yeah, *honesty* is why this won't work," he scoffed.

Mason shook his head. "You may be fooling yourself, but you aren't fooling me and you aren't fooling Liberty. We see your fear."

"I'm not afraid."

"Sure you are. Love's scary. It's a free fall into someone else's keeping, a sort of surrender. You think I wasn't afraid at some point in my life that the person I loved would suddenly abandon me or crush me when I allowed my vulnerabilities to show? Being abandoned by someone you trust with your heart, someone you trust to love you no matter what, is worse than any form of hate. It's the *indifference* that kills you, their ability to simply walk away from something like it's nothing when it meant everything to you. It sucks. I should know."

Sean looked down at his feet. "I already apologized for the past."

"You did, and I appreciate your apology. I'm glad you finally get that you were wrong, but it doesn't change what happened any more than your father's death changed who you are inside. You're the same person you were when he was alive, the same person you denied yourself to be. That's always been you. Don't you think it's time to be honest with yourself? We all fear we'll somehow be ostracized or condemned, but you get to a point you gotta care about your happiness more. Put all the fear away. There is no judgment here."

"I hate that there's a part of him inside of me. All my life I tried to earn his approval and I never even liked the bastard. I'm so afraid I'll end up like him."

"Then stop trying to live by his standards, my boy. Some people are just incapable of love, But, Sean, you're not. You're not him. I saw you tonight. I saw the moment you barked out a threat you couldn't follow. I watched you force your hands behind your back so you wouldn't be too rough. You won't allow yourself to hurt the people you care about the way he did. You're stronger than he was. Christ, look at your career choice. You help people recover from injuries while he spent a lifetime dishing them out. You're running from a demon that isn't chasing you. Give yourself credit for having freewill. You chose not to be like him and you're not. And now he's dead. It's time to let his expectations go."

Emotion choked him despite Mason's compassion and understanding. "You don't know what's in my head."

"Tell me. Do you think it'll scare me? Make me love you less? Not going to happen, Sean."

"This won't end well, Mase."

"It may never end."

"Everything has a shelf life."

"Well, why not wait for the expiration date before you throw it away?"

He couldn't keep having the same argument.

"Thank you, Doctor Phil. Now, if you'll excuse me, I gotta get dressed."

"Because you pushed too hard?"

"Stop psychoanalyzing me! You aren't that kind of doctor so stop actin' like you are."

A bit of Mason's calm fell away. Yeah, Sean was lashing out like a hurt child, but he didn't want to hear this shit. He had to hear about his faults all his life from his old man, never once feeling good enough. And now the bastard was dead and he'd lost his chance to ever see pride in his father's eyes.

It was such a double edged sword. He didn't agree with his dad on anything. The old fucker was a bigot, a chauvinist, and the worst sort of bully. He never accomplished anything notable in his life, yet expected Sean to somehow conquer the world. He spent decades trying to live up to the standards of a man he hated, a man who had no moral compass, a man he knew he was better than, but who somehow held the scorecard. Mason would never know how having that sort of a man for a father felt.

"I know you're trying to help but you've got no right to call out my personal demons. Fuck you and your perfect life! You have no idea what it's like to be raised by a man that hates you, to be told day after day that you're a loser, and no matter what you do, no matter what you accomplish, there's no proving him different."

"You're right. I'm just good old Mason, always there when it's convenient, but clueless when it comes to real life issues. Why should I know about pain? My life's a walk in the park. All I'm good for is that little extra, so you can get the affirmation you need and once and for all feel like a strong and worthy man."

Mason stood and paced, agitation showing through his calm exterior. "Why, Sean, was my love only good enough when his piece of shit imitation of affection wasn't available? This entire relationship, from start to finish, you've always chosen the slight chance at a knock off over a genuine thing. It's like watching someone trade a handful of priceless gems for a worthless doubloon. I've been forced to witness you hope each time might be different and each time you came back feeling worse for trying. You tried until the bastard died!

"Why has he always had this hold over you? Did you ever look at him with pride when he pushed your mother around? Has he ever done *anything* that impressed you? He wanted an emulation of himself! You hated who he was, but tried to please him anyway. Why? So some dickhead could give you an *atta'boy, son!* And forget about you in the next minute?

"Big fucking man *you* were. How did it feel to sit back with dear old dad and not have the balls to tell him what a prick he was when he ridiculed someone smaller than him? Did it make you feel good to stand *with* the bully rather than stand *up* to him?

"I loved you, Sean. I gave you everything I had

to offer and you passed it by for nothing. When he rode your ass about never having a functional relationship I bet you pretended he was right rather than chance him discovering the truth. All those times you could've told him just how wrong he was, just how little he truly knew you, but did you? Nope, because that would be admitting you fucked another man and that's pansy shit."

A hidden part of Sean's soul quivered deep within his gut. Everything he said was correct. He could almost see the torn corduroys and sloppy sneakers he wore as a boy, feel the shame and anger that filled his tiny chest when his father would spend hours putting him down. He hated that boy. He would never be that weak again.

But the fucker was dead and he certainly wasn't going to listen to it now. "Fuck you."

"Ah, but you already did," Mase sneered. "You fucked me for years and I let you. I trusted you and loved you without condition and I never once threw your faults back in your face." He turned and looked toward the ceiling. "Yet you still walked away. I surrendered heart and soul to you and gladly accepted all of your flaws, because, to me, your imperfections made you human. I wanted to show you the man I saw, give you the confidence he tore from you like strips of flesh. I was *always* proud of you, but I wanted you to be proud of yourself. Why did I do that, Sean? Why did I build you up so that you could just walk away? I never for one moment actually believed your shame could outweigh our love."

He was right, which made Sean's choices all the more difficult to bear. "Mason, please..." He didn't want to hear anymore.

"Please what? Let's talk about it. Your dad's dead so let's finally get it all out in the open. You think I don't see reality because I accept it, but I see more than you realize."

"I don't want to do this."

"Do what? Admit that you're afraid or admit that your father didn't have a clue when it came to people or love? Which is it, Sean? Was dear old Dad right? Are you just a pansy ass little —"

He jumped to his feet. *"Fuck you!"*

"Big words for a coward."

Sean never saw Mason act like this. Why was he doing this? He trusted him with the stories of his past, confided in him during their most vulnerable moments. And now he was mirroring his father's words, forcing Sean into a place he never wanted to revisit. Fuck him for using those memories as ammunition now.

"Come on, Sean, let's hear it. Could you possibly place more value in the opinion of a man who beat your mother than you could in your own views? Are you that lost that you can't see how wrong he was? He made you miserable. He was never going to change. If you would've married a woman he would've called her a good for nothing cow same as if you would've stayed with me he would've called you a faggot."

Without thought, Sean shoved forward, slamming into Mason, but he caught his arms and restrained him with surprising force. "Fuck you," Sean panted, his heart thundering in his chest.

Mason held him tight, his mouth close to his ear as his whispered, "He wasn't a man, Sean. A man doesn't bully women and children to make himself feel big. It's what's in here that defines the man." His hand rubbed over his back where his heart pounded. "When are you going to climb out of his shadow and embrace what you really are, a man *nothing* like the asshole that raised you?"

Sean's chest was too tight. His eyes blinked quickly as he continuously swallowed a knot that formed in his throat. "It's not that easy."

"Why does it have to be so difficult?"

"You don't understand. What you have here with Liberty, I've never had anything like that. That kind of security—"

Gripping his shoulders, Mason forced him back and stared into his eyes. "That's because you never *let* yourself have it! It takes faith, Sean, faith in something you don't get in a written guarantee. You have to trust the people that love you to catch you when you fall, to pick you up when you're down and accept you at your worst. Let go of the fear. We aren't him and neither are you. Don't let him control you from the grave. He's gone. His words can't hurt you anymore. They meant nothing then and they mean even less now."

Sean's shoulders shook as he fought the need to cry. Mason's brow creased with sympathy. "Come here." He pulled him into a tight hug and kissed his ear, whispering, "He couldn't love you because *he* was broken. There was never anything wrong with you. Believe me. You're easy to love."

"No, I'm not." Sean heard the hope in his own words, but didn't dare to go there.

"Then explain to me how, after only meeting you a few days ago, you've already made my wife love you?"

His head jerked. "Liberty doesn't *love* me."

"Really? Do you think she'd allow someone to do the things you did with her if she didn't care for them on some level?"

"She didn't have a choice."

"There's always a choice. Do you honestly think I would've let you force her into something she didn't choose? Do you honestly think *you* would've been able to force her?"

"I'm bigger—"

"It has nothing to do with size."

"Come on, Mase, she was scared—"

"I told you before. It takes strength to submit, not fear. The only person afraid back there was you. You were afraid we would tell you enough was enough and ask you to go. When will you get that we want you here? There's nothing you can do that's so evil we would turn our backs on you."

Sean dropped to the edge of the bed. His

voice was hard to find. When he finally spoke he sounded as if he'd swallowed a handful of razor-blades. "What you have with Liberty, it's beautiful. Why would you risk wrecking it by inviting me in?"

"Because we think having you with us will only add to the beauty of what we share."

"Aren't you afraid I'll take off again?"

Mason smiled. "We're both a little older and a little wiser. If you try to leave again, don't expect me to stand idly by like I did before and watch you go. Besides, there's a different dynamic when a female's involved. I don't think you could do that to Liberty."

"Awfully big gamble."

Mason kneeled before him resting his arms on his thigh. "Like I said, it's about trust, trust in each other and trust in the love we share." He palmed the back of Sean's neck and drew their heads together, looking him directly in the eyes. "If thirteen years didn't diminish what we feel, I doubt anything could. I love you, Sean."

He felt raw and exposed, as if Mason were looking into his soul. "I love you, too."

The soft press of Mason's mouth against his lips sent trickles of pleasure down his spine. Sean let himself be slowly eased back onto the bed and Mason crawled into the space between his thighs. At first they simply kissed one another, taking the time to relearn each other's taste and feel. There was no haste or urgency.

Mase smelled good. Strong and clean like

soap and linen and a little bit of Liberty. The weight of his body was something he'd forgotten, that delicious press of strength, more substantial than a woman, harder, more powerful.

Mason's fingers entwined with his. The pressure, when he squeezed his hand, was more fortifying than any handshake. This was an agreement, a consummation of the future they were all committing to share. Vulnerable and terrified to be trusted with something he so badly desired, he feared it would suddenly be ripped away from him, when he proved he wasn't good enough.

"Don't think about that now," Mason whispered over his mouth as if reading his mind. "Put the fear away. Trust this."

His tongue coasted over Sean's and he loved the rough feel of his jaw against his. He slowly caressed his way under the hem of Mason's cotton shirt. His skin burned his fingertips and his muscles trembled under his touch.

"Take this off," Sean whispered.

Mason spent another moment kissing him. They were each reluctant to pull away. Finally, he rose and shucked his shirt. He was beautiful.

"Wait," Sean whispered, talking a moment to look at him—*really* look at him. He was a long awaited feast for the eyes. Although many years had passed, time had treated him well. His, trim abdomen was still rigid and lean. Sean placed his palm on the side of his chest and ran a thumb over his dark, flat nipple, sharp at the tip.

Mason shut his eyes and breathed in the pleasure.

He repeated the caress on the other side, his eyes watching and greedily eating up every square inch of perfection that was Mason. Slowly, he moved his touch down his stomach, fingers tripping over every muscle like a ribbon laces over a Jacob's ladder.

Mason slowly lowered the zipper of his pants, one tooth at a time, the silence making way for the quiet interruption, echoing like a stampede of something magnificent to come. He stared at him as he worked his pants over his firm hips and his cock sprang free. Slowly, he shifted his legs out of the pants and returned to the space between Sean's thighs.

Mason leaned forward, bracing his weight on his palms as they pressed into the mattress. The heat of their cocks meshed as their flesh collided, a heavy weight of sensitive skin caressing and kissing. Mingling and preparing their flesh for what would come.

"Let me take you, Sean. Trust me not to hurt you and put yourself in my care."

Sean's chest rose and fell as seconds ticked slowly by. He cupped Mason's jaw, pulling him closer. Tenderly, he licked over his lips and whispered, "Yes."

Mason's mouth pressed down, his body gliding over his flesh, tongue probing deep inside. Sean's arms coiled around his strong form and held him there, needing his strength, coveting it, and never wanting to let it go. The scratchy hair of their legs added to the delicious friction as they moved together, rolling and rediscovering the other's body.

The kiss turned needy and urgent. Demanding. Sean gripped Mason's ass as their cocks nudged together creating a slippery trail along his belly. His balls drew tight and he needed more. "I want you."

Mason kissed over the stubble running down the thick cord of his neck. His mouth was like a scalding brand, marking and reclaiming him all at once. His fingers digging into the flesh at the side of his stomach was a pinch that released some of his building need. *Yes!* He needed to feel him, to know his possession was there, present, more than just a fantasy.

Mase's mouth moved to his hip as he bit down, sucking hard. Sean's cock twitched at the feel of his lover's mouth so close to where he wanted him most. Not until he was sure his flesh wore the purple bruise of his mark did Mason move on. Scooting down the bed he took hold of Sean's needy flesh and squeezed.

Sean watched him, eyes dark with lust and wanting. With torturously slow control, Mason leaned forward and seductively took Sean in his mouth. The sight of his lover's lips closing over his flesh, his lover's eyes watching him intently, had him hissing in pleasure. It was almost too much to tolerate.

Skin grew slick. The flat press of Mason's

tongue massaged the sensitive underside of his dick. His knees pulled up as he moaned long and hard. "Fuck..."

He felt Mase smile and heard his muffled chuckle as his cock was suddenly engulfed in burning pleasure as Mase took him to the back of his throat. Sean grabbed hold of his head and thumped his hips, guiding his mouth up and down.

His release tunneled through his body as if journeying from his toes. His spine twitched. His asshole tightened. Mason sucked harder, his fist pumping up and down, milking every ounce of pleasure.

Sean's orgasm ripped through him, unleashing something buried in the depths of his soul. He shouted as the hot release chugged from his balls. Mason's mouth released his cock with a suctioning pop as his hand continued to jerk out his release. Hot semen erupted from his dick, washing over Mason's hand, fingers, and splashing his belly. Sean tipped his head back and moaned at the unbelievable sensation as he caught his breath.

He was so turned on his overworked, sensitive cock still rested hard against his belly. Mason sucked on a finger and brought it to Sean's rear. Moving in tight, small circles, he massaged the muscle until Sean relaxed into him and Mason sank his finger deep. Another finger quickly joined the first. He began to fuck him with the two digits, pumping and scissoring, stretching and readying him.

Sean's feet pressed into the bedding. His ass lifted as he greedily rode Mason's hand. Finally, Mason withdrew his fingers and moved closer. His knees pressed into his thighs as the blunt tip of Mason's thick cock nudged his opening and he relaxed.

Although his fingers had just been inside, stretching him, Mason's supple cock had a girth that took patience. Slowly, he pressed forward and Sean felt as if his body would rip in half. He breathed through his teeth as Mason slid in to the hilt. They each sighed and held still for a moment, allowing each other to adjust to the pressure. He'd forgotten what it was to feel so filled.

Mason leaned forward and Sean's knees fell wide. The new angle pressed his cock into all the right places. As he began to move they never once took their eyes off of the other.

Their bodies, slick with sweat, glided as their grunts and moans echoed. Hands pulling flesh, bodies knocking, pumping, writhing, it was incredible. How had he ever walked away from this? This was so much more than two men fucking. This was love. This was possession.

Mason pressed deep and Sean tightened in ecstasy. With one final, hard thrust Mason came deep inside of him triggering Sean's second release. Hot spatters ejaculated from him as Mason slammed his hips forward a few more times, making sure he truly drained every last drop.

Their eyes met, and in that moment there was so much love and affection neither of them could put a voice to what they were feeling. Mason nodded as if to say, *I know. I feel it too.* And Sean had to blink back tears. What the fuck? Since he stepped into this house he'd cried more than he had in the last twenty years. He needed to get a grip.

Before he could degrade himself too much, Mason's thumb skimmed over the corner of his eye. He, too, wore a glazed expression. Rather than make some macho comment about the two of them, he instead remained quiet. Mason leaned down and kissed him softly.

"I love you, my boy. Don't ever leave me again."

Mason's honest vulnerability was a million times better than any pathetic denial of what was actually happening here. He swallowed the hard lump in his throat and whispered back, "I love you too, and I never want to lose you again."

CHAPTER 15

*L*iberty awoke late that night with the sense that she was being watched. She opened her eye to find, not just Mason, but Sean studying her in the illumination of the bedside lamp. They leaned over her, one on each side of the bed, heads both damp and skin smelling fresh with the clean scent of soap.

"Hi."

They smiled and at the same time said, "Hi."

She glanced at Sean, his eyes tired, but happy. "You're still here."

"I'm still here."

"Are you staying?"

"Until you ask me to leave. Do you still want me to stay?"

She looked up at Mason, but found no persuasion of any sort in his eyes. It was up to her. "I want you to stay."

"Good, because I don't want to go."

Sean leaned down and gently kissed her lips. The soft caress of Mason's mouth on the sensitive patch of skin where her neck met her shoulder had her nipples tightening. She'd never been kissed by two men at the same time.

"I'm sorry about the way I acted this afternoon. I'll never talk to you or treat you like that again," he said against her ear, his voice laced with promise, apology, and thick emotion. Her heart broke for him. He was not a bully. She saw the real Sean, the gentle Sean. Aggressive sex did not equate him to the man his father was. She hoped he could understand that.

Cupping her hand to his scruffy jaw, she smiled. "I know you didn't want to hurt me."

His gaze turned shuttered. "Sometimes...I react without thinking of the consequences to others and in that moment I wasn't sure what I wanted, Libby. Part of me *did* want to hurt you— both of you."

"Because you're scared."

His Adam's apple shifted as he jaggedly nodded. "Yes. I'm still scared, scared I'll hurt you and scared I'll somehow mess this up. But I'm speaking from the bottom of my heart when I say I don't want that to happen."

She understood that sort of fear, battled it every day. "Did Mason ever tell you about the first time we made love?"

He shook his head as her husband's hand

tightened around hers, knowing this was not an easy memory. She drew in a steadying breath.

"We decided to wait until after the wedding. I knew it would be different, but I didn't know how. My experience with men was limited and twisted to say the least. At first, when Mason would kiss me my body would react in so many wonderful ways, the slightest brush of affection would overwhelm me. I didn't know how to enjoy such things, how to know they were genuine.

"It took time and patience, the sort of patience I never expected a man to have." She smiled at her husband and laced her fingers with his. "Part of me anticipated making love while a greater part feared I'd hate it with him as much as I hated it with...others."

"Did you?"

She smiled sadly. "No. I liked it very much. But because of my past, any form of pleasure came at a price. He was so tender, so gentle with me and I *needed* that at the time. But as he fell asleep and my mind continued to turn over the experience, I somehow mutated a beautiful thing into something shameful and ugly."

A solid lump formed in her throat as she remembered her panic, tasted the regret, and felt every bit of worry she faced the night of their wedding. She swallowed back the uncomfortable sensations connected to that evening.

"Restless, I slipped from bed and locked myself in the bathroom. Despite all the wonderful things Mason said, all I could hear was my mother's hateful words." Her eyes closed as she reminded herself she was present and safe—with Mason—and Sean. "I hurt myself."

Sean's eyes showed deep concern as he gently asked, "Why do you do it?"

She shook her head. "I don't know. I don't want to, but... at one time that was the only way I could feel. Despite the ache, I was in control of the pain, I chose what to feel, but really I have no choice at all."

"We always have a choice," Mason softly whispered, reminding her of the mantra they diligently tried to live by.

"Mason taught me about choice. He spent hours listening. His eloquent advice was so tempting, but I was so screwed up it seemed impossible. Life couldn't be that simple. I knew, eventually, I'd wear him out and he'd leave. His life could be so much easier with someone normal."

Even now, such thoughts gutted her. She was not easy. Her OCD was tedious, to herself, others, and universally avoided by outsiders. People liked simplicity, order, and logic—all things she thrived to create, but complicated beyond explanation. Her disease demanded hyper-organization, yet made her world messy and complicated to the point of debilitating everyone else's life close to her.

"When he found me that night I needed medical attention. I refused to let him waste another day on someone as fucked up as me. He was so good and successful. I was convinced loving me would be a burden. But he wouldn't take that. He said, '*Love isn't something we choose, it's something we accept.*' He'd accepted what his heart wanted. My heart wanted him too, but I couldn't accept that I was worthy of anyone else's love."

Sean grasped her other hand and placed a soft kiss on her knuckles. "I'm glad he convinced you otherwise."

She smiled. "It took years, but I eventually accepted that he loved me, not because I might some day heal, but because I was lovable even with my faults. He gave me a manageable routine I could handle and anticipate, and one day I realized I actually held faith in what we had, believed he'd be there at the end of the day and all the days to follow. His love was the first thing in my life that I could truly depend on. Some times I relapse and my fears get the better of me, but most days I know, even if the curtains are crooked and some teacups are cracked, my husband will always love me."

"And I will," Mason whispered. "We know love can happen at first sight, but accepting and trusting another person's love can sometimes take a lifetime."

She glanced at Sean, his brow tense with a desire to believe and a deep-seated fear of depending on others. She had those fears too. "Honesty helps," she said. "When I stopped hiding my fears and started talking about them, I didn't feel so alone."

"I don't want to talk about my dad or my past. There's so much regret. It hurts too much."

"What if we told you none of that mattered? I know you as the man my husband loved for nearly half his life. You're a great shopping companion and a sore loser at cards and playful and silly. I know we have a lot to learn about each other, but I'm not interested in the guy you were. I'm only interested in the man you intend to be. That's the Sean I want to know."

"God," he whispered, shutting his eyes. "I'm not sure I know who that is."

"Maybe we can all find him together," Mason suggested.

He sighed. "This was not what I expected to find here. I wasn't prepared for any of this."

Mason chuckled, his fingers affectionately brushing over Sean's. "Neither were we." They leaned in and kissed just above her face.

"Mmm...I love watching you two kiss."

Sean grinned against Mason's mouth and slowly faced her. His head dipped and his lips found hers. "I love being able to kiss both of you," he whispered against her mouth and she moaned, skating her tongue against his.

"I think it's late and we all need to sleep. I have work tomorrow and you two have all day to enjoy each other, but for now I think our minds and bodies could use a little rest."

"He's only saying that because he's the oldest and can't keep up," Sean teased, his teeth softly nibbling her shoulder.

She giggled and Mason shoved him playfully. She sighed and admitted, "I am tired. Today was physically and emotionally exhausting."

Sean drew back, the playful glint vanishing from his eyes. "I'm sorry."

She shook her head. "It's over now. Tomorrow's a fresh start. I'm just so glad you're still here." She took his hand and guided it to Mason's. "My boys." They smiled and each kissed her cheeks.

~

"Middle name?" Sean asked as his knees pumped over the asphalt.

"Belle."

He chuckled. "You're parents actually named you Liberty Bell?"

They'd been asking questions back and forth all morning in an attempt to get to know each other better while Mase was at work. He didn't want his relationship with Libby to be solely defined by sex or their association to Mason. He wanted to know her as much as he wanted her to know him. What she said the night before mattered and it became clear he needed to figure out who he was in order to let go of the past and face the future.

"Not bell like the kind you ring. There's an *e* at the end. It's a girl's name."

He laughed. "Still, that's cruel."

She jogged beside him, her shorter legs working twice as hard to keep up with his longer strides. "No one ever said my parents were nice."

He slowed, hearing the exertion in her voice. When they'd both seemed a bit antsy, stuck in the house, sexual tension charging, he suggested they take a jog to burn off steam. If he was going to find new work he needed to keep in shape.

"What about your father?" He asked as they rolled into a cool down pace.

"I hardly remember him. Were you close to your mom?"

His heart constricted as it always did when he thought of his mother. "Somewhat. For a long time I blamed her for a lot of my dad's actions. I thought, if she could just stand up to him, neither of us would have to suffer. I wish I could take that back."

Her hand slid into his, the touch still slightly unfamiliar and jolting, but he appreciated the comforting gesture and accepted it. "Mason says so many of our choices can be explained by the developmental stage we were in when we had to make them."

There was no doubt Mase was the most edu- cated of the three of them. In a way, he was grateful for his wisdom, though he sometimes struggled to show it. "Does it bother you how often he's right?"

She laughed as they turned onto the driveway. "No. I depend on his wisdom and experience. It calms me down. He's so logical about everything. I don't know how he does it."

"That's just Mase."

"Yeah."

He opened the front door as they crossed the threshold out of the October sun and into the cool central air. Sweat trickled down his spine and into his shorts. "I need a shower."

"Me too. Mason will be home in a two hours. I need to polish the silver."

Understanding that the silver was a priority to her, he allotted time in his mental schedule, figuring he could use the hour to job hunt online. "Okay. Well, I'm gonna go wash up and I'll find you later."

"Okay."

As he showered, his mind wandered over their conversations. He was coming to know Libby on a personal level. It was a little backwards, considering how much they'd interacted on an intimate level already, but he liked finding out little details about the woman she was.

Every tidbit of information sent a pinch of excitement to his heart and by the time he was drying off he was desperate to return to her. He couldn't recall ever being so mesmerized by someone else or wanting to gorge himself on another's presence the way he wanted to with Libby.

Dressing in lounge pants and an old t-shirt, he smiled as he sniffed the collar, the gentle scent of fabric softener translating to how much love and care she put into every action.

She takes good care of you.

Drifting through the hall, he paused at the door to the study, his gaze drawn to her bedroom. What if he went in there? Nothing was stopping him, but she had to polish the silver. She might get angry if he disrupted her plans. Hesitating only a minute, his curiosity got the better of him. He just needed to see her for a moment then he'd let her go about her chores.

Tapping lightly on the door, it eased open and his breath sucked deep in his lungs. Libby turned, her body naked and freshly showered as she held a fluffy white towel to her breasts.

"Sean?"

"I..." His feet shifted, crossing the threshold. He had no reason to be there other than his desire to see her. All day they'd remained respectful of each other's personal space, but suddenly the distance was killing him. "I want..."

Her arms lowered, dropping to towel to her waist and baring her perfect breasts. "What is it?"

Approaching slowly, his fingers shook as he ran them over her damp curls. She truly took his breath away. Trespassing on uncharted territory, stumbling through the unrecognizable emotions clogging his mind, he asked something he'd never asked of another. "Can I make love to you, Liberty?"

Her lips parted as she blinked up at him. Hopefully she understood he'd never requested or desired anything like this before, from anyone. When she didn't immediately answer he worried he'd asked for too much. Prepared to back peddle, he drew in a breath and stilled as she lifted to her toes and pressed her lips to his.

His eyes shut on a sigh of relief as her arms slowly wreathed around his broad shoulder. His hands drifted to her bottom and lifted as the towel fell to the floor. Turning to the bed, he lowered them to the blankets as they softly kissed.

Shifting, he removed his pants as she pulled his shirt over his shoulders. His mouth traveled from her breasts to her throat, but he needed to be inside of her, was desperate for that connection.

Her knees bracketed his hips as he held himself against her sex. Their breath mingled as their gazes collided and held. The magnitude of their connection was impossible to ignore and he wanted to put a label on all the confusing feelings inside of him, but feared it was too soon.

His lips brushed hers as he inserted his length into her body and thrust forward. Her head tipped back as she moaned in pleasure and he gasped as their gazes severed.

"Look at me," he breathed, needing to feel the emotional link.

Her blue eyes found his as he cupped her face in his palms and slowly rocked. "I like when you look at me," he confessed, unsure where such vulnerable admissions stemmed from. "Stay with me."

"I'm here," she whispered, her hands softly sliding over his arms and back.

Keeping a slow pace he pressed and trembled with the extraordinary sensations bombarding him. As great as her body felt wrapped around his, it was the emotional bond that was quickly undoing his control. Something inside of him demanded he go slow and savor the experience, knowing it compared to nothing in his past.

She let out a throaty sigh and he knew he wouldn't last. Intense emotion filled his chest, contracting as if one more tender feeling would send him shattering into a million pieces. His face lowered to her shoulder as his arms wrapped tightly around her form, pulling her close.

His throat constricted as romantic sentiments rushed to escape. Her skin carried her unique scent he'd come to recognize and crave and he breathed it in, drawing more pleasure from each brush of her flash against his. *I love you.*

"Oh, Sean," she breathed.

His body trembled as his release came in an unpredicted rush, called forth by his name upon her lips. He shook and she held him as he filled her with jerking pulses of sweet ecstasy. A choppy breath slipped past his lips as he rested over her.

"I've never done that before, made love to a woman," he quietly whispered as he breathed in the soft scent of her hair.

Her fingers brushed over the back of his neck as her mouth pressed a silent kiss to his ear. "You should do it more often. It's nice when you take it slow."

A thought crossed his mind and he lifted his shoulders, still maintaining their connection. "Do you think Mase will be upset?"

She shook her head. "No. I think he expects this sort of thing to happen from time to time."

He swallowed. "Will you tell him?"

"Of course. I tell him everything. Don't worry, Sean. He'll be happy we did this. It's what he truly wants."

Licking his lips, he glanced away. "Libby... I kissed Mason the morning you and I played in the pool." He hated upsetting her after something so beautiful, but his shame was preventing him from moving forward. "I'm so sorry."

She kissed his cheek. "I know."

His gaze jerked to hers. "You do?"

She nodded. "I also know about the times you two fooled around in your room. Mason confides in me as much as I confide in him. Sometimes he just takes a little longer, but the truth always comes out."

"Are you angry?"

"I was hurt, but... I understood what happened. Sometimes a moment gets away from us. You touched me in the pool and I allowed it, Sean. In that moment I might have allowed a lot more, but I never intended to betray my husband. He knows about that and he understood as well."

"How do you do it?"

"Do what?" she smiled.

"Be so understanding and accepting."

Her smile turned sad. "There are a lot of things in life I can't accept, no matter how much I want to and try, things that make my skin crawl with no rational explanation. Luckily, this isn't one of those things. It took a long time for Mason and I to reach a point where we could explore our sexuality together. He's given me so much in regards to that, I could never ask him to dismiss the part of himself that calls to you, not when something in me calls to be with you too. It's new and exciting, but I like what we're doing. I like how *this* feels."

He pressed his lips to hers. "I like it too." It was terrifying how much he liked it. In truth, he loved it—loved them.

～

THERE WAS a thrill that came with each preparation that day, a sort of settled rightness that was no longer temporary and therefore more valuable. While two was nice, it was limited. Three on the other hand had always been a copacetic number in Liberty's world.

Three seemed the first true whole number. One needed three to form a whole shape. There were three primary colors required to make all the other shades that painted the universe. Three was strong, a foundation. Anything counted in threes seemed to manifest itself deep in her soul and sooth the outlining chaos.

That evening, her mind bathed greedily in all the comparable sets of three she enacted, each one tapping into some hidden affirmation that they, too, were now more solid than ever, because they were three.

Her fingers tapped over the three dinner plates, counting pleasantly in her head as she followed with three linen napkins, each one folded in thirds. As they ate, she divided the three courses and continuously counted three lima beans onto each bite followed by nine grains of rice.

Of course she felt Sean's gaze on her. Mason had once watched her with the same curiosity, but she never sensed a need to explain her proclivities, which was not always the case when others shared their table.

After dinner, she left the boys to talk while she cleaned the kitchen. As she cleared the table her heart fluttered, each time she saw them casually touch one another in an intimately telling way. After dinner they watched television, but her mind was preoccupied. Though they'd all shared many sexual encounters, she longed to be with them again—together as three.

"You tired, Lib?" Mason asked, gently rubbing her knuckles.

Her cheeks heated. "I'm ready for bed, but I'm not tired."

She laughed as Sean's head whipped around. "Really?"

He was so cute. "If you guys are watching this I can wait—" The television clicked off and both men looked at her with hunger in their eyes. "Or not."

Mason stood and Sean followed. Her husband held out his hand, "Let's go to bed."

Excitement danced in her belly as she slid her fingers into his and he hoisted her to her feet. Sean's arms wrapped around Mason's back as he pressed a kiss to his neck. "Lead the way, my boy."

The way they spoke to one another, the gentle way they were relearning how to touch and openly show affection took her breath away. She wasn't sure when the fascination would fade, but for now she savored each novel display.

Holding hands, the three of them walked casually toward the bedroom. Sean and Mason stripped as she excused herself to the bathroom and completed her nighttime routine. When she returned, they were both under the covers whispering and kissing.

"You started without me," she pouted.

They both turned, their gazes smoldering as they drew back the covers. "Never," Mason said. "You belong right here."

She breathed excitedly as she slid in the space between their bodies, so many emotions colliding in a knot that would soon come undone.

"Come here, Liberty Belle," Sean whispered pulling her chin in his direction as Mason's mouth caressed her shoulder.

Two tongues, each with their own texture and skill licked at her sensitive flesh as hands coasted under the covers and up her thighs. They slowly pulled her knees apart and moisture coated her folds.

The sheet was pulled away and her breasts were instantly covered with two different mouths, one soft and gentle, the other hard and demanding. Mason suckled her flesh tenderly, building a fire deep in her belly while Sean tugged with needful pulls at her nipple causing an eruption of pleasure in her womb. Her muscles contracted as her body came alive.

Their hands petted over her skin, tracing every soft curve, stimulating every nerve. Fingers reached for her sex and spread her wide, tracing her dew over her sensitized flesh. Lips kissed lower and Liberty suddenly found her wrists being pressed into the mattress beside her hips. Her body quivered as her control was removed. She wanted to let go.

Their large bodies skimmed over her, mouths

suckling, marking, tongues licking, blazing a trail of fire in their wake. Her knees were pressed wide and their mouths retreated from where she desired their kisses most, only to slowly return again. The fire built in intensity and need. The first lick over her smooth crease had her arching off the bed.

Hands tightened on her thighs. Liberty luxuriated in their hold, reveling in the sensation of being so desired and cherished. Rather than plunging into her core, two tongues licked at her folds, crossing and touching in a French kiss over her sex.

The hard scrape of their jaws was a perfect contrast to the smooth flesh of her pussy. She recognized Mason's touch as he licked over her clit. Sean's mouth latched onto her folds and sucked hard. Her thighs were stretched wide to accommodate both of them as their hair tickled her legs and belly. She lifted her head to drink in the sight of their two heads at her apex.

Sean's hair was coarser than Mason's, but equally as beautiful. Where Mason's hair was black with shards of silver, Sean's was gold with shocks of wheat and the rusty amber similar to the belly of a robin.

The slow awakening of her body was mixed with long kisses and detours of pleasure. It was fulfilling seeing them together without boundaries or fear. Some fundamental wall had come down over the last few hours. Tears stung her eyes as she contemplated how lucky they were to have each other and how special their future could be.

Mason pulled back and Sean filled the space between her legs. His fingers slid easily into her sex and his mouth latched onto her clit, sucking softly, drawing out her pleasure rather than rushing it. Such a contrast to the man she'd seen the day before. He was touching her with care, being careful and gentle.

Mason stretched out beside her and played with her nipples as he kissed her neck. He watched Sean eat her pussy from his position beside her shoulder as he whispered in her ear, "Doesn't our boy have an amazing mouth?"

Our boy. Warmth spread through her chest at the familiar endearment for Sean. She smiled and arched her back, pressing farther into Sean's wicked tongue. Oral sex was becoming an addiction. "Yes."

"Do you want to come, Liberty? I know Sean desperately wants to make you come. He's dying to drink you up. Aren't you, Sean?"

Sean moaned between her legs in agreement.

"I think that's a yes," Mason said as he pinched Liberty's nipple and she cried out at the bite of pleasure-pain that added to her building climax.

Sean's tongue darted in and out of her channel, fucking her softly with quick little strokes. His fingers strummed her clit, rubbing and teasing her higher and higher until she felt as though she would burst.

"Go ahead, Liberty. Come. Come all over Sean's tongue."

That was all it took. Mason's words triggered something inside of her. Her body seemed to snap as Sean's tongue pressed deep. His fingers applied pressure to her clit and her body fluttered and contracted as waves and waves of pleasure pulsed through her.

"Good girl," Mason praised.

Sean slowly withdrew. He seemed to not want to leave. Mason reached into the drawer of the nightstand and withdrew the bottle of oil and passed it to Sean. He then climbed between her legs and took Sean's place. He lined his cock up with Liberty's throbbing sex and stared down at her then leaned in and kissed her deeply, pouring so much passion and love into the kiss, emotion and gratitude flooded her.

Sean kneeled at the foot of the bed behind Mason. Her husband smiled and plunged deep inside her pussy. She moaned and held onto his shoulders as he began to fuck her. He buried himself as deep as possible, his pelvis kissing hers as Sean moved closer.

Mason's eyes closed as he breathed in a shaky inhalation. His chest swelled as he held still. Liberty knew Sean was readying him. She watched over Mason's shoulder, holding her husband close as Sean's muscles moved and flexed as he pressed his fingers into Mason. She could tell the moment he withdrew his fingers. Mason's body released some of its tension only to tense once more in preparation for Sean's cock.

As if needing the support, he leaned into Liberty, sealing their dewy bodies from breast to thigh. The weight of his body doubled as Sean leaned in and slowly entered him. The sensation of Mason's cock inside of her, stretching and twitching, as another man filled his rear was like nothing she could describe.

Her heart was fuller than it had ever been. She felt crushed and pulled, but in the most delicious way. She wondered what Mason must feel to be so full and so stretched over the hot coals of pleasure. She didn't know how he was tolerating so much. Just as pain could be good, too much pleasure could sometimes be torturous.

Mason breathed hard, his breath panting against her neck. She looked into Sean's eyes and gently squeezed her husband's shoulders to offer her support. Sean stared down at her. "Do you feel me filling him, Libby? Can you feel us both pressing into you?"

She realized she was breathing hard too. "Yes," she panted.

He smiled and then slowly moved, withdrawing and thrusting into Mason with one hard snap of his hips. His movement reverberated through her pussy and she moaned just as Mason grunted. Mason peeled his body from hers and kissed her lips. He seemed more in control now, as if he had just needed a moment to adjust and breathe it all in and gradually they all started to move.

Mason withdrew and thrust into her. Each pump of his cock echoed with a grunt as Sean then thrust forward as well. They developed a rhythm. Back, back, thrust, thrust, back, back, thrust, thrust. She reveled in the pattern, so familiar to her self-soothing.

Her hips lifted in cadence. The pressure built to an addictive degree, her greedy sex seeking more and more. The more comfortable they became with the position the faster they moved, their fluid bodies working into a rhythm of natural beauty.

Their skin grew slick and their various cries filled the bedroom. The wet slap of skin added to the striking cacophony of sound. With each hard flex forward, Mason's sac slapped against her bottom and she could feel the impact from Sean's body as well.

Faster and faster, harder and harder, the pleasure flourished. Mason suddenly stilled. Sean's hands moved to where she held onto Mason's hips and he squeezed. Mason seemed to take something from this unspoken message as he buried his cock to the hilt and waited.

Suddenly Sean drew back and pounded into Mason, the smack of the flesh hard, partnered with dueling male cries. Her body moved and slid with the force of their assault. Mason dug his fingers into her hip and his cock swelled deep inside of her, forced his body into hers until they seemed to exist as one.

Sean shouted, his voice raspy and hard. She watched, spellbound, as his shoulders jerked and his body shuddered with the fierceness of his climax. He was filling Mason with his come and that erotic thought set something loose inside of her and she instantly came as well, her sex clamping hard on Mason's cock buried inside of her.

"Jesus!" her husband shouted as he flooded her with his warm release. They collapsed in a knot of twisted arms and legs, no one looking at anyone, yet somehow all searching for the other.

She stared at the ceiling and panted. Her fingers latched onto other seeking fingers as they gripped one another. Mason. Her other hand was captured. Sean. Over her belly they found each other and grabbed hold.

Three. They were happily and perfectly three.

OVER THE NEXT few months they fell into such a natural rhythm that one would think it had always been the three of them. Sean never returned to the guestroom since that night they all made love as one. The master bedroom belonged to all of them. Liberty was equally his wife as much as she was Mason's and Mason as much his husband as he was hers. Sean couldn't imagine losing either of them. He'd never been happier in his life.

Although Liberty still led a regimented and particular existence, he'd adjusted to her quirky ways. He naturally sat in his designated seat and knew never to interfere with her mornings. Watching her was like watching a genius solve an algorithm. She had a purpose and method behind every move.

Mason told him often how much having him there had helped curb Liberty's compulsions. Sean had no other baseline to go by other than that first week he arrived, but Mase would frequently smile when he caught his wife laying down a dishrag without folding it in order to answer the phone or check on something in the oven. Sean's heart would warm at the sight of those smiles.

In the beginning, their sexual appetites were insatiable. But as time went on and he came to depend on their connection, they found a pace that suited them as a whole. Some nights the three of them would make love while other nights Libby would watch as he and Mase fucked. There were times he enjoyed watching the two of them, knowing it was necessary for them to share that independent connection as much as he needed the same with each one of them, autonomous from the whole.

He eventually found a job working for a company that arranged home care for veterans. His new job allowed him to keep his own schedule and base his hours on his client's needs. There was complete autonomy when it came to choosing his caseload, and that worked for their unique family.

He liked what he was doing now more than he ever enjoyed his profession. He worked partially from home and had taken over part of Mason's study to keep his appointments and records. He made house calls to his patients and enjoyed that he never worked more than eighteen hours a week.

Mason still had an intense schedule that bounced him from nightshift to dayshift and pulled doubles in between. There was never any jealousy. Rather, it seemed Mason took comfort in the time Sean and Liberty had to get to know one another. Sean knew it relieved Mason greatly to know that his wife was never truly alone.

He'd fallen more in love with Mason and found himself madly in love with Liberty as well. He was still awed at the emotions that came with living in such accepting circumstances. It had been some time after the first month together that he realized he no longer cared much about what others thought.

They'd been walking through town, Liberty to his left and Mason to his right. As Liberty slipped her hand into his, Sean naturally did the same to Mason. It just felt right that it be the three of them and fuck anyone who didn't get it. They got it. Mason and Liberty got him.

When others would stare at the three of them or whisper, they simply smiled and nodded and continued on their way. The majority of the time it was the three of them, but there were also times when it was just one on one. Those times were important too.

Sean never took Liberty as roughly as he had that day in the study. He was extremely careful with her. During those moments when he could tell she was craving a good hard screw, he would step aside and allow Mason to tend to her.

He recognized that this new softer side of him was incongruent with the man he'd always been. Sometimes he craved that harder edge, but Mason usually saw to it that he got what he needed without involving Libby.

It was Sean's choice to spare her his harder side. It wasn't something they discussed and he wasn't even sure how aware Mason was that he was avoiding anything but gentle love with their wife. It was just the way things needed to be and Sean was fine with that.

"Hey."

He turned and Mason stretched beneath the sheets, his face wearing a pink imprint from the pillow. The scruff on his jaw was dark over his tan flesh, creating a sexy shadow. Sooty lashes drew purple crests along his cheeks as his eyes peered at him at half-mast.

"Where's Lib?"

"Making breakfast. She's been up for hours."

"Mmm." Mason rolled onto his belly as he

stretched and groaned, his hands fisting and arms sifting under the pillows. Sean's hand cupped his ass and he stilled. Turning his head to look at him, his smile was slow and had Sean's cock coming to life.

"Horny?"

"Yes," Sean admitted, pressing a soft kiss to the other man's jaw. "I want to fuck you. I want to fuck you fast and hard."

Mase sighed as if the idea held appeal. His ass flexed under his palm. "Get the lube."

Sean reached for the oil and Mason reached for his cock. Sean caught his wrist and squeezed. "No. I want to take you and you're going to take it."

"Feisty this morning."

Rather than waste time with small talk Sean said, "On your knees."

The corner of Mason's mouth twitched. He knew better than to disobey him when he was feeling like this. "Yes, sir."

Sean drizzled oil into his palm and worked it over his cock. Mason climbed to his knees and waited facing him with equal authority. Crawling behind him, Sean roughly slapped his palm on his shoulder sending him down with a grunt. He grabbed his ass cheeks and spread them, pouring more oil over his crack, working the liquid in and out of his hole.

"Have I done something to upset you?" Mase asked as he planted his palms on the mattress in surrender. Sean needed that surrender this morning, needed to dominate and let out this thing that woke inside of him.

He didn't answer. Mason would know he wasn't upset, know he simply needed to assert himself in a way he couldn't with Libby. Reaching around, Sean grabbed hold of Mason's cock and squeezed. "When I fuck you it's going to be so deep and so good you're going to spill yourself all over these nice clean sheets. Then I'm going to ride you as hard as I can until you come again. Only when I feel like you've been thoroughly fucked will I take my pleasure. Head down."

Mason's dick swelled in his grip as he lowered his shoulders to the bed. Without preamble, Sean lined the blunt head of his cock up to the tight knot of Mase's rectum and thrust all the way in. His body jerked as he grunted at the intrusion. The tight hole gripped him, sliding over his flesh with warm flutters. He fucked him hard, like a man possessed. His hands gripped as his hips smacked against Mason's flesh, leaving a spattering of large handprints upon his ass.

Sweat burned his eyes as he forced his cock deeper and deeper, the tight grip of Mason's channel fitting him like a custom made glove. Yanking his hips back he gritted his teeth as he fought off his climax. Pressing hard he felt the moment Mason lost the battle and shot his load on the sheets. His body clamped around Sean's cock as he relentlessly thrust on, working past his own need to come.

Mason's fists wrapped in the bedding as Sean plunged into him. "Fuck, Sean! Don't stop!"

It would take a head on locomotive to impede him at this point. Harder, deeper, in and out. His nuts smacked into Mason's taint as he hoisted his hips higher. "Jerk yourself hard again."

Mase reached beneath his rocking body and took hold of his flesh. The pleasure was building to an intolerable point. The sound of their bodies punching into one another was a stimulus all on its own.

His ass tightened and Sean knew he was once again hard. He growled and dug his thumbs into Mason's flesh, spreading him wide, watching his big cock plunge in and out as he impaled him.

"Fuck, Sean, Fuck! I'm gonna come again!"

Suddenly, without thought, he ripped his body from Mason's and flipped him onto his back, lunging forward to capture his cock deep in his mouth. Mason arched into him, bucking his hips off the bed, and moaned as Sean sucked him deep to the back of his throat.

"Give it to me," Sean growled between licks as he swallowed down hard on Mason's thick cock. "I want to drink every last drop from you until you're as dry as the desert."

Mason's hands fisted in his hair. His hips rose off the bed, knees falling wide, as he fucked Sean's mouth. Sean found his own cock and jerked himself off, yanking with fast, rapid tugs. The first wave of hot come hit the back of his throat and he swallowed. In one fast move

Mason turned, pulling Sean with him until he was beneath him. Mason knelt at his shoulders, one hand gripping the headboard as he fucked Sean's mouth.

Come ran down his throat as his own climax burst forth leaving an uncontrolled mess like that of a teenager after his first wet dream. He gripped Mason's ass, shoved his finger in his hole and sucked him off until he had nothing left to give.

They collapsed, both of them completely incapable of moving or speaking. Breath sawed in and out of his lungs as Mason draped a tired arm over his chest and kissed his jaw lovingly. "That was incredible," he said to Sean, each word coming out on a panted breath. "Thank you."

～

LATER THAT DAY, long after Mason had left for the hospital, Sean was switching out some light bulbs that needed changing. Realizing the one fixture in the hall required a screwdriver, he frowned. As he was about to yell for Libby to grab him one, the phone rang.

Sighing, he climbed off the stepladder and went in search of a tool kit. He first looked in the linen closet, but there was nothing but perfectly ordered white linens there. He then went to the laundry room, but didn't find any tools there either.

He could hear Liberty's muffled voice as she

talked on the phone. "Where the fuck would you keep tools, Liberty Belle?" he murmured as he scratched his head.

He walked into the kitchen where Liberty stood by the fridge with the phone pressed to her ear. When she saw him come in the room she turned and quietly said, "I have to go."

He was about to write 'tool kit?' on her notepad when he noticed something peculiar about the tense set of her shoulders. He frowned as she turned further into the corner. He looked at the caller ID on the base resting on the counter. *Restricted.* That usually came up when Mason called from an office in the hospital.

"Is that Mase? Tell him we need a new flood-light bulb for out back."

"Mom, I got to go," she said and quickly hung up.

Mom?

"Were you looking for something?" She wouldn't meet his eyes.

"Who was that on the phone, Libby?"

She moved over to the counter, still not meeting his gaze. "No one. It was no one."

The phone rang again and she flinched. He leaned over and read the caller ID. *Restricted.* He reached for the phone.

"Sean, please don't." She looked up at him with pleading eyes. What the hell was going on?

Her hand held his wrist, squeezing ever so slightly, but he felt her trembling. Had something scared her? His thumb automatically clicked over the talk button when the phone rang again and her hand fell away as she turned her back on him.

"Hello?"

"Mason?"

"Who is this?"

"It's KarLyn. Look, I need to speak with Liberty—"

"This isn't Mason. It's Sean."

"Well, I don't know who you are but this is Liberty's *mother* and I want to speak to her."

"Why are you calling here?" He watched as Liberty's tight shoulders rose and fell.

KarLyn scoffed into the phone. "Pardon me, but that isn't your business. I don't even know who you are. I called to speak to my daughter, not some stranger answering her phone."

Sean studied Libby's overwrought body and recalled all the things Mason had told him about her mother and stepfather. Speaking with a calm he didn't feel, he said, "I would appreciate if you didn't call here again."

"Just who do you think you are? I'm her mother and I'll call my daughter whenever I damn well—"

"You won't call this number again unless you want the police coming to your home with a warrant for your arrest, do you understand me?" Silence. Liberty sniffled and he decided that was enough. "Do not call here again."

He hit the end call button and returned the phone to the charger. Liberty didn't move. Using a soft voice, he gently stepped forward and ran a finger over her arm. "Lib?"

She sidestepped his touch and moved to the counter where she'd been readying their lunch. "She won't call again. Thank you," she whispered.

"Are you okay?"

She nodded quickly, but still wouldn't meet his gaze. "Will you look at me, Libby?"

She took a deep, slow breath then turned to face him. "I'm fine. Really. I...I saw the caller ID and thought it was Mason."

She wasn't okay. She was definitely shaken. "What did she say to you?"

"Nothing."

Bullshit. "Libby, you know you can talk to me about this. Whatever you need, I'm here for you."

"I just need to move on. It's done. She called and now she won't call back. It's over. She just tries to call every few months. I don't want to give the issue another thought. I won't allow her that kind of control."

"Should we call Mason?" He wasn't really sure what to do in this type of situation. Mason should be made aware of what happened right away, but he didn't want to cross Libby. Maybe they should even call her therapist, that Dr. Young person.

"No. Mason's busy. Please don't bother him at work with this. I'll tell him when he gets home, but there's no need to make him worry while he's working."

He didn't agree, but he wasn't going to oppose her wishes until he had a bead on her state. He could sneak away and call Mase, but he wasn't really sure he should leave her. He nodded slowly.

"Lunch is about ready."

"Okay, Liberty."

They ate in silence. She didn't seem to notice how distracted she appeared. He didn't stare at her, but he also never took his gaze off of her, always keeping her in his peripheral.

When he finished his sandwich he reached for her hand and gave it an affectionate squeeze. She squeezed back and smiled up at him. Relief set in. There was his girl. "What do you say we go for a swim after this?"

Her smile bloomed. "That sounds great. Let me just clean up. Why don't you go get changed? I'll meet you there in a few minutes."

He watched her with keen eyes. She seemed genuine. He was reluctant to leave her, but also didn't want to make her think he was babysitting. He leaned in and slowly kissed her. "Maybe we forget the suits."

She smiled against his lips. "Okay. Let's listen to that new Beatles album Mason ordered. Why don't you go put it on?"

Unable to come up with another excuse he reluctantly stood and left her to clean up. As he walked out of the kitchen he paused and watched her for a moment. She seemed to be going about cleaning as usual, methodically washing the dishes and wiping down the counters. He turned and quickly headed to the entertainment room.

He was on his way back downstairs before a single note was sung. British voices filled the air as he returned to the kitchen. It was already spotless. Liberty stood before the sink, palms braced against the lip of the basin, a cloud of billowing steam curling up from the faucet.

As if in slow motion he watched her arm bend and her hand reach for that scalding fall of water. *"No!"* he shouted just as her fingers interrupted the flow and sent a cascade of burning water over her soft skin.

He grabbed her and jerked her away from the sink, furious that she deceived him. He shut the sink off and faced her. She was crying, her eyes unfocussed, her sharp thumbnail pressing into the pink, freshly burned flesh of her hand.

"What the fuck, Liberty?"

She didn't answer or even seem to hear him. She simply stared down at the immaculate floor, her nail worrying her tender flesh red until a piece of raw skin peeled away and pinpricks of blood raised to the surface. He grabbed her hand, wrapping his fingers around her tiny thumb.

"Stop it! Look what you're doing to yourself!"

She didn't look. Her teeth bit into her lip, the pressure turning her soft pink lips white and then purple as a bruise took shape right before his eyes. She was going to draw blood. "God damn it, Liberty, stop!"

Tears rolled down her cheeks and she began

to shake. What the fuck should he do? "I'm calling Mason," he said suddenly, not knowing what else to do.

"No!" she shouted. He froze and she fell apart right before his eyes. He caught her in his arms as she began to sob.

"Talk to me, Libby. Tell me what you need."

Her entire body shook with the force of her tears. "I need...I need to get it out."

"Get what out?" He held her tight, sensing she needed the closeness, needed to feel secure.

"I don't want to hurt myself, but I can't stop it. It's like a snake crawling through my veins."

"Tell me what to do to make it stop."

"There's nothing you can do! I just have to wait it out or exorcise it in ways that aren't good. Mason's going to be mad at me. I don't want to disappoint him, but I got to get it out! I want to get it out, Sean!"

"Mase is *not* going to be mad if you don't hurt yourself."

"I need to feel it. It won't leave unless I do something!"

"You mean like burning yourself."

She turned away as if too ashamed to verbalize. He wasn't a psychological person in any way, shape or form. At least Mason had taken a few psych classes in college and read up on Liberty's disorder. Why hadn't he taken more time to research what to do in situations like this? He always focused on the cause. She just seemed so well adjusted and normal, aside from being a clean freak. She made it easy to forget she was sick. He was totally unprepared for an emergency.

"Libby, let's talk about it."

She shook her head. "Talking doesn't work."

"Are you saying only pain will make it go away?"

"That or time."

Fuck! Fuck this bitch for calling and getting Liberty so upset. He ground his teeth together and thought for a moment, as he looked down and tensed. The entire time he had been holding her she had been scraping her nail along her skin leaving a mark. *"No!"*

When they were kids they called them sissy tests. They used to mark their skin as if to show how tough they were. Stupid thing to do, being that every single one ended as a permanent scar.

He restrained her and she hardly struggled. She simply looked down and continued to cry. He couldn't leave her alone. Reaching into his pocket, he pulled his phone behind her back and texted Mase. He didn't want to worry him, like Liberty had said. Mason's job saved lives and someone else may need him more than them at that moment. Thinking of a fast way to get Mase home with as little stress as possible he sent him a text.

. . .

WE MISS YOU. Lib and I wanted to see if you could take a half day. Y don't you see if you can get out early? Love ya.

AS HE SLIPPED his phone back in his pocket he looked down at Libby. She wasn't doing well. He had an idea, but wasn't sure if it would backfire. He sighed as he realized he only had one idea to work with. Hopefully when she came out of this dark place she would forgive him.

"Okay, pretty girl. You're coming with me."

CHAPTER 16

*L*iberty stared numbly at the wall as Sean sat her on the bed. "You with me, Lib?"

She wanted to say she was here, but she couldn't answer. Answering required talking and talking required feeling. If she let herself feel, let her mind out of the little trap that held her thoughts, she would shatter. The pain would swallow her whole until she squeezed it out with pain.

Her mother's hateful words echoed through her mind accompanied by haunting visions of her past. Sean kneeled before her, his eyes troubled, and she knew this was her fault. More sins. His hands pried her fingers apart and kissed the gouge she had left in her skin. Sighing, he turned and moved to the nightstand. He returned a second later with a long sash.

"Don't hate me, okay?" His voice was ragged.

He pressed her wrists together, her palms

curling against one another, as he wove the sash tightly around her hands, bounding them until her palms were flattened together as if she were saying her prayers. Her fingers could cross, but she could no longer scratch herself.

"Lay back." He eased her shoulder back and guided her to the bed. His touch was light and gentle. He was always so careful. She frowned as he untied her pants and slid them off her legs, followed by her panties. What was he doing?

He stood and watched her for a moment, brow creased as if in deep conflict. He paced and then came to stand at the foot of the bed again.

"Fuck," he whispered to himself and paced some more. Finally he seemed to reach some sort of decision. "God, forgive me."

He removed his pants and shirt. His penis was flaccid against the backdrop of his hard body. Liberty curiously watched him through teary eyes as he approached. He reached between her legs and briefly touched her dry folds. His touch wasn't sexual, but clinical.

"Good," he said on a shaky breath. He fingered the edge of her blouse. "I should have removed this before I tied your hands." He was nervous.

Shutting his eyes, he took three deep breaths. When he looked at her again the tortured creases bracketing his eyes were accompanied by hard lines of determination.

He pressed his hands into his hips. "Liberty, I think I can help you. So help me God if I make this worse I'll never forgive myself. I want you to know I'm only doing this because I love you. When you call my name it'll all be over."

She told her head to nod so he knew she understood even though she had no idea what he was talking about. She somehow sensed he was trying to help her. Forcing her muscles to move, her head shifted, but she barely budged at all. Sean squeezed his eyes shut and uttered an oath.

He slid her to her belly and adjusted her hands over her head. Then straddled her thighs, his weight something she craved. His palm coasted over her soft flesh as he mapped out her curves. Sharp pain suddenly lanced through her rear as the crack of flesh hitting flesh rent the air.

"One," Sean said as she cried out in shock.

He spanked her. She had never been struck like that in her life. Her flesh burned and her body quivered. Another crack sounded and white hot pain shot through her other cheek.

"Two."

What was he doing? He was hitting her. Fear suddenly trembled through her. Her hands were tied and he had her pinned. Mason wouldn't be home for hours. And why was he waiting so long for the next one. Two was *not* enough.

"Three."

Fire filled her veins and her flesh prickled. A deep throb spread in her belly. Something about that third slap against her ass settled inside of her. One thousand invisible needles pricked her skin in the shape of Sean's hand.

"One." He struck again. This time a little harder or perhaps it was just that he was now slapping already abused skin.

Her flesh plumped beneath the surface, feeling larger than it was. Visions of pink and red filled her mind and something small opened up inside of her.

"Two."

She cried out, visualizing that small hole that had unlocked in the shadows of her mind. It was like a bud, forcing its way open from within the claws of a tightly knit stem. Glowing, burning shades of gold and amber in a storm of blackness.

"Three."

The intense fire that lit along her flesh rushed through her pores, up her spine and into that small bud. An explosion of graceful vines burst forth in her mind, coiling around her psyche like arms holding her tightly together. Squeezing, choking away the hurt. Something was happening to her, something terrifying, beyond her control, yet just on the cusp of it. She feared this thing that grabbed hold of her, and at the same time, feared Sean would stop.

His thighs slid down her legs and then a fresh patch of pain lanced into her flesh.

"One."

Ah, another set of three. She took comfort in the perfect number, its dependable cycle taking hold of her once more.

"Two."

Hot. Burn. Sear. Penetrate. Deep. Encompassing. Craving. Holding. Hijacking. Dispersing. Throbbing. Aching. Wanting. Comforting. Her mind was a collision of emotions, so many contradicting feelings yet all of them uniformly right.

The intricate bud in her mind forced itself out into a radiant flower. It was something unique and new, something she'd never imagined or thought of before. Tendrils of sparkling vines twisted and turned within her, pulling her all together, holding her there so that she wouldn't come apart. She felt incredibly safe, warm, and centered.

"Three!" The crack of Sean's palm coming down on her flesh split the air.

She sobbed, much like she would at the peak of a climax. The flower burst into a thousand stars. Light flickered within her mind, winking in and out of her vision, a kaleidoscope of crystallized raindrops pouring over her, marking her with tiny prisms of light that would create new buds of pleasure. This must be what it was like when a star burst into a galaxy.

She was suddenly free, as if she were falling, but at the same time wrapped in a tight nest of feathers. Her senses awakened and the pain washed away. Her flesh burned in a way that centered her, made her feel as if she had come full circle. There was no shame. There was only this incredible, all-encompassing sense of rightness. A feeling she welcomed. She shut her eyes and dove into the sensations, letting them swallow her whole.

The delicious ache enthralled her entire being. Her mind let go. Her fears diluted, seeming suddenly silly and small. Every part of her was alive, mind, body, soul. Her heart beat steadily in her ears and she could hear Sean breathing heavily behind her. Not just Sean. She was panting as well.

His hand drifted over her baked flesh. Although he was gentle his touch cut right to her core. She moaned and he again reached between her legs. She was sopping wet. The barely there touch of his fingers so necessary she practically had an orgasm then and there, her hollow entrance trembling and weeping for him.

"Sean," she moaned his name, begging him to finish this thing he started.

"Fuck, Liberty, I should walk away now."

"Please don't leave me like this."

"Did I hurt you?" She recognized the guilt in his voice.

"No, but I need you to finish this. *Please!*"

His body began to tremble. "Libby, I can't, I'm not in a good place right now to touch you that way. I can't be gentle."

"Forget gentle. Please, Sean, I need you."

If he abandoned her now she would die. He brought her to this place. He created this need inside of her. She was like a bitch in heat wanting nothing more than for him to fuck her like an animal. This couldn't be over. A needy sob bubbled out of her, "Please don't abandon me. I trust you. Help me."

As if she said some sort of magic word he snapped. Her hips were suddenly hoisted into the air and his cock plunged between her wet folds, slamming in to her. He shouted and she immediately came around his hard cock. Her sex clamped down on him like a vise, so tight her body was squeezing him out, but Sean would have none of that. He held onto her, forced himself back in, burying himself to the root.

"*Fuck*, Liberty!"

She gave herself over to his care. His body slammed into hers again and again. It went on for days, weeks, years. She lost all sense of time and being. One orgasm whirled into another forming a tornado of pleasure. He held her tight and lost himself in her body. She felt his control snap and had never before felt closer to him. *This* was Sean. She realized then and there just how much he had been hiding himself.

When he came it was like a tsunami flooded her gates. Her mind could take no more. The most brilliant spectrum of color spread behind the lids of her eyes and a sense of absolute peace blanketed her.

For the first time in her entire life she was completely free. It was as if she were taking her first breath. She embraced the tranquility and let the world fall away.

"Get the fuck off my wife!"

~

THE SNARLED words startled Sean as his attention jerked toward the door, a chill running up his spine. Mason stood, still dressed from work. He'd obviously gotten his message.

Sean looked down. His softening cock eased out of Liberty who was nothing more than a marked up puddle of sweat and wild curls. Her shoulders moved softly. She had fallen asleep, fallen into subspace. Never in his life had he experienced anything so intense. She had come more times than he could count. She was magnificent. Incredibly strong—

"I said get off of her!"

Sean jumped and stared at Mase, temporarily struck dumb. "Mason, look, it looks bad, but you don't—"

"If you don't climb off of her this *instant,* so help me God I will kill you."

A cold stone of dread settled in his gut as ice seemed to form over his heart. He'd never seen Mason so angry, as if he held his control by a thread rapidly unraveling the balance they'd just found.

He knew it looked bad, but... "If you'd just let me explain."

Mason marched into the room as if he planned on steamrolling Sean. He quickly leaned back and stumbled off the bed. Mason's disgust was a living thing. It choked Sean and he was terrified that nothing he said, no amount of explaining would make this right. Old fears of rejection and not meeting certain standards stabbed his mind.

Mason staggered to a stop, his eyes locking in on Liberty's flesh. Her face was completely hidden by tangles of curls. Her arms still rested where they'd been tied above her head. Her thighs were sprawled. Wide, red palm prints marred the porcelain skin of her backside and thighs.

Sean winced as he noticed his come seeping out of her sex, mingled with her own juices. Mason's fingers shook as he reached out to touch one pink handprint on her skin. Sean wasn't sure if he even made contact. The punch that slammed into his face came out of nowhere.

He stumbled into the wall and knocked over a small table as he went down. Pain exploded behind his eyes as his skull rattled. The clatter of all those dainty little boxes Liberty lovingly placed all over the house, boxes too small to put anything in, caused a racket in the otherwise silent room. Sean quickly caught an especially delicate little box before it hit the ground and shattered.

Mason stood over him, shoulders bunched, fists held wide at his side, and scowling with a rage Sean had never seen. "I want you out of this house!"

And there went his heart. Sean could almost hear the crack.

"I trusted you with her. How could you...just get out!"

Sean swallowed. He deserved nothing more. He gingerly moved his jaw and it cracked. Slowly, he pulled himself to his feet and grabbed his pants. "I'll be gone within the hour."

He looked at Liberty, wanting to touch her one last time, but knowing he had lost the right. He suddenly felt sick. Was this him turning into his father? The marks on her body suddenly seemed so ugly and painful he cringed. He needed to get out of there.

~

MASON LIFTED Liberty into his arms, careful not to touch her tender backside. He was so angry he couldn't even allow himself to fully face what he just walked in on. At first he had heard the sound of bedsprings and grew excited. The scent of sex permeated the air, drawing him nearer. But then he had walked in and found Liberty's hands tied, not tied as if they were playing around with light bondage, but tied in a way her fingers couldn't escape.

Sean had been fucking her. Hard. Memories of that morning and how fiercely Sean had taken him came flooding back to his mind. The force, the intensity and greed Sean had used solely to satisfy a selfish desire. Mason was different. He was bigger than her and he had consented to such roughness, wanting a bite of pain. Liberty was fragile.

A soundless cry of worry had left his mouth

when he saw her collapse as if from sheer exhaustion as Sean filled her up with his release. And then he noticed her skin and wanted to murder him.

Splotches of angry shades marring her perfect flesh had him seeing red. How dare he lay a hand on her in such a manner?

She moaned as he brushed the damp hair away from her delicate face. Tracks of tears marred her soft skin. Rage, toxic, volcanic rage warred with his need to handle her gently.

He gritted his teeth as he carefully unknotted the sash wrapped around her hands and cradled her sleeping form in his lap. He wanted to find Sean and punch him again. Harder this time. He wanted to mark him the way he'd marked his precious wife, but he couldn't leave her like this.

She sighed in his arms, the sound relieving a bit of his tension. He kissed her temple and she stilled. "Mason?" She opened her eyes. "Where's Sean?"

Mason pressed his lips together not trusting himself to answer. He didn't want to further upset her. She didn't handle sudden change well.

"What's going on?" She sat up a little more.

"Careful," he said, worrying over her abused body.

"Where's Sean, Mason?"

"I told him to leave."

"*What?* Why? Like leave the room?" He didn't answer. "Mason, tell me you didn't throw him out."

She made to scramble off the bed. He tried to hold her with him, apparently needing to comfort her more than she wanted his succor. She pushed him away. Her refusal of his touch shocked him. There was a kind of panic in her eyes he didn't recognize.

Her rejection of his reassurance and comfort discomfited him and in frustration he shouted, "He hit you, Liberty. I want him out of here."

She shook her head and made an alarmed sound in the back of her throat. She looked at him with an expression he couldn't name. Not fear. Not anger. Not distress. Disappointment.

"How *could* you?" Before he had a chance to answer she turned and ran out of the room. "Sean!"

Baffled and suddenly frightened, he frowned. Had he given them too much time to themselves? A very real sense that he wasn't as secure in his position as he assumed took over. Memories of being blindsided thirteen years ago when Sean suddenly announce it was over choked him.

He didn't like feeling unsure of himself. This was ridiculous. If she had to make a choice she wouldn't seriously choose Sean over him, her husband. Or maybe she would. Maybe he wasn't enough and she loved him more. Not waiting around to find out, he quickly went after her.

Mason found her kneeling in front of the guestroom door speaking softly. "Please let me in, Sean. Don't do this. Please. He doesn't understand."

Her last words hit him like a punch to the stomach. Fuck this. "Liberty."

She only turned to scowl at him.

Well, this was his house too. "I want him gone."

"Shut up, Mason!"

He froze. She'd never addressed him with such a hateful tone. What was happening here?

"Sean, please open the door." There was nothing but silence as the minutes ticked by. Liberty sat naked on her knees by the door and Mason watched, speechless.

He observed silently as a tear slipped past her lashes. She pressed her palm into the door and he noticed her skin was red and scratched. He frowned, but before he could say something she whispered again. The pleading in her voice, the vulnerability…it disarmed him.

"You helped me, Sean. You got it out. The bad pain went away." She shut her eyes and more tears slid past her lashes. "That's never happened before. I've never felt so free, liberated to the point that nothing else mattered. Please believe me. You didn't do anything wrong."

Mason frowned and crossed his arms over his chest. His body shivered as it became clear they shared something completely apart from him. Despite his resolve and unshakable calm, every human frailty trembled. They were going to leave him.

"I look at my hands and I feel shame," Liberty softly confessed as she bowed her head and cradled her hands in her lap. "What I felt in there with you had nothing to do with shame. It was surrender, to a force *I* chose, not one that *forced me* into a choice. I found control in surrender. All of my life I've tried to combat those difficult moments and never once have I won. It was always stronger. But you helped me beat it, Sean. You." Her palm pressed into the door again and she whispered, "Please don't leave me." Without looking at Mason she stood on shaky legs and walked past him as if he were a ghost.

He flinched at the sound of their bedroom door slamming.

After a few moments he finally snapped out of it and pounded on Sean's door. "Open the goddamn door, Sean. I want to know what the hell is going on."

He listened for a moment. He could hear Sean moving, the sound of drawers opening and closing. He stepped back and leaned against the opposing wall and waited. He was torn between going after Liberty and finding out what the fuck really happened and what he saw. Having clearly missed something momentous and not finding any answers, his guts twisted in knots with each passing second.

After about fifteen minutes the door finally opened. Sean held a large duffle bag in his hand and a pillowcase filled with what looked like toiletries and additional clothes. He froze when he noticed Mason standing there. His eye was black and blue and Mason noticed the remnants of tears on his cheeks.

"Just let me get my stuff out of the study and I'm gone."

He was so torn. Part of him wanted him to go. Part of him needed—selfishly wanted—him to stay. He loved him, which made his betrayal all the more painful to bear, the sharp cut of disappointment bringing back the worst moments of his life—Sean, again, being the trigger.

Part of him was terrified he alone wasn't enough to make Liberty stay after Sean left. And part of him broke at the thought of seeing him walk out of his life again, of watching his family break apart. Why did he have to hurt her? Mason truly believed he was better than this. He trusted him with her safety. He still couldn't believe that he'd harm her despite the proof his wife wore.

Sean dropped his bag by the steps and headed toward the study.

"Wait."

Sean paused, but didn't turn around.

"Tell me what I missed. I don't understand," Mason pleaded.

"It doesn't matter. If you actually think I would ever lay a hand on her in anger then none of it matters."

Guilt lanced through his gut. So many of Sean's issues stemmed from his fear that he would one day turn into an abusive monster like his father. If he'd wrongly accused him of being just that, he'd never forgive himself. But what he saw…

"I fucking well can't imagine you hurting her. I trusted you! That's why I snapped when I saw her collapse beneath you, your handprint all over her delicate skin."

"What did Liberty say?" Sean asked, his back tense.

"She isn't speaking to me."

He turned and faced him. The black eye was turning into quite a shiner. Mason fought the contradicting urge to go over to Sean and soothe the bruise versus giving him another one.

"KarLyn called."

"What?" Of all the things Mason expected Sean to say, that absolutely was not one of them. His entire body tensed with fear. "Did Liberty talk to her?"

"Yes. She called and it upset Libby pretty bad. She told me she would tell you when you got home, but not to worry you while you were at work. I was scared she'd hurt herself. I could tell she was upset, but then, after we ate lunch together and some time passed, she said she was fine. I didn't really believe her at first, but she was really convincing and kept reassuring me I had nothing to worry about. Eventually I had to run out of the room for something. I wasn't real keen on leaving her so I was as fast as I could be. I literally was only gone for a minute or two. When I came back she was at the sink."

Mason swallowed, fear filling his stomach like bile. "Did she hurt herself?" he rasped.

"Barely. I got there just in time. I interfered before she could do any real damage. I watched her...she fell apart, man. I never saw her like that. I was so scared and I wanted you to be here to make it all better. I don't know enough about what she needs to know what to do in situations like that. I held her and she cried for a long time. Stupid asshole that I am, I didn't realize she was sitting right there in my arms hurting herself. She scraped the skin off her hands, leaving long gashes that'll probably scar, and she lost it again when I forced her to stop. Worse than before.

"I didn't know what to do. I texted you, but I didn't know if you were in surgery or if you would be able to leave. I had to do something. I needed you here. Then we sort of began to talk. She told me about it, the compulsion inside of her to get the pain out, to give it life. I'd heard similar things before, a long time ago when I used to spend time at this club downtown. There was this girl, Ashley. She, uh...she used to tell me there was this need inside of her to feel pain before she could move past her shit. Like she had to let it out or it would only grow bigger and bigger until she could think of nothing else. She was a masochist."

"Liberty is *not* a masochist. What she has is totally different."

"Agreed. Different. As in separate. Look, I may not understand the OCD thing, but I get masochism. They're two different things, apart from each other."

"You don't know what you're talking about."

"Don't I? Come on Mason, think back to a few months ago when I first showed up. We had a brief conversation in your study about how she needs an outlet. You may not like what you walked in on, but don't act like you haven't considered it. You know me. I didn't want to show her that side of myself. *Believe me.* I love her, but in that moment, when she was breaking in my arms, so frightened of a force she couldn't see, she needed it. It was either that or wait it out and watch her suffer through the emotional cycle while she agonized internally and slowly withdrew in order to come to terms with the pain.

"Sometimes we need to be restrained in order to unknot what's inside, have our choices taken away. I did that for her. *For her,* Mason. It wasn't about me. I gave her the outlet she needed and I witnessed the moment she broke free of what was inside of her. It was totally fucking beautiful seeing her liberated from the claws of control that held her hostage. I didn't really get it before, when you said she's aware she has it—"

"Ego dystonic."

"Whatever," Sean quickly continued. "I never really understood what you meant, but now I do. She hates it. *Really* hates it. She has such a strong will. I assumed she didn't mind being a little quirky. I mean, it isn't like she complains about it. But today I saw what's inside grab hold of her, saw her face it, knowing she lacked the strength to fight it. I saw her fear she might somehow disappoint you and her shame because that made her feel weak, and there was no perfect way for her to get it out." He shook his head. "I hated seeing her like that, so helpless, despising what was inside of her enough to actually mutilate herself."

They stood silently for a moment. Sean caught his breath after his long explanation then quietly said, "I'm sorry. Maybe I shouldn't have done it, but it was all I could think of and I know it worked for her. I felt it. She was free for those minutes we were in there. She went to that place where there's nothing but peace and I'd be willing to bet she's never felt anything like that before, finally at rest, her demons purged. All her inhibitions just washed away. She didn't have to be perfect. She just had to *be*."

His heart broke hearing the truth of everything he'd missed. How could he have judged so quickly, so harshly? Swallowing, chest tight with regret, he rasped, "I made a mistake."

Sean tensed. "I'll leave. This is your marriage. Regardless, I want you to know I would never hurt her, I mean really hurt her. Those marks will be gone in a couple of hours and the only scar she'll carry from this entire fiasco is the one she gave herself."

He shook his head. "Don't be an idiot, Sean. I meant I made a mistake when I thought you'd hurt her. I should have known better. I completely mistook the situation and it caught me so off guard I freaked. I'm sorry. Please don't leave."

Sean looked at him as he seemed to consider his words. "Is she upset?"

"Not with you," Mason said, thinking he would soon be making another long apology.

"You should go talk to her."

He sighed. "I'd like it if you talked to her first. She won't listen to me until she knows for sure that you aren't going anywhere. I've never seen her so upset with me."

Sean shifted his belongings in his hands then dropped them out of the way. "She's your wife, Mason. You love her regardless of my role in all of this. I know that and I know you know it too, but it means nothing if she doesn't realize it."

So many times he'd been given no choice but to be the voice of reason where Liberty was concerned, but suddenly he was without a logical excuse or the confidence he'd come to depend on. Truth be told, he was wrong and now terrified by the mess he'd created.

As his shame settled heavily on his shoulders, he truly understood the pain Libby had been battling all this time, only hers had manifested year after year, a million times heavier than the burden he now shouldered. God help him, but he understood how one could be driven to extremes to find the slightest relief from such ugly emotions.

Looking into Sean's eyes, he admitted, "I've

never let her down before, at least not to this degree."

"Mase, you're only human. No one's perfect. Talk to her. Tell her everything she means to you. All you have to do is be honest."

Swallowing tightly, he nodded. He couldn't do this without Sean. "All right."

Sean reached out his hand and squeezed, but as he turned toward the bedroom Mason dug in his feet. Sean twisted and Mason stepped up to him. He ran a finger over the nasty bruise circling his eye. "I'm so sorry for this. I'm sorry for all of it."

Sean sighed. "I could've made the same mistake if the roles were reversed. If I ever thought you were hurting her I'd do more than give you a black eye." He shrugged. "I'll live."

A dry laugh escaped, masking his regret. "I may not. She's going to kill me when she sees your face."

Sean smiled. "Don't worry. I'll eventually step in to help. It'll just be girl punches and slaps. I'll make sure she doesn't hurt you too bad, tough guy."

CHAPTER 17

*L*iberty turned as the door opened. She placed the broken pieces of her Tiffany jar back on the small table that had been knocked over and sat on the bed. She inhaled, ready to have her first big fight with Mason.

He looked as though he had just lost his best friend. His head hung as he softly asked, "Are you leaving?"

"That depends. Is Sean staying?"

His face paled as he stared at the bag on the bed like it was a dead rodent.

"Mason?"

He cleared his throat. "Would you be staying just for Sean?"

Her chest constricted. How could he think such a thing? "I love Sean, but I love you too, Mason. I love you both. I like the way things are. I don't want us to break up. You promised that wouldn't happen. You promised we'd always talk things out. The three of us, that's what I want. Not just Sean, not just you, but the three of us. A family. But the idea of you two fighting..." It broke her heart.

He shut his eyes as if he were fighting tears. She couldn't take any more of seeing him like this. She went to him and wrapped her arms around him. "I love you, Mason. No matter how mad I get, nothing will ever change that. But I will not let you blame Sean because you don't understand something."

He threw his arms around her and squeezed her so fiercely she wheezed. He pressed his face into her neck and let out a deep stuttering breath. "I can't lose you, Liberty. I'm nothing without you."

His lips chased up her jaw, sending chills down her spine. His raw words tickled her ear as his voice turned pleading. "I need you. I know you think you need me more, but that's bullshit. You're my world, Lib. Without you I have nothing. Losing you would leave a void no one could fill, not even Sean. I need you to realize that, to believe me when I tell you it's the honest to God truth. You're my wife. My everything."

Her breath trembled past her lips as she turned and found his mouth. Whispering against his lips, she promise, "I know. And I love you the same, Mason. These last few months have been wonderful, but I'll never stop cherishing the moments you and I steal away and reconnect. I need that. I need to know that there is still us."

"There will always be an us."

His lips pressed to hers in a kiss so tender and reminiscent of those quiet moments they alone shared. It was beautiful and promising, reassuring her that all worries that they might drift apart were unnecessary. He was here, her husband, always her beacon of strength and dependability, holding her close when the waters got rough.

Slowly, he eased her back onto the bed, his hands relearning her curves as his mouth whispered anointing promises into her soul. Yes, so long as they were one, they could handle a third, but Mason would always be her touchstone she relied on above all else.

She ran her hand over the back of his hair and waited until he regained his composure. "What about Sean? You're the one who said love is about trust, trusting those you love to accept you and not walk away when you aren't at your best. You can't make him leave, Mason. No matter how upset you are with him or me, you can't. He's part of us now. It's okay to need him too."

"I need him too, but only if that includes you, Liberty. Without you I can't manage any of this. You balance me."

She shut her eyes, finding his words comforting and reassuring. "To think, *I* am actually balancing anyone... Mason, you have no idea how great of a compliment that is." She sighed and kissed him again. "Did you talk to him?"

"Yes. I misunderstood what I saw. I overreacted and wasn't thinking. I know Sean would never do you harm. I don't know what made me believe, for even a second, that he could. I just... when I saw you tied—"

"He did that because he was protecting me."

"I get that now." He stepped away and took her hands. A burst of shame webbed through her chest as he examined the scratches she'd gouged into her flesh. Mason slowly pulled her hand to his lips and kissed the wound. "I'm sorry you had a bad day."

She gave him a sad smile and pulled him to the bed. They each sat down on the edge, but Mason seemed unable to let her go so she let him continue to hold her hand.

"Mason, something happened to me today. I can't explain it. When my mom called...I was taken off guard. I thought I was okay, but then the memories wouldn't stop. All I could hear was her voice, her words. I was a little girl again and I could hear myself screaming every horrible thing I wanted to shriek in that train station when he died. I felt despicable and ugly and dirty. Then I saw Sean and realized what I was doing to him, so I tried my best to stop it. I didn't want him to see me like that. I didn't want to upset him and I didn't want to disappoint you."

Mason shut his eyes and squeezed her fingers reassuringly. "Liberty, you could never disappoint me. Sometimes we win and sometimes we lose. Your struggles are mine. We're in this together, a partnership. Please don't think that if you have a hard day I'll be disappointed. I know how hard you try. So long as you keep trying I'm always proud of you."

"I know that, rationally I do, but sometimes when I'm in that dark place and all I can see are the repulsive parts...it's so temping to stop fighting for healthy and just give in. It's only my promise to you that makes me keep fighting it back. I feel myself slipping. It's relentless. I want to silence all my horrible thoughts, but I don't know how without..."

"Without breaking your promise."

"Yes," she whispered, hating so much that she would never be perfect. The idea of being even remotely normal at times like that seemed so overwhelming and daunting it made living a hardship of camouflage worth it.

They were silent for a long while, both re-flecting. Finally Mason asked, "What Sean did to you, did it make it stop?"

She blinked back tears. Not tears of sadness, but the same tears that shock a person's system when someone gives them an unexpected gift with immeasurable value, spoils that one never expected another to bestow, tailed by gratitude too magnificent to hold inside.

"It did." She wiped her eyes. "I never ex-pected...at first I just thought he was trying to protect me from myself, but then I wasn't sure what he was doing."

She shook her head, still baffled by how simple it had been for Sean to chase away the

LYDIA MICHAELS

darkness. He swept in like a breath, blowing away any trepidation, scattering her fears as if they were nothing more than dust and curled shavings forgotten during the making of the woman she was meant to be.

"At first I was shocked at what he was doing and angry and a little afraid, but then...it was like he hit a switch inside of me that I didn't know existed. I trust Sean with everything I am and everything I cherish. I trust him with you, Mason, and I have no words to portray how much you mean to me. When I convinced myself I was in no danger, I finally let go and placed myself into his keeping and I knew he wouldn't let anything harm me. I trusted him and I...I just let go."

She completely lost the battle with her tears and needed to take a minute to regroup. Mason sat patiently. After a few steadying breaths she said, "Everything fell away, all the pain, all the ugliness, all the memories, all the demands for perfection. I just...broke and I was suddenly free. It was as though I could feel *it* leaving me like a physical thing being purged from my soul."

Mason pulled her into his arms and held her as she cried. He kissed her hair, her cheeks, her eyes, as he rocked her. His soothing words of love fell over her like a spring rain. She shut her eyes and gave herself over to his care, suddenly feeling very, very tired.

Soon another set of hands were holding her. Sean. Warmth blanketed her flesh and flooded her veins. These were her boys. This was where she needed to be. She trusted them to always keep her safe even when she was hiding from herself. For years she danced carefully around an invisible presence so as not to wake the beast. Mason learned to step lightly too.

But not Sean. Sean was different. After years of sidestepping his own demons, he confronted hers head on and beat them for her. She knew they could come back, but there was a sort of clarity now that hadn't been there before. As if she could finally see the light at the end of the tunnel. For the first time in her life she believed that someday that presence would be gone completely.

They all were so exhausted from the day's events that the three of them, without words, crawled under the covers and lay resting in one another's arms. Liberty was at peace.

She slept serenely, slumbering so soundly she felt like she was once again a little girl, before she knew the world harbored predators and a mother's affection could come at a cost and a father's standards could break a man. No one passed through this life without some sort of stain on their soul. There was no perfect. There was good and there was evil, and even saints were flawed.

Her dreams were colorful. Warm and light like sunshine. The horizon was open, the clouds bluffs and wisps of cotton candy dotting the fathomless skies.

Life bloomed before her eyes and under her touch. Shadows were chased away by the luminosity as though she were drawing her first breath. Mason and Sean stood beside her in her dreams, exposed and vulnerable and completely real. She knew then that the light radiating from every beautiful crevice and cranny, seeping into every nerve, bathing her in heat and comfort, was love in its purest sense. Love that they were all worthy of, a love that was inimitably theirs and given without condition.

It was a beautiful awakening, a peaceful acceptance. Liberty and freedom rest in the wake of surrender. All those flawed pieces were merely the details that create the whole person. Embracing every imperfection, Liberty realized, was the key to breaking free. It was breaking perfect.

EPILOGUE

 *ne year later*

LIBERTY WIPED away tears as she continued to laugh and press her hand into the stitch in her side. Sean was bellowing in the backseat shaking with mirth. Mason was beet red as he pulled into the garage, trying hard not to laugh with them since they were basically laughing at his expense. It was good to be home.

The trip to the cemetery had been a long one, but something necessary so that Sean could finally have the closure he needed. As they stood over the grave of Mr. O'Malley, she and Mason held Sean, showing him, that no matter what, he would always have their support.

After a long period of silence Sean finally admitted that there was nothing there for him. He'd thought visiting his father's grave would lay some demons to rest, but realized there was no need for some sort of symbolic or poetic ritual. Once someone stood up to a ghost it no longer seemed as frightening, as influential.

His father was gone, his absolution meaningless. Sean only needed to pardon himself and he would find the peace he had sought all along. The moment he came to terms with his unchangeable past and accepted that he too wasn't perfect, all of his old ghosts were laid to rest.

They left the cemetery and traveled east, hitting a line of bed and breakfasts along the coast. Mason declared the trip should be salvaged and that they would make it into a honeymoon of sorts. This time, one that included Sean.

For as wonderful as it had been to visit so many neat places over the last two weeks, it was even better to be home. They'd laughed more in the past fourteen days then they probably ever had in their entire lives. It was an incredible thing to be in a relationship that was so accepting one never had to worry about making a mistake. The idiosyncrasies of their marriage, in Liberty's mind, were what made it perfect, each one of them filling a hole in the other.

They entered the foyer and she kicked off her shoes. Mason came up behind her, wrapping his arms around her ribs as he bit down on her neck. "You're going to pay for laughing so hard at my expense."

She giggled and melted into his hold. His

arousal pressed into her back. Sean came around to face her, all humor replaced with a mask of intensity that held her immobile. "It isn't polite to laugh at our husband, Liberty Belle."

"You were laughing too!" she protested in mock outrage.

He "tsked" and looked over her shoulder to Mason. "Hold her."

Mason's arms tightened, her nipples hardened, and Sean quickly unbuttoned her pants. Before she could even work up a good struggle he shucked her jeans and panties in one quick move.

Sean was incredibly efficient when he knew what he wanted. He moved to his knees and breathed deeply at the apex of her thighs. She shivered, loving the way he watched her. She was shamelessly wet.

"Hold her arms out, Mase," Sean said as he stood. Mason held her arms like a pagan sacrifice and ground his hips into her behind as Sean undid the buttons of her shirt and then quickly unlatched the front clasp of her bra. Her breasts fell free as he pinched the two pink tips hard, making her gasp.

"What happens when we forget our manners, Liberty?" Sean asked as he continued to toy with her nipples.

Mason slid his arms to her sides and splayed his palm wide over her midriff, his fingers reaching dangerously close to her wet pussy. He pressed her back so that his body was flush with hers, his arousal fitting perfectly in the cleft of her ass. The pressure was divine.

"I'd answer him if I were you, Lib," he whispered as he playfully bit at her neck.

"They get spanked," she rasped and Sean's nostrils flared.

"Do you need to be spanked, Liberty Belle?"

Her breath caught as moisture pooled and trickled at her folds. "I've been very, very bad."

"How many do you need to learn your lesson? Six, nine, or twelve?"

"Three sets of three, please."

"Did you hear that, Mason? Our wife wants nine. Do you think you could accommodate her?"

Mason thrust his hips forward and growled. "I think I could handle that."

"In the den," Sean barked, and she was suddenly lifted up and tossed over Mason's shoulder. She struggled because that always made it more fun.

"Quiet, wife," Mason said as he slapped her bare ass. The sting of his palm drove straight to her pussy, an appetizer of what was to come.

He put her down on the floor, her bare feet sinking into the plush ivory carpet, and quickly disrobed her of her shirt and bra. He turned and bent her body so she was face down over the arm of the white sofa.

Sean kneeled on the cushions before her. He already stripped and was now fisting his very hard cock. Her mouth watered. "Bend her over more," he said as he scooted closer.

She was bent over the wide upholstered arm, her palms sinking into the cushions just in front of Sean's knees, the rustling of Mason undressing sounded behind her.

In a soft voice that contradicted his intensity Sean said, "I need you, baby. Give me that pretty mouth."

She leaned forward and seductively pulled his cock between her lips. He moaned and she had to press her thighs together to try to contain her arousal from slipping down her thighs.

The heat of Mason's body fit behind her and the weight of his cock lay cradled in the crease of her ass.

"I want this ass." He pressed the blunt, smooth head of his cock into the tiny rosette of her back entrance, not to penetrate, just teasing her, showing her what would soon come.

She sucked Sean's cock harder and he moaned then quickly withdrew himself from the heat of her mouth, squeezing off his pleasure.

"Your punishment first," Sean decided.

Mason stepped back. His soft palm coasted over the round globes of her rear, caressing, admiring, mapping every inch. She gasped when the first blow came. Her sex contracted and she wished something were filling her. *Soon.* After the first set of three she was breathing heavily and quickly moving toward a state of bliss that would only improve as the night went on.

Sean cupped her face and kissed her tenderly. "You take your punishment so well, Liberty Belle." He moved off the couch and Mason took his place.

Mase kissed her too, but his kiss wasn't as refined. There was a demand in his kiss, a promise. Sean dealt out a set of three rapid strikes. She was quickly coming undone. "Suck Mase's cock, Libby and I'll give you some relief."

Her mouth chased after Mason's cock so fast it was almost comical. The moment her lips closed, Sean shoved two fingers far into her sex. She moaned and sucked Mason deep. His fingers knotted in her hair as he quickly thrust his hips. After only a few pumps of Sean's hand he withdrew and the void returned.

Sean's lips pressed into her throat as her head bobbed quickly up and down. Mason's fist remained knotted in her hair. Sean turned her chin. Her mouth fell empty and Sean's tongue quickly replaced Mason's cock. He ravaged her mouth, plunging his tongue in and out, sucking her lips, taking Mason's flavor.

When Mason's other hand knotted in Sean's thick gold hair he moaned into her mouth. Their lips were torn apart as Mason quickly directed Sean's mouth to his cock. Three quick thrusts over the other man's tongue and then it was her mouth being drilled.

Mason fucked both their mouths, driving deep over one tongue then the other. She soon found herself biting at Sean's neck, Mason's thigh, fighting to be everywhere at once. She needed them both.

Suddenly Mason released them and she was gripped under the arms and hauled over the armrest of the couch and onto the cushions. Her thighs were wrenched apart as lips, teeth and tongues bullied their way inside of her. Her ankles were grabbed and yanked wide, sending her plummeting down to the edge of the seat. Not that either of her men would allow any harm to come to her.

Sean buried his face in her folds and ate at her sex, slurping up every bit of her pleasure while Mason raised himself up and stepped over her, his feet sinking into the plush cushions on either side of her hips.

"Open." He tipped her head back and her mouth opened. His arm braced on the wall behind the sofa. He gave her little time to adjust to the new position as his cock filled her, tickled her throat, and shifted rapidly back and forth over her tongue.

Sean's tongue stabbed in and out of her at the same pace as Mason's cock and her muscles locked. His fingers moved in fast circles over the bundle of nerves hidden at the top of her slit. The moment her orgasm ripped through her she moaned and Mason's cock throbbed as hot come pulsed out of him and splashed against the back of her throat.

Three very different voices all moaned identical sounds of pleasure. Mason's hands tightened as he ensured that she swallowed every last drop. When he released her, Sean sat beside her for the briefest moment and then she was turned.

Her knees sank into the carpet, Sean's finger and thumb held her chin as he painted her lips with his wet cock. Mason groaned and then leaned in to lick the gloss away.

"Fuck that's sexy," Sean rasped.

Mason took her mouth in an intense kiss that left her dizzy. He guided her head to Sean's cock and directed her motions as she sucked him hard. Sean's hips thrust forward and Mason held her in place as Sean took her mouth. "Suck him good, baby."

Sean's hips dropped back to the cushion and her head was forced up and down. The slap on her ass from Mason's palm was so unexpected and so grounding, she almost came again. Mason released the back of her neck and Sean cursed, jerking his fist up and down over his flesh as Liberty fought to take more of him.

Red hot pleasure-pain bloomed over her flesh as Mason spanked her again. The image of her pink flesh had her insides fluttering and clamping and she wished one of them would fuck her. One more. She waited for it. Cried out for it. Needed it. Three perfect sets of three.

When it came she gave a muffled cry, almost delirious with pleasure, as she sucked Sean to the back of her throat.

"Now," Sean yelled and Mason tore her away from him and spread her out on the floor. Her protesting sob transcended to a moan of pleasure as hot spatters of Sean's come shot against her pussy. Mason's mouth dove into her folds, bringing her to a rapid release as he drank up every drop of her and Sean's passion.

They collapsed in an inelegant pile on the pristine carpet as breath sawed out of their lungs. They bathed in the aftermath of such intense play. Hands coasted over dewy skin. Fingers twirled in soft strands of hair. Lips delicately anointed curves.

Mason found her mouth and kissed her, pouring so much love into the gesture she nearly came undone once more. His mouth slowly pulled away and she was being kissed again, this time by Sean. She watched as they kissed, the affection so evident she felt as though she was embraced by it.

Now that the needy edge had eased they took their time caressing one another. The inferno they had banked slowly built again as they explored various erogenous zones. Soft sated sighs became needy pleas.

Sean smiled at her as he moved to sit on the couch. She followed him there, straddling his hips and he hugged her. "I love you, Libby."

"I love you too, Sean." Slowly, she lowered herself onto him. He stretched and groaned in satisfaction as her heat engulfed his length. When she was fully seated he kissed her tenderly then cradled her head to his shoulder.

"I love you, Mase," he said over her shoulder.

"I love you too, Sean," Mason replied as he leaned over Liberty's body and kissed him.

Moisture trickled down her backside and fingers gently massaged her opening. Mason's mouth kissed up her spine to her shoulder. "I love you, Lib."

"I love you too, Mason."

He stepped over Sean's knees and slowly pressed his cock into her tight hole. All three of them moaned as he sank himself into her. She adored it when they made love like this. It was the closest the three of them could be, each one feeling the other.

Once Mason had seated himself to the hilt, he reached around to Liberty's soft belly and held her to him, pressing her into his abdomen.

Her shoulders rested on his chest as her head fell back. She was completely encompassed within their gentle control. Sean leaned up and kissed the narrow column of her throat and slowly began to move. Like a seesaw, Sean would withdraw and Mason would slowly thrust. In and out, she was never alone, never without their presence. She was completely and irrevocably theirs, mind, body, and soul.

Their release was gentle this time, all the sweeter because of it. Slow gliding motions embraced them as one, never letting anyone go. Feeling the moment transcend into a timeless memory of serene beauty, she knew they would each keep it with them always.

~

Mason lifted his arm as Sean curled into his side. He kissed his temple and smiled. This was his family. He never imagined such happiness could exist. He thought about how far they'd come, not just since Sean arrived, but since that day he found Liberty in the hospital.

He smiled as he thought about the pile of books stacked sloppily on the steps in the foyer, waiting for someone to carry them upstairs to the study. The tacky souvenir mugs they had purchased on their journey were another wonderful example. None of them would match the white dishes and that was just fine. As he imagined the half-painted hallway they were still debating over he shut his eyes and his smile grew.

"What're you smirking about?" Sean asked as he snuggled closer.

Mason looked at the forgotten clothing littering the den. How far she had come. "I'm just thinking about our family and how perfect our life is."

Liberty walked in carrying three glasses of water. She handed them out and they each took a sip then scooted closer together as she crawled into Mason's other side.

"What are we doing for dinner?" Sean asked.

"Whose turn is it to cook?"

"Mason's. And it's your turn to do the dishes," Liberty said.

They each grumbled. "I guess I'll dig something out of the freezer. Or we could order pizza."

"Pizza sounds good," Sean agreed. As long as he was eating he wasn't very picky.

"Liberty? That okay with you?"

"Makes no difference to me."

Mason shut his eyes and allowed her words to seep through him. *Makes no difference.* A sigh of pure contented happiness left him as he held his husband and wife close.

Perfect.

LATER THAT NIGHT as Sean put away the last of the dishes and tossed the damp dishrag on the counter, he wondered when he had started considering this house his home. He couldn't think of an exact moment in time, but then realized it had nothing to do with the house, but the people inside it. Where ever Liberty and Mason were was his home.

He shut off the lights, leaving the rest of the mess until morning. He locked the front door and nudged Liberty's shoes out of the way so no one tripped over them. As he climbed the steps he heard them laughing and grew eager to join them.

Liberty's compulsions began to wane one tiny obsession at a time. After the first time he had helped her exorcise some of her demons, there was an obvious difference. He never thought much about spanking her again, but also never made any decisions not to do it.

One night Mason had to work later than usual and Libby was having a difficult time waiting for him. They'd watched a movie and she seemed restless. She stood and came to kneel beside him and then with such courage, she calmly confessed she didn't like what she was feeling and asked if he would mind helping her work through it. When he realized what she was asking he asked if she was sure. She was certain.

He kissed her for a while, slowly removing little bits of clothing. Once she was naked she laid herself over his knees in such a graceful display of surrender he almost found it hard to breathe.

It had taken fifteen that night. He always counted them out in threes because he knew that somehow made it easier for her. Five sets of three.

When the last mark was made he knew she'd escaped that dark place and reached a euphoric plane where there was no fear. They had made love afterward and Mason, having come home, found them on the floor and joined them.

Mason understood what was happening. He couldn't deny how much more at peace Liberty seemed after Sean would help her exorcise some of her demons, yet he was reluctant to use such force with her in the beginning.

As her OCD slowly became less and less obvious he began to envy the gift Sean could give her. One night Mason had offered and Liberty had eagerly accepted.

It was difficult for Mason at first, but then he too felt the transformation in his wife, saw the moment she transcended to that place of peace and let go of it all. After that it had just been something they did. It was never on a schedule, sometimes never discussed. Liberty learned to ask for help when she needed it and he and Mase had made a point never to let her go too long without such attention. Tense incidents became farther and farther apart.

Sean would never forget the day Mason came home early and found Liberty's tiny shoes piled one on top of the other right where she'd kicked them off in the hall. He had broken down and cried that day and Sean held him, completely understanding. Mason hadn't been crying because *his* burden had eased, but because *his wife's* had.

They all felt the relief as Sean's father's hold and Liberty's disorder diminished. Bound in ways no predestined mold could have designed. Like trying to swim upstream, they had each been chasing other people's ideals their entire lives. It wasn't until they realized that even the definition of perfect was broken, a geometric ray with no end, that they finally stopped trying to be something other than themselves and embraced who they truly were.

Three separate people, neither one perfect, each a little broken, melded so tightly together they had eventually become one.

. . .

THE END

**Want more edgy romance from Lydia Michaels?
Read Original Sin next!**

Claim your FREE book when you subscribe to Lydia's newsletter!
Click here to sign up for Lydia Michaels' Newsletter.

Are you follow Lydia Michaels?
Stalk her on TikTok, Instagram, Facebook, Goodreads, and BookBub!
TikTok @LydiaMichaels
Instagram @lydia_michaels_books
Facebook @LydiaMichaels
Goodreads
BookBub

Show Your LOVE
If you enjoyed this book, please don't forget to leave a review.

LYDIA MICHAELS' READING ORDER

MCCULLOUGH MOUNTAIN
Almost Priest
Beautiful Distraction
Irish Rogue
British Professor
Broken Man
Controlled Chaos
Hard Fix
Intentional Risk

JASPER FALLS
Wake My Heart
The Best Man
Love Me Nots
Pining For You
My Funny Valentine
Side Squeeze

CALAMITY RAYNE
Calamity Rayne Gets a Life
Calamity Rayne Back Again

THE SURRENDER TRILOGY
Falling In
Breaking Out
Coming Home

SURRENDER GAMES
Sacrifice of the Pawn
Queen of the Knight

MASTERMIND
Blind
Untied

NEW CASTLE
First Comes Love
If I Fall
Something Borrowed

ADDICTED TO YOU
Crush
Bang
Throb

THE ORDER OF VAMPIRES
Original Sin
Dark Exodus
Prodigal Son

STAND ALONES
La Vie en Rose
Simple Man
Sugar
Breaking Perfect
Hurt
Protege

About Lydia Michaels

Lydia Michaels is the award winning and bestselling author of more than forty titles, a certified life coach, and transformational speaker. She is the consecutive winner of the 2018 & 2019 *Author of the Year Award* from *Happenings Media,* as well as the recipient of the 2014 *Best Author Award* from the *Courier Times.* She has been featured in *USA Today, Romantic Times Magazine, Love & Lace,* and more. As the host and founder of the *East Coast Author Convention,* the *Behind the Keys Author Retreat,* and *Read Between the Wines,* she continues to celebrate her growing love for readers and romance novels around the world.

In 2021, Michaels released the groundbreaking, non-fiction series, **_Write 10K in a Day,_** to commemorate her career in the publishing industry. She looks forward to many more years of exploring both fiction and non-fiction writing, teaching about the craft, and learning from the others in the author community.

Lydia is happily married to her childhood sweetheart. Some of her favorite things include the scent of paperback books, listening to her husband play piano, escaping to her coastal home at the Jersey Shore, cheap wine, *Game of Thrones,* coffee, and kilts. She hopes to meet you soon at one of her many upcoming events.

You can follow Lydia at www.Facebook.-com/LydiaMichaels or on Instagram @lydia_michaels_books

<u>Read By Mood</u>

Billionaire Romance
<u>Falling In</u> | <u>Sacrifice Of The Pawn</u> | <u>Calamity Rayne</u> | <u>Blind</u>

Contemporary Romance
<u>Wake My Heart</u> | <u>The Best Man</u> | <u>Love Me Nots</u> | <u>Pining For You</u> | <u>Almost Priest</u> | <u>My Funny Valentine</u> | <u>Side Squeeze</u> | <u>Almost Priest</u> | <u>Beautiful Distraction</u> | <u>Irish Rogue</u> | <u>British Professor</u> | <u>Broken Man</u> (LGBTQ) | <u>Controlled Chaos</u> | <u>Hard Fix</u>|<u>Intentional Risk</u>

Emotional Favorites
<u>La Vie en Rose</u> | <u>Simple Man</u> | <u>Wake My Heart</u> | <u>Sacrifice of the Pawn</u> | <u>Crush</u>
Romantic Comedy
<u>Calamity Rayne</u>

Erotic Romance
<u>Breaking Perfect</u> | <u>Protégé</u> | <u>Falling In</u> | <u>Sugar</u>

First in Series
<u>Almost Priest</u> | <u>Falling In</u> | <u>First Comes Love</u> | <u>Wake My Heart</u> | <u>Crush</u> | <u>Original Sin</u>

Paranormal Vampire Romance
<u>Original Sin</u> | <u>Dark Exodus</u> | <u>Prodigal Son</u>

LGBTQ+ & Menage Romance
<u>Broken Man</u> (MM) | <u>Breaking Perfect</u> (MMF) | <u>Crush</u> (MMF) | <u>Hurt</u> (Non-Consensual) | <u>Protege</u>

Sexy Nerds & Second Chances
Blind | Untied
Teacher Student, Workplace, and Age-Gap Love Affairs... Oh my!
British Professor | Pining For You | Breaking Perfect | Falling In | Sacrifice of the Pawn

Single Dads & Single Moms
Simple Man | Pining For You | First Comes Love | Controlled Chaos | Intentional Risk

-

Dark Tortured Hero Romance
Hurt

Non-Fiction Books for Writers
Write 10K in a Day: Avoid Burnout

Made in United States
North Haven, CT
19 June 2024

53822811R00289